*Dianne,
Wonderful to meet you at [illegible]
Enjoy the adventure.*

CAPTURED HEART

a HIGHLAND HEARTS novel

Heather McCollum

HEATHER McCOLLUM

This book is a work of fiction. Names, characters, places, and incidents are the product of the author's imagination or are used fictitiously. Any resemblance to actual events, locales, or persons, living or dead, is coincidental.

Copyright © 2012 by Heather McCollum. All rights reserved, including the right to reproduce, distribute, or transmit in any form or by any means. For information regarding subsidiary rights, please contact the Publisher.

Entangled Publishing, LLC
2614 South Timberline Road
Suite 109
Fort Collins, CO 80525
Visit our website at www.entangledpublishing.com.

Edited by Libby Murphy and Liz Pelletier
Cover design by Heather Howland
Sketches by Irene Rea

Print ISBN   978-1-62061-057-2
Ebook ISBN   978-1-62061-058-9

Manufactured in the United States of America

First Edition September 2012

I dedicate this book to all the teal warriors out there battling ovarian cancer. May we all find our healing blue light. And to my teal army helping me SHOUT Against the Whisper! You amaze me constantly with your unending compassion, prayers and love. You all have Captured my Heart.

29 October of the Year our Lord God, 1518

Dearest Meg,

They are coming for me. I'm so sorry I must go to God now. I pray my Lord keeps you safe. Mistress Collins promises she will carry this letter and my journal to my brother. Pray God Rowland releases you to his care.

You must flee Rowland Boswell if he comes for you when you are grown. I fear he will use you. He is evil and his lies have condemned me to flames. He planned to kill young King Henry and Princess Mary and will stop at nothing to save himself. I took his letters detailing out his treasonous plans. They are hidden somewhere safe. Heed my words and find them! They are your only weapon against him.

Remember I love you now and for eternity.

Your ever faithful and loving mother,

Isabelle

Chapter One

English/Scottish Border: September 1535

Meg Boswell pressed her forehead into the damp neck of her horse as she clung to his mane. Fingers of moonlight stretched down, flickering against woman and beast as they galloped along the narrow road flanked by shadows and trees.

Aunt Mary's hasty directions beat in Meg's head: *Stay on the north road that follows the river up into Scotland.*

Good Lord! She couldn't even hear the river anymore. Was this still the right road?

Pippen's hooves clopped hard against the packed dirt. A crisp night wind tossed the leaves overhead, twirling many down to cover the road. Meg coaxed the crumpled parchment from her cloak pocket and smoothed it as she balanced easily in Pippen's sway. *God, keep me on the right path.* She blinked and held the scrap up to a flash of moonlight. Aunt Mary's blocky letters were engulfed in shadow. With her empty hand Meg touched her thumb and index fingertips together and drew them apart slowly as if honey stuck between them. A soft blue bubble expanded into the size of a chestnut, illuminating the poorly written words.

Rachil Munro, Alec Munro. Scotlind to west bi see.

Meg hastily snuffed out the blue orb and secured the note.

She reached out to Pippen with her senses. The horse's breath came in labored puffs. His lungs expanded and contracted, muscle fibers stretched with exertion, heart pounding, nearing its limit.

Meg swallowed past the clenching in her throat and pulled back on Pippen's reins. "Whoa," she breathed. She glanced behind her. Only darkness. No torches or snapping hounds. No hangman or executioner. No Rowland Boswell.

She sucked down the cool air. *Breathe deeply*. Panic chased people off cliffs, and panic had already ruled her day. Calm thinking must save her now, for she definitely needed saving.

Uncle Harold may be too afraid of English law to help, but Aunt Mary wasn't. Fear of witchcraft accusations chased all healers, even if she didn't have the curse that Meg had to hide. When they'd received word that Meg's father, Rowland Boswell, was half a day away and coming to retrieve her, Aunt Mary had packed up Meg and thrown her onto a horse. Boswell wrote that Meg was to be assessed for godliness and married to a prestigious man at court.

Assessed for godliness? In other words he planned to test her for witchery. And Meg wasn't going to sit obediently at home waiting to be examined, tried, and burned on the same false charges as her mother.

A branch in the thick woods snapped. Meg choked on

a breath, coughing on the acrid taste of subdued panic. She glanced once again over her shoulder.

Let no one see your light. Aunt Mary's words beat through Meg's memory in the silence. Eyes wide, searching the shadows, she pulled her bow to rest in her lap. *Nothing. 'Tis nothing.* She was well ahead of her father. She would get away.

Pippen nickered and twitched his ears. Meg stroked his sweaty neck as she scanned between the flanking trees. How many nights of terror would there be? Did this road lead to the Highlands like Aunt Mary had said, or would she need to ride across moors and mountains to the west? She should have taken more supplies, sought more direction. Yes, panic had ruled the day.

Pippen trotted a step or two, kicking up his hind feet. Meg patted the horse's neck. "Nickum's out there. He wouldn't leave us."

"Nickum?" Calling out in the silent night made her feel naked, revealed.

Unfamiliar yellow eyes reflected the moonlight as they peered out from the trees. Not Nickum. Meg put two fingers to her mouth and blew, sending a shrill whistle into the stillness.

The night breeze picked at her curls, tickling them across her check. She tucked the stray pieces behind an ear and touched Pippen's neck to assess his physical condition again. Contact with his skin made this quick and easy, second nature to her. Another thing to hide.

One small tap with her heels and the horse hopped into a trot and then loped into a canter.

Too bad none of her little curses fought off wild animals

and bandits and smothered witch's flames. Meg readied the bow and twisted in the saddle. Six sets of yellow eyes stared out from the trees. Her heart leapt. Wolves! As they stalked out into the open, Meg breathed and gripped the nocked arrow.

The wolves were smaller than Nickum, but they ran in a pack. They were skinny, hungry. Unlike Nickum as a cub, these hunters saw Meg and Pippen as a means to survive, a huge meal to keep their pack fed.

"Not without a fight." Meg raised, took aim, and fired, three separate movements strung together in lethal harmony as natural to her as breathing. *Just like at practice with Uncle Harold.* A yelp cut through the stillness as the nearest beast rolled off the path.

The warning should have scared them off. However, they kept to the hunt. The moon cast white across their gray snouts and tipped ears as they loped several yards behind. Meg aimed again. The creature dodged at the last moment and the arrow sliced off into the night.

Breathe. Imagine a direct line from your arrow to the target. Once more she shot, this time piercing a rump. The beast's muffled cry followed as he dodged into the woods.

Four more. She loaded, fired, and missed. She turned and clung low to Pippen, digging the heels of her boots into the horse's sides. Pippen plunged through the splashes of moonlight that filtered down between the leaves of the thinning trees. She peered under an arm. Her heart dropped into her stomach as one wolf snapped at Pippen's ankles.

"Go away!" she screamed. Fury pulsed, filling her and squelching fear. She didn't want to kill them and she didn't want to die.

The front wolf bent low, ears back, eyes narrowed. It plowed forward and the others followed. She notched another arrow, this time sitting up straight she aimed downward.

Whump! The arrow pierced the beast's back, and he careened off to the gully. She twisted to the other side, balanced on the charging horse. Pippen's coat slicked with sweat. The poor horse couldn't outrun them.

"Nickum!" Was he out there? Had the pack taken him down first?

Meg twisted. At the same time Pippen jumped, stretching his body over a fallen log. The arrow fired into the air as she clung to Pippen with her thighs, determined to hold on. He veered into the trees.

Wham! A branch slammed into her chest and plucked her off the horse. *Can't breathe!* She hung for a moment before falling to the hard ground. It happened too fast to scream. The impact rattled her body, as a spike of pain sparked lightning behind her eyes. *No!* She must remain conscious. She heard snarling, snapping. *Oh God!* She must stay… Then nothingness.

...

One must move slowly after a trauma, especially one to the head. Meg repeated the advice until the words began to make sense. Slowly the darkness began to make sense again. It had been night. She'd been riding somewhere fast. Her heart pounded. Where had she been going? She groaned and brushed at the tickle in her ear. North? Yes, to Scotland.

"My head," she whispered, and finally blinked her heavy

lids. She fingered the back of her hair and winced upon contact with a lump, sticky with drying blood. Nickum lay next to her, watching through glowing wolf eyes. Was there concern in his blank stare? Nickum whined and laid his muzzle on her chest. Definitely concern.

She raised a hand and splayed fingers through her friend's fur. "I'm still whole. If this isn't some awful nightmare, you've probably saved my life."

She ached everywhere as she rolled toward the wolf's mud-splattered coat. "Nickum." She pushed her face into the dense fur, needing the comfort of a warm protector. Upon contact Meg knew where all his scratches and bites were under the thick coat. Her fingers trembled as she searched for them. He had obviously battled.

"Any other hurts?" She closed her eyes and inhaled, focusing on the core of power that sat below her breastbone, just under the oddly shaped birthmark. She imagined it as a bright blue light like the one she could summon between her fingers. Meg pushed the power up and out of her hands to thoroughly search her friend. The muscles of his heart squeezed and relaxed with a strong steady beat, his stomach rolled half full, his bladder sat empty. Some muscles around one shoulder were bruised but it wasn't serious. She released a breath. "Just some scrapes and bites." She'd use ointment on them. She jabbed two fingers through his thick fur to yank off a small tick she'd detected on his neck.

She rolled gingerly to one side to stand with the help of a young oak. Nickum stood against her to add support. She breathed in again, but this time she let the bright blue ball of light spread through her own body, searching for injury. Bruises would darken her back and the arm that had taken the brunt of the fall. Thank the good Lord, her head injury was contained outside the skull. She opened her eyes and noticed dawn seeping into the dark blue sky.

"I will survive the night." She splayed her fingers through Nickum's fur. "With a bump on my head."

She glanced around. The bodies of three wolves lay nearby. Her fingers curled into his coat. "Let us find Pippen."

Pippen stood sweaty and trembling near a twisting creek. The creek tumbled along the face of a rock wall made up of towering moss-covered boulders. She whispered gentle words to her horse while she surveyed his injuries. She tied his reins loosely to a tree behind large holly bushes.

"Nickum?" she called softly, her gaze running the length of the rock face. Yellow eyes reflected out of a dark crevice. "You found a cave, clever wolf." Meg stepped into the pitch darkness toward him, totally trusting his instincts.

Out of habit, she glanced over her shoulder. Of course no one was there. She was alone in a cave in the forest. Yet the fear of discovery still kicked her heart into a run as she formed a small glowing orb between her fingers. The size of a currant, it illuminated the wide chamber once she walked past the narrow entrance. A deep earthy smell of moss and decaying leaves infused the sheltered space. She crouched in front of Nickum and scratched his ears.

Meg managed to pull several clay jars from her leather satchel with one hand while the other held the blue orb. It was better than a candle that could burn out, but she couldn't just set it in the corner to light the small shelter. Conjuring the light shot her blood through her body in case she'd need to flee.

The ointments she'd made with figwort and St. John's wort would help Nickum. But first she'd have to wash the worst of his bites. She forced a smile at her reluctant patient who outweighed her three times over. "Let's get you cleaned up."

By the time the horizon had lightened to dawn, Meg had managed, after one brief scuffle, to clean and apply some salve on the worst of the wolf's wounds. Nickum shot out of the cave as soon as she let go.

"Ungrateful," she called to his retreating tail.

Meg gingerly lowered onto her cloak and closed her eyes. She exhaled long and willed the tension to dissolve along her aching muscles. It had been the longest night of her life. Oh, how she would relish this sleep.

Minutes later the sound of thunder roused her. She groaned and covered her head with the cloak. The thunder continued… and continued. She pushed up on her elbows. A sunbeam shot into the cave opening instead of the rain she'd expected. She listened to the ebb and flow of the deep pounding and stood to peek outside. The source of the rumbling came from farther down the rock wall.

She stood by the opening to the cave listening, trying to discern the source of such noise. She should stay put, hidden in the dark cave. A voice? She swore she heard a voice, a man's voice. Meg's heart leapt into a sprint. Could her father have caught up to her?

Her eyes shifted to where she'd tied Pippen to a bush outside the cave opening. "Pippen?"

He was gone! Her only means of escape. She had to find him.

Meg grabbed her bow and quiver before slinging them over one shoulder. She stepped out and made a quick search of the bushes close by. No Pippen. She'd tied him to the bushes, hadn't she?

Meg jogged the path that lay along the rock face. She pushed past a bramble bush and stepped into…hell.

The clashing, scraping noise and grunts of men, the tangy smell of blood and iron mixed with campfire smoke. The sights, smells, and sounds of battle tangled around her where she stood, suffocating her. Meg covered her mouth with the inside of her elbow and squinted through the haze created by the sun heating the dew off the grass. Men ran everywhere, yelling, cursing, slashing. Blood-painted men lay scattered amongst the ferns and beaten down cornflowers.

There were two distinct groups scattered together, hacking and falling. One wore English clothing, the other Scottish kilts. Definitely a border skirmish. Not her father's doing. There on the other side of the meadow stood Pippen. Relief barely penetrated Meg's shock at the vicious carnage. She'd never seen a battle up close, only the aftermath, which was when her Aunt Mary took her to patch up injuries.

Why would a troop of Scotsmen be on this side of the border? Crossing these days was practically a declaration of war with King Henry VIII's reformation and Scotland's King James V's harboring of Catholic refugees. The two stubborn monarchs had made tensions between Scotland and England even more brittle. Had war been declared without Uncle Harold knowing?

A large Scotsman strode through the mist. His powerful stride pulled Meg's attention. The haze swirled around him as if he compelled it to move aside. His bare, muscled arms brought down smooth and powerful slashes against two of the English. Uncle Harold had told story upon story of the mighty warriors in the north, about their bravery and skill unlike the paid English military.

The Englishmen fought back as one, trying to lunge at him from opposite sides. Each time they attacked, their blades met steel, not flesh. Meg watched, frozen, as the Englishmen weakened under the Scotsman's claymore until in one swift stroke the fearsome warrior sliced through the shoulder of one.

She gasped and put her hand flat against her lips. Too late. The noise had carried. The Scotsman pivoted in her direction while the second Englishman retreated into the opposite woods.

Meg backed up until the sharp granite boulder dug into her bruised back. The man walked toward her, his eyes intent, assessing. His frown, piercing gaze, and the blood splattered across his untied shirt gave him the air of an ancient barbarian from Aunt Mary's history book. The man's biceps corded as he raised the sword so as not to drag it. Power, raw and unchecked, radiated from him as he stalked forward.

She tried to swallow, tried to breathe. She was squeezed between the rock wall at her back and the warrior's hard gaze with barely room to inhale.

Meg held up a hand, palm out. "*Stad*," she said.

The giant stopped his advance but clearly had not given up the hunt. Meg slid her arrow into position on the bow, pointed down, but if the Scotsman came too close, her bow would be of little use against his obvious strength.

"You speak Gaelic," he said in his ancient language. "Interesting." His deep voice pushed a fizzle of lightning through Meg. His gaze seemed to follow it down her length.

"Yet ye dress like the *Sasunnach*." The last word meant English and came out as a curse.

Meg didn't move. She couldn't.

"Where is yer escort?" he asked in English, although his Scottish brogue curled around the words, making them sound ruggedly foreign.

A movement caught Meg's attention. An English soldier walked up behind the warrior, a boulder raised over his head to strike him. *Good God!* Meg raised her bow, the arrow nocked.

"*Stad!* Stop!" she yelled. "Watch out!" Panic surged through her.

The Scotsman turned at the same time she fired. The arrow hit its mark in the flesh of the English soldier's upper arm. The force threw the Englishman backward, the boulder tumbling out of his grasp. The granite grazed the edge of the Scottish warrior's head, and he dropped to the ground.

Meg's hand flew to cover her mouth. The Englishman grabbed his arm where her arrow stuck out and took a step toward her.

"Hanover!" another Englishman yelled from the other side of the field. The injured man glared at her as he held his bleeding shoulder but retreated back across the meadow.

Meg touched the fallen warrior's chest, searching him for injury. The warrior would have an ache in his head from the mild swelling she sensed and a new scar, but he would live.

Thank you, Lord. Since when had she decided to side with the Scottish? Perhaps it was because of the valiant stories she'd heard growing up or because she was headed to her Aunt Rachel in Scotland, away from an English father. Or perhaps it was the strong jawline and wavy brown hair of the Scottish warrior.

Foolish! She sprinted back through the woods, desperate to get out of there before he awoke. She jerked to a stop. *Ugh!* She still had to retrieve Pippen! She huffed and continued her jog. Later. It was too dangerous right now with the English out there and the Scotsman waking soon. She dove into the cave and tripped over Nickum.

She groaned softly. "I've endured a beating." She crawled to the back of the cave, threw her cloak around her shoulders, and lowered herself onto the ground.

As her body began to calm, the weight of exhaustion pulled at her worn muscles. She would just rest awhile. And pray. She pulled the leather bag of medicines and her mother's last effects toward her without letting go of Nickum, then pushed her hand inside and sifted through the small clay jars, past the healing journal and grasped onto cold hard iron. Meg pulled her mother's key out and hugged it against her heart. Somehow the familiar weight of it grounded her.

What am I going to do? Warriors out there. Boswell following me. I'm practically lost. With no mount. Meg ran her fingers through Nickum's fur and held tight to the heavy key. She would rest, rest, and pray until she knew the men outside had left. Then she'd figure something out. She would survive, just like Uncle Harold had taught her. "Dear God, guide us to safety," she whispered. "Guide us to safety and to the truth."

Chapter Two

9 June 1517 — Figwort: shrub that grows as tall as a Scotsman, oval leaves, and small reddish-brown flowers during summer. Decoction to treat swellings, sprains, redness, putrid wounds, diseased parts, sores, and flesh rot. Crush fresh leaves into an ointment, with the cridhe of a stone.

Caden Macbain, chief of Clan Macbain, punched his way through the muck of darkness that strapped him down. The brittle lightning that arced through his head reassured him that he was indeed alive. As he opened his eyes, Ewan Brody's grim face split into a grin. Caden's friend and second in command grabbed his hand. Ewan's strength could carry Caden's large frame, but Caden shook him off. He'd stand on his own. Caden swore beneath his breath and touched the side of his head. His own blood stuck to his fingers.

"Bloody hell."

"Good to see you rise, Caden." Ewan studied him with an irritating grin. "I'd hate to have to tell your sister that an

Englishman killed you with a pebble."

Caden frowned and pinched the pain that had settled between his eyes at the top of his nose. "'Twas a bit more than a pebble." He surveyed the meadow. "The battle is finished?"

"Aye, you slept through the last of it." Ewan pushed the small boulder with his boot. "You're lucky the English have poor aim. He would have cracked your skull open if he had hit you straight on the head." He chuckled. "To be knocked unconscious by a *Sasunnach*—"

"Enough!" Caden roared.

Ewan backed away, although his grin stayed in place.

Fury, at himself, filled Caden's gut. He had been deaf to the English dog sneaking up on him. Caught off his guard…by a woman.

"Where did she go?" he demanded as he turned in a tight circle.

Ewan, Hamish, and several of the young warriors turned to search the clearing.

"Where'd who go?" Ewan asked.

"Bloody hell, she's gone," Caden said and strode to the rock wall. The woman with large, beautiful eyes. He hadn't imagined her.

"See to the wounded," Ewan said to the other men, "and set a guard in case the English cowards decide to regroup." The young warriors quickly dispersed to set up a small camp. "Caden, who is this 'she' you've misplaced?"

Caden studied the ground, but his mind filled in the memory. She had stood in the mist with the sun shining on her hair. Red highlights flowed through her deep brown hair over her slender shoulders to her narrow waist. Her lips—full kissable lips—had been parted, breathless, and totally begging to be plundered.

Long lashes framed her eyes. Hazel. More green than blue or brown. Although they had been round, she hadn't swooned nor frozen in fear. The lass had courage and skill. She'd fired her bow at him, or at the English. Caden frowned. Had she meant to shoot him and missed?

"Diana, goddess of the hunt," Caden said without a trace of humor. "She appeared like the huntress that my da described to us from the ancient stories," he mumbled, and peered through the forest.

He easily picked out the broken branches that marked her trail. He glanced at Ewan, who stared back like he'd lost his sense. "Bloody hell, Ewan, I'm not touched in the head. There was a lass here, and she shot the bastard with her arrow."

"So," Ewan said haltingly, his face a mixture of worry and checked amusement, "a pagan goddess saved your thick head?"

Caden scowled. "I know she isn't an ancient goddess, but I did spy a lass along the edge of this rock face." He plucked an arrow fletching from the twigs and traced the feather with his finger. "Her eyes were so wide." He pointed to the trail through the forest. Deep smudges in the soft earth showed that she'd run back along the rock face. "And she knows naught about hiding her tracks."

Ewan took the fletching from Caden's fingers and studied it. "Who is she?" he asked. "I'm intrigued. I will call a search."

"Nay," Caden returned abruptly. "The men would scare her." A worse vision replaced his concern. At least ten of the

English bastards had scattered from the battle. One of them might find the girl. What if she were alone?

"I don't have time for this," he grumbled and pushed past the bare branches. "I'm in bloody England on a mission, not to rescue foolish lasses."

Although she had saved his head. And she was the loveliest woman he'd ever seen.

She could be surrounded by battle-stung Englishmen ready to take out their vengeance and lust on an innocent lass. The thought tore across his chest, and Caden pushed off into a run along her trail of broken twigs and churned up mud. Hell, he could nearly trace her individual footprints.

He stopped at the rock wall where the grass had been flattened and chewed. No horse, but the woman's footprints led to a crack in the rock face. A cave. Caden ducked his head into the dark hole and pulled his dirk from his boot.

"Lass?" He blinked to help his eyes adjust to the low light.

A deep growl came from the rear of the cave and every nerve in Caden's body shot warrior's lightning along his muscles. He crouched, dirk before him, and squinted into the black. Bloody hell, the lass had walked into a wolf's den! He crouched, waiting for the beast to hurl his body at him. Waiting and listening for the faintest sound of human life. Waiting for his blasted eyes to adjust to the dark.

With another long blink, the outline of a huge beast standing over a lump came out of the inkiness. A foot. There was a small foot sticking out from under the wolf.

"Don't move, lass." Caden spoke in English using the most unaggressive voice he could muster with the blood pounding through him, urging him to lunge. "I'll lure him out."

The beast growled low again and Caden wondered briefly how heavy the creature was.

"Scotsman?" Her soft voice penetrated the darkness.

"Aye," he answered and blinked hard at the strange sight.

The woman sat up and pushed her hands against the side of the wolf.

"*Stad*, wait," he gritted out as calmly as he could.

Caden took another small step forward in the tight space. Even bent, his shoulders grazed the ceiling. The wolf leaned back on his hind legs and snapped as if he were about to jump.

"Nickum, no!" The woman pulled her legs out from under the beast. "I know him…well, perhaps not really…" She stood, her hand stroking the enormous creature.

She pointed at Caden. "Your weapon. Put it down and he won't attack, at least not unless you threaten me."

Caden lowered his dirk but kept it poised to throw. He could hit the beast right between its yellow orbs if it turned on the girl. The wolf relaxed into a sitting position. He stared at the two for a long moment.

"Ye have a wolf," was all he could think to say.

"My escort," she said with strength in her voice. In the dim light that filtered into the cave, she was a darker blur against the rock. "Your head? You are well?"

"That's the largest wolf I've ever seen."

The woman patted the beast's head. "I made sure he was fed well as a pup. He grew large…and protective," she stressed. "Your head?"

Caden replaced the dirk in his boot. "Will heal."

"You need to clean it." She motioned to the mouth of the cave. "In the stream. I have a poultice that will help it heal without taint. I can give you some to apply."

When he didn't move, she shooed him toward the door again. "Go wash it."

"I'm not leaving here without ye," he said, the words surprising him. Her eyes grew round. "Not until I know ye are safe," he added.

The woman stood bent over in the small cave. She picked up a bag and dug out a leather jar. "I am safe with Nickum."

When she threw it to him, he caught it but didn't move. The presence of the wolf and her odd behavior caught him there. For a long moment they all stared at one another.

"How," he said slowly, "do I apply it?"

The woman huffed lightly and moved forward. "Go out so I can see."

Caden stepped into the bright light, made certain they were alone, and turned to the woman. She blinked up at him. Her forehead drew together when she examined the cut on his head. Her lips, pink and soft, opened slightly. Caden shifted.

"Aye, my ointment will help immensely."

"Ye are a healer."

"A dab of this." She took the leather cup from his hand. Her finger brushed his, her skin cool, thin, not the overly oiled skin of the pampered, but soft nonetheless.

"I have men who could use yer poultices."

Concern warred with refusal across her lovely features for a long moment. He watched the tiny scrunch reappear between her sloped brows as she considered his request.

"Of course they could." She uncorked the vial, dabbed some on her finger, and reached up to touch the cut over the bump. Caden hardly noticed the intense sting with her so close, just under his chin.

She stepped back, dropped the vial back in her bag, and eyed him warily. "You handled that much better than Nickum," she said with a casualness that contradicted the stiffness in her stance.

"Yer wolf's name is Gaelic."

"I know some of your language," she answered.

"'Mischievous'?"

"I found him half starved as a pup, tangled in brambles, alone in the world. I pulled him out of so much trouble as he grew up, the name seemed fitting. He follows me everywhere."

The woman's eyes shifted past him into the forest, roaming, searching. Did she fear the English?

"My men are back in the meadow."

"Oh, yes. I…yes, I can help for a time, but then I need to continue on."

"Where are ye headed?"

She walked back along the face of the rock. Caden watched the natural sway of her hips and the soft folds of hair down her back as he followed. She didn't answer his question. There was a little leaf stuck in the auburn waves. He reached to pluck it out right when she stopped. Caden pulled up short, his fist in her hair around the leaf.

She turned, her hair wrapping around a shoulder.

"Ye have a leaf." He inhaled silently, pulling the fragrance and warmth of her closeness into his lungs. The flow of auburn silk smelled fresh, clean. What was that flower? Her gaze moved to his hand in her hair and then up to his eyes. So close, close enough to kiss. Caden dropped his hand and the leaf fell out on its own.

"North," she said.

"North," he repeated, having forgotten the question. *Och, what a fool.* How long had it been since he'd tupped a fine lass?

"I can pay ye with food," Caden said, his words blunt.

Ewan spotted them and strode across the green. "Sweet Diana, ye are real." He spoke in English and bowed to the woman, eyes lingering on her neckline. Caden scowled so hard his jaw ached. Ewan had a way with the lasses. He was slightly shorter than Caden and one of his most cunning warriors. The man had been known to use battle strategy to lure a lass into his bed.

"'Diana'?"

Ewan's eyes danced. "When ye shot yer arrow to save our chief's life, fair lass, he saw ye in a golden glow coming out of the mist. 'Tis truth it is he who named ye after the pagan goddess of the hunt, Diana. However, I must say that ye are much more bonny than any goddess could ever be."

She actually blushed over Ewan's rhapsody and tucked a stray hair into place. "'Chief'?" She glanced at Caden.

"Aye, he is our chief, Laird Caden Macbain, from the ancient Colum line of the Macbain clan, from Druim Keep at the base of the triple mountains, north of Loch Tuinn."

The lass nodded as if all that made sense. Perhaps she was familiar with their country.

"And I am Ewan Brody, cousin to Caden and part of Clan

Macbain. And what is yer true name, lass?"

Caden waited. What would she say? Would her name give a clue to her character like the one she'd given her wolf? A name could tell a lot about a person.

"Excuse me," she said and jogged briskly to a man sprawled against a tree trunk.

Ewan's eyes narrowed in confusion.

"Healer," Caden said.

"You don't know her name?"

"Not yet," Caden said and followed her across the clearing. "Beware, she knows some of our language."

Ewan cocked an eyebrow. "Interesting for an English."

"Odd."

"I need fresh water, fire, rags. Clean." She rattled off orders in fairly well pronounced Gaelic while she inspected the bloody end of Hugh Loman's arm. The limb had been severed.

Caden motioned to Hamish. "Get what she needs." The young warrior rushed toward the supply wagon. Caden called back over his shoulder so that everyone could hear his order, "and if anyone sees a large wolf around the parameters, don't shoot it." Several eyebrows shot up among the men, but not one question was voiced.

The woman stared at him and bowed her head slightly. A "Thank you" perhaps.

Caden inspected the state of his men around the camp. A skirmish had been anticipated, but not so soon after crossing the English border. Perhaps the young English king had ordered local militia to attack any Scot.

Caden took a long drink from a bladder filled with spring

water. He wiped some of the liquid on the back of his neck. "Bloody English heat." He would rather be home seeing to his clan's protection. Unfortunately, his mission required the journey. He frowned. This skirmish would delay them and he needed a truce before the first snowfall to save his clan.

Ewan caught up with Caden. "What's the lass doing out here on her own?"

"She hasn't said."

Ewan tilted his head to a tawny-colored horse tied to a tree on the other side of the camp. "Sean found him wandering about near the lass's trail. I'm supposing it is hers."

Caden nodded.

"Just she and the horse? Perhaps she's daft," Ewan whispered.

"Perhaps she is, Ewan. Best stay away from her."

Caden moved onto the supply wagon to check the rations.

Ewan followed him. "What was that about a wolf?"

"She has a pet wolf." Caden counted the barrels of mead then turned to Kieven, who was in charge of the food. "Fill all the containers ye have with that spring water before we move on."

"A pet wolf," Ewan mumbled and leaned against the wagon. "Most unusual."

Caden surveyed the clearing. "Where's Girshmel?"

"He's checking the road and perimeter to the creek." Ewan indicated the narrow river they'd been following behind him through the woods. "To make certain the English scampered home to lick their wounds. I wouldn't be surprised if Girshmel brought back an English head on a stick. He is an odd one."

Caden agreed. "Odd one," he echoed, though his mind

and gaze followed a very different odd one. The woman from the mist was unlike any lass he'd ever met. Alluring, capable, especially for an English lass. Perhaps it was the mystery shrouding her that caught at him. She shot a bow with accuracy, traveled alone through hostile countryside alongside a wolf, and although she was cautious, fear didn't paralyze her. Diana, the goddess of ancient Greece, no. Yet there was something special about her, something unique, and Caden would figure out what it was.

...

Meg moved among the wounded men, all of them Scots. The only English she saw were dead. She spoke to Caden's men in a mix of Gaelic and English; luckily Uncle Harold had made certain that she was schooled in Gaelic, but she rarely had chance to practice it. They seemed surprised, even wary, but eventually she won some nods. They were fierce men, large, grimy, and bloodied. She was extra careful not to reveal too much knowledge about their ailments, even though she could sense every scratch upon contact. She must seem odd enough to be wandering around in the forest alone.

Ugh! Would they give her direction away if they ran into her father? She'd have to ask their chief not to give out information about her.

The man who had lost his arm was named Hugh. Meg spent most of the day working on his stump. She washed the ragged edges of skin and applied a pungent herbal salve all over the raw end.

"Lass, that stuff smells like rancid entrails of an animal dead a fortnight," said one young warrior. "What does it do?"

Meg chuckled at the grim description. "The salve will dry the blood at the end," she answered slowly in his language.

She wiped a dirt-speckled arm across her damp forehead. The sun beat down on the open meadow despite the onset of autumn.

"I need to wash." At least her hands, and some of the larger stains from her surcoat.

"I will escort ye," the soldier offered. "I'm Hamish."

Meg shook her head and gestured to the unconscious man. "Stay with Hugh. If he wakes, he should see a friendly face."

An argument, to stay, darkened the warrior's face.

"And I need some privacy." She stepped away briskly.

Meg let the shade of the trees wash over her hot skin as she walked to the stream. Would her other aunt have any useful information for her? Her mother's sister, Rachel, had married a Scotsman and stayed up in the wilds of the Highlands. Uncle Harold said that Rachel and Isabelle had loved each other. Meg hoped that Aunt Rachel would be as fond of her when she showed up unannounced on the woman's doorstep with the threat of Rowland Boswell on her heels. That was if she could even find Aunt Rachel in the vast wilderness.

Follow the river that runs along the North Road until a large lake with a road around. Then head west until you pass a range of three mountains.

Meg shook her head and inhaled to stomp the edge of fear back down in her gut. She plunged blood-tinged hands under the tumbling water. She scrubbed her face, pushing back her hair.

Without a sound, large, grimy arms encircled her and yanked her off her feet. The stink of blood and sweat gagged her scream, making it come out as a squeak.

"You're mine, wee water nymph." The hard chest against her shoulders rumbled. Meg kicked backward but missed the man's knees. He laughed at her impotent squirming. "Girshmel Black," he said in English, "claims ye."

"Release me, or…or *go stróice an diabhal thú!*" The Gaelic insult was the only one Uncle Harold had taught her.

With one thrust, the man tossed her into the air, flipping her so that she faced him. "Ye want worms to eat me?" he asked and laughed.

"Let go!" she screamed into his broad, dirty face. His toothy leer showed brown crooked teeth. His breath smelled worse than the rest of him. She could sense the rottenness at the base of those teeth. They'd fall out within a year.

"Now why would I be doing something like that?" he asked.

"Because my wolf will eat you," she said and held two fingers to her mouth. Her whistle pierced the stillness. The man's eyes searched the forest and grew wide as his gaze settled on the opposite side of the stream.

"Are ye a witch, lass, or a kelpie?" the man asked. His eyes narrowed.

"And if the wolf doesn't kill you…" The Macbain chief's deep burr brought the smelly ogre around so fast that Meg's head whipped backward. "I will."

The warrior stood just inside the edge of the forest, his short sword poised, ready to fly. The intensity of his eyes, the hard line of his jaw, his flexed arms as he towered there without a shirt on, kicked her heart into a gallop. The man's kilt fell low on his hips. Droplets of water beaded along his tanned skin and his hair dripped. He looked like a natural predator fresh from a swim.

"I've claimed her, Macbain." Girshmel's statement sounded like the whine of a child trying to woo a sweet before supper. "The lass was all alone out here just waiting to be taken." His eyes shifted between Caden and the short sword.

"You cannot claim what is already mine," the Macbain chief enunciated in his native language.

When had she become his?

"Release her." The warrior tipped his wrist back, ready to strike. "Now."

"*Cac*," Girshmel swore and opened his arms.

Meg dropped onto the hard packed dirt. She scooted away from Girshmel's leather-clad feet, lost her balance, and tumbled.

Cold spring water caught Meg's scream as she splashed under the surface. Her heavy skirts twisted around and tugged her down into the swirling eddy. She couldn't find a solid footing on the slippery rocks. Hair was suddenly everywhere, snaking around her head, tangling, gagging her. She surfaced but sucked in a mouthful of water, making her cough violently while flopping in the waist-deep water.

Warm arms, solid against the current, wrapped around her waist. Meg grabbed hold. She pawed hair off her forehead and tipped her gaze to the chief's face. He held her securely, facing him in the water. He reached for her face. She held her breath as he touched her skin…and pulled a leaf off her cheek.

"Ye seem to attract leaves." He pushed her hair from where

it stuck against the sides of her head.

What does one say to that? "I...uh, thank you, Chief Macbain."

"Caden." His deep burr sent gooseflesh along her chilled skin. She shivered. "Caden."

"Sweet Diana!" the gallant Scotsman named Ewan called from the bank where he and several other men stood, witnessing her humiliation. "How did ye end up in the stream?"

Caden pulled Meg up against his solid, bare chest and lifted her sopping form from the water, setting her on the bank. For a brief moment her hand rested on the smoldering warmth of his chest, a light sprinkle of hair the only barrier between them. The Scottish warrior was all muscle and heat. Her healing senses told her that every part of him was toned and in perfect working order.

"Girshmel found her," Caden answered.

"And threw her in the water?" Ewan asked, confusion crossing his face. Several of the men chuckled. Ewan elbowed one who began to cough, a wide grin splitting his beard.

Meg wanted to crawl away from the stares and hide. She turned and hiked toward the meadow. She needed to get moving again anyway before her father caught up to her. Just the thought made her heart race. How many hours had she given to these warriors? Too many.

Water drained out of her numerous layers and she huffed in frustration. The heavy material dragged the ground, gathering a pile of fallen leaves with it. Her gaze searched the meadow but only kilted warriors moved about. She needed to find Pippen, get dry and warm, and head out.

"He tried to claim her," Caden answered behind her.

"Girshmel!" Ewan yelled for the offending man.

Meg reached the fire and splayed her hands before the flickering flames. She would need to dry first before moving on. She was impatient but not a complete goose. An autumn breeze chilled the air as the sun surrendered the horizon. Crickets chirped out to their mates in the growing dark as night settled amongst the thin tree canopy. Meg shivered as cold and exhaustion soaked into her. Uncle Harold had always said she was tougher than the faint-hearted maids in the village, but this was beyond normal. This was a nightmare.

"Garrett, a blanket," Caden called and moved close. His heat touched her back, and then his fingers. Meg held her breath. He worked at the buttons along her spine, brushing just enough to send shivers of a different kind down her body. Was he planning to strip her right there where she stood framed by the sunset? She stepped away, but he followed.

Garrett ran up with a wool blanket, and Caden placed it over her shoulders. He turned her to him and pulled the blanket closed beneath her chin like she was a child. Fatigue from her run the night before, the day's tending of wounds, and then the struggle at the stream, beat at her composure. She focused on the ground so he wouldn't see her resolve dissolving.

"I need to leave soon," she said. "Treating your men today has delayed me."

"You need to dry first. Pull off yer wet things under the blanket. They will hang and dry while ye warm by the fire."

Her chin jerked up. "Strip my clothes off? Out here in front of you?"

"Under the blanket."

"Under this blanket?"

"Unless ye prefer to undress away from the fire."

Meg pursed her lips. Did she really have another choice? The fire gave warmth, light, and safety. She glanced around at the men moving around the camp. None seemed to be watching. Where had that Girshmel gotten to?

She turned back to glare at Caden. Was this to be a war of wills, then? She stood a long moment trying to figure a way to win this first battle, but there was no way around this if she wanted to get dry and stay warm.

She huffed and let the sodden surcoat drop around her ankles. She peeled the clingy sleeves from her arms and let them drop, as well as the tied pocket. Meg lifted her foot to peel a stocking down and wobbled. Caden tried to grab her elbow through the heavy blanket but grazed her breast instead.

She jumped at the contact and glared at Caden, though he stared at a point somewhere in the distance. She frowned but continued to disrobe.

"I'm finished," Meg murmured and took a large side step over the mound of dress.

Caden glanced down and then back to her face. "Yer kirtle."

"Will stay on my body."

"The kirtle will dry quicker off yer body."

"I would be naked beneath," Meg snapped.

"No one will take yer blanket."

They stared at one another over Meg's tight fist where she held the wool closed at her chin. Even as she glared at him, she couldn't help but admire the strong length of his neck. A Celtic cross hung from a cord and rested on his well-muscled chest, a chest she knew radiated heat. Meg swallowed hard.

Caden stepped up to her on the other side of her clothes. "Ye are safe here now." His words were low. "I claimed ye. No one will harm what is mine."

"I am not yours," Meg retorted a bit breathlessly. Panic warred with her courage. How had she gotten into this mess?

He raised one eyebrow. "Would ye rather be claimed by Girshmel, then?"

"I would rather be claimed by no man." Meg tipped her chin higher as if she didn't stand there nearly naked draped in a borrowed blanket.

"'Tis safer to be claimed." He frowned, but something in his eye made her think that he wasn't too annoyed. "Yer kirtle," he said as if ending the discussion.

Damn! He was winning this battle, too! He was offering protection and she needed to get dry as fast as possible. Ugh! She ducked beneath the blanket and peeled off the thin, sodden material. With one hand she stuck it up through the hole and then followed it with her head.

"Garrett, hang these to dry for…" Caden said and waited.

She smiled bitterly. "Mistress Diana."

She moved to the other side of the fire where she sat down, cocooned in the scratchy wool. She wasn't about to tell these men her real name. Allowing her discovery was terrible enough. If they knew her name they could possibly give her away to her father. Fear and determination weighed on her shoulders as her mind replayed the frantic words of her mother's letter. She wouldn't let her mother's warning be for naught. She must escape Rowland Boswell.

Meg stared at two rabbits on roasting sticks above the fire. Her stomach growled. She hadn't eaten all day.

Caden turned to a young warrior. "Donald, make sure Mistress Diana receives some food." He glanced at her, his frown back in place. "For payment for helping my men." He stalked away.

Meg watched the muscles between the chief's shoulders. Their long lines flexed down through his waist to his narrow hips, barely concealed by the hastily draped kilt. She tore her gaze away. *Ridiculous!* Her life was balanced on the thin edge of disaster. She didn't have time to admire the contours of a Scotsman's muscled, solid, warm body. She swallowed hard.

"Me name's Donald Black, Miss," the young warrior said slowly in a thickly coated brogue over his English. He squatted on the other side of the fire and turned the rabbits on the spit. "I'm sorry for grinning back there by the stream. There is nothing humorous about a lass almost drowning."

Her face heated. "No offense taken." Her stomach growled rudely.

"The rabbit should be roasted right shortly."

She huddled down in the blanket, trying to forget the fact that she was stark naked beneath it while talking to strangers. Maybe she should rest, then start out again during the night. Her father probably wouldn't pursue her in the dark.

"For Mistress Diana," Donald said and presented the juicy meat off the spit. He also handed over a bannock, some cheese, and a bladder of fresh water.

"Thank you." She bit into the smoky, roasted meat with

barely contained joy. "This is delicious." She swallowed and took a bite of the bannock. "I don't think I've ever been so ravenous."

"Ye have no food with ye?" Donald asked, and sat across from her with his own fare.

"Some, and I intend to hunt." Where was her bow? Perhaps Caden had put it with Pippen. She'd seen her horse brought into the camp.

"Are ye going on a long journey, then?" Donald asked.

Meg tipped her chin and continued to chew.

Donald turned back to his food. "We're a long way from home, too."

She glanced at Donald's kilt. "Is Scotland far?"

"Several days on horse and maybe slower with poor weather." He grinned. "And the weather is always poor this time of year. I love me Highlands anyway."

Meg coughed around the rabbit melting in her mouth. "Highlands? You've come from the Highlands of Scotland, to the northwest near the sea?" She swallowed the food in a gulp instead of enjoying the bite.

Donald took a swig of spring water. "Macbain land doesn't border the sea, but 'tis close."

Perhaps these people could help her find her aunt. Caden seemed honorable. He hadn't once tried to spy under the blanket when she'd undressed. He'd saved her from that brute at the stream. Her father would never think to search for her within a group of Scottish warriors. And there was food—good food.

"So," Meg said with a casual air, "are you headed home, to the Highlands?"

"As soon as we complete our mission."

Meg chewed the side of her lip and glanced around the camp. "Your men are in need of more of my cures. Especially Hugh, with his stump."

Donald frowned. "Hugh has a wee son back home. Just born."

"I could go with you all on your journey and keep Hugh as well as can be. I think he will mend, but the wound needs to heal properly. And there's the fear of fever."

"I will speak to Caden about it," Donald said, and stood. "We would be most obliged if ye could help the injured. They have family back home. Thank ye, Mistress Diana."

Meg blushed. She would of course keep the men as healthy as she could, but guilt balled into a lump in her stomach for not telling them how much she needed their escort.

"Where are ye headed up in the Highlands?" Donald asked. "The Highlands are vast, and I don't want to promise ye that we take ye somewhere and then discover that it's way far away from Druim Castle."

What should she say? T'would be folly to tell them somewhere she wasn't really headed. She didn't know enough about the clans of Scotland to know of a place near her aunt's holdings. She groaned internally.

"Do you know of the Munros, Donald?" she asked tentatively. "Are their holdings near to Druim?"

His eyes seemed to grow wider and he tilted his head a bit. He blinked several times. "Aye, lass, I do. They border Macbain land." Donald jerked his head in a nod. "Are ye headed to the Munros, then?"

Meg's heart pounded. God was giving her a means to escape, a way to get to safety. "My aunt is married to their chief," she rushed out.

"Rachel Munro?" Donald coughed on some of the rabbit he was chewing.

"Yes."

He gave her a timid smile and began to hop from foot to foot.

"Are you having cramps, Donald? I have something for that."

He shook his head. "Are ye…I mean to say…is yer name really Diana? The chief will want to know yer real name if ye'll be traveling with us."

The Macbains bordered her aunt's property. They had treated her with respect, given her food and protection, and possibly an escort. She'd already told Donald where she was headed. Good Lord, she sat amongst them in nothing but a blanket. It was clear that she could trust them. "Of course he will. No, Donald, my name isn't Diana." Confiding released the knot in her stomach. She smiled timidly. "My name is Meg Boswell, and I'm pleased to make your acquaintance."

Donald mumbled something about finding his chief. He trotted toward the other side of the camp.

Meg ate the rest of the rabbit and bannock. Despite her foolish run without a plan, at the moment she was warm, well fed, and protected. Perhaps this plan would work after all. Perhaps God did intend for her to survive this journey.

...

Caden concentrated on keeping his eyes on Ewan as they discussed their best route for the mission. His gaze kept straying to the lovely lass drying by the fire. Flaming gold, her hair moved in the breeze.

"We can still make Yorkshire by noon tomorrow if we leave at dawn," Ewan said. "Today proves we aren't welcome in England."

"Aye," Caden agreed. "We best keep off the main road."

Donald jogged up to them, stopped, and moved back and forth between his feet.

"Donald, do you need to take a piss, man?" Ewan asked.

"Nay," he answered breathlessly. "The lass, well, she well, she said—"

"Spit it out," Ewan said, a smile softening his rebuke.

Donald swallowed hard. "She says her name is Meg Boswell. She wants us to escort her to the Munros."

Caden stared hard at Donald. The muscles in his chest contracted, his breath halted.

"That…that would make her Alec Munro's niece, right?" Donald asked.

"That would, indeed," Ewan said slowly, as if tasting some new brew of mead.

All three men turned toward the mystery woman sitting as royal as one could sit naked beneath a wool blanket. She couldn't be, could she? She was English. They were close to Yorkshire and traveling near the main road in and out of Scotland.

Caden strode across the clearing, barely aware that Ewan and Donald followed. His legs stretched out before him, his muscles taut.

She didn't resemble Alec Munro. In fact she was quite opposite the obstinate, stab-you-where-you-stand, burly Highlander with his red hair and fuzzy beard.

She watched them walk over to her. Caden stared down at her. Was she really Alec Munro's beloved niece?

She cleared her throat. "Donald and I were talking about how you could use my help treating the injured while you journey back to the Highlands. I would like to strike a deal with you. My help for your escort to my aunt's home." She paused. "I will not interfere with your mission here in England."

Caden's hands fisted at his sides. "I would have yer name if ye will be traveling with us." He watched her face for any signs of dishonesty. "Yer Christian name."

Her chin rose a bit, displaying the lovely line of her throat. The splash of firelight on her exposed neck darkened with a blush. "I didn't tell you my name before because I thought it was prudent not to give strangers that information while I traveled."

"Traveled *alone*," Caden reprimanded.

Annoyance flashed through her eyes but she covered it with a tight smile. "I travel with my wolf and my mount. Not alone."

Ewan opened his mouth to say something, but Caden raised his hand to stop him. "Yer Christian name, milady."

"My name is…Meg Boswell."

"Niece to Alec Munro?" Caden shot out, his blood surging within. His hands clasped and unclasped at his sides.

She glanced at Donald, who still fidgeted, and then back to Caden. "My mother's sister is married to the Munro chief. I wish to journey to their holding. Donald has said that their land borders yours."

"I told ye," Donald said beneath his breath.

The woman pushed off the ground to stand. Caden's gaze moved over her slight frame, down to the bare little toes that squeezed upon each other in the grass.

"I understand having a woman along may seem odd, but I promise not to interfere with your mission—"

"Our mission is completed," Caden said abruptly. His fists clenched.

"Well, then, I couldn't possibly interfere. I will just take care of your injured and will follow you back to the Highlands. A mutual gain."

A gust of wind scattered wood smoke this way and that. Several of the lass's curls tugged free of the blanket and floated out around her face. She looked like she'd been tupped, her hair in beautiful disarray. He could imagine it fanned out across the soft fur on his bed. One side of the blanket slipped, exposing the creamy milk-white skin of her shoulder. Caden's jaw ached.

"Have we set a bargain, then?" She chewed a bit on that luscious bottom lip.

Caden nearly groaned watching those lips, so soft, so perfectly formed.

"Aye." His gaze moved from her lips back to her lash-framed eyes. "We have set a bargain. Donald, make certain a tent is set up for Lady Boswell so that she may dress and sleep."

Donald hurtled away from them.

"And Donald, not a word to the men yet. I will tell them about our guest."

"You may call me Meg," she said. "I don't hold tightly to

formalities and we have a long way to go."

Caden watched her pull the blanket up to cover the bare shoulder and frowned. "Get some sleep. We leave England at dawn." He turned on his heel, dismissing her. The wave of lust, however, was harder to ignore.

Was she frowning at his rude departure, her lovely eyes glaring at his back? Meg Boswell was certainly no fainting flower. She had spirit and courage. She was most definitely glaring.

Caden let out a long breath. They'd be back on Scottish soil on the morrow. Why, then, did he welcome an excuse to slice someone through?

Ewan jogged to keep up with Caden's long strides across the camp.

Caden stopped and turned to him. "Alert the men that we leave at dawn for home. Make sure they understand that *Meg*," he said, stressing the name she bade him use, "is our guest."

"Are you going to tell her—?"

"Not until I have to." Caden walked purposely toward the cold stream. Perhaps another icy swim would remind his body about his goal. He slapped a low branch out of the way as he strode into the darkness of the trees, tearing the green limb from the trunk of a slender birch. He should be celebrating, not scowling. After all, he had completed his mission on his very first day in England. He had captured Meg Boswell, and she didn't even know it.

Chapter Three

27 July 1517 – Garlic: strong odor, green stalk that flowers white or pink in early summer, white bulb hides underground. Search among the rocks near the mountains of the north. Lorg an lus seo ann an uamh, an fuar uamh le moran na frith-rathaidean agus an blath cridhe anns am meadhon.

Prevents wounds from oozing. Relieves breathing ailments. Helps stomach pains. Raw juice or boiled for half a day mixed with clean water should be drunk to expel the evilness from the body, although its stench drives away all but family.

Meg spent the first two hours of the next morning checking behind her, but no one raced after them. The Macbains rode two across with a scout up ahead, Meg in the middle. They traveled so slow, too slow for her. Her journey would be faster if she progressed alone, though who knows where she'd end up? *Lord, give me patience.*

She sighed and pulled her mother's journal out and opened it across her lap. Balancing in Pippen's familiar sway, she thumbed through the sections of her mother's notes. After all these years, she knew the words by heart. The more she learned from Aunt Mary about the art of healing with plants, the more she realized that some of her mother's notes were not quite correct, even though her mother was considered a miraculous healer.

They stopped for a midday meal of honey cured meat and cold bannocks. Meg checked on Hugh and changed the dressing on his stump. He was still weak from blood loss and had been riding with another soldier.

Donald Black sat next to her, by a tree.

"You make a fine lady's maid," she said in Gaelic, and smiled at Donald, who handed her a skin filled with water.

Instead of smiling, he seemed confused.

"Or perhaps you are my guard," she teased.

Donald choked and she patted him hard on the back. Her sensitive touch told her that his heart rate had sped up. Perhaps she'd embarrassed him by naming him her maid.

"Milady?"

"No milady, just Meg," she chided. "I am sorry, Donald. I was only teasing." She indicated the water and food he'd brought. "You seem to have been stuck with the task of making sure I don't starve or wander off. I don't mean to be a bother."

His shoulders relaxed. "No bother," he said. "I have a sister at home. Ann. She's just your size. I've always watched after her."

"I will be happy to meet her when we reach the Highlands."

"Meet her?" He frowned slightly.

"We will be neighbors. I will come for a visit once I'm

settled."

Donald stood. "I need to check the horses."

She watched him walk off, and her smile faded. He thought she was strange. *Well, I am strange, but they shouldn't know that just by talking to me.*

Meg stood and breathed in the crisp, autumn-scented air. Colored leaves danced in the trees above as the bright sun glittered down. She loved autumn, the full harvests, the festivals before winter. She ignored the small stab of homesickness as she walked over to Pippen. Certainly the Highlanders had their own bountiful festivities. She ran strong fingers under Pippen's soft muzzle.

"I told you all would work out," she whispered. The horse nickered.

"Meg Boswell." Caden's soft, steady voice shot through her and Meg whirled around.

"I didn't hear you," she said and smiled timidly.

Caden stood only a step away. His normal half scowl was in place as he adjusted the saddle on Pippen's back. He tugged on the saddle as if checking to see if it was secure and then turned to her, crossing his arms. "What has ye watching over yer shoulder all morning? What makes a lass leave her family with only a wolf and bow for protection and a small satchel of food to sustain her?"

He was so tall, taller than any of the men in the village near her home. His intelligent eyes stared at her as if figuring her out. She didn't know what to say.

Caden stepped closer to Meg; his fingers pulled a small birch leaf from her hair. He was close, so close that she could easily lay her hand against his broad chest. At least he had a shirt on this time.

"I've deduced that ye aren't a fool, Meg." He indicated her leather pouch. "I've seen ye reading that book. And yer way with the injured," he said. "Ye're not addled, so it must be something dire to make ye run."

Meg opened her mouth but then closed it. She couldn't tell him that she was running from her own father, a traitor to his king, a liar, and murderer of her own mother. She was humiliated enough. "I appreciate your escort, but I—"

"I like to know what enemy I am making, lass." He stared hard, unblinking.

Meg swallowed. She hadn't thought of it that way. Was she endangering these men just by associating with them? Would her father take out his vengeance on the Macbains for helping her?

"I…mean, my mother…well, the man…" Her tongue couldn't form the terrible words. She studied the rounded toes of her leather boots. The flush that burned up her neck and cheeks wouldn't go away even with slow, steady breathing. The awkward silence stretched until she glanced back up at his strong features.

"I understand," she started again. "I should not put you all in peril." She focused on the blue specks in his gray eyes. "If you could give me some basic directions toward my relations, I will travel on my own. I would but ask that you don't divulge my name or the direction I am traveling if asked."

Caden watched her in silence. He uncrossed his arms. "Ye're running from something fierce."

His observation wasn't a question, but she tipped her head in a brief nod anyway.

He took a step closer and Meg held her breath. "Ye have my escort, Meg Boswell, no matter who chases ye." Caden's hands moved to her waist, and he lifted her up into the saddle. His hand lingered at her knee. "Just shout out if ye see that the devil's caught up to us, lass."

Caden removed the warmth of his large hand, and she breathed again as he turned away.

"Thank you," she said to the back of his head.

• • •

They traveled the north road, which really wound through the lowlands on a northwest direction. Caden watched Meg twist in her saddle for the twentieth time. She most definitely fled someone, someone she expected to follow. A brother? A father or guardian? Perhaps a husband or a lover? His jaw tensed and he rubbed a hand over the scruff that had grown there over the week he'd been away from Druim Keep.

Fortune's irony had landed Meg in his lap. There had been no need to steal her away, and now no worry about her running from them. She didn't cry or complain or beseech him for her freedom. In fact she was grateful for his escort, making this mission much easier.

Caden raked his hand through his hair, letting the guilt fall flat inside, as if it didn't matter. Because it didn't. The lass would play her part in their plan, a plan that must work or many in the protection of the Macbains would die this winter. The feud with the Munros was an old one, but it remained vicious with raiding attacks. The bastards had even gone so far as to burn the Macbains' fields, even though Alec Munro denied it. Without food stores for the coming winter, many would starve—mostly the elderly and the children. The threat of starvation had prompted Caden to bring the idea of using a hostage to the council. Someone the Munros cared about.

He watched his captive sway gently in her saddle. She laughed at something Ewan said as he rode next to her. The spirit in the lilting cadence licked along the row of men like wildfire racing across a dry heath. Soon every man within earshot grinned like a foolish arse.

Everyone except Caden.

With each pleasant exchange, the lass would hate them more once she knew that she was merely a pawn in a war.

"It must be done," he said on a low exhale and his horse's ears twitched. The faces of the children born under the Macbains' protection moved behind his eyes. The responsibility of their lives weighed on his shoulders. He wore the cloak of The Macbain, the cloak he had donned the day his father died. He'd do what no other chief had been able to do. And he would do it by kidnapping and using an innocent woman.

Caden sat up taller in his seat and tapped his mount forward to ride in front of the line, up where the lass's sweet laughter could not reach him.

...

They made camp as the moon rose in a small meadow that sloped toward a pond. Meg washed as best she could and sat by the fire waiting for the rabbit to roast. Even though they'd crossed into Scotland, the mood in the camp was tense. She sat silently, watching the flames as they licked up the large hare on the spit.

The glow of the fire made reading possible, so Meg dug out her mother's journal. After hours of contemplation during the day's ride, she was certain that her mother wanted her to run to Scotland. She flipped to the garlic entry. Garlic grew in many places, but her mother wrote that she should find it in the north. And her mother wanted her to learn Gaelic. Uncle Harold had told her many times that her mother had always loved the rugged Highlands where their sister had settled and that she'd wanted Meg to learn its ancient language.

She ran her finger down her mother's lightly slanted script to the last line of the garlic entry. "*Lorg an lus seo ann an uamh, an fuar uamh le moran na frith-rathaidean agus an blath cridhe anns am meadhon*," she pronounced with a slow cadence.

"'Find this plant in a cave, a cold cave with many paths and a warm heart in the middle,'" Caden said from where he stood behind her.

Meg's heart jumped, partly because he'd startled her and partly because, well, if she'd admit it, because it was Caden Macbain.

"A cold cave with a warm heart?"

Caden sat down on the log and turned the spit over the low flames. "What does that mean, lass?"

Meg huffed out a long breath. "I don't really know. I suppose there is a cave up north where I need to go to find…" Perhaps if she didn't stare at the amazingly large, ruggedly handsome warrior sitting so close in the deepening dark, her heartbeat would slow back to normal.

"What do you need to find?" His tone was casual and it brought her gaze back around. He sat close, watching.

She couldn't quite tear her eyes away from that gaze. "I...I don't know that, either."

"Something to do with the devil who's chasing ye?"

Meg tipped, just enough that he noticed. His eyes never left hers. She glanced down at her hands. She was a burden to these men.

"So ye do read." Ewan sat down on the other side of Meg and peered at the open book. "English and Gaelic?"

"Mostly English, some Gaelic," she answered in his language. She concentrated on keeping her breathing normal, even.

"Most unusual." He turned the rabbit on the spit. "Ye are the most unusual lass I've ever met."

Meg forced a little laugh. "I'm just an average Englishwoman raised in the countryside."

"Hardly," Ewan continued. "Ye shoot the bow as well as the goddess Diana." He motioned to the rabbit, which Meg had shot earlier. "Ye tend the impaired and injured." He moved his hand in the direction of the men milling around securing the horses. "Ye read." He tapped the book. "And ye're brave enough to journey alone without an escort."

"Foolish enough," Caden remarked.

She frowned at Caden, but he'd already beaten her to that particular facial expression. His favorite. She certainly didn't want to call attention to the fact she was far from the usual English maid, but she also didn't want this mighty warrior to think she was totally daft. If these men thought her clever, then they'd be less likely to try to trick her or take advantage of her lack of Highland knowledge.

"As I've mentioned numerous times, I had an escort. My wolf, Nickum, was and still is my escort." She pointed toward the woods. "He never leaves me. The first night we journeyed I thought six wolves would surely take us down. Nickum was just waiting until they tired before he attacked. As soon as I fell off of Pippen, he was right there to protect me."

Both men stared at her. Caden's teeth clenched shut, but Ewan's mouth hung open like a gasping fish. "Ye were on the ground with six hungry wolves?" he all but yelled.

"Well, I had shot three of them with my arrows," she explained and turned her gaze to the snapping flames. "So it was really just three wolves by that time."

"Ye could have been killed!" Ewan continued. As his hand brushed hers, she could sense his rapid heartbeat, his empty stomach, and full bladder.

"I was lucky that I didn't hit my head on a boulder when I fell."

"No, woman! The wolves, they could have torn ye apart," Ewan said.

Meg shook her head. "Not with Nickum following me." She turned to Caden. "So you see, I did not foolishly run away without an escort."

She waited for them to agree, acquiesce, or admit that she did know what she was doing, even though she really didn't. Instead, silence ensued as they all watched the rabbit turn.

"So ye are running away?" Ewan asked, the normal humor in his tone gone. "From who?"

Caden's eyes bored into her but kept her face forward. She needed to tell him something. She'd called his bluff before about leaving them, but she'd be foolish to do so. This band of Highlanders was her best chance of reaching her aunt safely.

"My mother died when I was five summers old." She hesitated. "A wicked man accused her of being a witch just because she helped people who were sick or injured. He had her burned."

Meg watched the sharp tongues of flame dance under the rabbit with the night breeze. Her mind touched on the awful dreams she'd had since her uncle had taken her away, the dreams born of whispers about her mother, whispers of how she screamed in the flames.

"And now he chases ye," Caden said.

Meg watched the fire. The bowing flames entranced her. She could almost imagine the image of a body moving in the blaze, screaming in the flame. She turned to him. "I do not want to burn, Caden."

"Holy God, why would anyone want to burn ye, lass?" Ewan asked.

"He thinks ye are a witch, too, because ye…help people," Caden answered.

"He doesn't know me." Meg focused on the fire. "He hasn't seen me since he took my mother away." She picked up a stick and pushed it into the dirt. "He might accuse me once he has me."

"Are ye a witch?" Ewan's whisper held a bit of awe.

"There is nothing but good in what I do. I have no dealings with Lucifer," she snapped.

"I…I didn't mean to—" Ewan stuttered.

"I need to get away from him."

"He cannot just take ye without yer guardian's permission," Ewan said. "Unless ye think he would steal ye away in the middle of the night." He gave an odd little laugh.

Meg squinted at him from her peripheral view.

"He could take ye if he was yer legal guardian," Caden said, his voice even.

The statement hung amongst them while Meg's stomach knotted. She wrapped her arms around her middle and leaned toward the warmth of the fire.

"Is he yer—" Ewan began.

"I think the hare is roasted through, Ewan." Caden cut him off. "Let's get our guest fed and to bed. We leave with the dawn."

Meg would have retorted that she wasn't a child, but Caden's words stopped any further interrogation. And she was tired. Down to the bone tired. She needed to keep her wits about her and exhaustion would only work against her. Tomorrow she'd enter into the heart of Scotland, the land of rugged mountains, raw beauty, and deadly secrets.

• • •

The moon was high when Caden laid his head down on the mossy ground outside Meg's tent. Perhaps her pet prowled nearby, perhaps not. Donald and four others were on the first watch and Caden had sent Ewan to sleep far away from the lass, far away from her pleasant expressions that had returned quickly after her anger cooled.

Caden watched the clouds blow across the sky, past the moon on their way north over the moors, over his home. Meg turned inside the tent, her body pushed outward against the confines of the draped blanket. He was only a few feet away. One roll and he'd be up against that warm outline.

"Bloody foolish," he whispered and closed his eyes against the sight of her backside molded by the blanket. He would keep his distance. The lass could lure any man with those long lashes and hazel eyes, the lushness of her mouth, the silky hair that lay around her soft curves. Half his men watched her like eager pups. If she weren't so beautiful he'd swear she was spelling them. Her strong, gentle spirit was bewitching enough. She had no need for magic.

Though Meg Boswell was not to be touched. She was a pawn to be used for a higher purpose, not a simple wench with which to dally. If she came to harm while in his protection, a peace might never be settled. And peace was more important than anything else.

Caden drifted in and out of sleep, as was his usual slumber on journeys. He was never parted from his sword and never completely unaware of those around him.

He first heard Meg's voice vibrate along the razor's edge of a dream.

"No, leave her alone. Let go…" she mumbled.

Caden's eyes snapped open, his fist tightened around the hilt of his sword. Darkness still shrouded the camp. His eyes sought out the guards walking the perimeter. Nothing seemed out of place.

"Go," Meg muttered. "Mama…don't go. No, don't take her

away."

The lass was dreaming. Her words pressed hard into his chest, clenching, making it more difficult to breathe. Pressure born of guilt perhaps or a need to protect the weak, whatever it was, it wrapped around him, made him ache to confront the foe in Meg's dreams, to slay her demon.

"Caden," she murmured on a breath.

Caden sat upright. Had she just called for him, called for him to save her?

"Help…" Her word tumbled into a whimper.

He pushed under the flap at the back of the tent. Meg lay wrapped in a binding cocoon of blanket, yet she shivered. Bloody hell, the lass was too delicate to be sleeping out on the cold ground as they traveled farther north. Thoughts of what she would be enduring if he hadn't found her made his heart beat even heavier.

"Macbain," she mumbled.

Caden knelt down, unsure what to do. "I'm here lass, ye're safe," he whispered near her ear. "Sleep. I will watch ye."

Meg muttered something but calmed with his words. She shivered again. There was no other blanket so he reached under the tarp and grabbed the blanket that was his pallet. He covered her with it and stared. Another quake jolted under the woolen, and her face crinkled as if she were in pain.

"More night terrors," he murmured and stretched out beside her. She rolled into his side immediately. His body radiated heat and Meg's soft nuzzle against him fueled it even more. She whimpered. He turned toward her and pulled her against him, cradling her. "Hush, lass. I'll chase away the bad.

Dream of the good now."

Meg's face relaxed, lips parted, the trembling ceased. Caden lay wrapped around her, listening to soft steady breaths, basking in the warm air escaping on exhales against the hollow of his throat, inhaling the sweet flower smell of her skin. He tried to close his eyes, tried to close his mind to the thought and sensation of her in his arms.

She's a hostage, a pawn. That is all. He said the words over and over again in the silence as he guarded her against the cold. With each repetition, the mantra turned more and more hollow until it sounded like a lie.

For four long days, Caden rode near Meg, watching her examine the journal, listening to Ewan expound on some native flora, and grumbling about the flush most of his men exhibited when she tended their injuries. And for three more nights, Caden stretched out next to her, muting the cold wind that skittered under the tent, and soothing the nightmares that tortured her. Each night he would start off with intentions of leaving once she settled into the depths of slumber. Each night he ended up wrapped around her soft, sleeping form only to disengage and roll out from under the tarp just before dawn.

Each morning his blanket was folded and laying over his horse's saddle. She never said a word.

...

Caden rubbed his jaw and took a washing gulp of spring water. The sun set below the tree line, and several of the young Macbains he'd brought secured the horses. Meg walked gracefully between the injured. She spent some time changing

Hugh's bandages. Caden discussed the two possible routes for the next day with his scout. When he turned back, she was staring at him from before a newly lit campfire.

She didn't turn away. He nodded before he thought better of it. Ewan conveniently appeared. Caden scowled and flexed his shoulder muscles.

Her lips seemed inclined to turn upward at him just because Ewan knew how to talk to lasses. She barely uttered a word to Caden, yet each night she turned into his warmth, his name often whispered on an exhale. That whisper alone was more enticing than a hall full of willing maids.

It would end as soon as they reached Druim Keep. One more night, perhaps two, if he decided to circumvent Munro land.

Two more nights, he decided. No need to risk the Munros stealing back his hostage. He couldn't push them too hard with a lady traveling with them. *Aye, two nights*. He leaned back near the fire to wait for everyone to fall asleep and the guards to walk on the far perimeter. Then he'd check to make certain his prisoner was warm enough.

Caden laid on his back with Meg snuggled into his side. His mind drifted in and out of dreams until the sound of a horse shot through his consciousness and snapped open his eyes. He didn't move, but the fingers of his left hand found the hilt of his short sword. Had he dreamt the horse nickering outside the tent? He breathed slowly. A low growl sent his blood rushing through his limbs. Damn. Was it her bloody wolf or some other beast? He shifted away from Meg's warmth and sat up, eyes and ears trained on the back flap of the tent.

The horse whinnied and trotted away at the same time a voice cursed from the other side. "*Cac!*"

The growl increased in volume.

"Nickum?" Meg opened sleep glazed eyes. She sat up and blinked. "Caden, what?" she started, and quickly assessed the sleeping arrangement. "Caden! You're sleeping with me!"

What could he say? There was no time to explain.

Nickum growled and snapped outside the tent.

"Nickum!" Meg called, her voice strained. "Caden!"

"Bloody beast!" a guttural voice yelled outside and Caden leapt up, yanking the blanket flap aside.

Girshmel stood, his sword in hand as the large wolf advanced toward him.

"Girshmel, what the bloody hell are you doing here?" Caden demanded.

Caden heard Meg stand behind him.

"Ho!" Ewan called, running up to the tent with a short dirk and a torch. His hair stood up at odd angles. "What is bloody going on?"

Donald followed Ewan and froze when he saw the wolf. The two perimeter guards also emerged from the night.

The wolf's stare moved between the men and Meg. The beast growled deep and snapped, fresh spittle flying from his muzzle. Girshmel stepped backward.

"He'll stop snapping if you put away your weapons," Meg advised crisply. Moonlight flickered through the moving branches. Splashes of white danced over the small crowd where they stood near the tent.

Ewan tucked his dirk in his boot and Caden tossed his

sword into the tent. The guards dropped their weapons. Nickum turned to Girshmel and crouched as if preparing to pounce.

"Keep a hold of that sword, Girshmel," Caden said lowly. "When the beast tears your throat out, it will save me the trouble of finding out why you were sneaking into Meg's tent in the middle of the night, with a horse waiting outside."

"What...I—" he began.

Nickum growled, ready to spring. Girshmel jumped and dropped his sword in the leaves. Nickum kept his eyes focused on him but backed up to sit beside Caden at Meg's feet.

"I thought I heard something, someone with the lass. I just thought to make sure she was safe." Girshmel held up both of his hands. "I didn't know it was you, chief, in there alone with her."

Meg gasped and ducked into the tent. "He was not invited," she bit out. Incoherent mumblings ensued with jabs of what could be colorful insults, yet she spoke them so softly Caden couldn't quite make them out. Caden's balled-up blanket hit the side of his legs where he stood just outside along with the hilt of his sword.

Ewan turned toward Caden. His face was filled with shadows, flickers of torchlight, and condemnation. *Hell!*

"Nickum," Meg called from inside, and the wolf nosed his way into the tent. Caden heard the beast lower its bulk onto the ground. At least the lass would be safe and probably warm with the wolf.

"I'm thinking you two may have something to discuss." Girshmel glanced between Ewan and Caden. The man picked up his sword and stalked out of the circle of torchlight.

"Girshmel," Caden said, his words hard as stone. "Do not go near Meg Boswell again. Am I clear?" What was hopefully clear was the promise of death under his words.

"Aye…chief," Girshmel said without a backward glance and disappeared into the night. Caden listened to Meg's muffled curses until she settled.

"Donald," Caden said. "Put a man on Girshmel…quietly."

Donald retreated with the guards.

Caden grabbed the blanket and sword and walked toward the dying fire.

Ewan followed. "You've been lying with her. Bloody hell, Caden! She was a maid."

Caden pivoted close to Ewan so that their words wouldn't carry. "She's still a maid."

"You mean you've lain next to her these nights—"

"To keep her warm. To help her sleep," Caden finished flatly.

"How bloody gallant of you," Ewan answered with unveiled sarcasm. "And here I thought you just liked to scowl at her."

Caden and Ewan stood only a breath apart, each of their faces rock hard.

"Ewan, she will hate us, all of us, when we reach Druim."

"You even more so for making her soft on you, stealing her honor—"

"I have barely touched the lass and have definitely not stolen her honor."

Ewan threw his arm out toward the tent. "You came from her tent where you two slept against one another! The guards, Girshmel, Donald…they all saw you."

"I'll make sure they understand what did not happen," Caden gritted out.

Ewan stepped back and tossed the lit end of the torch into the fire. "No wonder the lass moons over you."

What the hell was Ewan talking about? "She smiles at you, Ewan, not me."

Ewan ran his hand through his hair, making it stick out even more. "Aye, but her eyes follow you, Caden," he said low. "They search you out."

They both watched the thin blue and red flame of the torch catch along the dry wood left in the pit. So the lass did watch him. The heat of her stare wasn't just his imagination or the lust built by nights of inhaling her sweetness.

"She's simply a pawn to force the peace, Ewan. Don't get attached. She *will* hate us."

Ewan turned toward him. "What if she doesn't hate us?" he asked on the rush of an exhale.

Silence shrouded them, waiting, listening for a reply. The little flame snapped and crackled, flashing light against their faces as it grew.

Caden turned his head, his eyes locking with his friend's. His voice was low, cold, unbreakable. "Then she's mine."

Chapter Four

1 August 1517—Hedge Woundwort: reddish in color, hairy plant that flowers in summer.
Found in shady places, hidden away from the world. There are many paths to take to find Woundwort's ring of flowers. When in doubt, one should take the third path to the right.
Stamp the plant in vinegar and apply as a poultice to take away hard knots and inflammation. Use the leaves for healing persistent wounds.

Meg noted the subtle changes to the countryside as they traveled northward. Gently rolling meadows turned to coarse, mossy fields erupting with steps of jagged rock. They'd left the North Road two days before for another road that had dwindled to nothing but a pebbly path. Deciduous trees flapped their brightly colored leaves amid soaring pines under a crystal blue sky.

Meg let Pippen follow Donald as they wound their way along the edges of cliffs and down through autumn-colored valleys. Here snow already touched the tops of the mountains, and she kept her borrowed wool blanket tucked tightly around her. More than once she sent a prayer of thanksgiving that she wasn't alone, starving, freezing, and most likely lost. Or worse, prisoner of those dishonorable English soldiers.

Although she didn't speak about her thankfulness because she was still furious over Caden's trespass and embarrassed by everyone's knowledge of it. For they surely must know, even though no one said as much. How could they not know that their chief had bedded down with her? Meg was fairly certain that she was still a maid. If Caden had taken liberties with her body, she would have woken up. Wouldn't she? Just how much of her dreams about the Macbain chief was truth?

No one talked about the disappearance of that ogre, Girshmel, either. Donald had said that the man was a mercenary who'd been living amongst the Macbains for a couple months. Since he'd obviously offended the chief, he'd left. Because the man had taken his horse, it didn't appear that Caden had murdered him or Nickum eaten him. He'd simply left the morning after the incident.

Meg wondered what Donald would say if she asked him about the horrible drama of the other night. If only this long trip could be over. She could start over with her aunt's clan, where no one knew of her humiliation.

Donald held one finger against his lips. "Quiet now, lass," he whispered. "Dangerous terrain here." He pointed up to a line of trees above them. "Ambush territory."

Meg glanced around her. She drew her bow across her lap and nocked an arrow. Her gaze moved between the narrow path and the tree line above. She hadn't thought about enemies other than her father after they'd crossed into Scotland. Of course there were enemies even within one's own country. She just hadn't considered it so close to the Macbain border. Whose lands were they traversing?

After an eternity of watchful silence, the winding trail along the side of the mountain gave way to a moor filled with late blooming wildflowers and purple heather. The men pushed their mounts into a run across the sun-washed expanse.

Donald pulled back beside Meg. "We're almost home, lass." He pointed ahead. "Just past those boulders is Macbain land. No need to keep quiet now."

He kicked his horse into a gallop.

Meg twisted around as the men raced past her on both sides, smiles cracking along their dirty, fuzzy faces. She tapped Pippen and raced after them. The relief of almost being at her aunt's, the fresh wash of mountain air along her skin, the surge of her horse after days of sedate walking. The speed was more than her frown could take. She beamed widely. Halfway across, she glanced over one shoulder and her heart leapt high. Caden rode behind, restraining his charger to match Pippen's pace.

The sun beat down. The wind tugged at her loose braid, pulling several locks free to fly behind like errant ribbons. Meg's blood pumped under her skin, warming her as she bent forward along Pippen's neck and kicked lightly, giving him freedom to run.

Caden's mount surged up next to Pippen. He rode with the ease of someone raised on the back of a horse, much like herself. She narrowed her eyes and quirked the grin into a challenge.

"*Siuthad!*" she yelled to Pippen, urging him to stretch his legs against the speed of Caden's charger. Pippen flew across the wildflowers, hooves tossing chunks of soft peat behind him. Meg laughed and lay low over Pippen's neck. She glanced to the side. Caden leaned across his charger's mane, his eyes sparked with appreciation and suppressed laughter.

"Slow down, lass!" he warned.

"Ha!" She laughed and steered Pippen around the boulders out into another meadow that led to the shores of a large lake.

"Ye'll break yer bonny neck."

Meg flew past the other Macbains who'd already reached the second meadow. Pippen reached the lake in a splashing of hooves and she pulled back on his reins. She laughed and stroked her hand along his sweating neck. Her horse pranced in the shallows and then lowered his head to drink.

Caden's horse splashed to a halt next to her and she tried not to look at him. The world was too beautiful, the air too clear to frown with anger and justified embarrassment. Instead, she absorbed the wild glory of the landscape.

Mountains, some low and some soaring, encircled the valley basin where they stood. Snow-tipped green pines and trees of gold, red, and orange covered the mountain slopes. If God was the artist, He'd taken vegetable dye and delicately enhanced each tree up the hillside. The sun sparkled along the choppy waves in the lake and the wind blew fresh against Meg's skin. She breathed in a full gulp, letting it cleanse her.

Caden maneuvered his charger next to Pippen.

"God lives here," she said, her words edged with whispered

awe.

Caden's voice was also hushed. "Aye, 'tis more than just beauty in it. There's spirit and courage and strength." He dismounted into the knee-high water and led Pippen and his charger out to dry ground. "'Tis why men fight for her," he said.

"You mean fight for *it*," she said and stared down into his eyes. Clear air and sunshine filled her. Alive! She was more alive here than ever before. He reached up for her and before she could react, he plucked her off Pippen and set her on the ground.

She would have gasped but there wasn't time. Pippen was now at her back and Caden stood tall as a mountain before her. She glanced down and then straight before her. Both positions seemed awkward. She finally tipped her head way back until her gaze met his again.

"You mean fight for *it*, the land, the mountains," Meg corrected.

"Aye." He stepped back and pulled Meg away from the horses. He pointed toward one mountain.

"Druim Beinn," he said.

"Ridge Mountain," Meg translated.

"Druim Keep, my home, sits at its base."

"You own all this land?" she asked. "Up to that mountain?"

Caden's finger traced along three mountains to the east and west. "From there to there, all the way to where we stand, lass, belongs to the Macbains."

Meg's eyes roamed the vastness. "And which way are the Munros?"

When she turned to him, his face resembled stone, his eyes

dark.

"What's wrong?" she asked.

"Much."

He touched her hair and the space between them seemed to dissolve as he moved closer. A shiver ran through her that had little to do with the cool wind.

"There are things ye must be told and I will tell ye, Meg."

He touched her back and she instantly registered his rushing blood, his contracting biceps, and his tight muscles. The vessels in his head flexed with tension. He must have an ache in his head.

Meg concentrated on his physical parameters instead of the way his fingers threaded down to the ends of her hair. She should move away. She should breathe. Meg drew in a breath as he cupped her cheek in a warm palm.

"First…" he trailed off as his lips lowered.

Good Lord, what is he doing?

Meg's heart pounded as his breath touched hers. His lips followed. Warm and powerful, Caden's mouth moved gently over hers. She inhaled his piney masculine scent. Twisting bubbles tickled inside her stomach. Her head slanted on its own, unknowingly allowing the kiss to deepen. She sensed the energy filling his body, blood rushing even faster, heart thumping in rhythm with hers.

Good Lord, what am I doing back?

Caden growled low and lifted her into the shelter of his body. Meg's fingers moved up to the soft waves of his hair, the same waves she'd been staring at for days. Giddy excitement, mixed with something far deeper, ran through her body like a poison, spreading to the ends of every extremity. She all but clung to him as her legs wobbled like a freshly born colt. She breathed and kissed and tasted while a tingling ache grew heavy in her abdomen. What new malady was this? Madness and necessity all wrapped together.

Pulling back, Caden rested his forehead against hers. She breathed in his essence, not wanting to let go.

"Meg," he said, his lips so close to hers that they brushed them in a feather-light kiss. He was talking again. She tried to pay attention. "There are things ye need to know—"

Nickum howled. The warning snapped Meg out of her fog and into alert.

"Nickum?" She pulled out of Caden's arms. Something was wrong. Nickum stood at the crest of the hill near the tree line. Her wolf wouldn't expose himself in daylight and wouldn't call out unless under dire circumstances.

Meg took two steps away from Caden and turned at the same time Ewan's voice rang out through the glade.

"Macbains! Batail!" His tone poured ice water through Meg's flushed body.

"Meg!" Caden shouted at the same instance she heard an arrow *zing* through the air. A small patch of meadow grass beside her leapt into the air as the arrow punctured the serene hillside.

"God's teeth!" she swore on a gasp.

"Get down!" Caden ordered.

Zing!

The sharp pain ripped through Meg's shoulder, slamming into her with enough force to yank her body to the ground. She flew off her feet and into the lake.

Icy mountain lake water filled her mouth as she gasped, clogging her airways. Bubbles and splashing filled her ears. Red water swirled before her eyes as she blinked into the murk.

"Nay! Meg!" Caden's voice sounded far away even when his arms lifted her. The weight of the water in her hair pulled her head backward and the heavy clothes anchored her limbs. She couldn't move, couldn't open her eyes, could hardly draw a breath. Her self-defense surfaced enough to make her cough, lake water sputtering up and out. Caden turned her gently in his arms.

"Bloody hell!" he cursed. He ran then, with her cradled against his chest.

The jarring hurt, but she couldn't respond above a whimper. She was too heavy, too cold. Nickum's whine seemed near and far at the same time. Was this really happening? *Please be a nightmare!* Although while everything else seemed fuzzy, the pain was very real.

Caden lowered her to the ground, the heaviness of a blanket anchoring her. "Stay with her," he said. Nickum's fur brushed her face. "Let no one touch her." His warm lips touched her forehead and he was gone.

Meg tried to open her eyes but they were too heavy. She fought for consciousness. At least her ears worked. Steel slid and clattered against steel. Men yelled curses in Gaelic, their words slurring into each other in a cacophony of anger and retaliation. A malevolent storm of human angst, hatred mixed with the desperate need to survive, judge, and execute. Hot tears leaked out of her eyes.

"There she is," a rough, familiar voice called. Nickum growled and moved over the top of her, his back foot against Meg's cheek. "*Cac!* That wolf is guarding her."

Girshmel. It was Girshmel! He'd joined the enemy, whoever that was.

"I'm not going near it," another voice said in fast Gaelic. "That's the largest damned wolf I've ever seen."

Nickum rubbed against her as he sat back on his haunches, preparing to leap. A silent scream. *No, Nickum, they'll hurt you! Run!* Nickum growled and snapped, making one man yelp.

"Bloody coward," Girshmel snarled. "The chief will want her. She's Meg Boswell, the Munro's niece. Valuable and a sweet little tidbit at that."

"Then you get her," the other voice said.

"You idiot, give me your bow," Girshmel said.

No! Nickum, run! Her words trickled out on a whimper. Nickum stood his ground over her, growling and snapping. She heard the bowstring pluck and the arrow rip into Nickum. Nickum cried out but didn't move, just leaned into her. She choked on a straggled breath as she detected the torn flesh and muscles with her unnatural abilities. Blood surged through her friend with energy to fight or run.

"There now, he's weak. See his eyes? He's stunned. Pull the lass out by her feet," Girshmel said. "Hurry, Macbain might come back."

Nickum didn't growl. He didn't do anything when rough hands grasped her ankles. *Oh, Nickum. What have they done?* The man pulled. She focused on her leg muscles to kick at the man, but blood was flowing out of her too fast to give her muscles the energy they needed to fight. Oh, God, she was losing too much blood!

Nickum's muscles contracted, and he sprang away. The man dropped her ankles. She tried to block out the sound of teeth and ripping flesh. She tried to roll, pull herself away from the carnage, but her blood-starved body wouldn't cooperate. Fresh tears leaked from her closed eyes.

"Shite!" Girshmel yelled over the gurgling sound of blood and screams. She heard him fire another arrow. Nickum's cry rent the air. Meg couldn't even flinch, let alone try to help her friend.

"Damn, he's coming!" Girshmel poured out a string of obscenities, and she heard his feet pound away. The other man's screams died with his breath and Nickum's bulk collapsed beside her leg. Meg lay there trapped in agony, unable to move. The numbness that blanketed her body moved higher until she could barely contain the glimmer of consciousness. Perhaps it would be better to surrender.

"Meg," a faint whisper of a voice called to her, urgent, full of fury and something more, desperation perhaps. "Meg!"

Caden. She sighed inside the tiny wisp of conscious thought still aflame. Caden had returned. With the sound of his voice, she gave into the blackness.

· · ·

Rachel Munro sat before the fire in the great hall stitching a shirt for her husband. The flames crackled and she warmed with contentment. She barely remembered her life in England, growing up as a merchant's daughter with her sister, Isabelle, and brother, Harold. She'd married Alec Munro, the new chief of the Munros, soon after Alec's father died. The old Munro had been business partners with Rachel's father, and she had convinced her father to bring her along on one of his trips to the fabled Highlands. She'd never left since, except once when her sister had given birth down in England.

Rachel loved the Highlands, the rugged beauty, the solid, simple life. She'd fit in easily with these passionate people. And of all the passionate people that she fit with, Alec Munro was definitely the one who kept her on her toes, even today after all these years.

She watched him play a game of chess with his old friend, Phillip, at the long table across the hall.

Alec slammed his hand down on the oak planks, making the wooden pieces jump and Phillip curse. Her husband was full of bluster, pride, and passion. A true Highlander. She loved him fiercely. Thank the good Lord she hadn't returned to England like her father had wanted, like he'd made Isabelle do. She doubted that Alec would have let her go, but if she had, she'd probably ended up wed to an English dandy or worse, a monster like the man her sister wed.

Rowland Boswell was elegant with a courtier's handsome façade, but he was also demanding, cruel, and suspicious. If only their father had known what an atrocious match he'd forced on Isabelle. That his choice in suitors would ultimately lead to his gentle daughter's death. And if Rachel couldn't get Isabelle's daughter out of England, the same could very well befall the child.

Rachel frowned and stared down at her finger where a tiny

bead of blood swelled up from a pinprick. Even thinking of the dreadful man was dangerous. She closed her eyes and formed a pea-sized blue glowing orb between her other thumb and forefinger. She passed the lighted sphere over the minute hole and sealed the skin.

"Devil of a man," she cursed, and snuffed the light.

"Talking to yourself, wife?" Alec asked, and peered down over her head.

Rachel tilted back. "Just pondering how I can get you to brave English soil to rescue my niece."

Alec huffed and pulled on his wiry beard. He scraped the second chair along the stone floor to face the fire and flopped into it. "We've been through this, Rachel."

They had, many times. Around and around, Rachel knew all the arguments against it.

"I've been forbidden to set foot on English soil, Rachel. That weasel of a man got a bloody royal decree."

She poked the needle through the linen. "Bloody royal decree. I know."

"I don't fear for *my* life," he defended.

She didn't look up, but reached out and patted his arm. "Of course I don't want you to die, husband, but no Englishman could best you."

"I'd forfeit my lands. You and Searc would be landless, homeless." He stared into the crackling fire. "Is one girl worth the lives of the whole clan?"

Rachel watched her minute stitches. "You risk our clan every time you refuse a truce with the Macbains." Her words were feather soft, floating on a whisper, because they didn't need to be any louder.

Alec's fist slammed onto the wooden arm of the chair. She had held her needle still with her words so as not to jab herself again. She rarely jumped anymore, but it was good to be prudent, nonetheless.

"Why do I bother to come sit with you, woman, when you plague me so?"

Rachel watched him from the corner of her eyes. "Because you love me, you stubborn old mountain of a man."

He turned his head from the fire. His eyes sought hers and she swallowed against the increased pace of her heart. The silent promise reminded her of long ago days when he would chase her through the wildflowers across the moors. Alec stood and leaned in front of her, his hands braced on each of the wooden arms. She tilted back, no longer able to see her work, and returned his stare.

"Aye, that I do," he said low and leaned forward, kissing her lips gently. The gesture was so sweet that Rachel yelped when he shoved his arm under her legs and lifted her. His unfinished shirt slid from her lap to the rushes.

"Alec! What are you about?" she called as he strode with her across the main hall. He leered at her and she couldn't stop a giggle from erupting.

"I think I'm about to remind you, lass, just what a randy old mountain man you're strapped to."

She laughed and clung to his neck.

The towering double doors to the keep banged open with a gust of autumn-chilled wind. Alec planted his feet and turned.

"Geoffrey," Alec said, and let Rachel slide to the floor.

"What are you doing here?"

Geoffrey was a Munro who had been living with the Macbains, covertly keeping an eye on the Munro's most dangerous enemy.

"Caden Macbain," he breathed in large gulps of air, as if he'd run the whole way from Druim Keep.

Rachel placed her hands on him. His heart rate was too high, but he was young and could handle the exertion.

"Caden Macbain asks for you to come," he said and handed Rachel a rolled parchment with a bit of grime-splattered plaid tied to it before resting his hands on his knees.

"I'm not bloody likely to walk into that death trap." Alec swore and tried to grab the letter, but Rachel was too quick.

Geoffrey straightened. "Not you," he said, finding his breath. "Lady Munro."

"*Mac an donais!*" Alec swore. "And neither is my wife. Has the Macbain hit that thick head of his?"

Rachel scanned the parchment. Her breath caught in her throat, her eyes narrowed, and she turned to Alec. She held out the bloodied rag.

"Did you send men to attack the Macbains at Loch Tuinn this noon time?" she asked.

Alec grabbed the scrap of material. "Lies," he grumbled. "As if I can tell this is Munro blood. Phillip!" he yelled, though the man was right there. "Did you send out men to Loch Tuinn?"

"Nay," his second in command answered. "We trained in hand to hand all morn and worked the rest of the day to fortify the north wall."

The knot in Rachel's stomach loosened, but she frowned all the more. She handed her husband the parchment. "Margaret," she called.

A young woman came running in from the back storage rooms.

"Come with me, girl. I need to pack my things." She turned to Geoffrey. "Wait for me."

He nodded while Alec shook his head.

"You are not going, Rachel," Alec said firmly. Her husband was the most stubborn man she'd ever met, but she was his match.

Rachel turned back to him slowly. She indicated the letter. "The Macbain has brought Isabelle's daughter here and she's been shot at the loch, by who we don't know. Meg may die without me." She shook her head, never breaking contact with his eyes so that he could read her unmoving sincerity. "I won't allow Isabelle's daughter to also be murdered. I'm going."

Alec took a step toward her. "He thinks we attacked them. He'll keep you as hostage, woman."

"He pledges that he will not keep me if I help Meg. You read it."

Alec dropped the parchment to the floor. "A Macbain won't keep his word."

"His father may not have, but we've heard that Caden is different."

"Nay!" Alec yelled, his face turning bright red. "He's still a bloody Macbain, without honor. I will not let my wife just walk into his trap. This is all a lie!"

"Geoffrey," she said calmly, though she held her husband's

burning gaze. "Did you see an injured woman brought into Druim Keep this day?"

"Aye, milady. All the men said it was Meg Boswell."

Rachel's stomach clenched with a mix of frantic worry and excitement that her niece was finally away from England.

"And just how did the Macbains end up with your niece?" Alec jumped on the question. "Steal her away from England? Using her against us! Nay! You aren't going, wife!"

Rachel shut her eyes for a long moment, then walked to her husband. She touched his blotchy face. His heart raced as if in battle, every muscle in his body tightened, his stomach clenched. Worry. The corners of Rachel's lips turned up.

"I love you, too, Alec." She stared into his blue eyes and stroked her hand down to sit on his upper arm where she squeezed. "I have to go to Meg. She's all I have left of Isabelle. You know I can save her."

Alec breathed out low. "Nay, woman. Do not go."

"I will be safe. And I know you have half a dozen faithful Munros over there that could secret me out if need be." Rachel sensed Alec's blood slowing in his veins. His chest relaxed. "You, husband, get to fight on the battlefield to save your family. Let me save mine."

He stared at her a long moment and Rachel knew she'd already won, but she would wait until he gave his approval. Husbands must appear to be in control even when they weren't.

Alec continued to stare while he spoke out to the room. "Phillip, prepare a group of twenty men to escort Lady Munro to her niece. Let Macbain know that we were not at Loch Tuinn today and that if anything unpleasant should befall my wife, I will have his head for Christmas supper. I expect her returned within the week."

Rachel leaned in and kissed her husband hard on his lips. She turned and ran with Margaret up the stairway.

• • •

"She is growing hot." Caden's voice rushed about the room. His hand lay along Meg's cheek.

"Shock turns to fever fairly quickly in a wee lass," Caden's housekeeper, Evelyn, said and tucked a blanket around Meg.

Caden took up the damp rag from a clay bowl and washed Meg's forehead. This wasn't supposed to happen. Meg Boswell was to be used to force a peace, but she wasn't to be harmed in the process. The mission: to quickly take her from her home in England, to bring her safely up to the Highlands, and then give her to The Munro in exchange for a promise of peace and the return of their livestock. Simple.

Bloody hell! He should have anticipated the attack, should have shielded her, had her constantly surrounded by his men.

Evelyn shook her graying head, her hands on her ample hips as she peered at Meg, studying her. "A bonny lass. Hard to believe she's niece to a witch."

She touched the heavy cross that hung from her neck. "She's but a wee thing." Evelyn's gaze turned to the hearth. "Smart of her to keep that beast around, I suppose." She eyed Nickum lying unconscious on his side before the fire.

Caden stood on the opposite side of the bed. Meg did seem small in it. He had broken the shaft of the arrow that still lay in her torn shoulder. She lay flat under the light blanket. She was pale, like the dead, her dark lashes stark against ashen cheeks. Her shallow breaths barely moved the blanket. He watched them closely for several seconds to make sure they continued a regular rhythm.

Nickum whimpered but did not rise. Ewan and Donald had pulled the arrows from his body and wrapped him tight, but more was needed to bring the animal back.

His gaze returned to Meg and he ran a palm against her cheek. "Where is her aunt?"

"I sent Geoffrey with your letter as soon as you gave it to me."

"Send for Fiona from the village," he ordered. "She knows the ways of healing."

"You need more than herbs to fix that," Evelyn said, pointing to Meg's covered shoulder.

His chest numbed, hollow, empty. "Send for Fiona. If Rachel Munro doesn't come by midnight, I will bring her."

Evelyn opened the door to the chamber. "What's this?"

Caden turned to see corridor filled with warriors.

Ewan peered over Evelyn's head, and into the room. "We're here to see if there is anything we can do."

"Anything you can do?" Evelyn asked.

"Aye, for Meg," Donald said. "The wee lass helped most of us on the mission."

Ewan spoke loud. "Aye, even saved The Macbain's hard head, she did."

Evelyn's gaze moved between the men and Caden. She shook her head. "The chief will have need of you if the Witch Munro doesn't come. And perhaps two of you to help hold the lass when Fiona pulls out the point of the arrow."

"I will help," Hamish called from the back.

"So will I," Kieven stated, and tried to shove through. "She saved my leg from turning black."

"*Stad!*" Evelyn called and yanked Ewan and Donald into the room. "Kieven, be a help and find Fiona. Tell her to bring her cures."

Kieven's footfalls sounded through the stone corridor.

"Hamish, we'll call you if you're needed. Now all of you go back down and find something to put in your bellies. Did you bring any game back from England?"

"Aye," another man called. "Meg even helped with that."

Evelyn snorted. "For a Munro, you all think rather highly of the miss."

"She isn't a Munro, she's a Boswell," another insisted.

"Well you think rather highly then of an English lass with Munro blood in her veins," Evelyn countered and shooed the rest of them away from the door.

Donald stood near Nickum at the hearth. "You think he will die, too?"

"No one is dying," Caden said with determined patience, barely concealing the threat in his voice.

Evelyn moved back to the other side of the bed. "I'd say that your men are not the only ones thinking highly of the English Munro."

Evelyn had been his nursemaid, his housekeeper, his friend, especially when his mother had died. And she'd always been able to see the truth in him even when he wasn't sure of it himself.

He stared down at Meg's pale forehead. "If she dies, we have nothing to bargain with, Evelyn. There'll be no chance for peace."

There. That was a plausible explanation for the twisting in his gut. He met Evelyn's steely blue eyes. "The Munros may even blame us for her death."

"Even though it is one of their bloody arrows in her?" Donald asked.

"They may say it wasn't them," Ewan retorted. "Alec Munro didn't ride with them."

Caden's eyebrow rose. "Did anyone see his son, Searc?"

"Nay," Ewan answered. "Nor did I see Gormal or Phillip. But the bastards called themselves Munros."

Caden frowned. The door flew open, hitting the wall.

"That would be because Munros were not at Loch Tuinn at noon today." A comely lady with a long braid stalked regally into the room. She shed her outer fur-lined cape, let it fall to the floor, and moved directly to Meg.

"They called themselves Munro," Ewan repeated.

Sharp blue eyes flashed to Caden. "Someone is tricking you, Macbain," the woman said. She was shorter than he'd thought she'd be, but there was no missing the strength she possessed in her resolve.

"Rachel Munro has arrived," Fiona announced as she and Hamish hefted a large kettle of water to set over the hearth.

"You mean the Witch Munro," Rachel said softly and gave Caden a sardonic smirk before turning back to her niece. She touched Meg's cheek with the flat of her hand and frowned. "Heat the water. Rip these rags. Mix these herbs with fresh water. Turn her on her side. I'll brace her; you push through swift and straight, Macbain."

Caden waited for Rachel to grasp her firmly and he held her back right where the barbed tip poked through. She seemed so fragile in his hands, so small. Rachel nodded. Bloody hell, he hated to do this! *One, two, three!*

Meg screamed, even through her unconsciousness, as Caden forced the arrow through her shoulder and out the back. Blood welled up, spilling out of the holes.

"Hold her on her side! Move!" Rachel placed her hands flat against the ragged flesh on both sides. "Keep her still." She closed her eyes, inhaled, exhaled, her cheeks puffed out with the volume of air, and then shrank with her exhale. A bright blue light glowed out from under her hands.

"What bloody witchcraft..." Ewan whispered.

Evelyn murmured and made the sign of the cross. Donald took a step backward, toward the hearth. Only Fiona seemed unimpressed by the strange process. Rachel continued to hold Meg between her hands, eyes squeezed shut. Her face pinched tight as if she struggled against a great weight.

Seconds ticked by with Caden's heartbeats, hundreds of them. The blue glow softened against Meg's skin, softened until it faded to nothing.

"Catch her, Macbain," Rachel whispered and slumped into a sitting position on the side of the bed. Fiona jumped to steady Rachel while Caden lowered Meg back to the plump tick. His eyes sought out the ragged holes. Neither one bled.

"Good Holy Christ the Lord," Evelyn said, her hand pressed against her lips. She peered close at the holes. "They are…healed."

"Fiona," Rachel said, her voice weak. "Pack a poultice of hedge woundwort leaves on each wound. Change the dressing once a day and it will heal completely without issue."

Caden raised his eyes from Meg to her aunt. Rachel Munro was drained, like a wet cloth rung out until not a drop of moisture remained. Her courageous spirit was dimmed, her flashing eyes sunken.

"Ewan," Caden said. "Help Lady Munro to the fire to sit."

At first he thought she would argue, but then she leaned on Ewan's arm as he helped her shuffle across the room. "I will be fit again once I rest," she announced and accepted a cup from Fiona.

"Evelyn, have a room made ready for Lady Munro."

"Nay, Macbain. I will remain with my niece," she said.

The flames crackled in the hearth, throwing shadows across the stone walls of the room. No one moved. Caden nodded to Evelyn, setting everything into motion once again. He sat on the bed next to Meg. Color crept back into her face. He touched her forehead. Warm, not hot. His gaze drifted to Rachel where she sat slumped before the hearth. The witch had taken the lass's fever, too. At what cost to her?

"She still must sleep, Macbain, for my healing to take hold." Rachel's words carried despite Ewan and Donald sloshing the pot of dirty water out through the door, and Evelyn and Fiona carrying blankets in and out. Evelyn's eyes stayed on Rachel as if the woman might grow horns and a tail at any moment.

Caden brushed a finger along Meg's cheek and then stood. He walked to the hearth, around Meg's wounded pet. Fiona took the empty cup from Rachel.

"Fiona," Caden said. "Can you make some of your poultice for Meg's beast?"

Rachel's eyes flickered open and her head came up to stare at the animal as if she hadn't noticed his massive presence before.

The maid's large eyes showed a healthy amount of fear.

"Donald and I will put it on the beast. I would not have Meg wake to find her beloved friend dead after he stood his ground over her." Caden's gaze connected with Rachel's. "He saved her life while we fought off…whoever ambushed us."

Rachel's eyes softened as if she understood that it had taken him much to recognize the possibility of trickery in the attack.

"Did you already remove the tips?" Rachel asked.

Caden nodded. "He lost a lot of blood."

"Fiona," Rachel said. "Mix some feverfew with the same poultice you will make for Meg." She paused and closed her eyes, head falling against the straight back of the chair. "Once I'm rested, I will *pray*," she said, "over the beast as well."

"Pray?" Evelyn said low, and shook her head as she headed out the door.

"Yes, pray." Rachel opened her pale blue eyes. She leaned forward and caught Caden's hand to leverage into a standing position. "My gift is from God," she said as they stepped toward the bed. "I am no Lucifer-worshipping witch, Macbain."

Caden tipped his head briefly, and she relaxed into his arm. He helped Rachel down. Side by side with her niece, there were few traits showing their blood connection. Only their build and long slender fingers were similar.

"Is this gift passed on through generations?" He placed a blanket over the woman.

"Yes." Rachel turned toward Meg. "Sometimes to our detriment." She closed her eyes and began to breathe in a slow steady rhythm, falling instantly asleep.

Caden moved around the bed to sit in a chair near Meg. Long lashes lay like fans against soft skin; light freckles sprinkled across the gentle slope of her nose. Her eyes moved behind the lids following her dreams.

Meg's pink lips parted on an exhale. "Caden…"

Caden leaned over the bed. "Ye're safe, Meg," he whispered.

A quick glance showed that the room lay empty as Fiona had gone to the kitchens to prepare the poultices.

"Caden," Meg murmured.

He ran his thumb across one smooth cheek, down to her jaw near her ear, then followed the soft lines of her neck. "Sleep, lass. Ye're safe and well." The same words he'd used each night while she battled her dream demons.

Meg released a sigh and surrendered to a deeper slumber. Caden sat back on the rickety chair.

"Interesting," Rachel said from her side of the bed. Her eyes flicked open. "She calls for her captor in her dreams?"

"She doesn't know that she is a captive," Caden said, his words gruff but without remorse. "She believes that fate brought her an escort to you. She runs from some man, I think her father." Rachel frowned and Caden continued. "In all truth she would have died on her way here alone, if I hadn't run into her."

"She has not had an easy time avoiding death while in your care, either, Macbain." Wise eyes assessed him sideways. Rachel pushed up on her elbow.

"I ask you not to tell her," Caden said. "If she thinks she's a guest—"

"So Meg is a hostage?" Rachel asked.

Caden paused. He inhaled slowly to help the twist in his stomach that he ignored. Just because his plan had deviated from the original one, he wouldn't give it up. Bargaining for peace was his best chance at saving his people.

"Aye. Your niece is the only thing I have left to bargain with. I will release her to the Munros when your husband agrees to a peace between us."

"You also have me now," Rachel said.

"I gave my word that you could go." Caden's jaw hardened. He wouldn't break his promise.

"Even when your larders are empty and your cattle have been raided away?"

"I do not go back on my word," he all but growled.

A softness tugged at the corner's of her mouth. "So I told Alec. Very well. You be the one to tell her."

Simple words, but powerful. The tightness in his chest relaxed. The news must come from him. He owed Meg that much for using her need for escape as an easy way to ensure her cooperation.

"Why do you think it's her father who chases her?" Rachel asked.

He leaned back. "She mentioned that her mother was killed." He'd leave out the fact that a lot of what he'd learned had been from Meg's nighttime talking. "That a man had accused her of being a witch and had taken her away to be burned. She fears this man would legally be able to take her. She never mentioned a father." He rubbed at the tension above his eyes. "Who else would it be?"

Rachel's lips pinched. "So the bastard has realized his jeopardy."

"What's his name?" He would have a name for the one who tortured Meg in her dreams?

"Rowland Boswell. He's got some title in England, but it doesn't mean anything except that he can play court games. Isabelle, Meg's mother—my sister—discovered his treasonous plans. She thought that if her husband was caught, her daughter would lose everything. Colin Macleod tried to rescue her but she wouldn't leave. Knew she was close to ruining Rowland's plans for good. I don't think my sister knew just how far Rowland would go to punish her."

"So the marriage wasn't one of love?" he asked.

Rachel snorted and swore under her breath. "My sister was...dutiful. When my father demanded she return to England and marry, she protested once, but when Father threatened to take his revenge on the Macleods, she returned."

"You were more fortunate."

"Father did not approve of my praying and how I wouldn't hide it. When he heard Alec wanted to marry me despite my talents, he blessed the union."

"Isabelle had similar talents?"

"Aye, though only I knew. She hid them completely. Boswell created those charges of witchcraft. They were lies."

They sat in silence. Caden watched Meg breathe.

"Could Meg have your talent?"

When she didn't answer, his gaze raised to her. A smile haunted her lips. "As far back as I've been able to trace, every woman in my line has." Rachel pulled back the sleeve of her kirtle. A brown shape lay against her skin. She held it up so that the light of the fire caught it, revealing a large birthmark.

"The mark of the dragonfly," she said. "My mother had one on her leg, her sister on her hip, their mother on the bottom of her foot. Isabelle's was also on her foot." She lowered her arm. "We're fabled to have stemmed from a great healing witch in the tenth century, from somewhere in Denmark."

Maybe Meg didn't have one. Perhaps the lass was without this power. He'd watched her carefully with his men and had never seen a blue light. None of their wounds had healed quickly like Meg's had. "I haven't seen a dragonfly on her."

"Have you seen her naked?"

"Nay," he snapped, but then smoothed the edge from his voice. "There's been no mark on those areas exposed. And she healed my men with constant care, not magic."

Rachel shrugged and relaxed back down into the hay-filled tick. "How unfortunate."

"Unfortunate?"

"Death stalks all of us, Macbain. Talents such as mine fend it off for a time."

He'd never thought of it that way. His whole life he'd heard stories of the Munro Witch, how she healed with dark magic and that her soul would pay the price. Yet he saw no evidence of demonic presence or a dark nature. She didn't pray to Satan or require a payment for her dark arts. Would he have paid it if she had?

"Aye, in this cold, war-loving land, God's gift to heal is more valuable than gold," she said.

Caden squelched the question of Rachel's two buried sons. "Either way, your niece is extremely valuable."

Rachel didn't answer but snuggled down under the blanket next to Meg.

More valuable than gold? Perhaps a strange birthmark and an ability to heal with magic would make his hostage even more valuable. Munro would eventually want to marry his niece off. She would have to wed someone who didn't condemn her for this gift, if she had it.

Caden ignored the tension in his shoulders. He needed to think of every way possible to make his bargaining chip even more important.

Meg's eyes remained closed, her breathing even. He closed his heavy eyes and leaned back into the hard seat where he planned to stay the night, remembering Meg's kiss at the loch. Her softness and smell, the joy on her face.

He rubbed at the tightness in his chest. His mind turned to explanations, words, scenarios. He'd show her the children, introduce the families she was saving. He would show her, ask her how to save them, nudge her in the direction he'd chosen. Peace.

Caden needed peace to save his clan. He wouldn't let her hate him. Nay, he wouldn't let her, for he intended to kiss her again.

Chapter Five

15 September 1517—Honeysuckle: white, bell-shaped flowers in summer. The scent is pleasant and can be used in soaps and lotion (my favorite scent). Flowers throughout the summer months spread its sweet smell far and away. Ah, Saorsa! Use a decoction of the flowers to treat breathing disorders. The syrup may also be used to treat lung and spleen complaints. Use weakened syrup to treat nervous headaches. An ointment can be made with the plant and boiled animal fat to ease the burn from the sun and to rid ladies of spots.

Meg's eyes flickered open to a dimly lit stone wall. Heavy tapestries hung on the walls. Where was she? She inhaled swiftly. The loch! She gazed down at her shoulder where a poultice lay tied against her skin on the front and back. Tightness lightly pinched her skin.

"Hold him," a woman's stern voice instructed near the fire. The sound of a body being dragged across the stone floor pushed Meg into a sitting position.

"Nickum?" she whispered.

Caden held her best friend against his chest. A woman with a long braid pressed her hands to the wolf's side. He'd been shot, at the loch, standing over her. Meg's heart raced as images and sounds flooded back. How long ago had it happened? She was about to call out when she saw a familiar blue light grow along the crack between the woman's hands and Nickum's fur. The same blue light that Meg could conjure.

Caden stood solid. He didn't jump back in surprise at the unnatural light. He peeled a poultice off higher up Nickum's body, and the woman ran her glowing hands through Nickum's fur.

Meg edged over to the side of the large bed and pulled back the blankets. She'd been stripped to her thin smock. She shivered as her toes touched the rock floor.

"Unbelievable," she murmured at her own strength. Shot clear through, but no fever raged and her shoulder was nearly healed. Had the woman used her glowing light to heal her?

Nickum's legs twitched and a low growl issued from his clenched mouth.

"Hold still, beast," the woman growled back.

Caden glanced toward Meg. "Meg, ye are standing?"

"I can help," she offered, but her voice had lost its usual strength.

The woman's eyes lifted briefly and returned to her current patient. "Help as you can, niece."

Niece? Her aunt Rachel. Meg knelt down before the warm fire and touched Nickum's face as her wolf opened his yellow eyes. "All is well, Nickum," she crooned and stroked the dirt-covered fur around his muzzle.

Her aunt snorted. "I suppose that would be the most help you could give right now. Keep him calm, Meg." She turned to her and smiled, a twinkle in her crystal blue eyes. "And it is good to see you," she said.

"Good to see you, too." Meg brushed Nickum's fur.

Caden's eyes sought hers. "Aye, 'tis good to see ye awake again." His words rumbled through her. They were like warm molasses bread with melting butter.

Meg's stomach growled. "How long have I been asleep?"

Rachel sat back on her heels and Caden lowered Nickum to the rug. Meg moved to run her fingers over her pet's wounds, but grabbed air instead when Caden hoisted her up.

"A day and a night, lass." His words were gruff but he lowered her with tenderness back into her still-warm blankets.

"A day?" she began and stared over the top to Nickum bent around himself licking his wounds. Meg glanced at her wrapped shoulder. "Yet I'm so well." Her stomach growled again. "In fact, I'm ravenous and thirsty." She turned to her aunt, who seemed to be asleep in the chair next to Nickum, and lowered her voice. "Did she…ummm…the blue light…did my aunt…?"

"Aye," Caden said as he tucked the blankets back up under her chin. "She *prayed* over ye." The corner of his mouth turned up in a grin that looked dangerously seductive on his unshaven face. "A talent of hers and apparently one yer mother had and all the lasses in yer family."

Meg heard the question in that statement clearly. She blinked several times. "The light has the power to heal?"

"With what I've seen last night and this morn, I agree with

yer aunt."

"You agree with her?" What was he talking about?

"Aye, the light is a blessing," he said and walked toward the door. "I will have some food and drink brought up for you two." He stared for a moment and his smile retreated, leaving frost in its place. "Ye and Lady Munro are guests here."

He shut the door behind him.

"A blessing?" Meg murmured into the mound of blankets. She made a small cave underneath and produced a pea-sized orb of blue light. The glow illuminated the pitch darkness under the heavy layers. Could she heal like her aunt Rachel? Had she contained the power all along and simply never tried to use it? Aunt Mary had never mentioned an unnatural ability to heal, although she wasn't blood related to Rachel and her mother. Uncle Harold was their brother.

Meg heard a shuffling sound and squelched the light. Her aunt lay down next to her on the bed, her expression weeping with exhaustion.

"The healing steals my energy," she said, but managed to keep her eyes open as she lay on her side facing her.

Meg pulled another throw over her aunt.

"I'm Rachel Munro, your mother's sister. I haven't seen you since you were born, child." Rachel reached out and touched her hair. "You have your mother's reddish waves and her slender build."

"Thank you for healing my shoulder and helping Nickum."

"I understand your beast protects you. Having a protector is prudent. Smart girl." She closed her eyes. "Let us talk more about the little light you hide when I wake from my nap."

Meg's breath stilled at the casual words.

"And child." Rachel's lips slurred a bit with the heaviness of exhaustion. "The Macbains seem to think we know each other well." Her eyes caught Meg's. "Let's allow them to continue that thinking."

• • •

Caden sucked in a breath for patience as he entered the hall. The three remaining elders, Ancients Kenneth, Bruce, and Angus, swore it their duty to advise the young laird on clan matters. They reminded him often that although Caden was chief, he was not much older than ten and twenty. What could he know of tradition and ancient justifications?

The three had convened in the great hall when they'd heard of Caden's return with The Munro's niece. They sat before the fire of the main hall. "And the Munro Witch is here, too." Ancient Kenneth chuckled and shook his head. "She's a better hostage than the niece."

Caden watched Angus stare hard into his mug and take a swallow as Caden strode toward the back kitchens. He coughed around the ale when he spotted Caden and jabbed his finger in the young chief's direction.

"Caden," he coughed. Bruce pounded his back but Angus pushed off his friend's hand. "Must you pummel me every time I choke?" Angus threw his hand toward the opposite wall. "Caden's emerged. He just walked toward the kitchens."

All three men pushed out of their seats and hurried across the room just as Caden returned to the hall. He stopped before them, arms crossed over his chest, frowning.

"Now that the Munro Witch herself is here, we will use her, too," Ancient Kenneth started without preamble. He raised his eyebrow above his missing right eye, which he squeezed shut. A Munro had plucked it out thirty-some years ago with a mace. He'd spent decades returning the favor.

"We can keep her here, and not let her return to that devil." Angus rubbed his whiskered jaw.

"I promised the woman unheeded passage before she came," Caden answered in even measure, despite clenching his fists. He could walk away, ignore them. He was The Macbain, after all.

"Now why did you go promising a thing like that, man?" Bruce yelled from over the rim of his tankard. He'd been the best friend of Caden's father and could bellow just as loud.

Caden frowned at them in silence. Inside, he counted to ten in Latin.

"We are your council, Caden," Ancient Kenneth reminded him. "We should know your rationale."

"I didn't have time to bicker over details when the lass lay up there dying, so I promised it, and I would do it again. Rachel Munro saved Meg, and without the English girl we'd have nothing to bargain with." Bloody hell! He protected what was his. He wouldn't allow Meg to die.

"Aye, but to have the witch herself, now that would get Alec Munro over here quick," Bruce said, as he pulled on his gray-streaked beard. "I'm surprised that we haven't seen his ugly face yet."

"Rachel must have lied to him about her whereabouts. That devil would not have let her come here in the middle of the night," Angus answered.

All three old men nodded in unison.

Caden regarded them as they washed down several more swigs of ale. He waited. The three old warriors knew well that their chief could just walk past them without a word. Yet he never had. He'd always shown them respect, even if he didn't follow all their commands. Which was just, because Caden was The Macbain, not they. He listened to their commands, but only issued his own. They respected him even if he was hellbent on peace.

Bruce's belch echoed in the empty hall.

Kenneth set down his ale and wiped the thick scruff around his mouth with his sleeve. "So when do you plan on telling the English lass that she's our prisoner?" His thick brow quirked slightly with a more personal question. "I hear she's quite bonny. Your men seem foolish over her." Kenneth had been Caden's father's second in command, and his cleverness uncovered all unspoken truths.

Angus snorted and coughed. "Foolish youth."

"I will tell her soon," Caden answered. "For now I need her cooperation, so no one is to treat her with anything but hospitality. For now she is a guest here at Druim, and so is Lady Munro." He bowed slightly to the three warriors. "I must check on my men and their families."

Caden jogged down the steps and into the courtyard where his soldiers drilled. Caden wanted to drill with them, for it was easier than his intended course. He raised his hand as they hailed him. "Later," he promised, and strode through the open gate of the bailey and down the short lane into the village.

He knocked on the cottage closest to the keep. Bess Tammin stood at the door with her six-year-old son clinging to her skirts. She was a comely young widow who had lost her husband last year in a vicious raid with the Davidsons. Caden tipped his head to her and grinned at the boy.

"Chief Macbain." She stepped aside to allow him to enter. "Would you care for some ale or something hot, perhaps?"

"I came to see if you were faring well, Bess, and Peter here." Caden stooped to pull the boy's hand so that he stepped away from his mama. "Seems you're getting big and strong," he said, despite the lad's thin arms. How much thinner would he get this winter if his plan for peace didn't work?

Peter beamed up at Caden. "I can start training with the wooden swords in the spring," he said, pride puffing up his small body.

Caden studied him. "I can see a fierce warrior in you, Peter. I'll be happy to add you to the ranks." He tussled the boy's shaggy head. He watched Bess, his face growing serious, though he kept a light tone. "You have enough food?"

"We make do." She reached out to touch Caden's arm. "I hear you've returned with the Munro niece." Hope lurked in her eyes as she pulled Peter back against her side.

"Aye."

She rubbed her son's arm. "Your plan will work, then. We can use her to bargain for our grain and cattle back?"

Caden's stomach clenched in the same tight ball he'd held inside since the mysterious fire that burned their fields. "I will find food for the winter."

She smoothed Peter's hair. "I know you will."

Caden tipped his head to Bess and held his fist to his heart to Peter, who imitated the fierce pledge.

Nine more homes to visit. He breathed deep to lessen the tightness in his middle and strode to the next door.

Caden counted down each one, answering the same questions and promising food to each troubled face. Ten homes in all. Ten each day. That was his routine. So unlike his sire, who had holed up in the keep, planning sweet revenge and victory no matter what the cost. Caden wanted something different; he wanted peace because peace meant food. Without it, many of his people wouldn't survive the winter. The Munros had raided most of their cattle the night the fall harvest had been burned. Even though they didn't take credit for it, the council was convinced it was their most hated enemy's work.

He knocked on the last door. Hugh Loman answered.

"Get back in here, Hugh," his wife's voice called.

Hugh's eyes pleaded with Caden. "She's driving me to bedlam," he said and then grinned.

"Hello, Caden." Elizabeth Loman came to the door, their infant son swaddled against her chest. "Hugh's not fit enough to come back to train," she said, placing her hand on Hugh's forehead.

"There's no fever, woman," Hugh said, and ducked. "Meg took care of it on the way home."

"That she did," Elizabeth said, her eyes growing wet. "Thank God for her, then," she added, and turned toward Caden. "Is the lass well? I would like to pay my respects before you trade her off to those devils."

Worry, gratitude, determination with a bit of fury all flew

across Elizabeth Loman's face.

"She is well," Caden answered.

"I will use some of our ration to make her my special bread," she said. "She deserves more, seeing how she took care of my Hugh."

"Come to the keep," Caden said. "Tell Evelyn I want you to have enough grain for your bread."

"We have enough, Caden," Hugh said, but Caden knew just how little they had. With a new bairn, Elizabeth needed all the food she had for her family.

"I understand, Hugh," Caden said. "Tell Evelyn. We have enough."

Elizabeth dabbed at her eyes before withdrawing back into the cozy home.

"She weeps at everything," Hugh said to Caden and stepped outside with him. "She's up most the night."

"He's healthy, the bairn?"

"Aye and quite hungry." Hugh's laugh turned sour. "I didn't mean that we don't have enough, Caden. 'Twas a joke about bairns."

"I will trade Meg to her uncle soon," Caden said. "Then there will be enough."

"I've never doubted that you'd find a way," Hugh said.

Caden strode back toward the bailey. Ten houses finished for another day. When his fury welled inside him, demanding an attack based wholly on revenge, he'd remember the faces of the wives and children. When Meg stared at him with those big trusting eyes and he thought for a moment about keeping her, he'd remember his people. They made him accountable, made him who he was. His people made him The Macbain.

• • •

"Here it is," Meg said. She pulled the heavy key from her leather bag and handed it to Rachel. They sat in two wooden chairs close to the dancing flames of the hearth in their room. They sat completely alone since Nickum had begged to escape.

"Isabelle left you this?" Rachel ran a finger over the iron scrollwork in the handle of the key.

"Yes. The pattern is not really a pattern at all."

"'Tis odd," Rachel said. "My sister liked to leave clues and guesses about. She liked games when she was a girl." She focused back on the key. "A chest to unlock, perhaps."

"I think she secreted the proof away that she mentioned in her letter." Meg pointed to the parchment lying open on Rachel's lap.

"Why did your uncle give you your mother's letter now?"

"Really, it was Aunt Mary, although Uncle Harold didn't stop her." Meg fiddled with the edge of the woolen throw over her lap. "It was right after the anniversary of my birth and Uncle Harold received a letter from my father saying he was coming to claim me. That it was past time I was married. He wrote he had a match in mind but wanted to ascertain that I was free of witchcraft first. That was when Aunt Mary said that one of my mother's patients had brought the letter with the journal and key after I'd come to live there. They didn't want to frighten me with the letter, so they held it back until now."

Rachel squeezed Meg's hand. There was gentle strength in her grasp, warm and full of power. "So you ran away."

Meg looked down at her lap. "Do you know how they test for witchcraft?"

"Torture, for the most part."

"They examine you, prick any bumps or birthmarks to see if you bleed. They dunk you in ponds or see if you burn."

"Meg," Rachel whispered. "I tried to get her to come back to Scotland with me after your birth." Her eyes filled with regret, like little pools of blue. "She was so sad there until you came into the world. Then she spent her days pouring her love into you."

Silence weighted the air between them while the fire crackled and spit and warmed their legs.

"Harold kept you safe," Rachel said, as if coming awake again. "Always liked him, and that wife of his has spirit."

Meg felt a stab of homesickness. "Aunt Mary is fierce. When I was a young girl and she gave me the healing journal, she said I had to learn to read so I could hear my mother's advice on how to fix people."

Rachel pointed toward the book. "And you think Isabelle wrote clues in it."

"I'm certain." Meg flipped the pages open. "Each of her descriptions has a little something extra and some of the descriptions are obviously not correct, like where one would find an abundance of garlic." She pointed out discrepancies and odd sounding descriptions as she read the words. "I don't know what it all means. 'Find this plant in a cave, a cold cave with many paths and a warm heart in the middle.'"

"You know Gaelic?" Rachel asked.

"My mother asked my uncle to make sure I learned it.

I think she wanted to make certain I would understand her clues."

"Harold speaks it as well?"

Meg shook her head. "Whenever a Scotsman came through, Uncle Harold would ask him to give us both some instruction. Then we studied on our own. Although I'm not very fluent."

"Oh, I'd say you translated that quite well," Rachel said.

"Caden." Meg's voice quieted and she cleared her throat just a bit. "He translated it on the journey north." She tipped her gaze back down to avoid her aunt's stare. The steely look heated the crown of her head as she bent to read.

"Was the journey north long?" Rachel asked.

"Five nights, not counting the one Nickum saved me from a pack of wolves."

"Wolves?"

"Yes, right before I ran into the skirmish and met Caden."

Her aunt's eyes froze Meg's breath. Meg tried to smile. Her cheek twitched and it came out lopsided.

Rachel's face softened. "He is a handsome man, Meg. Strong and most likely virile. God makes them that way here in the Highlands. When you meet my Alec you'll see."

Meg shook her head. "Caden and I…there's nothing between us." She stared at the page, though her eyes didn't see any of the words.

Her aunt chuckled softly and began to hum. Together, they continued to study the journal while Meg spent the rest of the day avoiding the subject of Caden and how he meant nothing to her.

The next morning Meg requested a bath. Lake scum and

road dirt still coated her skin.

"Ye've been ill, lass," Evelyn protested.

"I am well." Meg moved her shoulder under the poultice wrap. "And I am desperate to smell like my old self. I even brought a bar of soap." She pulled the lilac-scented bar from her leather bag.

"'Tis nearly winter," Evelyn tried once more.

"I've yet to see someone die from bathing," Rachel said as she dragged a brush through her long, gray-streaked hair.

Evelyn murmured low and frowned. She made the sign of the cross across her chest before she left the room.

"Did you see that?" Meg asked her aunt.

Rachel tossed the brush on the bed and began to plait her braid once more. "They all do it here, except for your Caden."

"He is not *my* Caden." Meg frowned and glanced at the door, then back at her aunt. "Does it bother you?"

"There are rumors that I am a witch because of my talent to heal. Those who do not know me are frightened by the power. Their little signs give them the courage to interact with me, I suppose." Rachel shrugged slightly.

"Are you… I mean no disrespect, Aunt, but what you do, what you did to help me… Are you a witch?"

Meg's aunt finished tying a leather cord at the end of the long braid. She held her hands flat, parallel to one another, and a blue light began to glow between them. "I've had this power since I was a child. I had a mother who taught me how to use it. I've never worshipped anybody but God, our Lord and our Savior Jesus Christ, child." Rachel held the light easily, contained between her hands. "Our power is a gift from God, as we are gifts from God." With that she laid her hands together as if praying and the light disappeared.

"My mother—"

"Also had this gift, though she rarely showed it. I remember that after you were born, your skin was very yellow. Your mother held you in her arms and I saw the blue light wrap around you. And then you were all pink and healthy and Isabelle was exhausted." Rachel tipped her head. "Aye, my sister knew how to use her gift, but she was very careful not to let anyone see."

"Maybe my father saw."

"Never." Rachel placed hands on Meg's upper arms, forcing her to see the truth in her stare. "Rowland Boswell lied, Meg. Lied to ensure your mother would never be heard." She lowered her voice. "You also have your mother's power, though I suspect you don't know anything about using it."

Meg remained still.

"You aren't evil, child. Special, yes, but not a witch. Not evil." Rachel smiled then, as if her words solved everything.

Could her blue light and the ability to assess people's illnesses and hurts be a gift and not a curse?

"Aunt Mary taught me how to use plants to heal, but if I could do more… Could you…?" Meg pursed her lips for a second. "Would you teach me? How to use this…*gift* to help people?"

Rachel's happiness engulfed her whole face, making the years wash away and a radiant woman stand before Meg. "I've always wanted a daughter to teach." She nodded, her eyes shiny pools of restrained joy. "Aye, I will teach you how to use your talents to heal."

Evelyn pushed into the room and waved in two men carrying buckets of water. They placed the iron buckets against the fire to warm.

Donald came behind them with a bathing tub and set it on the floor near the hearth. He grinned at Meg. "Ye look fit," he said, but it came out like a question.

"Fit and better smelling after this bath," Meg said. "Thank you all for bringing it up." Her gratitude included all the men who flushed and bowed before leaving.

"Donald," she called as he left the room.

The man poked his head back in around the corner, his brows raised. "Aye?"

"Hugh—how is his arm?"

"Well, I believe," Donald said. "Haven't heard otherwise."

"Thank you," she said, and Donald disappeared. She turned to her aunt. "The man's arm was completely severed during the skirmish. I took care of him with herbs and clean wrappings along the trip back. I should check on him."

"Ye're hurt," Evelyn said as she coaxed the fire into a blaze and stirred the warming water. She stood and wiped hands on her apron. "I'll return with several bathing sheets." She shook her head. "Taking a bath in the autumn and wounded," she muttered as she strode out the door.

Rachel shooed Meg toward a chair and took up a brush. Rachel ran it down the length of her wavy tresses.

Meg moved her shoulder under the poultice. "I'm not *very* wounded."

After Donald returned to fill the tub and left the room

again, Rachel helped Meg undress. Her eyes skimmed Meg's stomach, stopping on the birthmark at her navel.

"The dragonfly. I wondered where you had it hidden. Your mother's was on the bottom of her foot. All the women of our line have one." Rachel slid back her sleeve to reveal her own small brown birthmark. "The mark shows we are…special."

Special, as in being more than human? As in being a true witch? Meg shivered at the implication and stepped into the warm water. Her aunt certainly didn't seem like an evil witch. She used her powers to help people. There was no darkness in that. Maybe her strange power was something other than a curse to be hidden.

Rachel unwrapped the poultice from Meg's shoulder.

"This will mark me also," Meg said, in awe of the healed hole over the spot where her shoulder connected to her chest. White puckered skin covered a hole, the size of an arrow shaft. She ran fingers gingerly across her shoulder to touch the other puncture mark on her back.

"The scars will fade in time." Rachel helped Meg lower into the water. The heat infused her muscles, coaxing them to relax in a warm embrace.

Evelyn walked in carrying a stack of cloth as Meg leaned her head on the lip of the high-backed tub.

Meg moved her shoulder around. "A miracle," she said. Out of the corner of her eye, Meg noticed Evelyn move her fingers across her chest and kiss her cross.

"A miracle from God," Rachel added with a wink.

Meg closed her eyes, giving into the languid pleasure of the warm water. "Ahh," she sighed. "Never underestimate the healing power of cleanliness."

• • •

Caden pushed through the double oak doors into the keep. He shook his head, dotting water droplets against the stone wall of the entry chamber. After an hour of training his men in the autumn heat, the frigid water of the loch had cooled the familiar fire in his limbs. If only it had cooled the fire in his loins that reignited each time he thought about Meg. He frowned and strode into the great hall.

One woman sat before the fire, her fingers toying with the ebony queen on his father's old chess game. Several of the kitchen servants peeked out from the back entry.

Caden walked to the hearth, where Rachel Munro stared up at the tapestry above the granite mantel and tapped the playing piece back in place.

"Ironic," she said. "The woman who started this bloody feud generations ago had Meg's coloring. Auburn hair. Even greenish eyes."

Caden glanced at the woven images of the tapestry he'd memorized as a child sitting beside his father while he and the council planned raids and victories against the Munros.

Rachel's pensive gaze moved to Caden. In the firelight, her eyes sparked. "And now a woman will end it."

He held his frown. Did Rachel Munro want the feud to end? Did she resign herself to the fact that her niece was worth more than stubborn pride and vengeance?

"Alec Munro will agree to a peace for her?" he asked.

Her eyebrows rose with the hint of a shrug. "My husband is

not the agreeing type."

The knot tightened in his gut but he kept the practiced mask of indifference. "He will agree to return our cattle he reived and give us half his harvest for burning ours."

Rachel's lips thinned. Her voice was low but strong. "Munros had nothing to do with the burning of your fields."

He watched her steely eyes until she blinked, but she didn't turn away. "Our cattle were seen being driven away by Munros."

"Reiving cattle and burning fields are very different offenses."

Caden continued to pierce her with his gaze. Even in her seated position, Rachel Munro held her ground as firmly as if she were an armed warrior.

"Offenses meant to starve a clan into submission," he said low, the beast of fury held in check only by his growing respect for the woman's courage.

She huffed and turned her eyes to the fire with indignant stubbornness. She was a good match for Alec Munro. "Meg is well. I must return to Munro Keep on the morn."

"Without your niece."

She flipped her hand in the air as if his statement was foolish. "Of course."

Caden looked quickly about the room to make certain Meg was still above. "You will tell Alec that I desire peace. I will return his dear niece alive and a maiden." Rachel's snort interrupted him, but he continued. "When our cattle are brought back with a wagon of grain."

Her attention returned to him. The anger had left replaced by something that resembled weariness. "And is my sister's daughter important enough to Alec to cause him to break his oath to see the Macbains punished—?"

"Punished for a dispute over one woman that happened nearly a century ago."

"Alec was raised with the tradition of hate." She shook her head and picked the white queen up. "I think he's actually frustrated with your sudden weakness," she said lowly. "There is no glory in beating a starving dog."

Caden breathed deeply through his nose to stop the anger from erupting. He brought forth the faces of the children he'd visited earlier in the day. Their faces kept him sensible. No, he'd never grovel, but he'd never give up, either, nor give into a moment of fury when so much was at stake.

"Meg is important to The Munro," Caden said, his teeth clenched. "We have it from a very good source that he dotes on his niece."

"What source?" Rachel snapped.

His anger relaxed a small measure. "Someone who is intimately aware of your family."

"Fiona," she murmured and leaned back in the chair. "Should have dragged her back."

"A shame you threw her to the wolves, Rachel," he said. "She still seems to care for you, the way she tended you the other day." The timid healer had begged for shelter and protection months ago when she'd fled the Munros. Fiona had sworn her allegiance to Caden quickly, but with tears in her eyes.

"Care for me," she said, a subtle sneer to her tone. "If she'd truly cared for me she wouldn't have lured my son to her bed."

Apparently Rachel wasn't done mothering her thirteen-year-old son. That was none of Caden's concern. "You will leave here on the morn and tell Alec that he can have his lovely niece back when the cattle and grain wagon arrive."

Rachel continued to lean back in the chair. She held the white queen up before the flames as if studying her delicate features. "She is lovely, isn't she?"

Caden ignored her question. "You will tell Meg that you wish her to stay here until you've made her room ready."

"You've kissed her," she said.

His gaze snapped to the woman.

"Munros were at Loch Tuinn," he said in answer. How else would she know about the kiss he'd given Meg before she was shot? "They saw the kiss and reported back to you."

Rachel shook her head, but her grin stayed on her lips. "Every time Meg says your name, her voice lowers as if the very thought of you warms her."

Caden watched her, not sure what to say. Was she purposely diverting him? His mind skipped back to his previous instructions. "Then you will convince your husband to accept my terms if either of you want to see Meg again."

Was it a bluff? No, definitely not. If they didn't agree, he'd keep Meg. His hard eyes reflected the promise enough to sour Rachel's foolish grin. She made a little huffing sound.

"Now why would I lie to my dear niece? Telling her to stay here while I make Munro Castle ready for her? To make it easier for you? So you won't have to guard her?"

Caden spoke slowly, relishing the upper hand he once again held. "Nay. To make it easier for *her*," he said. "Right now your niece is happy. She has freedom here, and safety. If you tell her she's really a prisoner, a pawn in this bloody feud, you'll strip that from her, making this place of sanctuary into a hell. A hell that could go on for weeks if you cannot quickly convince Alec to take my terms."

He bent forward so that his hands rested on the arms of Rachel's chair. The strong woman refused to retreat from his stare. "Do you really want that for your dear niece?"

Her hand rubbed across her mouth as if she tried to rub away a bitter taste on her lips. "I suppose that's check," she said and set the queen before the ebony king.

"Checkmate." He tipped the king into the queen, knocking it over and drawing a slim smile from the woman.

"I don't call checkmate until my king is dead." She indicated the white king on the other side of the board.

"He's cornered," he said low and straightened, giving her space.

"Cornered for the moment, but not dead." Rachel stood. "If you'll excuse me I'll see to helping my niece dress for the evening meal. I'll let her know that I will be leaving," she said, "to ready her rooms."

He watched Rachel climb the steps until she was out of sight. "Checkmate," Caden said as he turned to the flames, his frown the only evidence of the subtle twisting in his gut.

Chapter Six

24 October 1517—St. John's Wort: yellow flowers with five petals in summer, stands straight and sturdy. Grows well where the mist of mountain springs and rushing waterfalls can quench its thirst. Ointment for hard growths, bleeding under the skin, wounds, and insect bites. A mild decoction to prevent bladder leaks. Decoction to treat lung complaints and worms of the body. Be aware that strong potion may cause skin burns.

"A banquet for me?" Meg asked as her aunt lifted a thin smock to fall over Meg's head to her ankles.

"To welcome you and introduce you to all of the Munros." Rachel pushed Meg's canvas stays down around her waist, then turned her away so she could pull the strings to tighten the corset, displaying Meg's waist.

"I don't need anything so elaborate," Meg, said frowning. "I just want to meet Uncle Alec and my cousins." She would bring up her request to stay once she was with the Munros. Her aunt must realize she had nowhere else to go. Perhaps once on

Munro land, Rachel would suggest a small cottage where Meg could set up a new home.

Rachel's fingers froze in the laces. "You only have one cousin," she said, and then continued to tie.

"Oh, Uncle Harold said—"

"My brother does not know that my two sons were killed. Only Searc remains." Rachel turned back to the bed to pick up the loaned farthingale.

Meg stepped into it and her aunt brought it up around her waist. "I'm so sorry, Aunt," she said. "You couldn't save them with the blue light?"

Moisture glossed Rachel's eyes.

"Forgive me," Meg said. "I shouldn't have asked."

"Nay, child." Rachel shook her head and sat on of the bed. "You should know. Our powers do nothing when God has already claimed a person." Her hands fisted in her lap. "Both were dead before they were brought to me."

Meg sat next to Rachel. "In battle?"

Rachel sighed. "Two different ones, about a year apart. Alec wouldn't allow me to come with them. Thought a battle was no place for a lady, especially his wife." Her lips pursed tightly and she breathed in deeply through her nose. She seemed to hold the breath forever, or at least until she could speak without emotion. "He brought my sons back dead."

Meg laid her hand on Rachel's and squeezed.

Rachel turned to her. "Though, you can do plenty of good with that blue light when people still breathe."

The topic had turned but unease wrapped around Meg's shoulders. "Is it safe to use?" She glanced around the empty room. "Aren't you afraid you will be accused of being a witch?"

"I'm already called a witch."

Meg swallowed past the panic itching in her throat. "Aren't you afraid you might be killed?" People all across England were accused and killed for practicing witchcraft on much less evidence.

"Life is different up here in the Highlands. True, unfortunate women are prosecuted and killed. But I am no outcast. I am Lady Munro, protected and loved by my husband and clan. I pray and receive forgiveness from Father Daughtry when he visits. And every day I thank God for gifting me with the ability to help others."

Rachel pulled both Meg's cold hands in her own warm ones. "We have a gift, not a curse. We help people. God-fearing people." She shook her head. "Those who call me witch maliciously are powerless to harm me."

Meg stared at her aunt's strong hands. "I am an outcast. I have no husband and clan."

"Not yet, but one day soon, perhaps. Until then, you are under Munro protection."

Meg exhaled slowly. "Thank you."

"Now, let us have a small lesson before I leave." Rachel turned her palm up. The blue orb started pebble small and swelled until it filled her cupped hand. "What do you do with your light?"

"I…well, I use it as a light to see by."

Rachel laughed. "I suppose that can serve you, too. Any other uses?"

"I can tell what is wrong inside a person when I touch them, but I don't use the light for that."

Rachel closed her hand and the light collapsed into nothing. "Next time there is a wound, try forming the orb between your hand and it. Then envision the light traveling from your hand to the wound or ailment, flooding it with the blue light. Imagine how the skin or organ should normally function or appear. The light will follow your thoughts."

"Could I hurt people by accident, if I think the wrong thoughts?" How horrible, to actually do harm with her magic. That would surely send her to Hell, or at least the witch's pyre.

Rachel tilted her head. "The light won't cause normal skin to turn abnormal." She grinned mischievously. "I've tried, but it didn't work."

Meg's eyes widened in shock, but Rachel winked. She stood and pulled Meg back up to continue dressing. "We cannot harm people with the light. Though once you start to heal someone, be sure to finish it. Unfinished healing can hurt."

A knock at the door stopped further questions. Fiona peeked around the door. When she saw they were alone she stepped inside and nearly ran to Rachel. They grasped forearms and leaned into each other, their foreheads touching.

"I hoped to catch you before you left," Fiona said.

Rachel ran her hand down the young woman's dark hair. "Are you treated well here?"

Fiona nodded. "I use the herbal lessons you taught me to help them here. Their healer died last year."

Meg watched the two women, who obviously knew one another well.

"Help me finish dressing my niece," Rachel said, switching

to English. "Perhaps you can weave her beautiful hair."

"I would be happy to. Lady Meg, ye are quite bonny indeed."

"Even in my smock and stays?" Meg laughed.

"And ye will be even more stunning in the dress I found for ye." Fiona lifted the blue damask and velvet gown off the bed. "The gown belonged to Caden's sister."

Caden had a sister? Were there any other siblings?

"Sarah left it when she married. I took it in a bit to fit ye." Fiona held out her hands in the approximate circumference of Meg's waist.

Meg studied the precise stitches. "Thank you for spending your day altering it."

Fiona waved her thanks away. "Let's get it on you so we can join the evening sup below."

"So how do you two know each other?" Meg asked.

Silence.

"You are quite close."

Rachel and Fiona pulled the heavy gown down over Meg, and she was lost in fabric for a long moment.

"Fiona trained under me at Munro Castle," Rachel said. "She's a very talented midwife."

"Talented as in…?" Meg asked.

Fiona shook her head. "Not like Rachel with her gift. I just use herbs and common sense."

"And strength, innate intelligence, and a wonderful calm manner," Rachel added.

Fiona blushed.

Rachel and Fiona each took a sleeve and pushed it up

Meg's arms to tie at her shoulders.

"Why are you not at Munro Castle?" Meg asked. Again, silence stretched a little longer than natural in a casual conversation. What were they hiding?

"Fiona had a disagreement with a Munro and decided to leave until tensions relaxed." Rachel spoke quietly, her eyes meeting Fiona's. "If you need me, Meg, or need to send a message to me, send it through Fiona. She is your link to me."

"I hope it won't take long to prepare for my visit," Meg said. "I'm anxious to see Munro Castle."

"Not long, but you never know. The weather turns fierce quickly here." Rachel let out a little laugh. "You could find yourself snowed in until spring at Druim."

Bubbles flittered around in her stomach at the thought. Would Caden be angry to be stuck with her for so long?

Rachel draped a velvet waistband embroidered with golden dragonflies around her waist.

Meg ran her finger over the dragonfly pattern. "They match my…" She glanced at Fiona. "…mark."

"The girdle was your mother's."

"Why didn't she take it with her?"

Rachel's expression darkened but her thin lips continued to hold a pleasant line as if it were a familiar mask she applied without thought or effort. "Since Isabelle turned her back on her gift, the girdle just reminded her of the secret she must keep." She frowned then. "Ironic that Boswell chose witchcraft as his weapon of murder, since Isabelle was so adamantly against using it."

"Why?" Meg asked. Why would her mother refuse to use

such a wonderful power?

Rachel's eyes were sad. "I loved Isabelle, but she was not like me in the least. She preferred to follow proper protocol, didn't like to cause any type of stir. Which makes me think that Boswell was tangled in something terrible for my sister to move against her husband in any way. Isabelle preferred to use natural means to heal, unless it was dire and then she masked her powers completely." Rachel shook her head. "She was always hiding."

Fiona pulled at the heavy folds of fabric until the cascade of damask flowed perfectly over the farthingale. "Perfect length," she murmured. "Now let's see about yer tresses." She ushered Meg to a chair where she combed, pulled, and wove a beautiful mass of curls.

"Don't bother with the hood, Fiona," Rachel said. "I brought my pearls to weave into her hair. The color is a perfect contrast for them."

Meg fluctuated between embarrassment, relief, and joy while the two women praised her soft, creamy skin and luxurious locks.

"Like a lady at court." Fiona tickled Meg's ear with one last tuck of curl. "Come see yerself." She motioned to a polished glass in the corner.

Meg stepped before the glass and gasped at the reflection. "Are you sure that is me in there?"

Knuckles rapped on the door and Evelyn stepped into the room. "There's a fair amount of waiting down in the great hall, to see ye sup with us." She stopped short. A large grin spread across her weathered face. "Well don't ye polish up fine, lass?

Right out of Stirling court."

Was Caden one of those waiting?

The flutter in Meg's chest quivered down into her stomach. "Thank you, Evelyn."

"I just need to put on my own jewelry," Rachel said, her tone cold enough to make Meg turn. Tension packed into the silent room, but Meg wasn't sure why. Fiona slipped out the door behind Evelyn without a word.

...

Caden sat in his father's high-backed chair at the head of the long table. Many of the men milled about the great hall. He frowned. Although they were always welcome, most sought their own comforts after a day of work and training. Apparently they had heard Meg was well enough to dine with them. Half of them were curious about her miraculous healing and her relation to the Devil Munro. The other half just wanted to gawk with hopes of winning one of her bloody smiles. Hell, the room even smelled better since most of the men had bathed before coming.

Ewan sauntered into the hall followed by two young widows from the village, and Donald's sister, Ann. They giggled over something he'd said. Ewan waved him over. Maybe a soft, willing lass was what he needed to lift the heaviness in his gut. Caden strode the distance to the far wall.

"Caden, how could you scowl in the presence of such loveliness?" Ewan spouted.

Caden lifted one side of his mouth into a grin and perused Ann, Gwyneth, and Jonet. "And how could you three keep your last meal down with Ewan's sticky sweet rhapsody?"

They giggled. Ewan laughed.

Across the room Angus broke into a fit of coughing and cursing while Bruce thumped him on the back. The council had gathered with the rest to see the witch's niece. Were they planning how best to use Meg? Or how to abduct Rachel Munro on her way home in the morning? Caden frowned and watched the three old men until Angus's fit passed.

When his focus returned, Gwyneth had maneuvered herself around the other two women who now flanked Ewan. The woman wore a stifling floral scent. She twined her arm around Caden's bicep.

"I missed you," she drawled, her eyes sparking with open invitation. Her lips teased upward into a sensual grin. She leaned into Caden, the tops of her breasts pushed up high above the gown's collar. Aye, it had been a long time since Caden had bedded the willing widow. Normally the sight would twitch its way down into his groin, but instead Caden's thoughts roamed to Meg's creamy white shoulder that had stuck out of the wool blanket at the fire, the night he'd discovered her true identity. His pawn, his lovely playing piece, his checkmate. The heaviness in his gut twisted.

"I think Ewan would be of lighter spirits this eve." Caden disentangled his arm while Gwyneth pursed her lips into a tight line. "Another night." He walked across the rushes toward a group who had hunted earlier that day. Ewan called his name half-heartedly behind him, but Caden continued on.

"More for you, Ewan," Caden mumbled, and joined his warriors near the fire. He stood next to Kievan next to the wall.

"I hear we have venison and goose tonight, thanks to you."

"Ah? I mean…aye," Kieven replied. The man turned toward Caden, but his eyes seemed stuck to some point across the hall.

Meg must have entered the room. Foolish, muddle-headed man. Caden turned and spotted her, poised and lush in a blue court gown, the gentle sway of her hips trapping his attention as well. She gazed out at the sea of curious faces, nodding to those she knew. She leaned toward her aunt and said something as they walked to the long table.

Meg's glorious auburn locks were twisted with pearls. Her waist sloped in from the farthingale, and her breasts rose full with each breath. Lovely hazel eyes sparkled with sincerity and snared all notice. Color infused her creamy cheeks as she blushed.

Caden pushed off the wall with the heel of his boot and strode across the room. Time froze, and he alone walked through the spell toward Meg. She turned in his direction and her smile faltered.

Had someone revealed the secret? Did she already loathe him? What had Rachel discussed as they'd dressed?

"Ye are well?" Caden asked as he stopped before her. Would she answer or glare at him?

"Yes," Meg replied, a gentle smile tugging at her lips.

He released his breath and rubbed his jaw, realizing just how tense it had been. If he'd been Ewan he'd have half a dozen comments on his tongue. Instead he just stared down at her in tense silence. "The gown suits ye."

Rachel snorted behind her niece. "Did I mention that

Highland chiefs are lacking in the fine art of compliments?" She leaned in, but Caden could still hear her words. "What they lack in words they usually make up for in action."

Color rushed up Meg's open neckline and into her cheeks. Instead of turning away, she stared up into Caden's eyes, her own sparkling with mischief and laughter. His iron will stopped him from descending upon that pink mouth and showing her exactly what type of action he had in mind.

"Thank you," Meg said and bowed her head. "I would also like to thank your sister for the gown. I was told it was one that she left behind and would not miss. Is she here?"

His sister? Here? Thank the Lord, no. "Nay. Sarah lives with her husband's family toward the sea."

"Near the Macleod holdings?" Rachel asked.

"Aye." Caden motioned for them to sit, though he didn't take his eyes from Meg.

"I will have to thank her when we meet," she said, and pulled her dress around to perch on the bench. He sat on her left side. The hum of voices rose again as warriors took seats. Ewan sat across from Meg with Jonet and Ann on either side. Gwyneth sat farther down next to Hamish.

"Sweet Diana," Ewan said, leaning forward on his elbows as if he spoke conspiratorially. "Do not venture into London. I hear that England's King Henry snaps up pretty young wives before they can rise from their curtsey."

When Meg laughed, Jonet frowned and Ann's eyes narrowed. Although Jonet practically fought off marriage offers and Donald's sister was a bonny maid nearing the age to marry, the two lasses acted like jealous harlots defending their territory.

"There are some Highlanders who use pretty phrases," Meg said quietly to her aunt. "Perhaps that's why he's the only man present with a lovely lady on each arm."

Caden watched the two women across the table from him. Word had spread that Meg was to be treated like a guest, but had everyone heard his command to hide her true status?

"I am Meg Boswell," she said, gifting the two women with a sincere smile.

Ann and Jonet glanced at one another and grinned back hesitantly.

"I am Ann Black and this is Jonet Montgomery."

"Are you both Macbains, living here?"

"Aye, we live in the village," Jonet answered. "Ann is Donald's sister and I live under the protection of The Macbain, as my husband was taken in battle." Jonet regarded Rachel with cold eyes.

"Donald mentioned you on the journey," Meg said to Ann. "I can tell he cares for you deeply."

Ann blushed and glanced down. "He is a good brother."

Meg turned her gaze on Jonet. "I am so sorry for your loss," she said. "Living alone must be hard. You must be a very strong woman."

Jonet tipped her head. "I have managed."

"You two are very fortunate to have one another, to have friends." Meg tasted the roast goose as she looked between the women.

Caden watched her delicate fingers pull some of the meat. So slender and dainty, yet he'd seen those same fingers probe bleeding wounds, too.

"I've never had a friend," Meg said as if just stating a fact. The only reaction she showed was a slight furrow in her brow. She'd been lonely. No wonder she'd befriended the wolf.

"No friends?" Ewan asked.

Meg shook her head. "I lived on a secluded farm with my aunt and uncle in England. Of course, Nickum is my friend."

"Nickum?" Ann asked.

"My wolf."

Jonet glanced nervously at Ann. "I heard the beastie's been walking the village at night."

"There's nothing to fear from Nickum," Meg added anxiously. "He hunts then."

Jonet's eyes grew round.

"Not people," Meg added. "Only other animals. Rabbits and such. He likes to keep guard, too."

Jonet and Ann bobbed their heads slowly.

Meg asked the ladies about their skills and lives in the village. She seemed to really be interested in them. Was she trying to win them over, befriend them as allies in this war? That didn't make sense since she knew nothing of this war, yet. Or so he hoped.

Ann and Jonet talked more and more. What was it about Meg that calmed people, almost lulled them into liking her? Her voice ebbed and flowed in the conversation. The cadence and pitch moved like a song. Caden warmed, his shoulders relaxing. He laughed out loud at one of her quips about the stench of warriors.

Meg turned to him, as did most of the table. "'Tis true, Caden," she said and his breath caught at the sound of his name in her lush little mouth. The ladies laughed, but Meg didn't. Her hand on Caden's arm clenched tightly.

"I...I forgot," she stammered out.

"She's pale." Ann filled Meg's wine cup. "Drink."

Caden placed his hand over hers. "What did ye forget, lass?"

"The attack at the loch," she said, frowning. "Girshmel was there, when I laid against the tree. He's the one who ordered the other man to shoot Nickum."

"Girshmel?" Ewan asked. "Ye're sure? Ye were unconscious."

Meg shook her head. "I could hear. He said..." Her brow furrowed. The entire table hushed, hanging on her words. "He knew who I was, my full name, and that I was The Munro's niece. That's what he called me," she said. "That I was valuable and that his chief would want me."

Caden's gaze lifted to Rachel. Her eyes were cold, concerned, dark. She shook her head. If Girshmel wasn't working for the Munros, then who?

"How could I possibly be valuable to someone up here in the Highlands?"

Silence fell flat around the table along with everyone's gazes.

"Girshmel is a warrior for hire," Caden said, drawing her attention. "He could be working for any of the clans around us. And yer beauty alone makes ye valuable."

Meg frowned as if she didn't believe his explanation.

"Also the fact that ye're English makes ye valuable, especially if they could ransom ye back to yer family."

"Did the man say anything else that you remember?"

Rachel asked.

"Nay, not that I could hear."

Rachel squeezed Meg's hand. "Then let us talk of better things."

Meg had slid closer to Caden during the tale and her thigh brushed his. Even through the many layers of material, the rush of her nearness surged through him. He could imagine the milk-white skin of her thigh pressed against his own. As Ann and Jonet continued to describe the intricate process of preparing wool for weaving, he lifted a cup, his arm brushing Meg's. The slight flush to her neck was the only sign that she appreciated his proximity. She didn't move away.

Meg laughed at Jonet's quip about male sheep being as stubborn as men and bowed her head, causing a curl to escape the tight weave of pearls. A copper honey lock slid against the delicate skin on the back of her neck. The stray turn of silk bounced up and down along her skin as she tipped and tilted her head. If they were alone, alone and without the bloody feud between them, he'd chase that curl with his tongue, savoring the taste of her skin, her delicate flower smell.

"What say ye, Caden?" Ewan asked from across the table.

Caden swallowed hard past the dryness that coated his throat and tore his eyes away from Meg's neck. Ewan's eyes held mischief and the edge of jealousy. "My mind has wandered from yer fascinating conversation about sheep," he replied, his teasing tone making Jonet huff in mock indignation. "What is yer question, Ewan?"

Ewan stared at Caden for a moment. "About Jonet's woven cloth. Would there be a market to trade it down in the

Lowlands, for grain?"

Meg glanced along the table. "Are you low on grain? Was the harvest not good?"

The talk around the table melted away. Angus choked on his ale at the far end, leading to a fit of coughing and cursing as Bruce tried to whack his back. Meg leaned forward across the table to see down to the end. Ewan's eyes nearly fell from his face at the display and Jonet punched his arm.

"Is he well?" Meg asked. "Perhaps I should check on him," she said, leaning back. If not for Angus's cough, she would have surely picked up on the tension in the suddenly still hall.

"Old Angus is always coughing." Ann indicated Meg's plate. "Finish yer meal. He'll wait."

Meg took another bite of meat. "Was the harvest a poor one, then?"

All eyes drifted to Rachel Munro, who ate the last bite of venison on her plate. The crafty woman continued to chew as if her niece hadn't just asked the most fury-invoking question she could.

"Some harvests are large and some are small due to unforeseen circumstances," Rachel said, her steely eyes daring anyone to throw the first stone. "Let us be thankful that the Lord provides this generous meat."

Meg murmured, "Amen," and took another bite of roast goose.

She leaned closer to Caden and the energy of her warmth flowed into him, making his muscles ache and his heart pound as if he were in battle. "I think," Meg started, but then linked with Caden's gaze and stopped. She sucked in her bottom lip for a brief instant, wetting its pink softness.

Angus began to hack again.

"I think…someone…" She moved her attention away from Caden, down the long table to Angus. "Should see about his coughing. Especially if it has been going on a long time. There was a man back home with a similar barking sound. He needed help. Perhaps Aunt Rachel could—"

"I am quite exhausted, child." Rachel rose.

Caden and Ewan slowly stood after her, Caden more reluctant at having to break contact with Meg.

"I think I will retire," she said.

Meg started to rise, but Rachel motioned for her to stay. "Perhaps you should speak to Angus about his cough."

"You know him?"

Rachel stepped away from the table. "Of course." She studied Meg, her eyes flicking to Caden. "Angus Riley courted me when I was fresh to the Highlands. Alec stole me right from under his nose." Though Rachel walked away, regal as a queen, her soft but firm voice carried to Caden and those nearby. "I doubt Angus would let me talk to him, let alone *pray* over him."

"Well hell," Ewan said and glanced down the table to Angus and back to Caden. "Not such an ancient feud after all," he said and then caught himself.

Too late; the words were out. Jonet, Ann, and Ewan stared at Meg. Meg watched Rachel pass the wall with the tapestry. The woman ran her hand over the weave before turning down the dark hall toward the stairwell.

Meg turned to Caden. "That tapestry. The one depicting the beginning of the Munro and Macbain feud shows an injured woman."

Caden took a sip of his ale. He must give her enough truth to think she knew it all. Enough so she wouldn't think he was hiding anything. "An ancient accident that the council likes to recall."

"Did she die?" Meg asked.

"Unfortunately."

"There were two clans involved?"

Bloody hell! Caden set his mug down casually. "Aye, Macbains and Munros."

"Oh." Meg glanced at Ewan as if she suddenly understood his comment. "Best to smooth out new misunderstandings before they reignite the past," she said and rose.

"Where are ye going?" Caden asked.

"To meet the council and my almost-uncle."

Upon seeing her moving their way, the three council members stood and walked to the hearth. Meg changed direction and followed.

Jonet laughed. "They're running from her."

Caden frowned at Ewan. "Perhaps they're worried they may slip and tell the lass there's a feud and that she's in the bloody center of it," he said pointedly.

Ewan rubbed his face with his hand. "I think I'm done for the night."

"I better follow," Caden said. "Who knows what they'll say when cornered?" Then what would he do? He watched her sway gently across the thrushes. She'd find out soon enough, but not bloody yet.

• • •

Meg had chased them clear across the room, but unless they made a spectacle of themselves brushing past her, she'd cornered them. "I am Meg Boswell. I understand that the three of you are very important to this clan."

The three men glanced warily at one another.

"You are the council?"

"Aye, we are," the man with a patch over one eye said. When the silence piled awkwardly between them he bowed his head stiffly. "I am Kenneth Macbain, a distant cousin to Caden's father."

Meg curtsied.

The man turned pink. "Kenneth. Call me Kenneth, or Ancient Kenneth."

"Ancient as in wise," Meg said.

"Ancient as in old as Hades," the third man said, pulling on his gray-streaked beard until he winced, then grabbed his mug from the mantel over the hearth.

Grumpy old men were often the funniest. "And you are…?"

"Bruce Fenegin." He stifled a belch.

She bowed her head and turned to Angus. Should she admit that she knew his name?

"Angus Riley," he said and tipped his head, though his gaze wouldn't meet hers for more than the briefest of seconds. Did the man still love her aunt? Poor soul.

Bruce belched and murmured an excuse. Kenneth stared at her with his one sharp eye. Angus watched the flames and drowned another cough with ale. Meg sat in a chair and the three followed. She felt comfortable with them. She'd grown up in the company of her older aunt and uncle and their few peers from the village. Older folk loved to tell stories and all one had to do to win them over was to listen. Maybe then she could get close enough to help Angus with his cough.

"So ye are here to visit," Kenneth said.

Angus coughed into his hand. Dry, like brittle wind; not a good sound.

"Yes, until my aunt returns for me." If she could only touch Angus, she'd know for certain what ailed his lungs. From the way he squelched the cough, Meg didn't think he'd like her probing him with questions…or her hands. He seemed to pretend the cough wasn't there.

She turned to Kenneth. "Has your eye been injured long?"

"Aye." He leaned back in his chair. "'Tis a bloody tale."

Meg matched his posture, a technique for dealing with difficult patients she'd learned from Aunt Mary. "I would like to hear a bloody tale."

Bruce laughed and farted at the same time. The poor man must be puffed up with gas. She'd send him some marjoram on the morrow.

Kenneth narrowed his good eye. "Ye seem like a slight thing. I'd not have ye pale and fainting over the details."

Meg laughed. "I have yet to succumb to vapors over blood and gore. I've tended a few fresh injuries."

"So I've heard," Kenneth said. He propped his hands on his knees. "Very well, then. I was but ten and twenty, young, brash, full of strength."

Bruce snorted and Angus chuckled. She turned her gaze to Kenneth, though out of the periphery she watched Caden relax against the hearth. Her heart picked up a pounding beat, but she feigned complete attention to Kenneth's description of the battlefield.

"We rode along Loch Tuinn one winter morn after riding the Macbain perimeter." He paused. "Something we do—" he moved his fingers in a circle "—ride the perimeter of The Macbain's holdings to watch for interlopers."

The fire cast a warm glow to Caden's sun-bronzed skin. Meg pushed her focus back to Kenneth.

"And then out of nowhere above us, the bloody Mun… the bloody enemy—" Kenneth swooped his hand down in the air "—charged down upon us." His eye grew round and his arms more animated until Meg found herself caught up in the old warrior's vivid tale of good versus ultimate evil. Details of slashing and swinging brought additional insight and corrections from Bruce and Angus.

"How many limbs were lost?" she asked.

Bruce screwed up his face to think. "At least six by my count."

She shook her head, sad and in awe.

"And a mace caught my eye." Kenneth flipped up the eye patch, showing a badly scarred, stitched-shut eye socket.

Meg stood to peer closer. "I'd have done a better job stitching."

Angus coughed into his fist and Bruce laughed. "Angus didn't have the steadiest fingers even then."

"I'm sorry, Angus," she said and touched his arm. Instantly, Meg assessed the man's lungs. They were stuffed with taint, thick as pond mud. St. John's wort brewed in hot wine or water could help some. She'd ask Aunt Rachel for help. She patted his arm. "You did just fine."

"I was torn apart myself." Angus slid up his tunic to reveal a long, white scar that spanned his chest. "I got this at the same battle."

"And I this," Bruce said and showed a jagged line along his inner thigh.

"Bruce, ye old bull, keep yer kilt down." Kenneth snorted and yanked Bruce's kilt back down. Bruce turned red while Kenneth, Angus, and even Caden chuckled.

"Quite impressive wounds, sirs. And to think you all survived to tell the tale." She shook her head, causing another curl to come down to tickle her neck. Good thing she didn't plan to attend court with hair so desperate for freedom.

Caden had quieted behind her yet his gaze warmed her. She tucked the strand but kept her attention on the three elders.

"That can't be your only tale of bravery," she said. And indeed it wasn't. Kenneth, Angus, and Bruce continued with story after story of battles of yore. They tried to one up each other continuously until she fell into a fit of merriment. The three attracted a small crowd with their flying hands and wide flung arms as they began to reenact the contests of strength and stealth.

She laughed again and leaned back in her chair. Caden still stood slightly behind against the hearth. Meg glanced in his direction and caught his eye. He was so handsome, like a gallant knight. She almost sighed. What was wrong with her? She certainly hadn't drunk enough ale to elicit such thoughts. She smoothed a hand over her fluttery stomach and wet her suddenly dry lips. His grin faded.

"Meg will choose!" Bruce hollered over the boasting and raucous laughter of the younger warriors.

All eyes turned to her. "Choose?" What was it that she should be choosing? "How could I ever choose?" she asked playfully, surmising from the way Angus winked and Kenneth pointed to his own chest that she was to choose amongst the three old warriors. "What are the criteria?" she asked, mirth tearing her eyes.

"The most brave," Kenneth said.

"The most cunning," Bruce answered with a belch.

"The most knightly," Angus said.

"The most humble," Caden added from his spot, causing the room to erupt in a pounding roar of deep chuckles and whoops.

She joined the laughter. What a wonderful group. She'd never felt so included. As the room quieted, Meg tapped one finger against her lip. "Hmmm…how to choose? You all have terrible scars." The three elderly warriors nodded. Kenneth even flipped up his eye patch. "You are all the bravest warriors I've ever heard of." To that snorts and murmurs came from the younger men.

"How about us, lass?" Kieven called from the back.

Caden's perusal wafted over her like the touch of silk on skin. "Tonight I judge the wisdom and experience acquired through a lifetime of strategy and battles." With her words Angus, Bruce, and Kenneth puffed up even more if that were possible.

Meg huffed in frustrated resignation. "Alas, I cannot rule for one against the other two. You three are cunning, brave, and strong." She stood and sunk into a deep curtsey. "I choose each of you." She rose and they bowed. "I know under the protection of the three of you, I would always be safe."

Kenneth grinned. Bruce shuffled his foot in the rushes. Angus just turned red. Meg's contentment took in the whole audience. "I'm afraid these exciting stories have thrilled me to exhaustion."

The room grumbled.

"I will see ye to yer room, lass," Donald called. He stepped forward and then hastily stepped back when another hand firmly grasped her elbow. Meg's breath hitched and her stomach flipped at the contact. From the strength, self-assurance, and fresh pine smell emanating from the man, she knew it was Caden.

They walked up the long, dark flight of stone steps in silence. They were alone. Would he kiss her again? He held a taper to throw back the shadows. When they stopped at her door, she turned to him. "Thank you for bringing me here."

The flame cast shadows over his face.

"For the first time in my life I'm not checking constantly over my shoulder. For the first time I am free."

Cold, restrained anger pulled at his features. He didn't look at all like someone who had just been thanked. Forget him kissing her.

"Caden?"

He reached around and pushed open the door to her chamber. He grabbed her elbow and steered her into the room and yanked the barrier shut between them. Meg stared at the solid oak as she listened to his boots fade down the corridor.

. . .

Caden stormed down the steps to the great hall, which had nearly emptied after Meg's exit. He headed for the doors, somewhere away from the sweet smell and thank-yous of his bloody beautiful captive.

"Lovely lass," Bruce called. "And quite bonny."

"That one's got spirit," Angus agreed. "Not afraid of a little blood."

Bruce belched. "She's a healer."

"She'd make a good Highland bride," Angus said.

"Hard to believe she's a Munro." Kenneth lifted his mug to his lips.

Caden's words started low. "Yet she *is* a Munro, favored niece of Alec Munro, your sworn enemy."

Kenneth's mug stopped in midair, his eyebrow quirking up over his good eye.

Bloody hell! They'd been so easily won over, all of them. "Yet the three of you and the rest treat her like Stewart royalty."

Angus hushed him. Caden turned toward the glowing embers in the hearth and kicked them, sending sparks and ash snapping in the pit.

"I believe," Kenneth said, "'twas your order to treat her like a guest."

Caden certainly remembered that order. As a guest, Meg wouldn't try to escape, making life easier on everyone—everyone except him. Now he had Meg thanking him for rescuing her, smiling and lowering her long lashes at him as she talked about never being free until now.

Free? Ha! What was freedom anyway? He had surely never witnessed it. There was no freedom being raised as a future chief. There was no freedom from the quest to feed his clan, from the faces of starving children that haunted his dreams. Freedom was a false sensation. Meg would learn it soon enough. She'd learn it and her smile would die.

"I know what I said," Caden ground out, trying to hold onto his fury. He had to get outdoors into the night air, where he could breathe again. "Rachel will leave on the morrow, she'll negotiate with Alec, and Meg will be gone within a week. Don't get attached."

"Don't be getting yourself in a temper," Bruce said.

"Aye," Kenneth added as Caden turned and strode toward escape. "Or else someone will start to think *you're* the one getting attached."

Chapter Seven

26 November 1517 — Melancholy Thistle: drooping pink thistle head, flowers in summer. Decoction of the flowers or root in wine to dispel all melancholy diseases.
Find the Scottish variety as it is the most potent for dispelling doom. I must find an honorable Highlander to show me the best locations.

"My Lizzie hasn't been the same since the bairn came," Hugh Loman whispered.

Meg stood in the shade of the small house and wrapped clean linen over his stump. "Does the babe wake her during the night?"

"Aye. Though sometimes I'll wake to find her just staring at little Geilis sleeping in his cradle." He nervously glanced toward the doorway and rubbed his hand down his face. "She won't eat and she cries at everything. Won't let me even out of her sight."

"Sounds like the same affliction that lay heavy in my neighbor's mind after her babe was born." Meg dug around in her leather pouch for what was left of her melancholy thistle root, just a bit now tied with string. Most of her healing supplies were in need of renewal.

"Ye frown," he said. "Do ye not have enough?"

"Just enough. Let's brew some for her."

"Thank ye," he said with obvious relief.

When they entered, Elizabeth turned from the cradle, her eyes wide.

"Is his arm worse?" she asked and whisked over to him.

"No, healing quite well," Meg assured her.

Elizabeth grasped Meg's hand to squeeze hard. "Thanks to ye." She curtseyed. "I owe ye my life, too, for without my Hugh I would perish and leave little Geilis with no one." Elizabeth's eyes filled with tears, and one large drop broke free to trace down her thin cheek.

Meg continued to hold the woman's hand. In a heartbeat, she could sense the imbalance in Elizabeth's brain, like a shadow penetrating the folds. The small organ in Elizabeth's throat was also stagnant, just as if it had been in the new mother back home.

"May I see your babe?" Meg asked as she peeked over the cradle.

"He's not here. I just…needed a break and…" Elizabeth's words caught in her throat and she rubbed her face. "Bess has him down the road. Just for a spell so I could rest."

"Of course." Meg patted Elizabeth's hand. "That is wise."

Simple words, but they had the effect of a boulder falling into Elizabeth's arms. She crumpled downward, shaking her head and sobbing. "Nay, I'm no good mother."

Hugh pulled her up and sat her on the bed.

"Heat some wine with this root in it," Meg told Hugh, and handed him the taproot of a melancholy thistle. He nodded and left them, though his concerned eyes glanced back to Elizabeth. Meg inhaled slowly through her nose and walked over to Elizabeth. She sat next to her and rubbed the distraught woman's back as she cried.

"Elizabeth," Meg whispered to catch her attention. "You just had a baby and you're tired. I've met several new mothers and at least half of them swore they were terrible at it."

Elizabeth just cried into her hands, inconsolable. Meg watched Hugh crouch before the low fire to stir the embers.

Meg stilled her hand on Elizabeth's back and shut her eyes. She imagined the place in Elizabeth's brain, the place that was shadowed. Then she imagined that place lighter, just a smidge at first, then lighter and lighter until the shadow was gone. Meg's thoughts moved to the darkness she sensed in the front of Elizabeth's throat and imagined it lightening until it also receded.

Thump! Meg opened her eyes. Hugh stared from across the room, the leather flask at his feet, pouring across the rushes.

"What are ye doing?" Hugh demanded and moved across the room.

Meg's gaze snapped to her hands on Elizabeth's back, expecting to see blue light emanating from them. There was nothing…just hands and back. Elizabeth sat up straighter on the bed and dried her eyes on the corner of a shawl.

"I believe she was comforting me, Hugh," Elizabeth said and offered Meg a smile before turning on him. "And what are ye doing, dropping the wine? That is what I'm supposed to drink. Right?"

"Yes," Meg said, still taking in Hugh's startled face. What had he seen? *Good Lord, did I glow?* Would the man call her a witch? The fire leapt in the hearth and fear cinched her stomach.

Elizabeth stood. "I'll be sure to drink this brew," she said. "Though just the thought of it and your kind words have brightened me already." She turned with a small loaf of bread wrapped in a cloth. "I made this to thank ye for tending Hugh."

"The aroma is wonderful. Thank you." Meg cleared her throat. She didn't miss that Hugh watched her. "Well, I best go. Donald is most likely outside." She passed Hugh on her way out. "I'll check on your arm again in a couple of days."

"Thank you," Elizabeth called.

Hugh said nothing.

As Meg turned she caught the quick movement of Hugh's good hand across his chest. The man had just made the sign of the cross! Her face flamed.

She walked down the lane with Donald, but her mind was frozen. Hugh had seen something that scared him, something she had done. Word would spread. People would cross themselves when they saw her, and they may even call her a witch. Yet helping Elizabeth was the right thing to do. Doing so gave her purpose and made her *curse* a gift like Aunt Rachel said.

"Are ye well, lass?" Donald asked. "Ye seem flushed."

Meg concentrated on breathing smoothly. She swallowed the worry. Like dry bread, it hurt going down and lumped in her stomach. Did it really matter what they called her if she could help people like Elizabeth? Yes, if she could be burned like her mother.

She inhaled deeply. Fiona could get her to her aunt if needed. "I am well, Donald."

Ann and Jonet waved. They came across the road winding among the thatched cottages. Jonet glanced beyond Meg's shoulder. "Good day, Gwyneth."

Meg turned to see Gwyneth, fresh and graceful.

Gwyneth stopped. "Anyone seen Caden? I have something important to discuss with him."

"Are you trying to get into his bed again?" Jonet asked in Gaelic and rolled her eyes.

Again?

"I'll just walk on a ways and let you lasses talk," Donald said. He gave his sister a warning glance and shuffled down the road.

Ann ignored Donald. "You caught him fair and square last harvest festival," she quipped, and Gwyneth let out a little chuckle. "The man's too wrapped up now in trying to find us food to fall into anyone's arms."

"The food shortage is that critical?" Meg asked, breathing past the sudden nausea at the thought of Caden with the raven-haired beauty. All three sets of eyes turned. They seemed surprised that she'd understood them.

Although they nodded in unison, the message each gave was different. Ann seemed to have let slip a deep secret. Jonet raised her eyebrows, like it was not really all that bad. And Gwyneth's eyes popped wide and overly innocent.

"Many could die this winter," Gwyneth said, switching to

English. "Unless we are saved."

"Which is why I think we should still have the harvest festival," Ann said. "We should be thankful to the Good Lord for what we do have and ask Him for help."

Jonet held her skirt and turned in a circle. "We could still have the dancing. The men could hunt."

"I have found us some grain, too," Gwyneth said excitedly. "That's what I want to talk to—"

"The chief," Ann finished and pointed.

Meg turned around and her stomach flipped. Caden walked toward them, a small bundle of cloth over his left shoulder. As he neared, the bundle moved and whimpered. His big hand all but covered it as he gave it two little pats. A baby—he carried a little baby on his shoulder, like it was the most natural thing in the world.

Caden walked with strength in each step, shoulders wide. Yet holding a small baby so naturally against his chest made him look so much more...well, *everything*. Stronger, bigger...it took Meg's breath away.

"Good day," he said. He frowned at Meg. "Where is Donald? He is yer escort."

Meg blinked. "You have a baby."

Caden patted the babe's back once more.

Meg peeked around. "And it's drooling down your shoulder."

"Bairns drool when they're sleeping," he said and a crack of a grin softened his frown. "Some lasses do, too."

Meg's face flamed instantly. Had she drooled when he slept next to her on the journey?

"The bairn belongs to Hugh Loman. I offered to bring him home from Bess Tammin. Where is Donald?" he asked again.

Meg glanced down the road and pointed to where Donald stood against another house. When he saw Caden he jumped away from the wall and came toward them.

"He didn't seem interested in women talk," Meg said. She stepped up to the baby. "May I touch him?"

Caden shifted the baby off his shoulder and lowered him into Meg's arms. She held the sleeping cherub with one arm and touched his softly curled hand. Air rushed through his fresh lungs, blood moved along his vessels in rhythm with his heartbeats. His body hummed with life, thriving, growing.

"He's healthy," Meg said and played with the baby's toes.

Ann and Gwyneth stood over the baby, cooing as his eyes blinked open. Jonet pushed her little finger in the baby's palm and he clasped it.

"Caden, I'd like to talk with ye," Gwyneth said.

"Aye," Caden said, though his eyes remained on Meg and the baby. "Talk."

"Ann and Jonet would like to still have the harvest festival," she said right away.

"There's no harvest," he said with flat finality.

"I found grain," she said with a tip of her chin. "My cousin lives with the Davidsons and talked with their chief about giving us five sacks of grain for our festival."

"We should thank God for what we *do* have," Ann added. She clasped Jonet's arm as if the scowl Caden gave her might knock her down.

"Folks will miss the festival," Jonet said softly. "The

dancing." She shrunk under Caden's glower.

Meg should try to help them. Wasn't that what friends did? "I like dancing. T'would be fun to dance."

Caden didn't turn back to Gwyneth. "Thank yer cousin. I will send thanks to Gilbert Davidson for the grain. Make yer plans, ladies."

The women beamed. Meg handed back the baby to Caden. "Thank you."

"Donald, stay with Meg, even if ye don't like woman talk." Caden turned toward Hugh's house, the little baby snuggled into his neck. His kilt hung around his narrow hips, and his large calf muscles flexed as he walked up the hill. The patch of baby drool dried on his shoulder.

"My, my," Gwyneth said.

"Gwyneth!" Ann and Jonet yelled at the same time. Donald choked on an inhale.

Meg ignored the comment. "I would like to help with the festival," she said and trudged past Gwyneth toward the keep.

"Why ye will be the main attraction," Gwyneth said, grinning. "The niece to the great Munro."

Meg's shoulders tensed with the innuendo in Gwyneth's comments. The silent worry that passed between Jonet and Ann couldn't be missed. Just what it all meant, Meg wasn't sure. It definitely meant something.

• • •

The last meal of the day had been painfully long. Caden sat before the fire and rubbed an oiled cloth over the razor edge of his sword. Ewan had played the courtier, but even his mood was forced. Caden's headache intensified with each of Meg's questions about the harvest and each of her pleasant expressions, because her bloody smiles encouraged lingering warriors to boast more chivalrous tales.

Now all was quiet, everyone to bed. Only the wind in the chimney and the occasional creak and skitter broke the silence. Now he could think.

Caden stood and hefted the huge sword straight up, pointing to the ceiling. Balanced in his grasp, the weapon became a deadly extension of his arm. With a toss of weight, the hilt floated in his grip. He turned the weapon and sliced through the air. The blade sang. He rotated and sliced across and then upward as if fending off attack from a mounted enemy. His muscles warmed, the tension sliding from his body as he performed the familiar movements. He paused to take off his shirt, leaving him only in the kilt draped low around his hips.

He took up the sword and worked through several movements, letting the fire and the dance melt his tension completely away. In the blessed peace of the motion, his thoughts sifted through pieces of information. Boswell's letter, Fiona's information, Alec's silence thus far.

Meg.

And here his thoughts solidified. Meg was at the center of it all. She showed amazing courage yet seemed afraid to face the possibilities of what she was. She was intelligent but had no idea of her worth. Her face was that of an angel and her innate happiness could turn the meanest warriors to babbling fools. What was he going to do with her?

Caden sliced against the silent air, spun on instinct, and

froze, his blade out before him parallel to the stone floor. The tip pointed toward the dim staircase, directly at Meg. She stood with a tallow candle before her, more apparition than woman in a flowing white robe. Her eyes were wide, hair free flowing around gently sloped shoulders.

"I couldn't sleep."

Caden straightened, lowering his sword. "'Tis not safe to walk alone at night."

She glanced around. "I don't see anything frightening or dangerous. Just a waning fire and lovely tapestries." She trod lightly to the hearth, set the candle on the mantel, and splayed her hands toward the heat. The edge of white cotton stuck out from under the robe to fall just on the tops of her leather slippers.

Under the chemise, she would be soft, supple, and completely nude.

Caden drew in a breath and exhaled slowly. Control, he'd mastered it early in life. He could certainly control his reaction to the lass. She turned and gave him the most sincere bloody, damned smile he'd ever seen. Her gaze flicked to his bare chest before flying back up to his face, but just the quick caress sent heat through his body, melting his resolve to stay distant.

"A lovely lass alone is always in danger." He took a step toward her and stopped.

She pursed her luscious pink lips. "Sounds like you think I can't take care of myself."

"I don't see yer beast nor yer bow. I would say ye are as defenseless as a bairn."

She cocked her head to the side. "A clever woman always

has a trick or two. Uncle Harold made sure of that."

Caden stared at her for a long moment, his face growing serious. "Do ye mean the blue light? Is it also a weapon?" More than just curiosity—he should know if she could truly defend herself if needed.

Meg's face fell, her eyes blinking toward the ground. "I… that's not what I meant." She met his eyes again, weighing him. "I don't know what I can do. I know it can fix what I sense is wrong in a person."

"Like yer aunt."

She nodded. "Do you know that people call her a witch?"

"Aye, I do."

"Do people call me a witch, then?"

"Nay, lass. I haven't heard that said."

Relief flooded her face and a measure of tension melted in Caden. "Is that what ye fear? That ye'll be called a witch?"

She shook her head. "To fear is foolish."

"I've heard yer nightmares. And fear is not foolish. Fear keeps men and women alive."

"My mother died because she was called a witch. I've been taught to be as far from being a witch as possible."

"Yet ye're a healer."

Meg sighed and wrapped her arms around herself. "With… talents like mine, it is almost impossible not to help someone when I know exactly what is wrong with them."

Caden took another step toward her. "Ye didn't heal the men on our journey with yer powers."

"I used my powers to discover what was wrong, but I'm only now learning that the blue light can change things."

"Rachel."

"She told me I should try. I've only tried once, but it seemed to help."

Caden stepped up close, his tunic nearly brushing her bodice. "If ye keep helping people with it, they will call ye witch."

Her face tightened. "I know. I...I can't just let people suffer when I can help, either."

"The world is dangerous for a lass and even more dangerous for a witch."

Her eyes narrowed as she stared up at him. "Don't call me that."

"Have ye put a spell on me?"

"I can't do that," she snapped. "If I could, the world wouldn't be so dangerous for me, would it?"

Caden pried her hand from her robe and placed it flat against his heart. The contact of her skin against his burned through him. He inhaled her scent, warm woman and summer flowers. He hardened beneath the kilt. "Meg, I learned as a boy to control my mind, my will, my strength."

She swallowed again.

"What do ye feel in me now?"

She hesitated. "I...your headache is gone. Umm...your stomach is working. Your heart is beating most rapidly."

"As fast as yers?"

"Perhaps."

"What else?"

"Your blood is flowing fast. Your..." She blushed deeply and her eyes dipped to his kilt and then back up to his eyes.

Caden stared down into her eyes and touched her chin. "I control everything about me. My mind, my body. When ye smile." He rubbed his thumb across her bottom lip and it dropped open slightly, showing her teeth. He moved closer, so close that her short breaths fell against his own lips. "I am always in control, but ye, lass, are making me lose it."

Caden's lips touched hers with restraint. Then the softness, the sweet honeyed taste of her mouth, crashed through the walls he'd erected. He pulled her into him, encasing her in his arms against his body. If she'd have stiffened just a bit, resisted, it would have snapped him back to the familiar confines he placed on his actions, but she didn't. Meg melted into him, her slender, softly rounded body melding into his muscle-hard chest.

His mouth slanted against hers and Meg let out a little moan. That small sound, barely audible at the back of her throat, had the effect of five cups of whisky. Her hands crept up to his neck, fingers catching in his hair. He explored her sweet rounded backside, lifting her to fit intimately against him. No resistance—nothing but warm, awakening passion. He raked a hand through her hair to cup her head.

Meg kissed him back, her hands reaching around to touch along his jaw, down along his bare chest. The kiss ended as they both sought breath against each other's lips.

"Your heart is wild," she murmured.

"Strong enough to withstand hours of battle or one of your kisses." He feathered another one across her lips before lowering her. Caden still hugged her into his chest, not yet ready to release her. Hell, he'd never be ready to release her. Damn, what was he doing? She was a captive, a pawn to force peace.

He was using her to save his people.

He relinquished his hold and pulled back. "Like I said, lass. 'Tis dangerous to walk the halls at night."

The sight of her hitched his breath. She was rumpled and flushed, her robe falling open to reveal sheer white fabric barely concealing the rosy tips of her nipples. Her hair had been ravished by his fingers, her lips swollen by his kisses. She stood solitary, open and vulnerable, even bewildered.

"Was this…just to prove your point?" she asked, still breathless.

He heard the hurt in her voice even though the words sounded angry. He should say yes, hurt her now, so the pain later wouldn't be so much worse. His gut twisted into a knot like the one on a deadly swinging noose.

Caden rubbed his hand across his jaw. "Did it?"

Fury blended with hurt in her face. Tears and outrage warred in her eyes. She pivoted and started for the dark steps.

Bloody hell! Caden grabbed her candle and charged after her. "Meg, stop."

She halted but didn't turn around. He spoke to the back of her head. "Perhaps I told myself it was to warn ye, perhaps it was just because I wanted to taste ye again." He moved close enough to inhale the clean scent of her hair as he breathed. "My control dissolved at yer first touch. Yer senses revealed my response."

Meg's stance relaxed, but she didn't turn around. He placed his hand on her shoulder and turned her slightly so that she could meet his gaze. "It was wrong, though. Ye are a…guest here, lass, and I took liberties."

"Perhaps I should leave here soon, then," she said.

The thought of her absence was like a little gnawing hole in Caden. He ignored it. "I'll send word to the Munros."

She took the candle from his hand. "Thank you," she said and walked up the turning steps. He watched the lovely sway until she disappeared around a curve.

Now to figure exactly what his "word" to the Munros would be.

...

How dare she kiss him! Firelight danced along the wall, but the spying woman stood back in the black maw of an archway. Shadows hid the hot tears pooling in her narrowed eyes.

"Little English whore," the dark figure hissed, just a scant sound above a breath. Caden Macbain's kiss had grabbed the woman's heart and twisted the bruised organ until even the simple act of inhaling hurt. Meg Boswell was a witch! She'd admitted it!

She was supposed to be a captive, prisoner of the dungeons beneath Druim, friend of rats and fever down in the depths of the castle. Not a guest, and definitely not a woman deserving of Caden Macbain's kisses. What was he thinking? *He must be spelled. That's it. She spelled him with witchcraft!*

The woman slid further into shadow as Caden walked past, back to the fire. She inhaled silently and imagined the warm masculine smell of the chief of Druim, laird of the Macbains, and possibly her future husband. *Ha! Not now!* Fury poured out with the soundless tears, coating her with armor, shielding her heart. *Not now!* If Gilbert Davidson wanted information,

information that would punish Caden for his treachery, then he would have it. And if Meg happened to have an unfortunate accident while at Druim, then Caden couldn't use her for his beloved peace and he certainly couldn't kiss her again.

The woman's face contorted into a mischievous grin under the mask of shadow as she watched Caden grab his sword and shirt and step out into the night. The angry tears cooled on her cheeks, drying away as a plan took root, a plan shaped by vengeance, a plan to keep the anguish away. Aye, the Highlands were dangerous. Accidents and risk abounded, especially for a weak English witch.

...

Caden and Ewan stepped out into the courtyard that sparkled with early morning frost. Warriors sparred in the field just outside the wall. Young lads with wooden swords mimicked their movements, even down to the wipe of a brow, a spit, and a curse.

"Ho!" A man on horseback rounded the corner of one cottage and slowed from a fast trot to a walk. Two of Caden's perimeter guards flanked him. "I seek the chief, Caden Macbain."

"I am he. Who are you?" Caden called and slid his sword free.

The man dismounted, a folded missive in his callused hand. "William Fraser, passing along a message from the court at Edinburgh."

"Edinburgh?"

"Aye."

"We seldom hear news from so far east."

Caden sheathed his sword, though tension remained in his shoulders. He took the parchment. "Come inside and refresh yourself." He signaled for the man's horse to be taken to pasture and water. "Frasers from the south, then?"

"Aye," the man answered on his heel.

Caden signaled his guards, who left the messenger to return to their post. Ewan followed.

"I would have you wait for a missive to your chief," Caden said. Asking for food caught at his pride. One last glance at the lads sparring and laughing in the field pushed the words from his mouth. "We are in need of oats here and any other surplus your clan might be able to spare."

The man's face pinched in confusion. "I will let my chief know of your need."

Caden unrolled the parchment and scanned down the formal, flowing script. He signaled Jonet, who was cleaning up from the morning meal, to take the messenger to the kitchens for some food.

When the man left the hall, Caden tossed the parchment to Ewan. The three council members walked over.

"Bloody hell!" Caden cursed. "Lies."

Ewan read the missive that still held the broken wax seal of James V of Scotland on one edge. His brow furrowed. "Since when are you helping King Henry spread his Protestant reformation up here in the Highlands?"

"Lies," Caden repeated, his mind searching. Had someone reported that he'd recently visited England? Did they say he was helping Protestants? There was no mention of kidnapping.

He thought of Meg and their kiss the night before. He shouldn't have lost control. *Bloody hell!*

"Munro?" Ewan asked. "The missive doesn't say who's accused you."

"Bloody bastard," Angus cursed.

Kenneth leaned into Ewan's shoulder and read out loud for the other two elders. "Caden Macbain is to cease his heretical and traitorous views and actions immediately or the full weight of the Scottish crown will fall upon him and his clan."

"*Cac*," Bruce swore and stifled a burp. "I say we raid Munro tonight. Storm the castle, too!"

Caden sat, his mind folding around this new information. Did it make sense for Munro to involve the crown to save his niece? There hadn't been time for the old man to send a complaint to King James since Meg's arrival. Could this have been a plan of his from before? Perhaps that was why he delayed in sending a reply concerning Meg. Or was there someone else plotting against the Macbains, as Rachel Munro had suggested?

He turned to Ewan. "Compose a response that refutes the charges and asks who is spreading such damning lies."

Caden slammed his fist into his other hand. If the world demanded war, then so be it. "No word from Munro by the festival and we ride the following night," he said striding toward the door. "Prepare a plan of attack."

・・・

"I'm desperately in need of some herbs," Meg said to Donald, and shook a little vial that only contained the dust of comfrey.

"I need to find some before the winter covers us over." This was true, but she also just wanted to get away for a while. She needed to sort out what had happened last night, how she could have lost control with Caden.

"I don't think Caden would like ye to venture out of the village," Donald warned, his eyes uneasy.

"You'll be with me and we will stay at the edge of the forest on Macbain land. Fiona said the forest grows an abundance of garlic bulbs, feverfew, and Devil's bit. Although it's late in the season, I'd like to see if I can find any. And mushrooms for the festival. I know which ones are safe."

"Ye are safer here." He crossed arms, his gaze roaming the bailey.

Hmmm, creativity was needed to sway the man. Just an exaggeration, not a full-out lie. She sighed. "Gellis has that ear ache." She shook her head and ignored her guilty flush. "And Ann, well…"

His gaze came around. "Something ails Ann?"

She scuffed the heel of her boot in the pebbly dirt. Ann had an irregular menstrual cycle, and Meg could tell from a touch that she was fine, but the feverfew could help bring on Ann's flux when it was late. She hated to worry Donald, but she was so cooped up in the castle and did need the herbs. A ride out was worth the price of a little exaggeration. "I shouldn't really say." She worked concern into her eyes. "'Tis a womanly issue."

"A womanly issue," Donald repeated and swallowed hard, his Adam's apple bobbing along his throat.

"Aye, and Fiona and I are completely out of feverfew."

He huffed long and ushered Meg toward the stables. "I

suppose we can just ride to the edge and peek into the forest to see if ye see this plant."

Pippen stretched his legs as they flew across the moor toward the soaring trees. The cold sting of winter air melted under the strength of the sunrays shining down on Meg's face. The leaves had changed color and most had dropped to the ground.

"Slow down," Donald called from behind as they neared the forest edge.

Meg circled Pippen in a wide ring. She ran her gloved hand down his neck and leaned in. "I know." She hugged the horse and scratched him between the ears. She stopped Pippen just inside the tree line and dismounted. "Free to run a bit. This time without wolves biting at your hooves."

Donald followed suit.

She unfolded a clean cloth and gathered small chanterelle mushrooms hidden amongst the moss. A little further in, she spotted the creamy white cap of the hedgehog mushroom. She ran ahead to dig it up and heard Donald mumbling behind her.

"These will add wonderful flavor to a goose dish for the festival," Meg called. Her eye caught a patch of withered feverfew at the base of a tall pine tree. She sunk to her knees. "Just what I need."

Crack!

Meg jumped at the sudden explosive noise. She stood and whirled around at the sound of Donald's deep groan. He slumped to his knees and fell over into the leaf litter.

"Donald!" Meg ran to the fallen man. A large dead tree limb lay next to him. She glanced around but saw no one.

A broken stump stood out from the tree trunk several feet above. How often did large tree limbs just let go and fall when someone stood beneath? Her eyes narrowed and she once more scrutinized the surrounding forest, but couldn't see anyone.

She probed the back of Donald's head. Her sensitive touch told her that he had some bruising around his brain where the heavy limb had struck, along with some minor bleeding on his scalp.

Aunt Rachel's words swam through the worry in Meg's mind. *Envision the body being normal.*

She placed her hands on Donald's chest and closed her eyes. She took a deep breath and summoned the blue light, imagining it pushing into the man. Meg followed the path of muscles and bone through Donald's body until she reached his injured head, imagining the brain healthy and clean, no blood.

"What's going on here?" A man's voice shot through her so hard that she gasped and fell backward. Her eyes snapped open, her gaze shooting around the trees.

"I…I…" Panic at being caught using her light choked her words. "He's been hurt. I was but trying to help."

A strong hand clasped her upper arm and pulled her to standing. Good Lord, what had he seen?

"Are ye hurt, lass?" He set her away from him and knelt to inspect her fallen friend. The man's voice was friendly and he had a mouth full of white teeth. He was tall and broad with a handsome face. His dark hair was clipped along with a short beard. He dressed and spoke like a Highlander. The man stood, his head tipped back to study the tree stump. "He's got a nasty bump on the head. Rotten piece of luck, that."

Meg breathed in relief that the accent wasn't English.

He glanced around before gazing back at her. "May I be of assistance?"

"Yes, I need to get Donald back to Druim. Just there, through the woods. I am Meg…a guest at Druim." Best not to give the stranger her full name. Although her accent told him she was English.

He led her toward Pippen, who stood just inside the tree line. "And I am Gilbert. Gilbert Davidson, a neighbor and friend to the Macbains."

"The one providing the grain for our harvest festival?"

"I wish I could do more," he said with a bob of his head.

"Thank you very much for what you can give." Meg took hold of her saddle. She yanked down on it, her foot in the rung of the stirrup, when the leather snapped. She fell back into Gilbert Davidson's arms.

"Good God ye've had a run of bad luck today," he said with a chuckle, and turned her toward him.

The hairs on the back of Meg's neck prickled as she realized that she was pressed between Pippen and this large man's chest. The man gave off an overbearing vibe. Perhaps it was because he stood so close. When she'd met the Macbains, all of the men stayed well away from her.

Not Gilbert Davidson. They were also very much alone, out in the woods with no witnesses and no one knowing that she was gone from Druim. She was trapped.

"Ye are a bonny lass." He spoke much too close.

She turned and he frowned, changing his handsome

features into something far darker. "The leather seems like it's been sliced through. Thank the Lord ye didn't plunge off yer horse."

Meg swallowed hard. How could it have been cut? The sharp edge of the leather showed that it hadn't just torn.

"I can't allow ye to ride all the way back to Druim bareback, milady."

"I can take Donald's horse," Meg countered, her gaze flicking about. The horse was missing.

"Never fear," he said with a gallant bow, "I still have my steed. I will take ye."

He grabbed her elbow and propelled her over to his horse.

"Really," Meg said, "I can ride Pippen back without a saddle."

"Too dangerous." He lifted her up onto his horse. His hands lingered around her waist and her stomach fluttered up into her throat. He jumped up behind her, settling his thighs intimately around her hips. She grabbed a tuft of mane as the horse jumped forward into a canter.

Gilbert leaned close to her ear. "Ye have such a lovely accent. Is home England?"

"Druim is the other way," Meg said, trying to keep her tone casual, but her heartbeat thumped wildly.

"I know a short cut," he said as he dodged between the trees.

"There is no shorter route than straight across the moor," she said. Her eyes shifted amongst the trees. Where was he taking her? Anywhere besides the safe haven of Druim would be disastrous, even deadly. Foolish! Feebleminded! What was she thinking?

He laughed. "What does an English lass know of the Highlands?"

Meg clung to the horse with her thighs and fingers as Gilbert veered around trees. "You're going too fast."

He snaked one solid arm around her middle, pulling her back against him. "There now, I will not let ye fall."

Movement ahead through the woods hitched Meg's shallow breath. She gasped as Gilbert's horse pawed its front hooves in the air and dropped back to earth with a high whinny, jarring her teeth.

"*Cac!*" Gilbert swore.

Caden sat on his warhorse just two trees away. The clamping panic in Meg's chest unfurled into hope and complete trust that her hero would rescue her.

"Caden!" Meg would have jumped off Gilbert's horse if the oaf wasn't clasping her to him like a shield.

Caden raised one hand and six Macbain warriors surrounding them unsheathed their swords in unison. He brought up the dirk from his boot and pointed it at Gilbert. "One twitch from me, Davidson, and Ewan will skewer you through your back."

Meg remained still, her eyes trained on Caden's strong jaw. Everyone seemed to hold their breaths.

"God's teeth, Macbain!" The man's blood rushed fast, his heart pounding with alarm. "I was but rescuing the lass. Her saddle's girth strap was cut."

"Rescuing?" Caden didn't even blink. "Taking her back to your holding, you mean. You're headed south."

"I got turned around," he said, and slowly raised his hands out to the side. "Could you fault me? She's lovely. I but lost my train of thought."

Before Meg could even consider arguing that point, Caden's charger lunged toward her, missing her legs by a brush of horsehair. In one swoop of his iron-like arm, he lifted her from Gilbert's seat and spun his horse in a tight loop. She leaned into his warm chest. Pine and leather scent completely enveloped her, soothing and thrilling at the same time. Meg's senses picked up Caden's tight muscles throughout his body, poised to attack. His heart beat a strong rhythm, pumping blood to his extremities, and his pupils dilated.

Every part of his body was prepared to rip Gilbert Davidson in two.

Gilbert had reared back in his saddle when Caden had advanced. He now leaned forward without seeming to care that six swords still pointed toward him. "Ye grab the lass like she was a possession, Macbain," Gilbert said in English, and shrugged. "Like a lover."

He winked at Meg, who just stared in shock at the man's audacity. "Or…a captive."

Meg's sensitive gift told her that Caden's muscles tensed to flick the dirk he still held. Didn't the idiot know that his taunts would snap Caden's control? Could killing the chief of another clan cause a feud between them? She couldn't be the start of something so dreadful. She needed a distraction.

"Donald needs tending." She pointed back the way they had come.

"You dare attack my man and take my…" Caden paused

for the slightest of seconds, "…guest."

Meg pushed hard on Caden's arm. "Donald was hit by a falling tree limb." She lowered her voice. "I tried to help him."

"Hamish, Sean," Caden ordered, eyes and dirk still trained on Gilbert. "Find Donald."

Hamish and a young warrior spun their horses around with their knees, keeping swords drawn, and tore off through the woods.

"What are you doing on Macbain land?" Ewan called.

Gilbert kept his eyes on Caden. "I was checking to make sure ye received my gift of grain. I didn't know I'd be treated like an enemy."

Caden lowered his dirk and the other four men lowered their swords. "We will repay the favor when you are in need."

Gilbert bowed his head.

"I take it you know your way home." Caden wheeled his warhorse around. He wrapped an arm around Meg and leaned into the charge. As they broke through the trees, he urged the horse into a gallop across the moor.

"Donald's mount," Meg called above the wind as she spotted a lone horse grazing half way to Druim.

Caden motioned to one of the warriors and the man veered toward the animal.

She turned and leaned her face into Caden's shoulder and peered back over it. Hamish and Sean rode out of the woods at a slower pace, and Donald rode upright on Pippen's bare back. "Thank God he seems well."

He grazed Meg's ear with his lips, scattering a million little shivers throughout her body. "More likely, thank Meg."

...

Three more days and still no word from Alec Munro. Caden leaned his head forward, arms braced against the hearth to stretch his shoulders. He stared at the snapping flames as they danced around the dry peat in the hearth. Rachel had returned a full week ago to the Munro holding and Alec had yet to demand the release of his beloved niece.

Did the old chief think to steal her away? Caden made it understood that Meg was not to again leave the village of Druim, even with a guard. Donald had healed rapidly under her care. The branch was examined but no evidence against Gilbert Davidson could be found. Nor had they figured out how her saddle had been cut. Perhaps Davidson had done the deed to give her a reason to ride with him.

Caden frowned. Too many questions lay unanswered and, bloody hell, all they could do was wait for a reply from Meg's uncle. Caden had a loyal maid in Munro Castle. She'd witnessed several curt exchanges between Rachel and Alec that had quickly led to behind the door shouting, but the topic was never fully overheard.

Perhaps Alec believed his niece was safe at Druim since she was being treated like a guest and not rotting in the dungeon. Wind whistled down the chimney making the flames dance and shudder. Did Alec think Caden wouldn't let a guest starve through the winter?

The door banged open, caught by the wind. The harvest festival was planned for the next day, yet winter already snapped at the heels of autumn. Hamish and Ewan strode across the fresh rushes strewn through the great hall. Hamish handed Caden a folded parchment.

Finally, Alec Munro's response.

"Did Gregory bring this?"

Hamish shook his head. "Someone I didn't recognize. Headed south once I swore I would take you the missive."

Caden studied the wax seal. A rose, red and thick as old blood. Not from Alec. The grand design smelled of England. He broke the seal, unfolded the thick parchment, and scanned the script. The hand at his side rolled into a fist as he read it through a second time, making certain to miss nothing.

"From England?" Ewan asked, his brow furrowed. "The messenger wore English steel, but no coat of arms."

"Aye," Caden said and passed the parchment to Ewan. Fury pinched inside Caden's chest as control battled to keep his fury within. Anger would just cloud reason.

"Is it from her father? Rowland Boswell is her father?" Ewan asked.

"Aye, and he wants her back."

"To test her for witchcraft," Ewan read.

"Bloody hell," Hamish cursed at the same time Caden slammed his fist down on the top of the oak mantel. Fire leapt up with breath from the wind as if God himself roared up on Meg's behalf.

"Says he'll give us food and weapons against the Munros if we give her over quickly," Ewan spat. "How does he even know she's here?"

"Good question," Caden said. "And apparently Boswell wants Rachel Munro dead, too." He glanced around the hall that had been decorated with dried flowers and ribbons for the festival. No auburn hair, bewitching hazel eyes, and lovely lips.

"The bastard lays it out quite succinctly," Ewan continued. "And if we don't comply, then he gives weapons to our enemies as well as turning over evidence that we've murdered Englishmen, aided Catholics, and kidnapped a loyal English girl." He threw the parchment down on a bench. "So we'll have two ill-tempered kings ready to hang us."

"King Henry's too far away to bother with us up here," Hamish said.

"Not if he thinks we're harboring Catholics and rallying against him. The man spooks at the hint of rebellion ever since the uprising in York over the abbeys being burned. He sent Suffolk with orders to hang men, women, and children," Ewan said.

"So what do you want to do?" Hamish yelled. "Hand the wee lass over to be examined, tortured, and burned?"

"Nay!" Ewan shouted.

"*Stad!*" Caden held up a hand. He looked to Hamish. "Send word to the Munros about Boswell's offer. Make sure Rachel Munro hears that her niece is not as safe as she thinks."

The heat in Ewan's eyes froze instantly into shock. "Caden, you're not planning—"

"I will not hand Meg over to Boswell, even though he has legal custody. We still haven't heard anything from the Munros, and winter is coming. We need to leverage this information, use it to our advantage."

Hamish headed to the door just as Meg blew inside, followed by Angus. Her hair lay in scattered waves around her shoulders, her cheeks pink from the brisk wind. She was fresh and alive, brightening the entire room at once.

Hamish tipped his head to her as he ran out.

Caden folded the parchment and set it up high on the mantel. He wasn't ready to explain that the devil had caught up with her.

"Smile," Caden told Ewan.

"What?" Ewan still wore a fierce, battle-hungry scowl.

"Smile," Caden commanded. "Else she'll wonder."

"You're not."

"I don't."

Ewan smiled and bent over Meg's hand. "Milady, ye are radiant."

Meg twisted her hair over one shoulder. "Thank you, though this Highland wind is fierce. Thank goodness the festival is inside tomorrow, or everything would blow away."

Her gaze rested on Caden. She tilted her head just slightly off center. "Is something amiss?"

Caden relaxed his fists that had clenched at his sides. He'd inadvertently taken a battle stance. "Nay," he said, though the lie tasted bitter. At some point the lies would have to be told, sometime soon. He frowned more.

"He doesn't smile," Ewan said.

Meg stepped forward and laid her hand on Caden's arm. He tensed as the soft touch coursed through his body. She frowned. "Does your head ache? Your neck, perhaps? Your muscles are very...tense."

"Ye can tell that by a touch?" Ewan asked.

Meg continued to study Caden's face, his eyes. She was

close enough for him to smell the flower scent she preferred, close enough to pull her into his arms and kiss her like the other night. "His stance, his solid arm. I sense unease in people easily."

Caden stared into her eyes, mesmerized by the golden flecks within the greenish orbs. "My arm is always solid."

A twinkle in her eyes washed away the crease in her brow. "Of course," she murmured. "I can help the ache in your head."

"I didn't mention an ache."

Meg stared up at him, and he noticed a small leaf stuck in her tussled waves. She paused for a moment. "No, you didn't. If you get one, I have something to help."

"Probably tastes foul," Angus said with a laugh as he took a drink of ale.

Her eyes opened wider as Caden reached for her hair and leaned near her ear. "I've never met a lass so in need of plucking."

He captured a little leaf, pulling it free. He held it so she could see it before letting it float to the rushes.

Sparkle came to Meg's eye with a healthy shade of rose staining her cheeks.

"Angus, where's yer cough?" Ewan asked.

Angus patted Meg's shoulder. "The lass gave me some brew to drink. Terrible stuff but," he paused and took a full breath in, "I breathe better than I have in years."

"Miraculous," Ewan said.

Caden studied Meg. The lass had been up to more healing. Hugh told Caden he'd seen a blue light coming from Meg's hands when she healed Elizabeth's sadness. The incident had scared the hell out of his most seasoned warrior, but now Hugh was spreading praises. His merry Lizzie was back. And now Angus's cough was gone. Would he be as accepting if he knew she'd used magic on him? Would his clan welcome a lass with unnatural powers?

Meg was indeed valuable in more ways than one, although fear of unholy magic and superstition was a solid part of the people in this hard land. Caden watched her talk with Ewan and Angus. She could melt the hearts of the crustiest old bastard. And yet Meg Boswell was marked for death as a witch. Evidence and family history pretty much confirmed that she could wield the same powers. He'd yet to find the dragonfly birthmark on her, although he'd love to explore.

Caden picked up the parchment on the mantel. Meg's nightmare. With a flick of his wrist, he tossed it into the fire. The hungry flames scorched the parchment until it crumbled, the wax seal puddled into a pool of blood. He turned away from the burn to the beauty walking across the hall. Valuable indeed, he thought. So valuable that…he would never let her go.

• • •

Heavy snow blew down from the gray sky in diagonal sheets the next morning. Meg shivered as she turned from the small glass windowpane. She stepped into the farthingale and stood while Fiona laced her stays.

"Snow already?"

"Aye." Fiona helped Meg into a green velvet gown that she'd chosen from several that Aunt Rachel had sent over. Her aunt had time to find her gowns but still hadn't sent word inviting her to Munro Castle. Did her uncle not want her to come? Did he know that her father might be searching for her? Meg sighed and tamped down her suspicions.

She focused on the image in the polished glass. The cut of the gown accented her waist and full bosom. After her encounter with Caden, she chose the softly flowing dress with the low bodice for the festival. Gwenyth would surely dress with seduction in mind. In this gown Meg should be able to keep Caden's attention. The brief thought of him following the lovely widow home again pinched Meg's stomach.

Fiona tied the bell-shaped sleeves at the shoulders. "The festival is late this year."

"Mmmm," Meg murmured, her thoughts on the healthy muscles sculpting Caden's chest the other night she'd seen him practicing in the hall, the night of the kiss. Laird Caden Macbain epitomized everything she could desire in a man. He'd escorted her north to safety without ever making her beholden to him. He even knew about her magic yet didn't seem to despise her for it or even seem to fear it, although Meg couldn't imagine him fearing anything.

She sighed. And she had told him that she wanted to leave. *Fool*, she thought, pulling her thoughts back to Fiona as she covered the ties of her sleeves with rolled satin braids that brought out the golden green color of her eyes.

"Snow's about on time," Fiona continued.

"It's barely into autumn." Meg selected a warm shawl lined in fur.

"This is the Highlands, milady. We have a day or two of autumn and then charge right into winter."

"Quite a ways north of England," Meg said, her heart

thumping. *Dear Lord, please let the foul weather slow my father down.*

"Yer blood will thicken in time," Fiona said knowingly.

In time. Where would she be in time? Life right now was so uncertain she barely dared to think about the future.

"Ye are lovely," Fiona said as she tucked one of the ribbons back into the delicate weave down Meg's back. "Queen of the festival, ye are."

Meg laughed. "Thanks to your handiwork."

"If only Rachel were here to see ye."

"Have you heard from her? News of when I can visit?"

Fiona's eyes focused on Meg's hair as she tucked and twirled the cascading curls. "They've been so busy over there getting that old, drafty castle in order for yer stay. I'm sure that's why she's been delayed in sending for ye. She knows ye're safe with me here."

Fiona did meet her eyes then. "If ye are in any need to go to her, I can get ye there."

"I wouldn't want to intrude," Meg said.

Fiona squeezed her hand. "Rachel loves ye dearly, like she did her sister. Ye would be no intrusion. Rachel just wants ye to be comfortable up here in the Highlands. Right now this is the safest, most comfortable place for ye to be."

"Thank you, Fiona."

"No fretting now. Go enjoy yerself."

Meg's smile spread into a genuine one as she stepped forward.

. . .

Garlands of braided grasses and dried flowers decked the doorways, mantel, and tables of the great hall. The rushes had been swept from the floor for easier dancing. Large tallow candles glowed at intervals on long tables. Several women from the village hurried about with platters of meat and trenchers of bread. The Davidson's gift of grain for the festival had arrived two days ago, just in time for baking.

Meg stepped down the stairs and into the excitement. Villagers shook their boots and cloaks in the entryway and carried in more treats to share. Roast goose, venison, and wild hares in aromatic herbs were displayed on platters. Bowls of nuts and sweet suckets sat at intervals. Brown bread lay with bowls of churned butter. Wild onions and sliced beets coated with herbs steamed from other bowls.

Ewan walked in with Ann on his arm. She spotted Meg across the hall and raised her hand. Meg waved back. Jonet and Gwyneth came in, quick on their heels.

Three musicians began a lively tune and several couples formed a line. The flute played a quick song accompanied by the harp, and pairs began to weave in a familiar reel. Meg tapped her foot with the tabor drum. She'd danced this pattern with Uncle Harold at the festival near her home.

Ewan escorted Jonet out to the floor while Kieven took Ann.

"Would ye care to dance, lass?" Kenneth asked.

Meg gasped, her hand to her pounding heart. "I do like to dance."

Kenneth tugged her along. "Come then."

They caught up to the end of the increasing line. The steps

came back to Meg easily and she laughed as she twirled, her skirts soaring outward. No longer chilled, she was glad she'd left the shawl at the table. Soon she and Kenneth had worked their way to the top of the line. They would run down the parallel rows, weaving and twirling between other couples until they reached the end.

Kenneth stood with her at the top. "Ready?" he huffed.

"Yes," Meg said, and they turned away from one another to bow and bend beneath the raised arms of opposite dancers. As she rounded the next lady to meet her partner in the center she caught sight of Kenneth grinning from the end of the row.

Warm fingers encircled her own. Caden squeezed her hand gently and then they parted to weave back among two more pairs before meeting again in the middle.

"Did you yank Kenneth out of the dance?" Meg asked Caden breathlessly. His dark hair was captured in a leather strap, revealing the cut line of his smooth jaw and sensuous lips.

"Would you prefer the grizzled warrior to the chief, then?" he asked with a slanted grin and released her hand as they wove down between two more pairs.

When they rejoined Caden glanced at her gown and frowned. "I will find ye a shawl."

"I am quite warm," Meg said with more than a hint of sauciness. They turned once more and the reel ended with a bow and a curtsey. When she stood straight, Caden's eyes caressed her form, all the way up to her face.

"The color suits ye," he murmured.

Perhaps it was the exhilaration of the dance, perhaps it was the kiss from the night before, perhaps it was the promise in Caden's eyes that more could follow. For whatever reason, lightness and cheer filled her. Even though her future was unknown, the present held so much potential that she was going to surrender her worry and embrace simple happiness. At least for today.

The musicians struck up another reel but Caden led her back to the table where they sampled the feast.

"Meg!" Elizabeth Loman sat gingerly on the bench with the baby. "Thank ye so much for the melancholy thistle brew. I am truly so much better."

Meg squeezed Elizabeth's hand and peeked at the blue-eyed baby. "I'm so glad."

"Ah, the fair Meg," Ewan sang, and stood over Meg's shoulder. When she greeted him, his gaze plunged down her low neckline. Before she could respond, Caden stood and shoved Ewan aside before he fetched the shawl from the other end of the table. Caden glared at his friend as he draped the warm fur over her shoulders.

Elizabeth laughed and returned to her husband by the fire.

"'Tis good to see you, Ewan," Meg said.

He bowed and moved further down the table.

She frowned at Caden.

"Ye shivered," he grumbled and picked up a mug of ale.

Under the table, Caden's thigh rested against the folds of Meg's skirts. She sensed the heat there, the strength of his muscles even without using her powers. He reached for the venison platter, brushing her arm and sending chills along her skin. She tried to ignore her increasing heart rate and the pool of heat sprinting through her blood, but it was impossible. She picked at her food and tried to swallow down the creeping blush.

Meg's gaze roamed the room, anywhere but at Caden. She focused on a little ball of fluff skittering out from the back corridor from the kitchens. It raced under her table. A slight tug on her skirt hem followed. She bent down and pulled the orange tabby kitten into her lap. The soft fur ran through her fingers as she stroked it.

A woman brought around a tray of bowls filled with steaming stew. She set one before Meg and one before Caden. She hovered near him, but her happy expression faltered a bit when she noticed Meg. Her eyes shifted to the tuft of fur in Meg's lap. "There's Peter's kitten. He belongs to my son."

"He's adorable," Meg said and handed the ball of fluff over.

The woman tucked the kitten into a large apron pocket. "Cook heard ye like yer stew a bit salty, so she added some with extra thyme to yer bowl. I make it without much salt."

Where had the cook heard that? She'd have to clear that up later. "Umm…thank you," Meg said. "You must be Bess Tammin?"

"Aye, pleased to meet ye," Bess said with a quick bob. There was definite unease in her eyes. "I better find Peter. He's supposed to be helping in the kitchens." She turned to Caden, a soft blush infusing her cheeks. "Good day to you, Caden."

She called him by his given name. Not chief or laird. They must be close.

"I'll be by to check on you, Bess, in a few days." Caden tasted the stew and grinned. "Your best yet."

Bess beamed as Caden spooned more into his mouth.

Meg wondered if he knew the woman cared for him, and her stomach sank. She glanced down at her own bowl. Had Caden visited Bess's bed also?

The widow walked across the room, a definite sway to her hips. When she turned to go back into the kitchens, the woman passed her hand over her chest in the sign of the cross. She met Meg's gaze and shuffled back into the darkness of the corridor.

Meg frowned. The woman probably called her a witch. She spooned a mouthful of stew into her mouth. The salty broth pinched her lips, but it was hot and flavorful. She dipped her spoon back in and a small mushroom floated onto it. Meg was about to lift it into her mouth when she noted the reddish color of the cap. She stared. Was that a deadly amanita mushroom? Could Bess have accidentally poisoned the stew? Meg dropped her spoon and grabbed Caden's arm.

"I think there's something wrong with the stew." She churned through her bowl. Two more of the deadly mushrooms surfaced. "Good Lord," she murmured and peered down the table at all the people enjoying the hot soup.

"What is it?"

"The mushrooms in the stew. They are poisonous. Caden, they're all eating it."

"I didn't taste any mushrooms." Caden spooned through the rest of his own bowl. He tilted the cup toward Meg. "No mushrooms."

She stared at the brown liquid. "Are you sure you didn't eat any?"

"I'm sure." He pushed her three small mushrooms around with his spoon. "These were in yer cup." He pulled a bowl from

Hamish, who sat on the other side of him.

"If you're so hungry for Bess's stew, I'll get you some more." Hamish tried to grab the bowl back.

"No mushrooms," Caden said.

Meg frowned down at the offending fungus as Caden checked several more bowls. No other mushrooms were found.

Caden stood. "Where's Bess?"

Gwyneth walked up then. "Caden, I need to tell ye." She lowered her voice, though Meg could plainly hear her, and she spoke in English. "Chief Davidson sent word that he's received a letter from an Englishman." She glanced at Meg. "Something about witchcraft."

Even though Caden didn't show any outward sign of worry, from contact with his arm, Meg sensed the clenching of his stomach, the jump in the pounding of his heart. Her own stomach twisted around the bread she'd just eaten.

"Witchcraft?" she asked.

"Where's Bess?" Caden growled, ignoring Gwyneth's announcement.

"My cousin said Chief Davidson said the letter mentioned Meg Boswell," Gwyneth continued.

"I'm aware of the accusation. I'll send word to Gilbert telling him to ignore it." He strode off toward the kitchens.

Gwyneth slunk back down the table to sit.

Meg sat, just sat, for a long while, as Caden's words sunk in. A letter about her, from England, sent to holdings in Scotland? From her father? And Caden already knew about it. The acid flooding her stomach churned into nausea. He must have received one, too.

Caden came out with a frowning Bess. "I didn't put any mushrooms in the stew," she insisted.

"What are these, then?" He pointed at the poisonous little tops. People all along the table peered into their half-eaten soup. Meg stared at the mushrooms, her mind whirling. Would she have been dead before her aunt could reach her if she'd eaten them?

Bess's lips pursed into a hard line. "I didn't put them in her soup, I swear. Perhaps cook had them on a shelf and they fell in."

"Cook doesn't keep bloody poisonous mushrooms sitting on her shelf," Caden said.

"You are aware of an accusation against me?" Meg asked softly. She tried to take a sip of wine but Caden intercepted it first and took a large swallow. When he didn't keel over he handed it to her and she set it down.

"Meg, the mushrooms—" Caden started.

"You are aware that an Englishman is calling me a witch?" she asked. Fury blended with shock and fear. *I'm in danger and he didn't even tell me.*

"I received a letter," Caden said and then glanced at Bess. "Figure out where the mushrooms came from and how they got into Meg's soup."

Bess curtsied. "Of course."

Caden swiped the mushrooms into the rushes and crushed them under his heel. "Until then, all of Meg's food will be tasted first."

Meg stared at the retreating woman. "And you didn't tell me," she said, her voice still low even though the thoughts in her head screamed. Angry tears threatened at the back of her eyes.

Caden's eyes were hard when he turned to her. Irritation, worry, anger? "I didn't want to concern ye."

"You didn't want me to know that someone was hunting me for witchcraft?" she asked incredulously.

All conversation around them had ceased.

"Ye were leaving England, Meg. I assumed ye already knew."

"I was leaving to visit my aunt." Well, it was true, but not completely. She blushed.

Caden stood and leaned down to her ear. "While watching over yer shoulder the entire time." He straightened and grasped her hand. "Perhaps ye, too, should have mentioned yer father."

Meg forgot to breathe. He knew it was her father. He knew that the man who was supposed to love her wanted to try her for witchcraft and possibly kill her.

"I want to read the letter."

"The missive was destroyed."

Meg stared with wide eyes. "Destroyed?"

"Fell into the fire," Ewan called from down the table. Meg's attention snapped toward him. Ewan waved his hand as if the whole affair was nothing to fret about. "The letter just mentioned the possibility of being examined for witchcraft. Ridiculous! Not worth acknowledging."

"Gilbert Davidson seemed worried," Gwyneth mumbled, and received a glare from Ann. Gwyneth shrugged and raised her eyebrows in a helpless gesture. "I'm sorry…I just thought ye should know." She bit into a piece of bread.

"Is there anything else you think I know that you haven't

told me?" Meg asked as Caden grabbed her elbow and hoisted her out of the seat. "Or perhaps I should ask Gwyneth? Where are you taking me?"

"Somewhere private," Caden mumbled. Murmurs meshed together around the table. Caden walked them past the staring musicians. "Play something," he growled.

Meg clasped the shawl closed across her collarbone to hide the blotchy blush that prickled its way up her chest. Her mind jumped from anger to fear. A letter, about her, sent out through the Highlands.

Her mother's warning beat inside Meg. She wouldn't let Rowland Boswell take her. She must find the evidence of his treasonous plans against King Henry. That was the only way to defend herself. She sank one hand into the pocket of her skirts, fingers curling tightly around the key she always kept near.

Caden reached the shadows near the stairwell and stopped to pull her before him. He placed heavy hands on her shoulders. His heart beat strong as his muscles tensed. She breathed in his scent, strength and man mixed with fresh Highland wind and pine. The man must bathe often to smell so good. Meg frowned. Instead of sniffing him, she should be yelling at him.

"Meg," he said and exhaled. "There is a lot I must tell ye."

She met his eyes. "I expect there is."

"When I met ye in England I was on a mission," he started. "Nay." He shook his head. "Before that ye must know there was a feud."

"A feud?"

"Aye, it started a hundred years ago, over a lass. Two stubborn chiefs wanted her."

"What does that have to do with any of this?"

Caden stared hard at her, his fingers curling into her shoulders, willing her to understand. "Ye have to know the whole story." He shook his head. "Not just the what, but the why."

She crossed her arms over her chest. "Continue."

"The chief of the Munros and the chief of the Macbains both desired the same lass."

"How unfortunate."

"The lady was not able to choose. So they met to fight for her, to the death. They fought valiantly, but the lady couldn't bear to have either one die over her. When the Munro sliced down to finish the Macbain, the lady dove between them."

Meg swallowed hard. "She died?"

"By the Munro sword. The Macbain slashed back in fury and killed the Munro and thus began a feud that's been fed through the years by raids and attacks, leading to more deaths and more hatred."

"Between the Munros and the Macbains?"

"Aye," he said.

"Then I am—"

The sound of the front doors banging open cut into Meg's words.

"A message!" a man called out across the sounds of the festival. "To be delivered in haste."

"Finally," Caden murmured.

"You're expecting something?" Meg asked, but he had already turned. Could this be the letter inviting her to the Munro's holding? She frowned at Caden's obvious relief.

She followed him back into the festival where the gaiety hushed.

"I am The Macbain," Caden told the snow-dampened man. "From where do you hail?"

"I am a Davidson. An Englishman brought this letter to be taken directly to…" His gaze moved past Caden to the filled hall. "Meg Boswell."

Everyone froze for the briefest of seconds and then turned in her direction. If she'd wanted to hide, these good people would have given her away. So Meg stepped forward, propelled by expectation and what she'd like to think of as courage. Although in all honesty, she just didn't want to stand out as a guilty coward by retreating.

"I am Meg Boswell."

The man handed her a rolled parchment sealed with a rose of dark red wax.

"Bloody hell," Caden said when he saw it.

Meg's hand shook as she unrolled the scroll.

Dear daughter,

Rumors abound over your disappearance from England. Some say you ran from the accusation of witchcraft. If you are innocent of such heresy, you would not have run away. Therefore, I believe the other rumor that you were kidnapped by Laird Macbain and his men to be used to manipulate a truce with the Munros. They will be punished.

Do not fear, dearest daughter. I am on my way, with King Henry's support, to rescue you from this nightmare. Be prepared to leave Scotland when I arrive. Your Uncle Harold and Aunt Mary travel with me and fear for your safety. If you are not at the Macbain or Munro holdings, I will assume you have run away in fear of God and his judgment. Your aunt and uncle will then stand in your place, as it was under their care that you were seduced by the devil.

You are once again under my protection and authority.

Your father,
Rowland Boswell

Meg's inhale was shallow and hitched. A long moment passed before she was able to swallow. All eyes rested on her. She turned to where Caden stood, appearing none too patient. His hands were balled in fists, his face grim, legs spread in a natural battle stance.

"Boswell," he said.

Meg drew a breath. "It seems the devil has caught up with me." She handed the parchment to him. "He's coming to take me to hell."

Chapter Eight

*20 December 1517—Feverfew: small white flowers
with yellow centers.
Give half a cup tea for fevers, nervousness, hysteria, induce
monthly flux, and treat low spirits. Infuse into honey for
wheezing. Bruise and heat mash into a poultice to stop pain and
swelling from bug bites, face ache, and earache.
Although often found in dry areas, the best plants are found
along damp, windy mountain paths.*

"The bloody hell he is!" Caden slammed his hand down on the table. The festival was over, everyone gone home except his council and Ewan. Meg had retired immediately after receiving her father's threat. For that's what it was, cloaked in a letter of concern.

"We did kidnap her, even if she doesn't know it," Ewan pointed out. "She wasn't running away because she was a witch."

"She *was* running away when we found her," Caden said.

"From Boswell, though, not a charge of witchcraft." He didn't care what Meg could do with her little blue light. The woman wasn't a witch. A witch had a pact with Lucifer, hurt people and animals, and usually had gnarled teeth and fingers and stringy gray hair.

Meg was no witch.

"The last letter promised food and weapons to fight the Munros," Kenneth said. "Do you think that offer still stands?"

"What are you saying?" Angus demanded. "The lass is innocent and sweet as honey. She fixed my cough. We're not just giving her up to those damned English bastards."

Caden's blood surged inside him. His muscles twitched with battle energy. Aye, he needed to kill something. And if Ancient Kenneth wasn't careful, it just might be him.

"I'm just saying…if the lass decides to go with him, I wonder if he'd honor his first proposal."

"He's English," Bruce said. "He won't honor anything."

Kenneth continued. "Maybe when he gets here, we can demand the food and weapons before Meg goes out to him."

"Meg is not going anywhere," Caden annunciated with such poison that his words drew fear out of Angus's and Bruce's faces as they took a step back. His gaze bored into Kenneth, waiting for the old man's challenge.

A slow grin spread across Kenneth's bearded face. "Ain't that telling?"

"What the bloody hell are you talking about?" Caden growled.

Kenneth chuckled. "Meg's not going anywhere," he said. "Sounds like you have a fondness for the Munro lass."

"She's not a Munro," Caden said.

"Oh, then she's what? A Boswell? A *Sasunnach*, an English?"

Fury welled up inside him. He slammed his fist onto the oak table again, making all the tankards and bowls jump and wobble.

"You think Boswell will kill her?" Ewan asked. "His own daughter?"

Caden concentrated on breathing and not grabbing his sword. His gaze followed a knot in the oak table. "Aye. The man killed his wife. Meg thinks it was because her mother found some damning evidence against him, something that showed him to be a traitor. I think the man is desperate to kill off anyone who could possibly bring out the truth."

"How can we keep her?" Ewan asked. "What she needs to be is a Macbain, legally, that is."

A Macbain? Of course, a Macbain! Caden's head snapped up, his gaze connecting with Kenneth's. The old man raised his eyebrows, waiting, as if he'd come to the same conclusion but needed his young laird to reach it on his own.

"Angus, where was Father Daughtry headed after us?" Kenneth asked.

"The Macleods' holding."

Caden nodded and Kenneth did, too. Aye, it was the best thing to do. Meg would officially be under his protection. A blood bond with the Munros would force a peace. And most important, a marriage union would keep Meg at Druim, with him…forever.

"Ewan, take a small group of men to Colin Macleod's to

fetch the good father. Leave before first light."

"Will he be giving the Englishmen last rites?" Bruce asked, and chuckled.

"Nay," Caden said. "He'll be performing a wedding."

...

Meg stared at the bright spot of sun trying to break through the gray clouds. The snow had finally ceased. She was so tired of her room that she had climbed the narrow stairs to the catwalk on the roof of the keep. The view allowed one to see the countryside all the way to the forest on every side. She breathed in the fresh, crisp air.

"Be careful," Hamish called as he walked the perimeter of the roof. "'Tis slippery."

She listened to his steps fade as he rounded the corner, watching over the people stirring below. Was Caden down there? Her eyes caught sight of a black beast sitting at the edge of the forest.

"You haven't abandoned me, Nickum." The wolf trotted back into the forest as if something caught his attention. Would he follow her back to England? Her father would probably have him shot.

The thought twisted Meg's stomach. Her nightmare had come to life. Returning with her father meant succumbing to examination, possible torture, and probable painful execution. If she refused or ran again, her aunt and uncle would be in her place and the Macbains could be blamed for an abduction they didn't commit.

"Dear Lord, help me." She trailed her finger in the melting

snow along the wall. *What can I possibly do?*

The door to the stairwell swooshed open and closed. She didn't even look up, didn't want to talk to anyone. She was too miserable to pretend courage right now, which is why she'd avoided the great hall for the last four days.

Warmth slid across her shoulders, a fur. A wooden soup bowl scraped along in front of her on the rock ledge. "Cook says eat. I've checked it already. No mushrooms. I'm checking all yer food."

Caden's voice made her stomach drop even more. Not only was she leaving behind the first taste of freedom she'd ever had. She was leaving behind…him. "Thank you," she said.

He leaned on the wall next to her but didn't touch her. "Eat the soup, Meg. Ye're going to need yer strength," Caden continued.

Tears stung the back of her eyes. Was he so ready to be rid of her?

Caden brushed the snow off the ledge. "We have a good life here in the Highlands," he said. "Raw and rugged. Nature's battle for survival can be ugly and harsh but breathtaking, too. We don't have a lot here, not like the English cities. We live hard, fight hard…love hard."

He leaned his back against the wall, and the warmth of his gaze fell on her. She sipped.

After a long moment her eyes met his. "Thank you for the soup." She rubbed her chin along the fur. Did he want to say something? She waited.

"The council and I have been talking," he said. "I…we don't want ye to leave."

Her breath hitched for a moment. "You don't?"

"Aye. The men and I. Ye will be in danger if ye return with Boswell."

Her heart sunk a little when Caden said it was the council and the men who wanted her to stay, although he had included himself. "If I don't go with him, you all and my aunt and uncle will be in danger."

"He can't make ye leave, Meg. The decision is yers."

She shook her head. "He's my legal guardian."

"What if he wasn't?"

"He is."

Caden paused and then spoke slowly. "Not if ye become a Macbain."

"Become a Macbain? How exactly—"

"Marry me, Meg."

Her inhale stopped inside her chest as it squeezed. Was he teasing?

Caden took her freezing fingers in his warm hands. "Wed with me and ye will be Meg Macbain with a full clan supporting ye."

"Wed…you?"

Caden moved closer. His stomach gurgled, churning. Was he nervous? On the outside it didn't show. She reminded herself to breathe.

He bent his head and brushed the warmest kiss along her cold lips. The simple touch held such promise. His hand moved to cup the side of her head, his fingers combing back her curls. He kissed her again, slowly, as if they had all the time in the world. Perhaps they did. Perhaps she could become a Macbain, protected, maybe even loved, free from worry over using her powers.

"I don't need yer magic, lass, to know that I affect ye, too," he said against her lips. "Marry me and we can explore more than just a kiss."

"It could put the clan in jeopardy," she said.

"The clan is behind me. And," he paused as if weighing his words, "actually our union could end the feud between the Macbains and the Munros. Honor will dictate that yer uncle, Alec Munro, must end it if there is a blood tie between our clans."

"So there is still a feud?" So much was coming at her, it was hard to keep everything straight.

"Aye, but the immediate benefit is that ye will be safe from yer father. Legally, anyway."

She pinched her lips together. "Next time there is a letter that regards me, you must let me read it before it gets destroyed. Understand?"

He seemed to ponder her request. "Marry me, Meg, and ye will read all that I receive."

She sighed. She'd only known him for three weeks. He was the most handsome man she'd ever met. Honorable and strong and his kisses melted her insides. No talk of love, only of safety and alliances. Marriages were started on much less than that. Disappointment was foolish though hard to ignore.

She smiled.

"Yes?" he asked, his own wide grin coming to the surface.

"Yes, Caden Macbain, I will marry you."

• • •

Colin Macleod rode at the front of the long line of his men. He glanced over his shoulder at the heavily draped priest. "You warm enough, Father?"

"Aye, though there's a good amount of nip in the air," the elderly man said, and sank farther into his cape.

Colin breathed in the frosty evening air. The fresh bite filled his lungs, dispelling some of his worry. He hadn't seen Rachel since Isabelle had left that horrible morning, dutifully riding home to marry her father's choice. Colin spit on the ground. Bloody horrid choice, too. Rowland Boswell had turned out to be the devil himself. If Isabelle's father had known the man would dispatch his dutiful daughter to the witch's flames, perhaps he'd have recognized Colin's claim. He rubbed a hand across his full beard. They'd been handfasted together and Colin had loved Isabelle so much that when she begged him to let her go, he did. Bloody foolish!

And now he'd meet her daughter. Would she resemble his bonny Isabelle or the bastard devil that had spawned her?

"Druim," Ewan called out and pointed ahead at the outline of a castle against three mountains.

Colin's eyes rested momentarily on the largest mountain, the farthest to the right. How much time had passed since he'd visited there? *I should have stolen her away. Boswell would never have found her up in our cave.*

The Macbain riders had reached him the evening before, requesting a priest to marry Isabelle's daughter in an attempt to save her from that very devil, Boswell. Colin would have ridden through the night, but the elderly priest would not have weathered the journey. So they'd left at dawn, riding at a comfortably brisk pace.

"Keep watch for English," Colin called, squinting as he scrutinized the hills and forest edge surrounding them. "Never know where the bastards might be hiding." He caressed the hilt of his sword. The thought of running Rowland Boswell through made his palm itch in anticipation.

"Colin Macleod of the Macleods of Lewis brings the priest, Father Daughtry," Colin yelled up to the guard in the watchtower at the open gates of Druim. Ewan and his men rode ahead to the stables. The villagers moved in and out about their daily business with the castle. This would change if the English laid siege to Druim. Or would Isabelle's daughter go willingly, like her mother? *Damn!* He swallowed hard. This time it wouldn't matter. This wasn't his fight.

The guard waved them into the bailey. Colin dismounted and helped the elderly priest down. Several boys ran to walk the horses and Colin tossed them each a silver shilling. "See you walk and water them well, lads," he said and led the way up the stone steps to the great doors.

The guardsman had descended from the wall and opened the doors. "Colin Macleod—"

"Brings his priest, Macbain." Colin spied Caden Macbain standing near a long table with several other men. He recognized the council to the late chief and strode forward, meeting the gazes of the wiry old advisors before grasping Caden's arm in greeting. "You've grown into your name, lad," Colin said to Caden. "Even taller than your father."

"Welcome to Druim," Caden replied and released the hold. "Ale for our guests." Several serving lasses retreated to the kitchens. Caden indicated a backed chair for Father Daughtry. "Thank you for making the journey to Druim. We have an urgent need for a clergyman."

"A wedding?" Father Daughtry laughed. "For the tormented bridegroom it can seem urgent."

Caden raised a brow at Colin.

"I have not gone into the particulars with the good father," Colin supplied. Because Colin didn't tell anyone anything unless absolutely required. And the good father tended to see wickedness behind every change in the regular running of things. The old man voiced his judgments in annoying length and detail, too.

Caden turned back to the priest. "Father, with this union a bloody feud will end. We wish to see it happen before any more lives are lost."

The priest's eyes gathered suspiciously. "Aye, then, it would seem 'tis urgent. Where is the lass?"

"Above." Caden indicated the steps.

"Have the banns been published?" Colin asked.

"I placed them on the door of the small chapel here five days ago," Caden said. His gaze bored into the priest. "I will swear on your bible that neither of us have been married before."

"There will be a fee that will be returned if what you say is true. What can you pay?"

"Several cows are coming behind us," Colin said. "For the celebration after the wedding."

Caden nodded his appreciation.

"I pay two for the short crying of the banns," Colin said. "A gift to then be returned to the couple."

Caden seemed to exhale. Colin's small smirk wouldn't be seen through his thick beard. The big Highland warrior actually looked nervous. And it wouldn't be about the English, but rather one little English lass.

"Has her family consented to her marriage?"

"I do." A woman's voice cut across the room as the front doors banged open. She dusted snow off her furry coat, plucked off her hat, and walked across the room. "I, Rachel Munro, aunt to the bride, give my permission for her to wed Caden Macbain."

Rachel Brindle, now Munro. She had Isabelle's coloring, though gray had crept into her fiery hair. Even though she must be over two score now, her skin still shone with vigor. This Brindle sister had thrived in the Highlands. Isabelle would have also, if she'd only given him a chance.

Rachel bowed her head to the priest in respect. "Father." The priest resided with each clan in the area for several months before moving on. Father Daughtry's frown made Colin wonder what type of confessions the feisty wife of Alec Munro must have voiced. She continued. "I am the bride's aunt by blood. I am all the family that she has here and I gladly give her to Caden Macbain in marriage."

"I suppose you will do." Daughtry retained his frown. "I would wash the dust from my hands and face before we proceed."

Caden gave instructions to several servants to prepare rooms for Colin and Father Daughtry. The wiry council of three headed out, mumbling something about washing up.

Rachel tilted her head at Colin and studied him. Not much passed the notice of that clever woman. "Colin Macleod. Still a hairy mountain of a man."

He scratched at his heavy beard. He'd planned to cut it off, starting with a fresh growth over the winter, but rushed out before the deed was done. The lilt of her voice caught at his chest. She was so much like Isabelle, but with more bite.

"Still bonny even in yer advancing years," Colin said with a grin.

Rachel chuckled but then grew more serious. "I'd heard you became reclusive after Isabelle's death."

"Ye mean Isabelle's murder."

"Agreed."

Colin rubbed his face. "As reclusive as a chief of a huge clan can be."

"Never married?"

Och! The woman liked to pry. "Ye still married to that boar Alec?"

Rachel laughed. "Yes, quite married."

"I'm sorry to hear about yer two boys, Rachel."

Her happiness faded and he regretted his words. "Thank you, Colin. I still have Searc."

Colin glanced toward the stairs. "Does she look like Isabelle?" He should know before he saw her. Perhaps it would be better not to witness the ceremony.

"No, although she has my sister's eyes. Not the color, though. They're hazel like yours."

"Then she takes after Boswell," he grumbled.

Rachel's face pinched. "No, not at all." She tilted her head at him like a hawk centering on a mouse.

"God help him!" a woman screeched from above.

"Make way!" Bruce yelled and hefted a body through the doors.

...

Good Lord! I've killed him!

"Angus! Oh what have I done?" Meg yelled as she flew down the stairs behind Evelyn.

"Oh my Angus!" Evelyn crooned.

Kenneth ran inside, swearing.

Caden left a large man covered with a beard and took Angus from Bruce's unsteady hands. He laid him carefully on the rushes.

"What's happened, Hugh?" Caden followed Meg to kneel beside the fallen man.

"I shot and…it's all my fault," Meg said. *What have I done? The wind, it came from nowhere! Oh God, I'm so foolish! How can I help him?* "Aunt Rachel! You're here."

"Ye shot Angus?" Caden asked, motioning to the bow she'd flung on the floor.

"I shot a goose, for the feast," she said. "Aunt Rachel, you must pray over Angus."

"Ye shot a goose?" Caden asked as two other guards walked into the keep carrying a huge dead goose, an arrow protruding from the bird's neck. The animal hadn't suffered after the hit.

"Nice shot," the bearded man said.

Rachel shook her head. "Angus Riley made me swear never

to touch him again. I can't help, Meg. I swore."

"That was years ago, decades!" Meg yelled. She placed her hands on Angus's chest, which rose with shallow breaths, and her other hand under Angus's balding head. When she pulled it back it was smeared with bright red blood. "There is bleeding in his brain. He must have fallen back and hit his head. Evelyn," she called. "Find a rag."

Evelyn ran out of the hall, tears flooding her eyes.

"What hit Angus?" Caden asked.

"The goose," Meg and Hugh said at the same time.

"Ye shot from the walkway above?"

"I always hit my mark," Meg said. She sucked in a slow, bitter breath that tasted of regret. She should have waited until the bird was well past the wall. "I just thought it would be an addition to the feast. I…there was a wind…I didn't…"

"'Twas a strong gust the lass hadn't counted on," Hugh added. "Pushed the shot bird back into the bailey on the way down. Angus was near the wall."

"Meg," Caden said. "We only shoot from the walkway when the enemy is attempting to scale the walls."

She breathed deeply, her eyes glistening as they pleaded with Rachel. "He'll die."

The whole room watched Rachel expectantly. "You harmed him. You heal him."

"I…I'm not sure," Meg whispered.

Evelyn ran back in, her face and eyes red. A priest followed, a piece of cold chicken in his hand.

"What's happened?" the priest asked, shoved the meat in his mouth and grabbed his cross. "Are ye in need of last rites?"

"Nay!" Evelyn yelled and lowered haltingly to her knees.

Meg pushed the rags under Angus's head.

Evelyn crumpled over the fallen elder and brushed the hair from his face. "Oh Gus, you have to wake up," she crooned. She turned to Meg and switched to English. "I've heard what ye did for Elizabeth Loman." The old woman touched Meg's hand on top of Angus's chest. "Please try."

Meg exhaled long and glanced at Rachel. "I will…try."

"Try what?" the priest asked.

No one answered. Meg glanced around the room. "Caden?" she asked, her eyes resting on the bearded stranger.

"Colin Macleod," Caden answered. "He brought Father Daughtry for the wedding."

Caden gave a slight glance toward Ewan.

"Come, Father." Ewan took the man's arm and tugged him away from the scene. "I will show you where you can unpack your robes in case Angus needs those last rites."

Meg studied the stranger. Something was familiar about him but it was hard to tell with so much facial hair. Would he run screaming if he saw her heal Angus?

"I was…a friend of yer mama's," he said in English, his voice gruff.

Caden's hand squeezed her shoulder. Was he waiting for her to throw the man out?

"Isabelle was quite a good shot, too," the man said.

So Colin knew her mother well enough to know she could shoot, something Meg didn't even know. She'd question him later. Right now she had to use all her concentration on fixing this terrible wrong that was all her fault.

Meg turned back to Angus. She had to do this, must do it, and with a blasted audience. *Good God, help me help him... please!*

Meg shifted and Caden moved with her, never colliding but working in concert as they arranged Angus out flat and cradled his head on a pillow of rags. He never said anything but his presence calmed her, strengthened her.

"Evelyn, keep his head steady," Meg instructed, her voice stronger. She laid her palms back on Angus's chest. "Some of the bleeding has stopped," she said to Rachel, who had moved closer.

"Stop the rest, imagine it as normal tissue," Rachel instructed.

Meg closed her eyes and explored the tissue in the brain with her powers.

Evelyn began to pray out loud as if what she saw terrified her, but she didn't move away.

"That's good to pray, Evelyn. God's work here needs everyone's prayers," Rachel offered.

Meg kept her eyes closed and imagined her magic warming through to her hurt friend. The convoluted folds of white tissue stitched together, the bleeding absorbing into the surrounding tissue. "The bleeding is stopped." She sighed, relief evident along her tight mouth.

She laid her hands back on the old man's chest as he stirred.

Evelyn gasped and leaned down to kiss Angus's forehead.

"What hit me?" Angus asked. "A damn English boulder?"

"A goose," Bruce said, leaning over his friend.

"A bloody what?" Angus tried to sit up and grabbed his chest, groaning.

"What is it, Gus?" Evelyn asked.

The pain-filled groan cut through Meg. Now what? She placed her hands on Angus's shoulder. *Good God!* "Bits of the clot that began to form are broken loose. They're sliding through his veins."

"Dissolve them," Rachel said, so close she nearly fell on top of the man. "Imagine them gone, faded into normal blood. Quickly."

The blue light leapt out of Meg's hands before she could even drop them back on Angus's chest.

Caden was at her side, lowering the groaning man to the floor. He slid his hand down her back. Now he would know just how unnatural she was. "Ye can do it, Meg."

This amazing man had a power all his own, the power to calm her.

Meg closed her eyes and followed the rushing clots as they tipped and turned through the tiny vessels trying to find purchase. Just like chasing a dodging hare with her bow, Meg sought out and dissolved the dark chunks of clotted blood throughout Angus's body. After long moments, Meg leaned back onto her heels, exhaustion dulling her. Caden pulled her into his chest to hold her up.

"What happened?" Angus blinked as Evelyn hugged him. "Woman, you're weeping all over me," he chided, but he squeezed her back.

"A goose hit ye," Bruce said.

"I heard that, ye twit." Angus murmured comforting words to the housekeeper. Meg had no idea that Angus and Evelyn were a couple.

"What was that pain in me, after ye healed me?" he asked, his eyes on Meg.

"Clots going through your body." Her eyes began to close. "I'm so tired."

Caden scooped Meg up in his arms. "The wedding will have to wait until later. Meg needs to rest."

"I am so sorry, Angus," Meg said as her head lulled onto Caden's shoulder like it belonged there, nestled into his neck.

"All is right." Angus fussed while his two old friends pulled him up by the arms. "Bloody hell, I'm covered in goose blood."

"'Tis your blood," Kenneth said.

Meg breathed in the warmth radiating off Caden's neck. She barely heard Rachel behind her. "I think she did quite well. Seems you will be blessed with a powerful healer right here at Druim. Make certain you thank God for her."

"I think we all better wash before the wedding," Angus called out.

Caden carried Meg into the darkness of the hall.

"Heavens, what have I missed? Has someone else been injured?"

"No, Father. My bride is tired, though, with the shock of Angus's injury."

"Oh, shall we delay the ceremony?"

"Not for long," Caden answered and moved on. His lips moved closer to her ear. "I would have ye safely as my wife as soon as ye can stand, lass."

Meg shivered, but not from cold. The intensity in Caden's voice caught her off guard. The blatant show of her bizarre abilities didn't seem to faze him. Amazing. He carried her up against his solid chest. What would it be like for that strong body to move against her own? Even exhausted, Meg's pulse flew. She surely wouldn't need to rest for long.

・・・

Meg stood before the polished glass, her reflection clear and elegant in the blue brocade gown. Stitches of gold thread wove subtle swirls throughout the skirt. The bell-shaped sleeves were shot through with a lighter-colored blue silk. Against her waist, Meg wore her mother's dragonfly sash that accentuated her curves. Fiona brushed Meg's long curls until they fell in a soft cascade down to the middle of her back.

Aunt Rachel placed a dainty wreath of dried summer flowers and small shoots of wheat on her head. "Lovely," Rachel said. "A perfect autumn bride."

"Is that why you came?" Meg asked. "Did Caden send for you?"

Rachel continued to arrange the wreath just so. "I received word that you two were being wed and I came right away."

"Uncle Alec couldn't come?"

"Oh…he will be along soon, I'm sure."

Meg watched her own reflection in the polished glass. She seemed the perfect bride, but inside her stomach twisted with questions and worries. Did Caden really want to marry her or was he only doing it to save her and to end the feud? Many couples married without love. Without love, would they be happy? There certainly was a spark between them. She was a virgin, but she knew enough about anatomy and birthing to know what happened in the marriage bed. Meg blushed as she recalled Caden's kiss as he left her exhausted on her bed that morning.

"Lovely," Fiona said, "a blushing bride."

Rachel took a sip from a goblet of wine, waited, and handed it to Meg. Apparently, everyone was still on alert after the mushroom incident. "Drink. It will relax you."

Meg sipped at the chilled drink, letting its languor spread down into her knotted stomach. Evelyn poked her head around the door. "They're ready below."

"Thank you, Evelyn. Is Angus fit?"

The woman actually blushed. "Thank ye, milady, for helping him." Meg waited for the habitual sign of the cross, but Evelyn's eyes were sincere and lacked fear. Could people here actually accept what she could do, when even Meg herself barely did?

"Time to wed," Rachel said.

Meg's stomach flipped. With one last glance at the regal woman in the polished glass, she turned toward a new life waiting for her below.

She rounded the corner to a hall full of people, Macbain people with others standing near the very tall Colin Macleod. She almost didn't recognize him without his bushy beard. Something about the man made her eyes linger. He was handsome and she could understand why her mother would want to be friends with him.

Meg caught sight of Caden near the hearth. He was tallest of them all and easy to pick out. The man stood out among his peers, obviously a leader, strong and ruggedly handsome. He'd shaved his short beard, revealing his strong chin and jaw. Slightly damp waves of brown hair hung to his broad shoulders.

He wore a fresh kilt, perhaps new.

Her heart leapt as she remembered the kiss that had consumed them in that very spot before the fire. And now she would pledge to honor and obey him forever. Meg took in a long breath to slow her wild heart.

"Ann and Jonet spruced up the hall after the festival for the ceremony," Fiona whispered.

Meg pulled her gaze from Caden and spotted the dried flower garland from the harvest festival with a few additions of heather for good luck. The effect decorated the hall like another festival. Beautiful.

"They are quite fond of ye," Fiona said.

The two ladies stood in the crowd with Ewan and waved. Meg mouthed the words "thank you" to them and indicated the swags. Her two friends beamed.

She walked behind Rachel and almost ran into her aunt when she stopped suddenly before Colin Macleod. Her aunt swiveled, staring between her and Colin.

"Oh my, Isabelle," Rachel said, and then the shock on her face melted into a grin.

"What is it?" Meg asked, but her eyes strayed again to Caden, who stood beside the priest. She straightened up to best show off the beautiful gown, forced what she hoped was a casual expression on her lips, and breathed slowly.

"Don't you think Meg is beautiful, Colin?" Rachel asked.

"Aye."

Meg glanced at him and bowed her head at the compliment.

The priest gestured for her to keep moving toward them at the front of the hall.

"I would be most happy to speak with you later, sir, about my mother." Meg gave a brief bow and continued on toward Caden and her future. One foot before the other, she almost floated as she focused on the man before her. Capable, full of authority and honor, Caden Macbain encompassed the strength of the mountains that rose behind his ancestral home. Serious eyes locked with hers, softened by his grin.

That's it, one foot in front of the other. The feeling in Meg's fingers tingled away. *Breathe in, breathe out. Forward.* She held onto his gaze, using it like a rope to reel her in.

The room hushed as she stopped next to him before the priest.

"Lass…" Caden leaned down to whisper near her ear. "Ye are the bonniest I've ever seen."

Meg forgot to breathe and the numbness moved up her fingers into her hands. Jonet ran forward and pressed a bouquet of dried heather and wheat wrapped with ribbon into her stiff fingers. Meg nearly dropped them.

"And who gives this woman to this man?" the priest asked and frowned at Rachel.

Rachel stood tall next to Meg. "As a blood relation, I do."

"Very well." The priest read through the promises, asking Meg and Caden in turn for their vows.

Meg's included obedience. Nothing was mentioned of love.

She moved through the words, the entire ceremony, on Caden's arm. If he'd removed it she would have fallen over. She concentrated on breathing and forcing her legs to hold her weight.

Caden's voice echoed with strength. "I vow to protect and

keep Meg until death."

He said the words as if he truly believed every syllable, every letter of every word. *Keep until death*. With each word, some of Caden's might trickled into Meg, filling her with vigor until she stood erect next to him, linked but no longer leaning. His calm and powerful presence built her up rather than make her seem small. He did not tower over but stood tall beside her.

"By the powers given to me by the Holy Roman Catholic Church, I pronounce ye man and wife," the priest intoned. He repeated the proclamation also in English. "Ye may kiss her," he said to Caden.

The remaining moisture in Meg's mouth dried like the heather in her bouquet. She swallowed hard and pulled in her bottom lip to wet it.

The door swung open and Ewan's head popped in. "Caden?"

Meg hadn't even noticed that Ewan had disappeared.

As Caden pulled Meg around to face him, he said over his shoulder to Hamish, "Find Father Daughtry a drink or two of ale in the back." Hamish nearly carried the flustered priest away as the warrior chatted about the early snow.

Aunt Rachel moved then, quickly toward the door. Meg tried to turn to where an unfamiliar young man brushed snow off his furs near the door, but Caden gently tugged her chin so that their eyes met.

"This is more important." His lips descended on her own, stealing her breath and her whirling mind. His large hand cradled the back of her head as he slanted across her mouth with all the promise and heat of a lusty man at leisure. When he pulled back passion sparked his eyes.

A dizzy whirl descended on Meg as he turned to stand beside her, gazing out at the applauding crowd. Rachel, Ewan, and the stranger were gone. Caden raised his hand to the happy Macbains.

"This marks a new era!" Caden's voice rose about the shouts of celebration. "An era of peace!"

More cheers. A smile grew on her face. Marriages had been sealed based on much less. Peace for these people she'd grown to care about, protection for her against her father. Yes, this was good.

Caden squeezed her hand as Fiona, Jonet, and Ann hustled forward. Was she going somewhere? As if he sensed her confusion, Caden ran his hand along her cheek. "'Tis late. We will start the celebration tomorrow…after."

"After what?" she whispered, but from Caden's intense gray eyes she was pretty sure she knew.

"We will finish what we began before this fire the other night, *bride*."

...

"What is Rachel's lad doing here?" Kenneth asked as he followed Caden out of the hall. Evelyn had quickly spread the word that the celebration would start after the noon meal the next day, and people had vacated amid raucous good wishes.

"I didn't invite him," Caden answered. He shifted at once into a familiar battle stance and looked to Hugh. "Double the watch tonight. More Munros may follow."

He definitely didn't need a horde of furious Munros scaling

his walls on his wedding night. He glanced over his shoulder at the three council members, who practically ran to keep up with him. "For that matter, I didn't invite Rachel, either."

No, he hadn't invited anyone but the priest. And he only did that because he had to make this official. An official, legal marriage to make Meg a true Macbain. And the wedding night would completely bind them as husband and wife.

Caden exhaled long and stomped down the guilt that kept fighting its way up his gullet. Meg knew that their marriage would end the feud. She had wed to save herself, also her relatives, and his clan. The only thing she didn't know was that for a short while, she'd been a captive. *A very well-treated captive.*

There was also the fact that from the first kiss, Caden's mind had worked across many scenarios on ways to keep Meg at Druim. Her reactions indicated that she didn't mind his touch; in fact, she melted into him. Would she still respond the same way if she found out that his mission to England had been all about kidnapping her? His words to Ewan the last time he'd laid next to her warm body in the tent haunted him.

"She's simply a pawn to force the peace. Don't get attached. She *will* hate us."

Bloody hell!

Caden walked through the archway into the kitchen. Rachel stood with Colin in front of her one remaining offspring, Searc, while he drank from a mug.

"Did you come alone?" Caden asked the lad. Rachel frowned and opened her mouth but Caden held up a hand. Amazingly, the woman complied. The youth seemed to be about fifteen, high time to be training with the young Munro warriors.

Already a head above his mother, he stood straighter. "Aye, my father doesn't know where we are."

"I'm sure he is starting to suspect," Angus said from behind. "Especially if any of his loyal Munro spies have told him of the wedding."

"I intercepted the latest information," Searc said.

"Why?" Caden asked.

"Because my mother intercepted the first."

Silence stuffed the tight room. Rachel's eyes were wide, disbelieving. Was the youth picking his mother over his father?

"A united Scotland is a strong Scotland," Searc said, his lips tight. "My mother has a plan."

"Searc," Rachel warned.

"I don't know all of it, but she's clever," he added.

Angus sneered. "More clever than that bull of a husband."

"Shut your mouth, Angus," Rachel said softly.

"And," Searc continued, "I know she wants peace." His gaze connected with Caden's. "I would give it to her."

An understanding seemed to radiate across the room. This youth, though already physically warrior-like, had an intelligence that let him see past the blood lust that had grown between their clans. Perhaps there was hope for the next generation of Scotland.

Caden nodded to the future Munro leader. Then he turned to Rachel. "You have a plan. I would hear it."

From her stance he already knew she wasn't going to tell him. Rachel crossed her arms over her chest and leveled a hard stare. "The best part of it is waiting upstairs for her husband," she said, though the jest did not reach her eyes.

Ewan cleared his throat on a chuckle.

She turned to Colin Macleod. "We need to talk."

And with that, Rachel Munro, steely grand queen with a secret plan for peace, dismissed him. Perhaps he shouldn't give her a bed tonight. Although…if Meg was part of her plan, Caden should thank her for giving him the warmest bed in Scotland.

...

Caden lifted the latch to his room and allowed the door to slide inward. The glow from the fire filled the room with a comfortable wafting of warm air. His breath caught.

Meg sat in the middle of the soft furs. She'd pulled the crown from her hair so that the waves of auburn cascaded down like a waterfall of silk. Her sleeves were draped over the edge of the bed, leaving her slender limbs bare. She only wore her white shift with her stiff bodice still tied about her. The tight cinching lifted the swell of her breasts so high that a little nudge would spill her soft flesh over the thin satin edge. She was a goddess, a temptress with innocent wide eyes. If the lass could see beneath his kilt, she'd be running for the roof.

He rubbed the back of his head.

"I couldn't untie the lacings," Meg said and pointed over one shoulder to her back.

He let out a ragged breath. "Aye, lass." He twirled a finger in a circle.

She came up on her knees. Caden brushed the fragrant

hair over one bare shoulder. He tried not to touch her skin—if it were as soft as he imagined, his fingers would never stop. He dove deftly into the hiding places between the ties, tugging at the knots until the bodice opened down her back. Meg sighed in relief.

"Tight," he said, his eyes lingering on the exposed nape of her neck and upper back where the shift dipped.

She turned on her knees so that she knelt before him. Her breasts no longer swelled up high, yet their heaviness was evident behind the thin material. Her nipples stood out among the folds.

"So…" she began and tilted her head to the side. "What do we do now?"

"Do?"

"To consummate the marriage." Even in the glow of firelight, Caden could tell that her blush was intensifying. "I know you…know," she indicated the bed, "what to do."

Bloody hell, yes! In the few seconds that she'd started talking, he'd imagined all sorts of things they could do…that they would be doing.

He smiled then, and tried to keep the devil out of it. "Aye, lass, I know what to do."

"Perhaps you should explain everything first."

Caden continued the kiss he'd begun downstairs earlier. He unbuttoned his shirt and pursued Meg's lips in a gentle kiss full of promise. He pulled back just enough to see Meg's flushed face. Her lips parted, wet and gorgeous.

"Should I…?" she started.

"I'll show ye, lass. Showing's more fun than explaining." He leaned on his hands over her as she bent backward until her legs straightened out in the furs.

"Soft," she whispered and leaned back flat on the bed.

"Aye, ye are soft, everywhere," he added as he combed his fingers through her hair, fanning it out around her face.

"No. The furs. They tickle."

Caden glanced behind him at her shapely legs and petite toes as she rubbed them in the pelts. The tension in his chest moved down into his groin. His jaw ached. He had to go slow. *Och!* He wanted to taste every inch of those lovely long legs.

Meg laid a hand on his chest and frowned. "Your heart races, your muscles are tense—"

"Ye're going to have to turn off those senses of yers to enjoy this. I'm not yer injured." He braced himself up on his arms and leaned forward, careful to give her room to breathe. "I'm yer husband," he said, exploring the depths of her glorious hazel eyes. Little golden sparks radiated out like rays of sun from her pupils.

"Beautiful," he murmured. Caden caressed up Meg's arms until he reached her shoulders and began to rub. After a long moment her eyelids closed like the sun setting until her dark lashes lay against her soft, pale skin.

"Mmmm," she breathed, as he worked down one limb again and into her palm, massaging each finger. When he was done with her digits, he laid his hands flat against her collarbone. Slowly he washed them down over her ample breasts, his thumbs teasing her erect nipples. Meg sucked in her breath and her lashes fluttered open. She watched. Downward, his hands traveled to her belly.

He kissed the softly rounded abdomen through her shift. "Lovely."

Meg's lips relaxed open as she inhaled. His hands continued their explorations lower, down to her hipbones and the crux of her legs. The bones were delicate handholds, firm yet fragile. "Mine," he whispered as he gripped them.

She shivered as passion played within her eyes. Caden brought his hands together over her mound, the tight curls beneath the fabric. Her breath hitched on a gasp, and she moaned and shifted on the furs.

Caden slid his hands down and up her long legs, marveling at the softness of her skin. He inched the thin shift higher until she was exposed to the tops of her thighs. Firelight flickered across her face and he leaned in for another kiss. His lips angled across her delicious mouth, not too hard. Cool fingers clasped over his shoulders. He touched his tongue to her lip and then slid inside for a taste. She didn't retreat. When she imitated him, he groaned.

He left her mouth and kissed the crook of her neck. She tasted clean, womanly, and sweet. His hand gathered the shift up and, in one swoop, pulled it entirely over her head, letting it pool into a mound of white cotton. Her two perfect breasts sat perched on her chest and he lowered his mouth to one, his hand to the other. Caden suckled at the peak and Meg pressed restlessly into the layers of furs, her breath coming out in little rasps of pleasure.

"Caden," she said on an exhale as he switched his mouth to the other nipple while his hands massaged them. Her legs rubbed along his, and he reached down to yank his kilt from his hips.

Slow. He had to go slow.

He pulled back to give her time, to give him time to regain his control. She was flushed, her lips parted, her eyes dark with passion. The sight of her raged through his blood like wild energy.

Meg's gaze dipped. He managed to remain still, expecting fear or worry. Instead, her bright eyes warmed, melted into deep pools. She caught her lower lip between her teeth a scant second before her tongue darted out to wet that same lip.

Raw desire filled his chest, knocking his breath out in a groan. "Och, lass, I'm trying to give ye time."

"Don't," she whispered.

One little word and Caden's years of self-control nearly shattered. In that single moment he knew he could devour his wee bride and yet lose himself in the heat of her embrace. She completely enthralled him.

He lowered his mouth to her stomach and inhaled the warm fragrance of her skin. Bloody hell, she smelled of heaven! He rained hot kisses along her skin to her navel, where he found the mark of a small dragonfly.

Meg leaned back on her elbows, frozen, not even breathing. The passion that had been growing in her body seemed to drain away.

What would the witch hunters have thought of the odd mark? The thought raced fury through his already taut body. He pushed the thought aside. His anxious bride didn't need his anger right now.

Caden lowered his mouth to the birthmark and kissed it.

She didn't move. He kissed it again. "Every part of ye is beautiful, lass."

She inhaled, her chest rising with a full, slow cadence.

He trailed nibbles over her stomach until Meg moaned softly and flattened onto the bed. He tasted her skin in leisurely kisses all the way up to her face, where he could stare once again into her passion-glazed eyes. He'd never tire of searching those hazel orbs.

Caden's hand moved from her hip to the vee between her legs. His knee parted her easily and his fingers found heat.

"Och lass, ye are so wet," he rasped out. Sweat beaded on his forehead as he fought to control the lust and passion roiling through him. He needed to be inside her.

"Caden," she murmured.

"Let loose," he coaxed and sunk his fingers into her. Tight and wet, her body gripped his fingers, making his length twitch in anticipation. She panted, her fingers digging into the furs.

Her hips began to thrust upward against his hand. Caden licked a hot trail of kisses up her stomach back to her full breasts, his fingers working below.

"Caden, please, I want you!" She bucked into his palm and her hand moved downward, along his overheated body to grasp him. Light fingers wrapped around him and he groaned against her skin.

He growled and withdrew his fingers.

"No," Meg said, her legs opening wider, an invitation that he would never ignore.

"That's it, open for me, wife." He leaned over so that his breath rested against her ear. "Open yer sweet lips for me," he rasped as he nudged his tip into her open cleft. He reached under her full, rounded cheeks, lifting. "Let me fill ye," he groaned as he surged forward, sliding through the barrier and completely embedding himself within her.

Meg gasped and Caden stilled, heart hammering, muscles rigid, holding, waiting. "There is only pain the first time," he promised, watching her squeezed-shut eyes. She gave a little nod, but otherwise didn't move. He held himself on his forearms that completely encased her head, careful not to rock within her tightness.

"I won't move until 'tis better." *Lord, it be better soon!*

Caden brushed her lips tenderly, then kissed her neck, breathing and touching the responsive skin. His hand cupped one moon-pale breast, palming it and brushing the taut nipple. His mouth replaced his hand as he licked and teased the sensitive flesh. Meg moaned and her hips moved upward, sliding along him.

The friction almost made him surge forward, but he held still. "Better?" he gritted out.

"Better," she panted.

Caden needed no other encouragement. "Open yer eyes, Meg," he said as he leaned over her face. His body coiled below as he moved his hand down between her legs. He rubbed and she moaned, moving against him. Her eyes flicked shut.

"Look at me, lass," he commanded and she opened her eyes. He wanted her to see his intensity, see the honest fervor in his face, see the one who brought her exquisite pleasure.

Passion and heat floated in those brilliant hazel orbs. Caden groaned and plunged into her. She moaned deeply, staring up into his eyes as they thrust together over and over again, giving to one another, taking from one another, sharing, building, marking each other.

Her fingers curled into the furs. The rhythm took over and her head tipped back as she arched, thrusting her breasts high.

He couldn't resist. His teeth nipped down on a pink nipple moving before his mouth and he swirled his tongue around it, pulling her breast into his mouth.

"Caden!" she cried, grinding into him.

Her plea sparked through him. Blood rushing, heart pounding, deep slamming, shooting him higher and higher. His body coiled. How much longer could he last with her hot channel sucking along his rock-hard length?

He feathered quickly against her sensitive nub. Meg's eyes flew to his, fluttering shut and then open again. He rubbed faster, his body meeting her own until her body tightened around him.

"Caden!" she screamed. With her head thrown back, she arched into the bed.

His forearms closed around either side of her head and he stared into her eyes. "Mine, ye are mine," he roared as he pumped into her body.

She shuddered. He continued in and out until her body stopped convulsing. Caden lowered, careful not to crush her with his full weight. He kissed her, his hand wiping the damp hair from her forehead.

How in bloody hell had he found such a match? Passion and spirit, beauty and courage. She was…everything.

Caden settled them onto their sides. Legs and arms

entwined, he pulled the furs, cocooning them as one.

She nuzzled into his neck below his chin. Her lips tickled against his skin. "Now we are truly wed."

He chucked low. "Perhaps we should go again just to make certain."

After several minutes, when their hearts slowed back to a normal pace, Meg moved against him. Bloody hell, he was hard again already. His breath caught when her wee hand tickled a path down his chest. "Meg, ye are too tender just yet."

A faint blue light illuminated the furs and then blinked out again. "Not so tender anymore," she whispered and slid her lush naked body alongside him.

Caden grinned and groaned at the same time as her fingers found his length. Aye, her gift was indeed a blessing.

...

Meg rolled within the warmth of the blankets and stretched her arms overhead. Oh, what a night! Her body ached in places it never had before. She stifled a giggle and sent a brief healing wave of blue light inside and out. She opened her eyes as she basked in the decadent caress of the fur against her naked skin. The curtains of the bed were pulled back and sunlight streamed through the narrow, glassed-over windows.

"Caden?"

No answer. A late morning sun slanted brightly into the room. Perhaps he had to see to his men. He was The Macbain after all.

She noticed a wooden platter with cheese, ham, and a drink. Meg pinched up the small piece of parchment caught under the mug.

Good morning wife. C.

Meg's brows furrowed slightly. *Thoughtful.* No mention of love, but thoughtful was a good start.

A tapping at the door made Meg yank the furs up to her chin. Fiona peeked in. "I've come to get ye ready."

"Ready?"

Meg dove below the covers when two of Caden's men carried in buckets of water for a bath. Fiona directed the men, who kept their eyes averted before turning back to Meg. "Yer wedding feast."

The men left and Fiona helped Meg to the tub of hot water.

Meg sank into the clean, scented water with a long sigh. "Heaven."

Fiona laughed. Meg was about to sink in deep and close her eyes when the woman pulled a brush through her tangled hair. "Och, but the wee folk were busy tying yer long curls into knots last night."

Hopefully the woman would just think Meg's pink skin was from the hot water and not the thought of exactly what she was doing last night.

Scrubbed clean, brushed, and cinched tightly into her gown, she descended the winding staircase with Rachel.

"You are certainly refreshed," Rachel said and winked at Meg. Meg focused on cooling her blush.

They walked up to the long table in the great hall. The three council members stood when they approached.

Kenneth bowed deeply. "Welcome, Lady Macbain."

Others in the hall did the same.

Kenneth cleared his throat. "And Lady Munro," he added, though quieter.

"Ah, there he is." Rachel walked toward the door where Caden stood with Colin Macleod. Ewan and Donald kicked snow off their boots.

Caden. Meg couldn't help but stare for a moment at her husband. Tall and straight and covered with a dusting of fresh snow. Flakes melted in his thick, dark hair. He turned, his gaze capturing hers, warming her from the inside out.

"Colin Macleod." Rachel again waved for them to move closer to the hearth, where they now stood apart from the bustle of preparation. Meg watched her husband stride casually toward her.

Caden's hand went straight to her hair, brushing it from her face. "Ah, I thought I spied a leaf," he said, blue-gray eyes reflecting the snowy sky outside. "They seem to have a fondness for yer curls."

"I've been inside. No leaves," she answered, her breath a bit shallow because he stood so close and smelled so good.

Caden combed his fingers down and leaned close to her ear. "Perhaps it was a downy feather from our nest above."

There was no controlling the blush now. "Thank you for the food, though I would have come down with you if you hadn't left so quietly."

He grinned. "Ye sleep like the departed, lass. At least when ye are worn out."

"Enough," Rachel scolded. "You'll make the girl ignite with her blushes."

"They are newlyweds, Rachel," Colin said. "We should

leave them be."

"Oh no, Colin Macleod." She frowned. "A truth needs to be told."

"A truth?" Meg turned to the clean-shaven man. Without his beard he came across as much more civilized. His brown hair was shot with red and his eyes seemed familiar somehow.

Rachel nudged him with her elbow. "Go on."

"I…" He rubbed a hand down the back of his neck as if it pained him. "I knew yer mother, lass."

"Yes. Were you close?"

Rachel seemed almost giddy. "Meg, you aren't blood related to a monster after all."

What were they talking about?

"Isabelle," Colin said, "and I were handfasted in the Highland way."

"Married," Rachel translated.

Meg's breath held in her lungs as her mind whirled around what they were getting at. "You mean…"

Rachel clasped both their hands. "Meg, meet your real father. 'Twould seem you are a Macleod."

Chapter Nine

1 January 1518 — Heather: green, wiry shrub, small leaves with white or purple/pink flowers in mid to late summer. Find in rocky soil on northern moors and mountains in the Highlands. A brew from the plant will break stones in the urine. The decoction calms nerves that plague the heart and suppresses coughs. Its fragrance sends the mind to the western sea.

"My father?" Meg stared at the man, weighing him, the one who'd let her mother go. He was big, a Highlander for certain. His hand came up to his chin as if to pull at the beard that was no longer there.

"I didn't know," he said low as if he read the hardness of her eyes.

Was she that transparent? Meg concentrated on presenting a blank face.

"If I'd known she was with child, I would never have let her leave despite how she begged me to let her go." Colin's voice had turned rough. "Isabelle was always dutiful, and when her father threatened to bring England down on the Macleods... she just gave in."

"I don't think she knew she was pregnant yet," Rachel said softly. "She would have told me."

"I saw ye once," Colin said. "I came to drag her back to Scotland. I saw ye peek out the window when I found her in the garden." He shook his head. "If I'd known, I wouldn't have left without both of ye."

Rachel clasped Meg's hand. "All these years, I thought you were Boswell's daughter. That was until I saw Colin without all that fur hiding his face." She glanced between them. "Meg, you look exactly like him."

The council of three came closer, having overheard the startling news.

"Bloody lucky for Caden, not too much," Bruce said.

Two men that had ridden with Colin from Macleod territory walked over, their gazes curious. Narrowed eyes studied Colin and then moved to her in unison. A slow grin broke through the beard on the tall Macleod with fuzzy red hair.

"She is your likeness, Colin," the man named Seonaidh said. "Most fervently." He slapped Colin's shoulder. "See, man? You do have a direct heir. Shame she can't grow a beard and throw a sword, but an heir just the same."

"Aye, but she can shoot," Colin boasted.

Meg's own happiness pulled at her lips. Colin Macleod was her father, not Rowland Boswell, traitor to the English crown and murderer of her mother, the monster who wanted to torture her.

"I remember, I think," Meg said, the memories hazy and

mixed with fear. She slid her hand in her pocket where her key sat heavy, and she pulled it out.

"The key," Colin said.

Everyone in the circle moved closer in, heads bowed to see the intricate scrollwork etched into the handle. Jonet, Ann, and Donald had joined the group. Meg could barely see the key in her hand with everyone intent on studying it.

"My mother left it for me," she said.

"Aye," Colin said. "I gave it to her when I came to England." His large finger touched the odd lines carved into the iron.

"What does it unlock?" Meg asked.

"Nothing," he said, still staring at the piece.

"Then what is its purpose?" Caden asked from his place behind Meg.

Colin raised his eyes above her to Caden. "Isabelle made a map." He moved along one line up to the right until the end. "This is the way to the cave where we handfasted, our place in the mountains."

"Which mountains?" Caden asked.

"The large ones behind Druim."

No one said anything. Meg swallowed hard. "'*Lorg an lus seo ann an uamh, an fuar uamh le moran na frith-rathaidean agus an blath cridhe anns am meadhon*'," she recited.

"Find this plant in a cave, a cold cave with many paths and a warm heart in the middle," Rachel translated.

"Plant?" Colin asked.

Meg shook her head, excitement sparking through her. "The description comes from her medicine journal." Her gaze moved to Caden. "We are so close."

"The papers?" Colin asked, and everyone turned to him.

"If ye mean the letters Meg's been trying to find that prove Boswell planned to assassinate his king," Caden said, "then yes."

Colin's mouth opened as he stared between them. "Is that what they were? Are?"

"You didn't read them?" Meg asked with disbelief. First he let her mother go because she asked him to, and then he didn't read the letters that would have shown how much danger she was in.

"She made me swear not to."

"Why would ye do a thing like that, man?" Angus blustered.

"They were in English anyway," Colin said and reddened. "I only read Gaelic."

"Well bloody good ye didn't just do what she asked," Bruce said. "A man should know all to see what is best to be done."

Angus agreed and Rachel snorted. Meg ignored them both.

"Can we get to the cave?" she asked Caden. "Now."

"Right now there's a blizzard blowing," Ewan said.

"And a wedding to celebrate," Jonet said, indicating the filling room.

"Climbing a mountain is no activity for a wee lass," Angus added to the jumble of comments.

Meg kept her gaze locked with her husband's. "The letters would be a wedding gift," she breathed. "And it would ensure Rowland Boswell would leave us alone."

"Rowland Boswell *will* leave ye alone," Caden vowed. "Ye are under protection of the Macbains."

"And the Macleods," Colin added.

"And the Munros," Rachel said.

Tears stung behind Meg's eyes. She was not alone in the world. Regardless of her talents, she had support and family.

"Thank you," she managed to say, her happiness broadening as Caden let his own fill his face. There was pride there. For her? For the peace he was restoring to this part of Scotland? No matter. He was truly happy. Caden's joy filled her with joy.

Was that love?

"We will still journey to the letters," Caden added. "Just not in a snowstorm, wife."

She laughed. Yes, it was love…or at least the beginning of it.

"To the celebration, then," Ann said, and several "ayes" followed.

Meg rose on tiptoe, her hands on Caden's shoulders. He took the hint and lowered his face to hers for a soft, slow kiss.

They pulled back from one another. "I did try to wake ye, lass, but alas ye would not stir. I think ye were up too late last eve." Caden's eyes sparked with mischievous intent, warming Meg with a blush that heated all parts of her body.

"Aye, husband, I was."

He kissed the tip of her nose and took up her hand. "I will let ye rest tonight."

"Don't you dare," she whispered and ignored the flush that infused her face.

Caden raised his eyebrows at her wanton comment and laughed.

"Here, here!" Ewan yelled. He came forth with a tankard of bridal ale for Meg as they walked to the table. He nodded at Caden, an indication the drink was safe, and grabbed one for himself and Caden. "To the happy couple!"

"*Sláinte mhor!*"

"*Sláinte mhath!*" the people cheered to their health.

Meg let the honey ale slide down her throat. Nothing more had come from the mushroom incident, but Caden wasn't taking any chances.

"Today we celebrate before God and his witnesses, my union to Meg." He hesitated for a heartbeat. "To Meg Macleod."

A cheer rose up from a corner of the room.

"That would be part of yer clan, lass," Colin said.

Meg waved in their direction.

"And we celebrate peace. May God bless us with strong children and a united Scotland!" Caden roared and the room answered.

Caden scooped Meg up in his arms and she laughed. He wobbled, pretending to stumble. She gasped and clasped her arms around his neck while he chuckled and smacked his shoulder. The simple act grew into joy as they laughed together. Instead of putting her in her own seat, Caden sat down in his own with Meg on his lap.

"I cannot properly meet people perched on your knees," Meg said.

"Perhaps I want to keep ye safely tucked against me," he said, his face dimming a bit.

"Surely we're safe." Meg's gaze skating across the happy faces, many of whom had formed lines for the first dance.

Caden's gaze watched the throng. "An enemy could always

slip within."

Meg rubbed Caden's rock-hard arm. "Relax and enjoy, husband," she said, though she was glad that he took possible threats seriously.

"I never relax," he murmured.

Meg drew close to Caden's ear and shivered. "I won't stray from those I know well tonight."

"Ye are cold," he said.

"Just when the doors swing open."

"Which is about every minute," he grumbled at the mass of merrymakers.

"I'll just fetch my cloak upstairs," Meg said, and Ann stood with her.

"I'll go, too." Her easy jump up stopped Caden from standing. "If the two of ye end up in yer room together, we won't see ye the rest of the night."

Everyone within earshot laughed. Meg linked with Ann's arm and they strode through the throng, greeting and smiling until they were in the dimly lit stairwell. They climbed quickly.

"Thank you, Ann. The celebration is very merry."

Ann leapt up onto the next flat stair. "God's teeth!" she cursed and grabbed hold of Meg. Meg grabbed onto a chiseled hand hold in the wall next to her to stop them both from tumbling down the long flight of stone.

"What is it?" Meg asked.

"I don't know, pebbles or something on the step."

The last thing Meg wanted to do was answer questions about her magic light, so she slid her hand carefully over the step that had thrown Ann. "Dangerous. Pebbles rolled all along the step. They weren't there when we descended. And the wall torch is extinguished here."

Meg sensed Ann's heart rate rise again as she, too, realized that this was not an accident. Who were the stones meant for? What if she'd been alone and hadn't been able to catch herself?

"Let's find a broom. There's one by my hearth," Meg said. "We'll sweep them to the side on the way back down."

Ann took a deep breath and held tight while they gingerly walked up the remaining steps. They lit a torch from the fire in Meg's room to light the steps better and walked back down together. Meg relit the extinguished wall torch while Ann swept the pebbles to the side.

"We'll clean them up later," Ann said. "We should tell Caden."

Meg sighed. "He's liable to question everyone in the hall."

"He should," Ann said. "We could have been killed, ye could have. And after that mushroom mistake, I'm looking over my shoulder, too."

"I'm just glad you came with me." Meg squeezed Ann's arm. They left the broom on the stair.

Cape and torch in hand, Meg and Ann made their way down, carefully watching the dim steps.

As they rounded the corner under the darkened archway, a hand shot out and grabbed Meg's wrist.

She dropped Ann's hand to take back her confined wrist and her cloak dropped to the floor. With one jerk and twist of her wrist downward, just like Uncle Harold had taught her, Meg was free. She brandished the torch before her. Fire would surely keep the ogre away.

Gilbert Davidson's face froze for a moment in surprise. "I would like to pay my congratulations to the bride," he said and bowed. He tried to grab her hand again but she moved the torch in a quick jab. Quickly, Ann hurried down the steps, glancing back.

"You weren't invited." Meg wasn't sure if he had been, but after their last encounter, she doubted that Caden would invite the man.

"I brought more grain and noticed the gaiety. When I realized ye had married The Macbain, and so quickly, well, I wanted to wish ye many blessings." His insinuation that there was a carnal reason they had to marry quickly beat at Meg's composure, but she wouldn't let down her torch or her guard.

"Your well wishes and grain are appreciated, but you may want to let me pass before Ann returns with Caden."

"Yer husband had to step out to inspect the barrel of grain I graciously brought. Too bad the Munros burnt all their fields this past harvest."

The Munros? Her uncle was responsible for these good people nearly starving?

"Ann will find someone else to come."

Gilbert's face hardened, making the glint in his eye razor sharp. "What if they can't find *ye*?"

Meg's instincts flooded her with energy. She turned on her heel, ready to walk back into the great hall, when he punched the torch right out of her grip. The flame slid, spitting and sparking along the stone floor. She leapt forward to run, but he pushed her shoulder with enough force to spin her. She flattened up against the rock wall.

He leaned in, his palms flat on either side of Meg's head. "A quick kiss and we'll be on our way."

...

Caden rounded the corner as Meg kneed Gilbert Davidson with a quick thrust. Gilbert grunted and she ducked under his arm and slammed right into Caden's unyielding chest. He whirled her to the side and grabbed Gilbert up by the throat, ramming him against the same stone wall.

"Bloody insolent ass!" Caden seethed with fury. "Do you think to accost my wife in her own home?"

Gilbert tried to make a noise but couldn't get it past Caden's grip.

"Accost and abduct," Meg said as she huffed, catching her breath.

Caden dropped Gilbert but drew the dirk from his boot, holding its point a mere inch from the pulse at Gilbert's neck.

"A misunderstanding," Gilbert said. "I was trying to make up to your lady for that mixup in your forest." He glared back at Caden. "So I asked for a friendly kiss. I was unaware of what an insecure, smothering groom ye are, Macbain." He shook his head at Meg, completely ignoring the threat of the dirk. "A pity for ye, milady."

Meg's eyes snapped fire. "I am not your friend and have no need of your pity. I much enjoy my husband's smothering and he is most secure in his abilities to love me so well that stars swim before my eyes."

Caden lowered his dirk and stared at her, unable for a moment to say anything in the wake of her boast.

Meg pointed to the torch that still sparked on the ground. "Luckily, I had a torch, else I'd have had to break his nose or gouge out his eyes to stop him from carrying me away." She directed a glare at Gilbert so scathing and resolute that the insolent's foolhardy expression wavered.

Caden grabbed him by the shirt. How dare he touch Meg! Try to take her from him!

"Like I said, just a bridal kiss and then I'd escort her back to you, of course." Gilbert tried to connect with Meg's gaze. "My comments were about no one finding ye here because we'd returned to the party already. Why in hell would I bring the wrath of The Macbain down on me by stealing his bride? I just bloody brought you more grain."

Could Meg have misunderstood? Gilbert certainly scared her, attacked her enough that she was forced to defend herself. Caden breathed deep to control his fury and released his hold.

Gilbert straightened his shirt. "Such a temper. Would ye really start another war over a woman when ye just ended one? And I thought ye were the wise one."

"Wise enough to know that my height would stand out above an oat field, making it difficult to burn without being seen." Caden had always had his suspicions about the man. His father certainly coveted the Macbain land.

"I have no idea what you're talking about, Macbain."

"You know I am responsible for protecting and feeding my people," Caden said, his dagger still in his fist. "If I find out a *neighbor* has declared a silent war against us, I will kill him."

Gilbert's Adam's apple wobbled in his throat. "If ye kill me, Macbain, ye'll have England to worry about."

Meg's breath hitched.

"Are you in league with the *Sasunnach*?" Caden demanded.

"Nay, but some in these mountains are. They pledge themselves to Henry in an attempt to befriend the land-greedy king."

"And you have no interest in selling your principles for protection from English guns."

"Nay," Gilbert said, his grin fading to something like a feral grimace. "For someone who has just publicly proclaimed yer desire for a united Scotland, ye seem to be itching for another war."

Caden slid his dagger back in its leather scabbard. "Leave or stay if you wish." His unblinking eyes met Gilbert's. "Either way, never touch my wife again."

Meg stumbled into Gilbert, her mouth near his ear. What was she doing? "Tell Girshmel my beast survived and is hungry for him."

Caden pulled her back and brushed her through the archway. The lass risked too much.

Meg sank down in her chair and closed her eyes. Bloody merriment still filled the hall so he couldn't whisk her upstairs.

Caden sat down next to her and watched her breathe. He replayed the whole incident in his head while he waited. Gilbert was a problem, but he'd deal with that after the festival.

After a long moment she peeked out. "You're...grinning?" she asked, worry marking her voice.

His eyebrow rose. "So well that stars swim before yer eyes?"

"The bridal ale is strong. I'm sorry if I—"

He held up a hand. "No apologies needed, wife. I'm just glad I had a chance to give ye something to boast about."

Caden moved closer and kissed her lips. His heart slowed with her nearness, with her safety. He pulled back. "Are ye certain he didn't harm ye in any way?"

"I am unharmed." She sat up straighter. "Just worried that we have a new enemy."

Caden laced his fingers through hers. "A united Scotland is a distant dream." His expression turned grim. "Hot-tempered Highlanders butt heads more often than not. We're a fierce lot, but our strength can also become our weakness."

She leaned into him. "We've just taken a step backward, haven't we?"

"Nay, lass, don't think of it that way. I believe Gilbert Davidson was always an enemy. Now he's one that I know of, which makes him much less dangerous."

Ewan walked up. "I saw Gilbert Davidson."

"He cornered Meg alone. I think he had more in mind than giving the bride a friendly kiss."

Ewan scowled. "He fits the description of the tall man Angus saw with the torch."

"He denies it, of course," Caden said.

"He was hiding something," Meg said.

Both men turned to her.

Meg sighed. "Remember when I said that Girshmel was part of the attack at Loch Tuinn?"

"Aye," Ewan said.

"Just now as we were leaving, I mentioned that he should tell Girshmel that Nickum was still alive."

"That's why ye did that," Caden said. "Ye risked too much."

"He showed all the signs that he knew exactly what I was talking about and was nervous," she answered.

"Ye got that just by touching him?" Ewan asked.

"Thanks to her gift," Caden said, his eyes not leaving Meg. "She can tell when someone lies by the way their body reacts."

"Amazing." Ewan grinned at Caden. "So ye'll be able to tell if Caden ever lies to ye."

"Girshmel is working for Davidson," Caden said, chewing on the information. "At the loch, Girshmel said that his boss would want ye."

Caden watched Gilbert laugh his way through the crowds with another Davidson at his side.

"Simon follows him constantly, like an obedient dog," Ewan said.

Caden relaxed his fist and grabbed a drumstick. "Davidson's afraid to walk alone."

Meg stared, her mouth dropping open. "Are you going to let him leave?"

"Aye," Caden said, and took a bite.

"He's dangerous."

Ewan winked mischievously. "Don't fret, milady, for yer husband is wise. Let the wolf return to the pack and wait to see if he truly is the leader. Because it's the leader that must be thwarted."

Meg turned to Caden. "You think he's helping the English? Maybe Boswell?"

"Davidson brought it up, not me," Caden said. "I won't know if I capture him now unless he confesses under…pressure.

If we do that, we could still lose the leader. Best to let Davidson think he's safe. And I wouldn't want to curse our wedding day feast."

Wine followed the ale, along with roast goose and fresh herbed bread. Baked apples with honey were served with strong creamy cheeses. Caden tasted each thing Meg wanted to eat first, but nothing seemed out of place. Bess hadn't found who had poisoned Meg's soup, and he hadn't seen her here today. Father Daughtry sat at one end with a tankard and a full plate. The cleric laughed around a little hiccup and grinned sheepishly. Gwyneth sat with him and Ann joined them after making sure Meg was all right.

Caden ordered several of his warriors to follow Gilbert around the celebration until he left. Meg relaxed into his side, contentment in her features. The beauty of it pressed inside Caden's chest. How could one wee lass fill him with such power, such calm and happiness? It was beyond anything he'd ever experienced.

"I'm so happy here," she murmured. "Here with you. I'm glad I can help our people in some small way," she said. "I am finally part of a family."

Och, he had to tell her everything. Yes, she was part of this family and he'd hoped that none would tell Meg her initial status as captive. Maybe none would, but he would always know. She needed to know, deserved to know, and she should hear the truth from him.

She yawned and leaned into Caden. "How long do these parties last?"

It was his chance. He'd carry her above now and love her

until stars swam before her eyes. Then he'd tell her everything. Not just the mission but the reason for his desperate act. He wouldn't let her leave their room until she understood. Aye, it was a good plan.

"Until I can no longer stand the constant brush of yer leg against mine and that amazing flowery woman scent ye give off." His eyes dropped to her low neckline and the soft swell of breasts pushed above its satin edging. "Until I can no longer pretend to concentrate on routine discussions about horses and government and must carry ye above."

He leaned in close so that to anyone else it would seem like they were kissing. His lips brushed hers. "Until I can no longer contain my lust for my beautifully curved wi—"

Before he could even finish the word, Meg closed the miniscule distance between their lips, kissing him wantonly. She pulled him closer with one hand behind his head as he tilted her face to deepen the kiss.

A cold *whoosh* of air blew in as the doors banged open again. Meg shivered but continued the kiss.

A scream pierced the hall.

• • •

Meg jerked backward, her fingers squeezing Caden's arm. Everyone turned toward the entryway. A woman wobbled in, covered with snow.

"Where is my brother?" she screamed. "Someone find Caden!"

Brother? This must be Caden's sister. Meg's stomach tightened, and her hand flattened against the beautiful skirts. *I hope she doesn't mind me borrowing her gowns.*

"Sarah?" Caden turned. "Bloody hell."

He stood and strode out amongst the hushed people. Meg followed, excited to greet Caden's sister. The woman was fairly tall, her hair dark and matted from the melting snow caking it. Red, swollen eyes searched the crowd. She'd been crying. However, the enormous belly was what pulled everyone's attention. She was pregnant, more pregnant than anyone Meg had ever attended. She waddled more than walked.

"Caden, the bloody bastards took Eòin!" she screamed. She held her girth. Her protruding stomach stuck out so far, Meg wondered how she didn't fall forward.

"What are you doing out in this storm and in your condition?" Caden asked. "Where is your husband?"

Poor woman.

Sarah kicked Caden's shin and shrieked, a howl that funneled up through the room, silencing even the most distant attendee. "I said, they took him! The bloody Munros are going to kill him!"

"Munros took Eòin?" Caden asked calmly and signaled to Ewan. Ewan leapt up and signaled two other men. They waited near the entrance.

"Get Rachel and Searc," Caden said to Donald.

Sarah sobbed. Meg made a move to help, but Caden blocked her advance. This stress wasn't good for the baby. If Sarah thought the Munros took her husband, she wouldn't want Aunt Rachel's help.

"When they came up to the house, Eòin made me hide outside around back. I watched them take him away! He's probably dead already!"

"You recognized them as Munros?"

"Of course they were! Who else would take him?" She grabbed his arm, leaning into him. "I know you have a plan, brother, but we have to use the Englishwoman now! Send word that you'll kill her if they don't return my Eòin." She swallowed. "I can't raise this bairn without its father."

Meg's breath hitched. She stood perfectly still, her eyes on the woman. Use the Englishwoman? A plan? There were no other Englishwomen around.

"Sarah, much has happened since we last talked," Caden said, his hands balling into fists at his sides. Without moving his gaze he said, "Fiona, why don't ye take my bride upstairs?"

"I think I'll stay," Meg said, her words flat, hiding the twisting of hatching betrayal in her gut.

Sarah sobbed harder. "How could you be marrying at a time like this? You were on a mission to England, and then you were back so soon." She shook her head as if she couldn't believe all this. "Where is the niece of the Great Munro? You captured her, everyone says so. Ransom her now."

"The plan changed, Sarah," Caden said slowly.

Meg stood in the center of the filled room. No one moved, no one breathed. Was she even breathing? She couldn't tell. Nausea warred with numbness, causing pinpricks of light to spark in her periphery.

Caden had planned to use her.

He'd been on a mission down in England. There was a blood feud. Ugly thoughts whirled through Meg as she pieced details together. Never any words of love, only peace. The voices in the room seemed muffled as if she heard them at the end of a long tunnel. She sucked in air between dry lips. No, she couldn't lose consciousness, not when there was so much she needed to hear.

Sarah glanced around wildly. "Where is she? In the dungeons or upstairs?" She stomped her foot while holding her belly. "Get her, Caden. I don't care if your save-us-all plan has changed. Ride against the Munros." The last command ended with tears, though the strong woman did not crumple. "Bloody hell, Caden, I'll get her myself!" she yelled. "Where is she?"

Meg's legs worked on their own as she stepped forward.

Caden manacled her wrist but she walked past him, getting as far forward as she could.

"Hello, Sarah," Meg said, bringing the woman's tear-filled gaze to focus. "I am Meg…Boswell, Macleod, Macbain," she said in Gaelic. "Your new sister, the English prisoner."

Chapter Ten

17 April 1517—Shepherd's Purse: green, slender, white flowers, pods of yellow seeds, foul odor.
Drink to stop internal bleeding and flooding. Ointment for wounds about the head. Apply poultice to angry flesh and to staunch external bleeding. Plant juice on a bit of wool. Placed in the nose, it will stop heavy blood flow. Find Shepherd's Purse far across wild heaths.

"Meg," Caden said from behind her.

She stood firm. A room of people watched. Were they waiting for her to break down before his sister, run away screaming, faint? She wouldn't give them a show, and she wouldn't back down from the increasingly red, blotchy woman.

In the space of a heartbeat, Sarah pulled back her fist and whipped it toward Meg's face.

Caden's hand caught it before it made contact. Meg didn't even flinch.

"Let me go, Caden!" Sarah yanked her fist from him. "How

could you marry a Munro? A bloody English Munro?" She leaned to the side, trying to get a hold of Meg's hair. She caught the sleeve of Meg's gown and ripped it down, exposing her arm.

Self preservation kicked in, and Meg grabbed the material with a twist of her body. She might be a captive here, but she wasn't going to be stripped in front of an audience.

Caden jumped between them, as did Ancient Kenneth.

"Sarah Macbain." Kenneth spoke low, in the authoritative tone of a father. "Calm yourself, lass, and hear your brother out."

"The Munro's English niece roams free through Druim Castle. She eats Macbain food! Dances to Macbain music while her bloody uncle kills my husband! I will not calm down!" Sarah's last word came out with a moan, a familiar moan.

Meg had heard it in women down in Yorkshire. She was in labor. Sarah bent over, her large belly hanging. Kenneth and Kieven helped her sit down.

"Meg," Caden said. "We need to talk, lass."

"I think enough has been said for now," Meg replied. Even a glance at his beguiling, secret-keeping features hurt too much. Instead, she watched his sister twist with pain. It had to be equal to what she felt inside.

Oh God, had Caden married her only to force her uncle to do something? Was this marriage really a prison sentence? Panic and fury sluiced through her. Meg could hardly think straight with everything slapping at her confidence. One glance revealed that despite Sarah's noise, Meg was definitely the focus of everyone in the hall. They all knew that she was really a captive, that Caden was using her, that her marriage was a farce.

She caught sight of Gwyneth. The woman gave her a sad shake of pity, her lips curled into a tight pucker. The gesture knifed through Meg with such force she nearly doubled over with the moaning woman. She needed to get out of the hall, away from the stares. She had to think.

Sarah's guttural cry struck a chord in Meg. She needed to get out of the hall, too. Perhaps they should go together. She might have been made a fool, but she was no fool when it came to healing.

"I need to touch her," Meg said. "She's in labor."

Caden grabbed both of his sister's arms. "Be still, Sarah, or you'll harm the bairn."

Meg walked behind Sarah and reached to touch her shoulder.

"Oh." Meg exhaled and yanked back. Her gaze met Caden's. He certainly needed her now.

Sarah howled with a new pain.

"Take her upstairs. There are two babes inside. Things are dangerously cramped inside."

"Two bairns?" Kenneth asked. "How do ye—"

"Move!" Caden's voice rippled through the gathered Macbains. They pushed backward in unison as he heaved his sister into his arms.

"Ride to the Munros, Ewan," Caden called, and the three men at the door strode out into the snowy afternoon.

"There were no plans to take her husband or anyone," Rachel said, and glanced at Searc, who agreed.

"That was before you two disappeared," Caden answered.

"Aunt Rachel, we'll need you up here."

Meg ran behind Caden. "Fiona. Bring your herbs, especially calming herbs. Ann, Jonet, come help."

Her friends followed.

Friends? Enemies of the Munros, who knew all about Caden's plan. Enemies who jumped to help her because they loved Caden's sister? Or because they respected Meg? She massaged the ache at her forehead.

Caden carried his sister into Meg's original room and laid Sarah in the middle of the bed.

"Stoke up the fire," Meg ordered.

"What can we do?" Jonet breathed.

"I need clean linens, a sharp knife, strong string, some rope, and a pot of water to be placed in the fire to heat," Meg said.

"Get them out! Yer English bride and her witchy aunt!" Sarah moaned with another wave of pain. "Throw them in the dungeons," she whispered as she strained.

Meg ignored her. "Aunt Rachel, what do you think of a rope around the rafter that she can hold onto?"

"I've seen it done with success."

Some women found it easier to push when they held themselves upright from a suspended rope.

"I mean it, brother," Sarah yelled, her voice once more strong. "I want them out. I'll not have my bairn brought into the world by a prisoner."

Caden looked between them, his gaze resting on Meg. "What do ye want me to do?"

Sarah's eyes grew rounder still. "You ask her what to do?" She moaned and grabbed her belly.

Meg moved close to Sarah, careful to stay out of reach.

"Caden, hold her arms."

He hesitated, and Meg shot him the most brutal loathing she could summon. There was no time for hesitation. Either he supported her during this horror or he didn't. "Do you want them all to die, then? Both babes are in danger and so is she if we don't help."

Caden grabbed his sister's wrists, and Meg hid her relief in a handkerchief she swiped across her forehead. No, he hadn't chosen her over his clan, but in this little battle he'd chosen her over kin.

Sarah cursed in Gaelic until another pain gripped her. Meg waited until it subsided and walked up to Sarah. Some patients needed tenderness and love. Others needed a hard kick or a big dose of reality.

"I'm sorry we've met under these circumstances," Meg said.

Caden restrained his sister as she attempted to claw at Meg. Meg didn't flinch, knowing that he would stop any attack.

"Regardless, you need my help."

"Get away from me!" Sarah spat.

"Sarah!" Meg yelled. "You have two babies in you who are going to die shortly if you don't work with me to get them out. Do you want your babies to die?"

Fresh tears gushed from swollen eyes as Sarah shook her head. "Nay!" She breathed out long and seemed to calm a bit after several in and outs. "Two, ye say? Are ye sure?"

Meg wasn't about to go into the complexities of her talent. She moved forward and ran her hand over Sarah's distended belly. "I've delivered twenty-two babies. I can tell. And they need to come out quickly, as the cord oftentimes wraps around one or both."

She caught Caden's eye and gave the briefest of nods. Time was running out.

Sarah's breath hitched during the contraction. Meg came closer, locking gazes with the woman. "Breathe with me, Sarah," she said and counted, moving her hands in to indicate an inhale and then counted down to show how to hold the exhale.

Jonet, Ann, and Kieven barreled back into the room with the supplies, Fiona quick on their heels. Gwyneth peeked around the doorway but retreated when Sarah groaned. Thank goodness! Meg didn't need her jeers or pitying glances.

Meg and Rachel directed everyone, and within minutes the rope was looped over a rafter at the end of the bed, the water heated, and linens draped.

Caden released his sister's hands, but he leaned into her and kissed her sweaty forehead. "Sarah, follow Meg's instructions. Listen to her. She knows the ways of birthing and healing."

"Find Eòin," she cried.

"I will," he said. "That's my job, sister. You do your job, too. Listen and obey Meg." He paused. "I don't want to bury you and your bairns."

Sarah started to inhale on another pain.

"Out," Meg ordered him. "This is only for women now." She flapped her hand toward the door.

"Meg…" The contours of Caden's face tighted with barely controlled fury or…pain. "We will finish our discussion."

Meg clasped Sarah's hand. "I don't believe you ever chose to start a discussion with me."

"Then we will bloody hell be starting one," Caden swore.

Meg brushed Sarah's hair from her forehead. "Time to get your babes out of you."

Sarah closed her eyes to rest between contractions. Meg surveyed her womb through her senses. The girl baby would come first. She breathed through the umbilical cord. The second baby, a boy, needed help. The cord wound around his fragile neck and each tug and wiggle pulled it tighter. Soon his throat would collapse under the strain.

"Don't push yet, Sarah," Meg said. "Jonet, wipe her brow with a wet cloth. Ann, lay a drape toward the end of the bed, under the ropes."

Rachel oversaw the other preparations. She laid out the knife and thread to tie off the umbilical cords.

"You knew," Meg said softly, moving closer to Rachel. "That I was a captive…and you left me here."

Rachel hesitated at first. She gave a brief nod, her features strong, unrepentant. "You were in safe hands here. Not knowing your true status alleviated the fear."

"And my marriage? You've orchestrated this whole thing, this plan to trick your husband into accepting this peace, isn't it?"

Rachel exhaled long. "Don't close your heart to Caden. A man doesn't tie himself to a woman when there are other options, unless he cares for her."

"Which he's never mentioned. I…I don't know what to think, about him or even about you." Meg walked to the fire to help Fiona spoon the hot wet linens from the boiling pot.

Fiona touched her arm. "She's right. Ye were always safe. I could have gotten ye out of Druim whenever ye needed or wanted to go."

"Hmm…perhaps I should have known that before I said 'I do.'"

Evelyn bustled in with more linens. Caden stood just beyond, feet braced, arms crossed over his chest as if waiting for the call to battle. His gaze ran the room, connecting with Meg's. A hard stare, full of fire and strength and passion for his beliefs. A chill seeped across Meg's back and shoulders, in sharp contrast to the sweat that snaked between her breasts.

She pulled up the last dripping cloth and placed it over the heavy pole used to hold the clean linens. Sarah screamed and Jonet slammed the door shut.

"I see the bairn's head," Ann yelled.

Meg met Fiona's eyes. "After this, you will get me out."

Fiona stared, sad understanding in her eyes, and crossed to Sarah. Enough talk of deception. Time for new life and miracles. Meg followed.

The little girl came into the world with a full head of dark hair and lusty bellows. Meg cut and tied the cord and passed the healthy baby to Rachel, who washed off the blood. Evelyn cooed over the pink baby and brought her up to Sarah's sweat-streaked face.

"She's spunky," Evelyn said, smiling. "I can tell already you'll be chasing after her."

Sarah kissed the baby.

"Sarah." Meg touched the woman's stomach to assess the boy's progress. "Rest for now."

Sarah leaned back and closed her eyes.

"Are ye certain there's another bairn inside?" Ann asked.

"Most certain." She checked the baby girl. Blood rushed through her little body with vigor, lungs filled and compressed, fluids moved and cleared. Healthy and hungry.

"Is there a wet nurse?" Meg asked.

"I'll get Elizabeth Loman," Jonet said. "She can help until Sarah's milk comes in."

Men's voices raised and pitched on the other side of the door. The door banged open.

"Sarah!" A mud-streaked man charged into the room. "I'm here, flower!"

"Eòin," Sarah called weakly, but didn't rise. "We have a bairn. A wee lassie." Her hand flapped in the direction of the baby girl in a cradle near the fire. "There's another to come," she said and tears slid down her face. "You're well?"

The man grabbed Sarah's hand and squeezed. "Aye, I'm fine. Why did you not wait at home?"

"The Munros took you. I had to do something."

"They were fools, didn't know the land. I was away from them within the hour."

So the Munros were also fools, Meg thought, and frowned at the dirt the man tramped into the room. Birthing rooms should be clean, orderly.

"And they were not Munros," Eòin said. "One spoke with an English accent and the other referred to the Munros like he wasn't one of them."

English? Meg's heart slammed inside her chest. "Have you told this to Caden?"

Eòin surveyed her as if he wondered who she was. "Aye, quickly."

Sarah groaned. "I think the other bairn is coming."

Eòin paled under the dirt.

"Out!" Meg ordered. "While you men seem intent on slicing life out of this world, we women must do our job to bring life into it. Out!"

Eòin kissed Sarah's hand and stepped away. "When can I see my wee bairns?" His gaze drifted over to the hearth.

"Soon, now go." Meg moved to the end of the bed. "Ann, Evelyn, help Sarah up to hold onto the ropes.

Sarah groaned. "I'm so tired. I can't do this."

Meg glanced at the closed door. Luckily, Eòin hadn't heard that or she'd have him and his dirt back in here. She moved up to Sarah's head and smoothed the hair away from her forehead. "Sarah, you rode through a Highland blizzard to find help for your husband. You birthed a beautiful, healthy baby girl. You punched your brother's hand with enough force to make him wince."

"Caden winced?" Sarah asked, the spirit in her eyes igniting.

Meg hadn't actually seen that, but *she* had certainly winced. She raised her eyebrows. "Yes. Winced, I'm telling you. You are strong, Sarah. You can do this."

Sarah shook her head as another pain gripped her.

"Sarah, repeat after me. I am strong and powerful."

Sarah shook her head.

"Come now, say it. I am strong and powerful."

"I…am…strong and…powerful."

"That's it. Keep saying it." Meg lifted Sarah toward the ropes. Jonet and Ann looped each arm into the supports.

Rachel stood close.

"I am strong and powerful," Sarah said and swallowed. "I can do this!" she howled.

Meg checked the progress. A small head appeared. "Push now, Sarah!"

Sarah bore down.

"That's it. Now breathe, and bear down."

The little head broke free. The thick cord lay around the neck. With the next push, the shoulders slid out, giving Meg room to wedge her fingers between the cord and baby. Evelyn peered over her shoulder and gasped.

"What?" Sarah panted from above.

"Nothing," Meg said, "just bear down one more time."

Sarah pushed and the tangled baby came out, his body blue and still. Meg pulled the cord away from his neck. "Evelyn, the blade," she said calmly, and sawed through the cord around the neck. Then she cut the baby's cord at his navel and tied it. "Get Sarah down while I help him," she said as confidently as she could. She turned to Rachel. "The afterbirth needs to come."

"He's not crying!" Sarah wailed.

Meg carried the limp baby away in a linen, wiping away the birthing fluid, opening his little mouth. Ann laid a blanket on the rug near the hearth.

"He's dead," Ann whispered.

Meg shook her head. The child was still there, his spirit. She sensed a weak flicker of life just waiting to be fed into an inferno. "His throat has collapsed so he can't pull in breath." Her hands trembled as she spanned his motionless chest.

"Aunt Rachel," she called.

"Sarah is hemorrhaging, a rip that runs deep inside, Meg. I

need to help her."

Meg took a full breath. Could she save the baby? She had to try. She closed her eyes and imagined an open throat all the way into his little lungs. No fluid, nothing but open space.

"Yer hands," Ann gasped.

Meg blinked. The blue light glowed along the part between her hands and the baby's chest. "'Tis a gift from God, Ann. Pray for us. Pray for the babe."

Ann began to pray softly next to Meg while Sarah sobbed in the background. The room lay still, waiting for Meg to rise, to pass judgment, to say the terrible words every mother shrank from. The babe's life essence began to fade even though his airways were now open.

"Why aren't you breathing, tiny one?" Meg whispered, and wiggled the baby. Did he need some air to start the process, to know what it was like to fill his lungs? She leaned over and covered his mouth and nose with her own mouth.

"What are ye doing?" Ann insisted.

Meg blew into him until she sensed his lungs were full. She pulled back and pressed down on his chest until the air funneled out of his small chest. "Just like that, in and out. You can do it." She blew in again, sat back, and pressed the air out.

She sensed a gentle expanding of the baby's chest. "That's it, precious." The air returned on an exhale. Two more inhales and exhales and the baby twitched his legs. He opened his mouth, and a small cough forced more fluid from his mouth. Meg tipped him to his side and swabbed his mouth. She wiped his small frame briskly, causing him to whimper and finally cry out weakly.

"Meg," Ann laughed despite the tears coursing her face. "Ye brought him back to life."

Meg wiped at her own tears. "God did that."

"Is that…?" Sarah started from the bed.

"Your son," Meg said and brought the boy over to his mother. He was beginning to pinken.

"He…he wasn't moving," Evelyn said and kissed her cross. "I saw him. He was the color of death."

"Meg saved him," Ann said. "There was this blue light and she breathed in his mouth and—"

"God saved him," Meg insisted, but she was too tired to worry over what they all thought. Saving the baby had sucked the remaining energy out of her. She sat next to Sarah. Rachel collapsed on the other side.

Sarah grabbed Meg's hand. "Thank ye, Meg. I…I am so sorry for before," she said. "Thank ye." She cuddled the baby's cheek against her own. Jonet brought the girl from her cradle so Sarah could see them both.

"They are both healthy," Meg said. "You are a very fortunate woman."

"Fortunate to have ye and yer aunt here," Fiona said and Ann and Jonet agreed. Evelyn made the sign of the cross, and somehow it didn't annoy Meg. She soaked in the fresh beauty of the now-pink face of the boy. How could her magic be evil when it could bring that sweet babe back from the edge of death? Aunt Rachel was right. Her magic was a gift from God.

Rachel instructed Fiona from the bed. "Don't pack her with anything; just keep her clean. I need to rest."

"Of course ye do," Fiona said. "Ye, too, Lady Meg."

Meg concentrated on putting one foot before the other on her way to the bedroom door. A hallway full of anxious men greeted her. Silent. Expectant. Worried.

"You are a fortunate man, Eòin," Meg said in his native tongue. "You have a healthy daughter and a healthy son." The men around him cheered. The heaviness of Caden's stare fell on her, but she ignored him.

"And Sarah?" Eòin asked, trying to peer into the room.

"She'll be fine, thanks to Rachel Munro."

Relief flooded the man's face.

"Wash and then you can see your new family."

Joy lit his entire face as he turned, the men following him. Caden stood alone in the hall. She turned down the corridor to her room. Her room? Their room? She hesitated, her hand supporting her on the wall. Where else could she go? She must lie down before she fell down. She took one step and her legs buckled under the boulder of exhaustion.

Caden scooped her up. "Ye are more worn than when ye healed the others." He kicked their door open, and set her in the middle of the bed.

Meg finally allowed her gaze to fall on him. Concern furrowed his brow. Her touch told her that his blood pumped hard, and his heart hammered. His head ached and his stomach contained a large dose of bile. Good, he deserved a sour stomach. She sighed, closed her eyes, and relaxed into the plump tick.

Caden leaned forward, his breath tickling her ear. "Thank ye for my niece and nephew, for helping my sister." As Meg drifted into the healing oblivion of sleep, Caden's final words nestled into her aching heart.

"I am sorry I hurt ye, lass."

. . .

Meg woke to inky blackness. Only the embers of her fire lit the room, barely enough for her to see that she was alone. She stretched. Much better. She peeked through the glassed window slit to a gray pre-dawn glow, and then stirred the embers in the hearth and struggled out of the once-beautiful gown.

Tears pressed against the backs of her eyes. She was in a strange country far from home. Aunt Rachel had left her a prisoner of a blood feud. Rowland Boswell wanted to test her for witchcraft, and after yesterday's public glowing there would be plenty of evidence supporting a guilty verdict. Even if she wasn't his daughter, he wanted her dead.

And then there was the farce of a marriage she was caught in. The thought that Caden had tricked her, seduced her, was using her without telling her…her empty stomach pitched.

What choices did she have? Fiona could secret her away from Druim, but then where to go? Boswell had sent letters to all the surrounding chiefs. Maybe Colin Macleod would take her in.

"I need to think," Meg murmured at the red coals and rubbed away the hardened crystals of tears that had dried in her sleep. She dressed in a plain gown of wool over her smock and pulled on a fur-lined cloak. With a tallow candle before her, she walked in its splash of light to the door leading to the castle roof.

She nestled the cloak around her head to shield her from

the biting wind. The snow had stopped but lay in little drifts on the slick granite. Dawn blossomed at the eastern edge of the world, rays of sun soared from the golden center, lighting the day.

A guard walked around the corner and stopped. "Meg?"

Meg glanced at Hugh Loman and turned to lean against the waist-high wall. "Good day to you, Hugh. How is your arm?"

"Ahh…'tis good," he mumbled. "Milady, what are ye doing out here?"

"Is a prisoner not allowed the view?" She caught sight of a flock of geese high above. They flew with such freedom.

"Milady? Nay…I mean ye aren't a prisoner. Ye are Lady Macbain." He grew silent for a long moment. "Ye look all ye want." The door whispered open. Footsteps sounded, perhaps another guard to take Hugh's place. When the footsteps halted behind her, Meg turned.

Caden stood tall, all washed and crisp. Probably smelled like bloody pine, too.

""Tis slippery up here," he said, and came to stand with her at the wall. "Ye could fall."

"Mmmm…" Meg stared at him. "A dead hostage is much less valuable."

...

Caden studied his wife. The darkness beneath her eyes had faded with sleep. She wore a fur that couldn't possibly be keeping her warm enough up here. Her hair was a glorious tousled flow of reddish gold in the dawn glow. The long tresses tugged and twisted around her pinched face devoid of her smile.

He'd known it would disappear the second she understood, but the absence stole some strength from him.

"'Tis not that, lass."

"Then I am not a hostage?"

"Nay, not the second after ye became my wife."

"Before that, though, the whole time, the whole journey here, my time here…I foolishly thought…everyone knew…everyone but me."

He'd rather watch the back of her head. The loss of that sincere twist of her lips created an ache like a knife wound. He wouldn't turn away, though.

"You used me, Caden. You bound me to you."

"I was saving ye from Boswell, too. The plan was a good one."

The sadness glistening in her eyes was a fist to his gut. He almost doubled over. He deserved these punches.

"A good one," she said. "And you succeeded."

She shook her head. "You should have told me. Maybe not at the beginning; I can see the reason in that. A happy captive is an easy captive," she mocked. "Sometime before the wedding, before the wedding night. Somewhere in there you should have told me."

"Ye are right." He kept his gaze locked with hers so she would see he spoke truth. "Saying nothing was easier. We were happy. Ye knew that ye were ending the feud. I hoped ye wouldn't have to find out—"

"That I was a prisoner. Don't you think that would have slipped out from someone at sometime in my life here?"

"By then perhaps, well perhaps it wouldn't have mattered."

She turned back to the bailey. "Lies have piled up and I don't know where I stand with anyone. Especially you."

"My response to ye was no lie." Caden pulled her hand and placed her palm flat on his tunic.

She yanked it away. "Your physical reactions to me could stem from a base need and nothing more."

Was the simple need to tup her the cause for the ache piercing Caden, the chill freezing him as she turned away? If that were truth, this bloody pain would have disappeared by bedding Meg. Yet the plague of her sorrow, righteous anger, and betrayal infiltrated his every thought, his every muscle since the moment Sarah blew in with her own blizzard. Even with her powers, Meg couldn't read his mind and he barely knew what lay in his heart himself.

Caden exhaled, ready to give her the only thing he could at this point. "I will tell ye whatever ye wish to know. Anything."

"Was your mission to take me?"

"Aye."

"To end the feud with the Munros?"

"Aye."

"They burned the harvest?" Meg's hand rested against her slender throat.

"The fields were too dry. The flames ate through them faster than we could haul water. We lost our grains, most of our root vegetables, and our herds."

"Condemning you all to starvation."

"My people…women, children, the elders…they would die this winter if I couldn't find a way to bring food." Caden ran his hand over his jaw. "So I've demanded a wagon of oats from the

Munros as well as our herds returned. And with our marriage I've asked for a truce."

Meg swallowed. "So you are using me to force this peace? Our marriage is just a tool to leverage the truce."

Bloody hell, he couldn't let her think that. "The original thought came from wanting to save ye from Boswell." He could stop there, but that wasn't all of it.

"Ye are very important, lass. We learned that Alec Munro had a niece in England. At first I meant to just ransom ye back to him for our herds and grain, but with the information that he loves ye like his own… Ye are like his own daughter, so our union forces the peace. The priest's blessing and the consummation make it unbreakable. He has no choice but to agree to peace."

"My uncle Alec thinks of me as his daughter? Aunt Rachel's husband?"

"He loves ye and will agree to our terms to save ye," he said but his gut hardened even more from the blank amazement on her face.

Meg's eyes glistened frustration tinged with fury. "Perhaps if you'd explained things to me from the start you wouldn't find yourself stuck with a useless hostage, tied in a useless marriage."

"What are ye saying?" Caden's hands formed fists at his sides as his blood raced hard, throbbing in his head.

Meg turned her full self toward Caden. "You've been tricked, Chief Macbain. I've never even met my uncle Alec," she said, shaking her head. "I only just met my aunt this past week. I am not his beloved niece."

Caden gripped the top of the wall, his fingers digging into

the rough granite. "Bloody hell. Where is Rachel?"

At the same time Hugh Loman's holler ripped through the breeze. "Riders, ho!"

"Now who the…" Caden stopped when he recognized the broad rider leading the long line breaking through the forest, his sword raised. "It's about time." He grabbed Meg's frozen fingers. "Time to meet yer uncle Alec."

...

Meg stood straight backed near the hearth in the great hall as Aunt Rachel blew into the room beside her son Searc.

"Anything more I should know before yer husband storms Druim, Rachel? Searc?" Caden asked. "Besides the fact that Alec Munro doesn't even know Meg."

Meg could hear the taut wire in his voice, like thin metal stretched near its breaking point. Guilt was irrational, so why did the emotion gnaw at her? She wrapped her arms around her chest. She wasn't at fault because she was useless in all their foolish, idiotic scheming.

"Meg, are you all right?" Rachel asked.

"All right?" She chuckled. That's it. Fury was stronger than guilt. She'd stick to fury.

"Don't close your heart, Meg," Rachel said. "So many lives were at stake."

The door banged open again and Meg heard Caden curse. The three elders stalked into the room.

"You've done it!" Bruce bellowed. "Smoked the old fox out of his hole."

"Alec's come," Rachel said as if bracing herself.

"With a full contingent of men. Even Phillip rides," Caden finished. "Ewan!"

Ewan came forward as Caden walked to Rachel. "Milady, a token to slow the bull. Unless blood is your goal for today."

Rachel pulled a folded parchment and a handkerchief from her pocket. She held out the slip of linen. "He'll know I am safe if you wave it before him. Tell him Searc is with me."

Ewan swept the square of material from her fingers.

"You sent Fiona to me," Caden said. "Told her to lie about Meg, that Alec cherished her and was about to journey to England to save her." He took in Fiona, though the maid's gaze latched onto Rachel. "Even now Fiona is loyal to ye."

"Yes." Rachel grabbed Fiona's hand so that they both stood next to Meg before the flames. Searc kept trying to stand before his mother. Aunt Rachel had many protectors. Meg shivered at the tense chill of the room.

Caden swore and turned in a small circle as if waiting for something else terrible to befall them.

"Alec was forbidden to walk on English soil," Rachel explained, focusing on Meg. "Boswell saw to that years ago and Alec wasn't willing to risk his clan to save a girl he'd never met, even if she was of my blood."

"So now I have her but Alec won't agree to my terms because he still doesn't know her," Caden finished. Meg's stomach twisted at the way he spoke of her like she was some item to be traded. There was no emotion except wrath in his eyes. He'd been tricked just like she'd been tricked.

Rachel frowned and pursed her lips. "You are married now, completely and fully consummated. Any children who come from you will have my blood running in them. He will agree to peace."

"So the wedding was part of yer plan, too?" Caden asked.

Rachel let out a laugh. "I wasn't even here when you proposed, Macbain. That maneuver was all yours."

Meg's stomach pinched so hard she almost gagged.

Caden wasn't to be shot down. "You sent letters, letters signed as if from Boswell, threatening to take Meg back. To push me into protecting her."

Meg held her breath, not knowing what she hoped would be true. Rachel was already shaking her head. "Nay, we received the same letter." She slid the folded sheet from her pocket.

"Weapons and food," Angus said. "Wonder if the man's carried loads of grain up in wagons or if he's bought it from some foolish Scot up here."

Rachel opened up the letter she brought. Meg saw the slanted scrawl and shivered.

"My letter doesn't say anything about food." Rachel held it out to Caden. "Where is your letter?"

"Destroyed," he said and read down the parchment.

"Destroyed?" Searc questioned.

"Better to say it never made it to my eyes than to have it sitting around."

Kenneth read over Caden's shoulder. "How would Boswell know that we need food?"

Caden's attention moved back to Rachel. "He's working with someone in the Highlands. Someone who gave him that information."

"Not us," Rachel said. "He'd rather shoot us than talk to us."

She snatched the letter back. "And if he has that information, he probably knows that Meg is either still here or at Munro Castle."

"Then he is coming," Meg said and all eyes turned to her. "For me."

Caden's eyes met hers. "He can't have ye. Ye're mine."

Meg's heart soaked up the words. She was his. He claimed her, but was it because he cared for her, or just like one of his clan, she'd become his responsibility?

"Ye're ours," Kenneth and Bruce said at once and nodded to one another as if agreed.

"No one takes a Munro," Searc said.

"Nor a Macleod," Colin added.

Meg's stomach churned. "Then he's coming for us."

• • •

"*Mac an donais!* Ewan Brody, your blood will wash my blade if you wave that scrap before my nose again! Get the hell out of my way! *Rachel Munro, where are you, wife?*"

The roar thundered through the hall as the doors blew inward with the force of the wind and words.

"Meg, meet your uncle Alec," Rachel said and waved her hand in the air to get her husband's attention. He pivoted and charged toward them, much like an enraged bull. Ewan followed, squinting a newly blackening eye.

Alec Munro reached Rachel in the space of two heartbeats and grabbed her by the shoulders. He surveyed her up and down and then stared hard into her eyes. "You well, woman?"

"Quite well, husband," Rachel said. "Your blood is racing

too high. You need to calm down."

"You lied," he said ignoring her recommendation.

"No," she said calmly, into the face of the storm. "I said someone needed my help and you assumed it was Magis with her cough. I just didn't correct you."

Alec ran his rough hands down his face as if he wanted to pull the skin from his skull. "We'll not discuss this before enemies," he said. His eyes shifted to Searc. "And you?"

"Followed her," Searc finished.

"On your own, without telling anyone? Foolish boy. They could have slaughtered you."

Caden stepped in front of Meg. "We have much to discuss."

"There is nothing to discuss, Macbain. My family and I are leaving, unless you want a bloody battle to occur right here at your holding where women and children roam."

"May I present yer niece, Munro," Caden said and guided Meg to his side.

"I am pleased to meet you, Uncle Alec," she said in Gaelic.

A small bit of bluster melted out of the man. "We will take our niece home, too, then, or are ye still trying to hold the lass as a hostage?" he said in English. Meg noticed that he watched her for a reaction. He didn't get one.

"She isn't a captive, but she is staying," Caden said evenly. "She is my wife now, which would make us…kin."

The whole room of Macbains held their breaths as the words sunk in. Meg's dizziness began to return but once she remembered to breathe, the world righted itself.

"*Kin*," Alec spat. "I am yer sworn enemy, Macbain. I will never call ye kin."

"Husband," Rachel said, her hand on his arm. "Meg and Caden have married. Their children will have my blood in their veins. By your honor, you must call a peace between our two families."

"Peace?" Alec growled.

"Which would include the return of our herds," Kenneth interjected.

Alec spit on the rushes at his feet. Not a good sign. "Priest!" he yelled. "There must be a bloody priest around here to annul this ridiculous union."

"No priest here now," Bruce said. "And they've consummated the marriage."

"I can attest to the bed sheets," Ann threw in.

Meg nearly stepped into the fire. Instead of suicide she shut her eyes.

"And they didn't rise until late in the morning," Evelyn called from across the hall.

Heat splashed across Meg's face like someone had thrown hot soup on her. She took a step closer to the hearth. Maybe if the edge of her gown caught on fire, there would be so much chaos no one would notice her death by humiliation.

Everyone started talking at once, with Uncle Alec yelling Gaelic curse words in random eruptions of rage. Meg inhaled slowly. She didn't hear Caden say anything, but his warm palm cupped her hand. The words came up and out of her.

"Uncle Alec." Meg opened her eyes.

"Shhh!" Angus sputtered. "She's saying something."

Meg bent a smile. She kept her focus on the blustering, tall, shaggy faced man. He'd be intimidating in any situation, but with barely yanked-in fury he was a monster. Caden's hand squeezed again gently.

"Uncle Alec, I'm sorry this has all happened, but the truth is that Caden Macbain and I are truly, before the eyes of God, married."

Alec seemed to suck in his fury enough to address her without shouting. "Meg, I'm afraid that yer marriage was not legal, not without yer family giving their permission."

"I gave her my permission," Colin said.

Alec's eyes darted to Colin, then back to Meg. "I thought the Boswell devil was her father."

"Turns out Colin Macleod is Meg's father," Rachel said.

Alec snorted and pointed a finger at Colin. "Then consider yerself an enemy of the Munros."

Holy Mother Mary! Instead of peace there was to be more war. Meg was about to explain that Colin hadn't known and therefore hadn't given his permission at the wedding when Rachel stopped everyone. "Alec, I gave my permission for them to wed."

"What?"

"In fact, I orchestrated Meg's abduction from England in hopes that she'd be a beauty like Isabelle and that Caden would fall in love with her."

All eyes turned to Aunt Rachel. Jaws dropped. Alec's face twisted with shocked betrayal.

Rachel continued. "And now they are married and we can move forward in peace." Her mouth sat firm, but her eyes glanced down, her fingers catching at the folds of her skirts.

Alec's face grew red as a beet, his cheeks puffed in and out, his hands fisted against his legs. "What gives ye…" he shook his head, so overcome with fury. "What the bloody, blasted hell gives ye the right, woman, to end this glorious war…especially when I am winning!"

Rachel didn't even flinch. "I have one son left," she said softly.

"Brendon and Brandubh died as warriors," Alec replied as if that fixed everything.

"For what purpose?" Caden's voice was low.

Alec twisted around, eyes hard and damning. "They died for something greater than themselves."

"Ye mean the feud," Caden pronounced calmly.

"Aye, the feud, the cause my father taught me to continue, to uphold until justice is served."

"A feud that began over one woman a century ago," Caden said. "One woman who couldn't make up her mind over who she loved the most." He shook his head. "And because of it how many have died?"

"Elspet was pure, a symbol of goodness," Alec said, throwing his hand out to the tapestry depicting the start of the war. "I fight for justice and for the glory of Munros, as my father did before me and his father before him."

"So ye war for one woman and for the sake of tradition."

"For glory," Alec said but his voice had slid a notch.

"Meanwhile our bigger enemy, England, plans to rule our lands," Caden said, his voice rising for all to hear. Meg noticed that the room had filled. A dozen Munros stood along the wall near the doors while Macbain warriors packed in with swords ready.

Alec spit again in the rushes.

Caden continued. "While we spend our strength and resources feuding with other Scotsmen, the English organize their armies to seize more and more of our country."

"The feud keeps us skilled, trained, and ready," Alec insisted.

"At what cost?" Caden didn't wait for a reply. "I have no brothers left, ye have but one son. I have no uncles and a handful of cousins. What good are corpses against the English?"

Alec puffed up his chest. "Ye still have no right to force a peace—"

"No right?" Caden cut in. "I have no right to keep my people alive?" Caden opened his arms to indicate the men, the women who'd been helping with the meal, Bess's boy, Peter. "Do ye look into the faces of Munro children, Alec, and think 'Ye may die, child, because a woman died a century ago and now I want glory.'"

"Nay…I…" Alec frowned.

"I married to save my people," Caden said.

Meg stood numb at his words. Could the people in the room see her die inside a little?

"Sacrifice by one to save many makes sense. Sacrificing many to vindicate one is foolish. Sacrificing many to build up one's glory…is tyranny."

The room rippled with hushed agreement; angry and inflamed Macbains hung on every one of Caden's words. Meg's flush rose high into her face, but no one watched her, no one except Bess Tammin, who sent her a small grimace of pity where she stood with Peter.

Alec Munro indicated the awe-like trance of the Macbain people. "And if I refuse your threat of peace, I come across as a callous murderer of children."

"That," Caden agreed. "And ye and yer son will be sleeping for some time in my cold, rat-infested dungeon, since my men stand ready around yer forces outside. Rachel can go."

One of the elders grumbled. A cough barked softly into someone's fist. Somewhere in the filled hall a baby began to cry and was hastily taken away. Everyone seemed to hold their breath. Meg certainly did.

"Peace or tyranny, Munro?" Caden said.

"Shut yer mouth, Macbain," Alec answered. He stared hard at Rachel and scrubbed a hand through his tousled hair. "And ye want this peace so bad ye planned behind my back, woman?"

"I had no other way to salvage my only son. A mother will sacrifice just about anything to save her child."

"I should have let ye on the battlefield with us," he grumbled. "You'd have made us invincible and ye wouldn't have meddled." Alec seemed to age now that his bluster had seeped out, deflating him.

"I'm sure I would have meddled." Rachel stepped over to Alec's side.

"Aye, woman, ye would have. God's teeth," Alec swore. He placed his heavy hands on Rachel's shoulders. "Peace? I can barely stomach the word."

"How about alliance then?" Caden offered. "A united Highlands against the English, who try to take what is ours."

"And any other fool Scots who take up with them," Alec added.

"So…dungeons and tyranny, or an alliance over a drink of whisky?" Caden asked.

Alec rubbed his mouth through his thick beard. His face was granite, chiseled into a stubborn line fed by generations of self-righteous hatred. He had to know that everyone hung on his every breath as he drew each one out, weighing his options and Caden's words. He must see the logic in them.

Alec finally locked eyes with Caden. "Let's start with a drink and we'll go from there, Macbain."

The room erupted in cheers.

"We can discuss the return of our herds," Caden said. He released her hand and walked over to Alec, indicating the long table beyond. He never turned around.

Meg stood there with Colin at her side as everyone moved toward the table. Swarms of smiling people moved through the hall, which was thick with excitement and relief. Peace was being forged. Important details and oaths would ensue.

Much more important than one single woman, already forgotten. She was just a tool that helped bring it about.

The future glowed with the bright hope of peace and security for the Macbains. And she was now one of them. Why then did she want to weep?

Chapter Eleven

11 February 1518 — Brooklime/Water Pimpernel: blue or pink flowers in early summer. Bruised leaves on burns, swelling, or gout. A brew of leaves and flowers nourishing but bitter. Sweeten with honey.
Found in shallow fresh water streams and rivers fed by walls of water, which slow and freeze in the coldest months, protecting everything behind it.

Caden stood and glanced around at the happiness bubbling around him. The Munro warriors had been allowed inside, depleted of their weapons. People slapped each other on the backs. Whisky and ale flowed freely and food from the interrupted wedding feast was being brought out to share. His people would eat tonight without worry that this might be their last full meal.

Caden's gaze swung out at the crowd of people and frowned. There was one face missing.

He took a swallow from the wooden quaich and handed

it to Alec. Alec took the cup, swore softly, and tipped it back, whisky flowing into his mouth. A loud cheer rose around the table as the peace treaty was ceremonially sealed.

"Sit down, Caden," Alec said, handing him the quaich. "We have much to figure out between us and I need more whisky to do that."

Caden took the cup. "No more until we've agreed on the details, else you won't remember them." His gut gripped tight as he frowned. "Where is Meg?"

Rachel pointed to the hearth. "I thought she walked with us."

Colin sat down at the table. His eyes locked on Caden's with a hint of disapproval. "She retired to her rooms."

Alec bit into a drumstick. "Sit, Caden. Celebrate your peace. You've been fighting for it your whole life."

That he had. Since as long as he could remember, Caden had always questioned the reason for the feud. Long ago as he'd sat on his father's hairy knee and learned the legend, he'd frustrated his father into shouting with his "why" questions.

Caden slowly sat back down to enjoy the feast, although the joy around him seemed dull without her. "She should be here."

"Let her rest." Alec nudged Phillip next to him. "We will discuss your food shortage," he said, handing Caden another drumstick. "I won't have my niece going hungry this winter."

Caden had been waiting to negotiate this topic since he first concocted the plan to steal a country lass from England. Things had worked out so differently than he'd planned. The outcome for his people, though, was the same. For the hundredth time he forced his focus away from his bride and back to his people.

"You have my cattle and sheep, Munro."

Alec laughed. "That I do, Macbain. How about I return half to you?"

Caden studied the old wolf. This would be enjoyable. "How about I allow half of you to return home?"

...

Caden walked up the dark stairs, leaving the hushed laughter behind. His room was dark, untouched, empty.

"Where are you, lass?" The hollow emptiness of the room mimicked the ache in his chest. He'd held it at bay for the last hour as he worked out the details of the peace with Alec. The only thing they hadn't agreed upon was the recompense for the burnt harvest because Alec still refused to admit that he'd had a part in it.

Caden leapt up the steps leading to the roof two at a time and pushed into the gusty night chill. He hadn't realized he had been holding his breath until he released it with the sight of her.

Meg stared out at the night, her face braced into the wind. He walked up behind her and pulled her against his chest. "We started the day here and now we're ending it here."

She stood frozen in his arms. "Yes." She didn't turn to him, just stood like a fragile statue wrapped in fur and fine wool.

Caden rested his chin on her head. "The peace is settled."

"Good."

"I was just a lad when I swore I'd bring peace."

"A worthy goal. You must be very happy."

Happy? He should be uproariously out-of-control happy. How many nights had he dreamed of this day? How many times had he vowed to the frozen ground over his brothers' graves that he'd end it? Hundreds.

Caden turned Meg in his arms so that she stared at his chest. He lifted her chin with his finger. "Do I look happy?"

She blinked. "It's dark."

"Do I sound happy?"

"Perhaps you should return to the celebration. Happiness is lacking up here."

"Why aren't ye down at the celebration?"

"I was tired." She pulled her chin from his grasp, but he wouldn't let her turn away.

She was tired? Yet he found her up here and not in bed. Pointing out that fact would only irritate her more.

"My people won't starve this winter." Caden peered out above Meg's head. "The peace that I've spent my whole life envisioning has just become reality, yet…" He stared back down. "Yet it wasn't right."

Meg's gaze tipped up, and the filtered moonlight reflected in her eyes. "Wasn't…right?"

"Nay, ye were not there to celebrate it."

"I didn't think you noticed." Meg's voice was strong, without self-pity, but he heard a small hitch in her words that gave her away.

"I noticed." He touched her hair as it flew this way and that with the shifting breeze.

He should say more, but what? How could he explain something he didn't even understand himself? When he'd realized she had left the hall, it had been near to impossible not to follow. Only the constant reminders of his duty to finalize the peace had kept him below for the longest hour of his life. This steadfast desire to see her happy, too, didn't make sense.

He ran a thumb over her cheek. "Ye are the woman who made the peace possible."

"We both sacrificed to make this happen."

Sacrifice? Is that how she saw it? He frowned.

"For I won't put up with mistresses," she continued. "You agreed to marry me to forge your peace. Now you're stuck with me."

Caden was fairly certain from Meg's tone of voice that this had to do with more than some imagined threat of a mistress.

She shivered in the cold and all he wanted to do was carry her back to his room and warm her. Right now, she didn't give any signals that she was remotely willing. Bloody hell, women were complicated.

He replayed her words. Sacrifice, being stuck with her. She was worried about her place here, maybe even about his attraction to her. The thought struck him hard and he thanked God he hadn't continued to match Alec whisky for whisky, or he may have missed it.

He exhaled. "Nay, lass, ye have no reason to fear mistresses." He moved his lips closer to her ear. "I've thought only of ye since I warmed yer back in the tent each night on the way north."

She tipped her head to see his expression. Did she search for sincerity?

"I was quite angry about that," she murmured.

He tried to keep his neutral expression. "Ye did a fine job of letting me know."

"You're lucky my wolf didn't eat you."

He chuckled, feeling a warmth flow back into him at her lighter voice. When had her happiness become so important? He wrapped her in a hug.

His grin faltered at her still-rigid stance, and he inhaled the sweet scent of her hair. This was not an easy fix. "I am sorry, Meg. I should have told ye, let ye know everything and then decide on yer own. Perhaps…I worried ye wouldn't choose my plan."

"I trusted you," she whispered.

He brushed the top of her head with his chin as he stared, unseeing, across the winter landscape. "Can ye forgive me for capturing ye to force the peace? For not telling ye everything from the start?" He held still, his chin resting on the soft waves. What if she couldn't ever really forgive him? His gut tightened as he waited.

She nuzzled into his chest. "I suppose I can."

His chest expanded and he kissed the top of her head. He felt her body relax into his embrace. A beginning.

...

Meg held Caden's hand as they walked into the great hall the next morning. Aunt Rachel and Uncle Alec sat at the long table with Ewan and Kenneth. Ann and Jonet stood with Evelyn, who held several more links of dried flower garland.

"And just when we thought ye'd sleep the day away," Ewan called. "Food for the couple. They must be famished."

Meg blushed but kept her head high. She had nothing to be ashamed of—that was, as long as her screams hadn't carried below. Just the thought made her stomach clench. They sat at the table and Evelyn brought out some oat porridge and venison.

"Never seen ye sleep past dawn," Evelyn said to Caden. She winked at Meg. The woman actually winked! Perhaps she'd forgiven her for being a witch after she'd healed Angus and helped end the feud.

Caden's leg rubbed against Meg's under the table. "Where are the men?" he asked Ewan.

"Hunting for more game."

"With the herds returning, we don't need to send out as many hunting parties. I'd rather keep the men close in case the English decide to brave the cold," Caden said. "We need to be ready when Boswell decides to show up."

"Perhaps a response to his letter requesting Meg would be best," Kenneth said.

"Where to send it?" Caden asked.

"You think he's close?" Meg asked.

"I do. He thinks ye have something that could hurt him."

Meg's gaze switched to Colin. "We need to retrieve those letters. Are you certain they are still up in that cave?"

"As far as I know," Colin said. "They're well hidden. I doubt anyone else has found them, especially without the map." He referred to the key. "The other trails are deadly."

Meg's heart sped. "With those letters, Boswell can't touch any of us."

"Could ye lead us there?" Caden asked Colin.

"It's an easy walk up hill…for a Highlander."

"I could ride Pippen," Meg offered.

"And there's a waterfall in front of the cave entrance."

"Walls of hard water. The phrase is in her journal." She glanced up remembering. "*An fuar uamh le moran na frithrathaidean agus an blath cridhe anns am meadhon*," she recited slowly. "A cold cave with many paths and a warm heart in the middle."

"The waterfall is difficult to get past," Colin said. "Even in the summer, when the water doesn't freeze the skin from yer bones. By this time of year, it's fed by snow above on the mountain. Soon it will freeze solid until late spring."

"We also need to travel to Munro Castle before more snow makes it impossible to move the herds and bring the grain wagon," Ewan said.

"I think I agreed to too much last eve," Alec grumbled. "Giving grain when we had nothing to do with the fire." He shook his head. Rachel pressed her finger to her lips in a signal to hush, making Alec frown.

"Says he had nothing to do with it," said Bruce, "though Angus here saw him."

"That's a lie!" Alec shouted, his eyes narrowing on Angus, who turned a mottled shade of red and set his tankard down. "The bastard lies because Rachel chose me over him."

Rachel let out a loud sigh. "I think my husband should help lead the herds over, don't you think, Alec? You get cranky when you're cooped up inside too long."

"I get cranky, woman, when people lie about me!"

Angus walked down the length of the table toward Caden. Bruce followed and Kenneth straightened as if the three were one, standing against Alec. Alec's chest puffed up even more, and the tension crackled in the air. Meg's gaze moved between sides.

"Perhaps we need more whisky," Rachel said. "Bloody egos."

Angus glanced at Alec's fuming face, but focused on Caden. "I...that night...I saw someone out by the field with a torch."

"A Munro," Bruce insisted.

"Liar!" Alec threw back and began to slide his reclaimed sword free. Searc stood beside him.

Caden's hand slapped hard down on the table, making most everyone jump. "Let Angus finish."

Meg touched Angus's hand. He certainly had something to tell. The man's blood raced with almost dangerous speed through his aging veins. His stomach twisted and contracted, as did his bladder and bowels. The muscles in his eyes clenched and Meg could see them twitch every so often.

"Yes," she said encouragingly, "let him speak." *Before he explodes*.

Angus swallowed. "I've been meaning to say...well, I couldn't see who it was very well...not at all, actually."

"Ye said it was Gregor Munro," Kenneth said.

"Alec's cousin," Rachel added for Meg.

"I said I thought it looked like Gregor," Angus clarified.

"Gregor wasn't there," Alec said.

"He would never do something like that without my father's order," Searc chimed in.

"Now that I think about it, the man didn't have Gregor's height." Angus squinted and met Caden's eyes. "I was mistaken. I don't know who set the blaze, but there was someone with a torch."

"Well now," Alec said, his tone coming down two levels. "Angus Riley telling the truth."

"Thank you," Rachel added softly with a small smile to Angus, who turned a deeper shade of red.

"And I'm sorry I stabbed ye, Rachel," Angus added.

"You stabbed my aunt Rachel?" Meg asked. What was their history?

Rachel bowed her head. "An accident, a long time ago. Your mother saved me."

Alec seemed to growl and Rachel ran her hand along his arm. Could she calm him with a touch?

"Should be apologizing to me." Alec ran his hand along the scabbard at his waist as if he needed only a flinch from Angus to run him through.

"Angus, Bruce, Kenneth." Caden interrupted the growing unease. "Let's discuss who else may have started that fire. Then we'll plan to travel to Munro Castle. Colin, we'll discuss retrieval of the letters later tonight."

Meg rose from the table. "And I had better check on Sarah and the twins."

"Could ye bring Isabelle's journal back down?" Colin asked. "I'd like to see it…her handwriting again."

"We can pick out her clues in the discrepancies, even though we no longer need them." Meg sighed. They were so close to the letters, yet it would take a small army to reach them safely.

"Very smart, my sister," Rachel commented as she followed Colin toward the hearth.

"And brave," Colin added. "And so is her daughter."

Meg walked to the steps. Brave? Barely. So much had changed in her world over the last weeks. She conjured the little blue orb to illuminate the steps as the torch had been doused in the stairwell. "To think you could do more than light my path," she whispered to the orb. The sound of voices at the bottom of the steps caused her to douse the light and glance over her shoulder. "Brave? Not very," she said and hurried up the steps using one hand on the wall as a guide in the darkness.

As she neared the top where the steps became shallow and more treacherous, her foot came down on round pebbles. She yelped and wobbled, nearly losing her balance. Several pebbles plunked down the winding granite steps, but Meg fell forward, catching the top step on her hands and knees.

She steadied herself on the landing and illuminated the steps. Round pebbles lay even along the top two steps. She frowned. Not again. In the chaos of the last two days she'd forgotten to tell Caden about the rocks left before. Was someone really trying to hurt her? Or was she just being paranoid? After all, her marriage to Caden had just saved them from starvation.

...

As Meg entered Sarah's room and closed the door behind her, a cloaked figure moved down the corridor to the steps. The figure bent in silence and tumbled the pebbles back out into an even layer across the step, then hurried below.

...

Meg pinched her fingers and drew them apart to form the ball of blue light to illuminate the stone steps. Her heart sped up slightly and she fought the urge to worry over what Caden would think of her light. "The pebbles were left on three different steps at different times."

"I'll post a guard," Caden said as he brushed a hand across the steps where little rocks were pushed aside.

"Do you think someone isn't happy that I'm here? First the mushrooms, then the pebbles." Maybe it was her healing. She hadn't been hiding her newly discovered abilities and word had spread about Sarah's son.

He didn't answer. "I don't want ye walking the castle by yerself."

"At all? I'll be a prisoner again."

Caden sighed long. "Ye were never a prisoner."

"Mm-hmmm."

Caden pushed through the door to their room. A cheerful fire blazed in the hearth, washing back the shadows with splashes of orange and yellow about the room.

"You knew we were coming up here soon?" she asked. They'd been eating and talking with Munros and Macbains and Colin. There were lots of plans to be made and the snow wasn't making anything easy.

"If ye hadn't asked soon, I was going to just carry ye up anyway."

His words teased but his tone was serious. She touched his arm and sensed the tension. He was worried, too.

Caden's eyes held hers. He swept his shirt off over his head. The leather thong fell away from his hair, allowing it to wave down around his square jaw. Meg's gaze roamed over the chiseled muscles of his torso and the low-slung kilt across his narrow hips. Intense and purposeful, his movements made him resemble a hunter stalking his prize. A silver Scottish cross lay near the hollow of his throat and reflected the fire against his tanned skin. He was rugged and powerful.

He caught her chin and gave her a kiss. Meg nearly flinched at the tightness in his neck and shoulders.

She moved to the bed and patted the furs next to her. "Sit."

When he did she twirled her finger. "Turn around." She placed hands on his shoulders and began to rub. "Relax."

"Warriors don't relax."

"Maybe that's why warriors go around frowning so much. They all have aches in their heads."

"Will ye use the light on me?"

"Not unless you really want me to and then I might be too tired to…I just mean to work the tension a bit," she said and kneaded hard into the muscles of his broad shoulders. Hours of sword play had sculpted his body into an amazing display of strength. Meg's gaze slid down his bare back, smooth skin over steel and sinew.

Caden groaned low as she worked some of the knots around his neck. "Where did ye learn to do that?"

"Farmers get very sore muscles from working the land." She forced her attention back to Caden's bunched shoulders. "Uncle Harold liked me to work the knots out of his back. Said my little knuckles could bully the knots right flat."

Uncle Harold and Aunt Mary must be so worried about her. Guilt added to her fear that they'd been hurt or suffering.

Meg sniffed and her hands moved lower down his bare back. She rubbed hard across the underlying tension down his sides, stopping at an old scar. The tip of her finger traced the six-inch puckered line. "You must have been young."

"Aye, ten and three, I think."

"How did it happen?"

"A Munro blade."

"You could have died. You were just a boy."

Caden turned, catching her hand. "Boys died, my brother died. He was just sixteen." He cupped her face and gave her a quick kiss. "When he died and I became the heir to my father, I vowed that I would find a way to end the feud. I didn't know that I would win such an amazing lass in the process."

He brushed her hair back from her shoulders, his thumbs running small circles along her collarbone. A shiver ran through Meg that had nothing to do with the chill in the air, and everything to do with the heat in Caden's eyes.

His gaze moved across her body. "Lass, ye have far too many clothes on."

Meg wiggled off her slippers, letting them fall to the floor. She moved up onto her knees, then reached behind through the closure of her skirt to untie the lacing holding up her stiff farthingale. The layers dropped with a *swoosh*. Caden stopped his advance at the sound. She pushed up onto the furs and leaned back into the pillows at the headboard. When he didn't move, she untied her garters and worked her stockings down her legs. She dug her toes into the soft pelts.

Caden's eyes traveled the length of her skirt, over her bodice, and up to her eyes. Meg wondered if she appeared as hungry as he did. The silent charge of their stare twisted through her, coiling in her stomach and below. She drew a tentative breath and reached for the bottom hem near her ankles. She gathered the layers of material in her fingers and inched them upward so that they slid along her bare legs. Inch by inch she let the folds tickle the sensitive skin until the voluminous skirts bunched around her waist, exposing her pale thighs against the dark furs. Caden's eyes opened just a hint more and dipped to follow the line of her long legs, his roguish grin fading into one of amazement.

"I thought Highlanders were never surprised," Meg said, though the tease came out breathless.

"Rarely, lass." His voice was low, rough.

His hot gaze traveled up to the dark cave her skirts had created at the vee of her thighs. Meg's fingers released her skirts where they sat at her waist. Deftly, she untied the top of her bodice where the swell of breasts pushed upward, nearly to overflowing from the tightness of the ties below.

Caden rested a finger along her ankle and trailed it up her leg to the knee as he leaned across the bed. His warm palm cupped her bare knee, and as he bent over, his hand slid down the slope of her thigh. He kissed her, and his hand gripped the sensitive bend connecting her leg to her hip. He fingered the satin edge of her straining neckline, untying the lacing at the top of her bodice.

Hot kisses along her neck made Meg inhale and she tilted back to give him access to her flushed skin. As her shoulders pressed back into the pillows, the supple flesh broke over the satin scrap of a collar. Caden groaned as her breasts swelled out into full view, perched before him. He cupped them both, his mouth finding one nipple while his thumb strummed the other.

Meg's heart pulsed, spreading fire down through her loins as he sucked on one breast and then the other. Her fingers tangled in his hair and she moaned softly, her hips rising on the wave of passion. Her body trembled with heat, and she moved her legs, wanting more, needing more.

"Caden," she rasped, and raised her leg to rub against the hardness through his kilt. "I need you in me." She moaned as the sensations of his mouth sent a direct assault against her core, drenching her with need.

Caden's hand found its way past her many layers of skirts. She cried out as he thrust two fingers inside. "Och, lass, ye are soaked."

"More, Caden," she cried, wanting to be swept up with the force of him inside her. The tide of passion pushed aside any embarrassment and she reached down to find him. He stepped back and dropped the kilt from his hips.

Her mouth went dry at the sight of his huge, muscular, warrior body. "Don't hold back." Her legs spread against the fabric. "I need you."

In a heartbeat, he grasped her to him, lifting and turning her around to face away, just off the side of the bed. She wondered if her legs would hold her as he worked to untie the back lacings of her skirts. The ties broke in his hands, leaving the gown still attached around her waist.

"Bloody hell."

"Leave them." She pressed back into his hard body.

Caden reached around to her front, cupping her breasts

while he kissed the column of her neck. He brushed her hair to one side and teased the tender flesh of her nape. Meg's legs wobbled as she let out a low moan.

He steadied her by pushing her legs against the edge of the bed. His hands bunched the layers of fabric upward until chilled air slid across her backside. Caden leaned against her ear. "Open yer legs, bride."

She leaned forward to brace against the high bed. His fingers found her once more and he teased the flesh until she panted.

"Please," she begged.

He pressed against her globes seeking entry, and she arched, tilting back into him. He thrust deep, edging her toward the precipice. The fabric rustled as he pushed into and out of her straining body. She moaned. He reached around her again to pinch and pull at her nipples, lifting her breasts as he kissed and sucked along her neck. New sensations raged through her body from the new angle.

Over and over Caden plunged into her as she strained back to meet him. He reached up through the skirts to find her and rubbed until Meg could stand no longer.

She cried out as the world shattered, bending forward onto her hands on the bed. Caden followed her over the precipice as he pumped into her from behind, his roar filling the room.

...

A lone wolf howled from somewhere on the mountains behind the lit castle, sending a chill down Gilbert Davidson's back, which he ignored. Absently, he stilled his horse that pranced and twitched his ears where they stood on the lonely moor.

"I'm telling ye, she's practically chained to the Macbain's side with fifty warriors surrounding her, watching everything."

The hooded figure sat tall and lean on horseback in the shadows, like a wraith waiting to take someone's soul. "What you're telling me is that you failed."

Sweat broke out on Gilbert's brow despite the freezing Highland wind slapping his cheeks. "Simon, tell him how we were followed," he said, raising his hand to indicate Druim. "I feared for our lives in there. I think Caden found out we burned their harvest."

"Watched the entire time," Simon added and bobbed his head with vigor.

"Did you restrain the woman who's working for you?" the man asked, his profile and horse as still as the mountains before him.

Gilbert pursed his lips. "I've sent word that I want Meg alive. No more cut saddles."

"You sent word, but have not confirmed that she will adhere to your order."

"I…uh…" The heat rose in Gilbert's face and his gaze dropped to the mane of his horse. "I couldn't get close to her."

They were bloody lucky to just get out of Druim. He'd heard about the damned truce, which would make annihilating his neighbor trickier. With English troops and weapons and mercenary muscle he just might be able to finish what his da had quietly started, the absorption of the Macbain territory all the way to Loch Tuinn. The land was rich, fertile, and had a pristine water source. Druim castle was by far better fortified and more comfortable than the drafty old keep on Davidson land. Then maybe he'd expand his empire over Munro territory as well. His English companion certainly had no love for the Munros and could supply him with more weapons and resources.

"I should have sent Girshmel to take her," the Englishman said in a clipped tone. "I'd have her now."

"More likely Girshmel would have been shot on sight if the lass's wolf didn't eat him first," Gilbert said in defense.

The cloaked man turned toward Gilbert. His dark eyes glowed with the reflected moonlight that washed his face. Gilbert's breath caught against the lump in his throat. Even though he outweighed the man by far, the power the Englishman wielded turned his stomach cold.

"The lass remembers Girshmel from Loch Tuinn," Gilbert sputtered, and wiped the sweat from his forehead with the back of a sleeve. "She wanted me to tell him that her beast survived. I don't know how she knew he was with me."

"Did you see her wolf?" the man asked.

"Nay," he answered, glancing over the surrounding moorland. "From what Girshmel says it's the biggest beast he's ever seen. And if it survived, well, there must have been magic involved."

"I have no doubt that Meg is a witch like her mother and her aunt."

"She doesn't look like a witch." Gilbert glanced back at the castle. "I would hate to see such a luscious morsel burn." The man's stare made Gilbert swallow hard. "They say she's Colin Macleod's daughter," he rushed to add.

The man lowered the hood from his head and leaned forward across the black horse until he was within inches of Gilbert's nose. Gilbert didn't move but stared back into the lit black orbs. "Meg Boswell is my daughter. Her life and all her possessions belong to me."

Black and cold, the words slid down through Gilbert as though they had come from Satan's own mouth. He nodded. He'd have signed the cross before him, but doubted it would protect him. After all, would God really help him survive the deal he'd made with the Devil?

Chapter Twelve

5 May 1518 — Devil's Bit Scabious: slender plant, can grow up to the waist. Most of the root seems to have been bitten away. Legend says that the devil himself found it and bit it to destroy the plant in envy of its goodness, but no matter what the devil did, the plant still grows everywhere even with a stumpy root. Collect whole plant in early fall for drying. Brew for coughs, fevers, and internal pain. Purifies blood. Used as a wash externally, it heals skin eruptions and spots. A heated wash can be used to rid the head of scruf, sores, and flakes. Large doses will expel worms from the body.

Found in many places, in open meadows and on wild heaths.

"Caden's not here?" Meg glanced around the freshly swept great hall as if she might see him lurking in the shadows.

"Nay," Angus said from his seat by the fire. "There's a storm brewing, and it might bring a foot of snow. Caden left with Alec and Colin at dawn to bring the herds from Munro lands before it starts."

"More snow." Meg lowered down onto a stool near the hearth where the three elders sat.

"Och, winter is just getting started, lass." Bruce spoke around a bit of hay he had tucked between his teeth.

"I thought we'd ride to the third mountain today," Meg said.

"Not with that storm coming and too much to do moving the herds," Angus said. "Can't be helped. Yer letters will have to wait. At least they're snug in that cave."

Evelyn brought over a mug of warm milk and some bread to dunk.

"Thank you." Meg opened her eyes wide. "Please tell me my aunt didn't ride away this morning, too, without me being able to say good-bye."

"Nay, Rachel is above, helping Sarah wash the twins," Evelyn said.

Meg dipped the crusty bread in the warm milk. "After I break my fast, I'll help and then have a tour of the kitchens and larders if you have time. Even with food coming in, we will need to be careful. I should know how little we are starting with."

"Bright lass," Kenneth said.

"Wise and frugal," Angus boasted.

"Knew it the moment I saw her," Bruce said.

Meg had just finished the small meal when a horn sounded from the bailey. Three long blasts. All three elders stood, their gazes bouncing around the large room.

"There's no one else to protect her," Kenneth said. "Where's my sword?"

"Protect who?" Meg asked. "From what?"

Bruce pulled his sword from its scabbard along his side.

"You don't carry your sword? Are you already an old man?"

"God's teeth, there must be a sword around here," Kenneth said.

"Why do you all need swords?" Meg asked, watching nervously as Angus hefted a war axe down from above the mantle. She worried for a moment that its weight would topple him.

Kenneth jogged from the back of the great hall, brandishing a short sword. "To protect ye, lass."

"Protect me? From whom?"

The front door banged opened and the wind swirled in, shifting the fresh rushes across the floor like a hundred invisible feet.

Ewan strode in. "Meg, ye need to go upstairs."

She tried to step around the elders even as her heart hammered in response to Ewan's tone. "Why?"

"The English have come," Rachel said from the stairwell.

"Is Rowland Boswell with them?" Meg asked, turning between her aunt and Ewan.

"He rides in front," Ewan said.

"That bloody bastard," Rachel murmured as she walked up and linked arms with Meg.

Meg shook her head even though her stomach twisted. She rubbed a hand against it absently. "I won't hide from him."

"I prefer he not know ye are here," Ewan replied.

"Of course the English pig knows she's here." Angus spit on the rushes. "Or he wouldn't be riding over to pay us a little visit. Convenient, too, that most of the warriors, including Caden, are away."

"Aye, as if someone told him," Kenneth added and glanced again around the room as if his sword would suddenly appear.

Ewan watched Donald stride back inside. "More reason to lock ye away, Meg."

"He's asked for an audience," Donald said. "Says he brings Meg's aunt and uncle from England."

Meg gasped. "They're with him?"

"There's an older couple with him, a man and a woman. They're rather chilled through," Donald said.

Meg's hands went to her neck. Her poor uncle and aunt were traveling in this cold. Aunt Mary wasn't frail by any measure, but she wasn't used to Highland wind and snow. She had to get them inside.

"Ewan." Meg's voice rang with authority. "Let them in. I doubt Boswell provided them with appropriate clothing."

"Milady," Ewan started. "Meg—"

"Do you think he will just throw me over his shoulder and carry me away?" Meg broke in. "Would you let him just take me?"

"Never," Ewan swore, his eyes hard as flint.

"Then just let Boswell and my aunt and uncle in. Not their whole army." Meg turned to Rachel. "Do you think the villagers are in danger?"

"He only brought a group of ten men," Donald said.

"We hardly have that many left here." Ewan spat and clenched his fist over the hilt of his sword.

Bruce cleared his throat and brandished his ancient blade.

Ewan said, indicating the three old warriors, "Not including the three war lords in here."

"I'm sure you can defend me as long as I stay inside," Meg said.

"You would still be safer above stairs."

Meg locked eyes with Ewan. "I will not hide from that man, nor will I let him think that I am fearful of his accusations."

Fury burned hot inside as she thought about her aunt and uncle in Boswell's clutches. She wanted to be downstairs when they came inside in case they needed help. And truth be told, she wanted to see Rowland Boswell—needed to see him, the man of her nightmares. She needed to see that he was just a vicious man without any true power over her.

"Let them in, Ewan." And to soften her order, she touched his arm. "Then don't leave my side."

Ewan stared down at her fingers against his sleeve and sighed. He pivoted on one heel and he and Donald marched back out into the cold wind.

Meg turned to Rachel. "If they're hurt, will you help me?"

Rachel moved forward and squeezed Meg's hand. "Of course."

Long minutes ticked by. Evelyn walked into the great hall and stopped. "Why are ye all staring at the door?"

"Didn't ye hear the horn?" Angus asked, barely taking his eyes off the door.

"Nay, I was in the root cellar, taking count of last year's vegetables."

"The English are at our gates," Kenneth said.

Evelyn passed the sign of the cross across her bosom. "And you're going to fight them?" Her voice squeaked as she watched Angus heft the ax.

"No one is fighting anyone," Meg said. Luckily, none of them could tell from her voice that her pulse raced like thundering horses. "The group of English is small. Boswell has brought my aunt and uncle from England and wishes to talk with me."

"Holy Mother Mary!" Worry pinched Evelyn's face as if Meg had just said Satan had requested an audience. "I'll let Cook know that we may have to defend ourselves." Before Meg could stop her she raced to the kitchens, probably to sharpen the knives.

The solid oak doors rattled and Ewan pushed into the entryway. Two people shuffled in behind him, followed by a man of medium height draped in black wool and furs.

Meg moved forward, but Ewan held up a warning hand.

"Let them come inside to the hearth," Rachel suggested.

Ewan led the swathed, snow-covered people to the blazing hearth, where they turned from one side to the other before they began to uncoil faded plaids from around their bodies. Meg watched them hobble about, unwrapping to reveal the two people who had raised her.

"Aunt Mary! Uncle Harold!" Meg ran across the room, hugging their wet, chilled bodies. As she rubbed their arms she sent a small bit of magic through them, raising their body temperatures. She was quick and discreet, and ignored the man in black who stood apart, slowly exposing his expensive English clothes as he too took off his wet apparel.

"Meg," Mary crooned as she held her close. "I thought never to see you again."

"I thought you'd gone south," Harold said loudly and

winked at her. "Boswell swore you were up north."

"They came at my insistence," the man in black said as he straightened his courtly jacket and walked toward the hearth. "Hello, daughter. You are lovely, your appearance so very much like your mother."

Meg turned, eyes raking down him. He was lanky but with a heavy lidded appearance of someone well fed and not concerned with his station in life. He walked with authority, head slightly tilted upward so that his dark, close-set eyes peered down past a hawkish nose. He was neither handsome nor ugly. And the power he radiated seemed to slow down everyone's movements, as if they were afraid to offend. Meg knew the people in the room didn't care what he thought about them, but they still seemed to hush while they watched the proceedings.

"Then you, sir, do not remember my mother, as we look very little alike," Meg said, staring back into those dark, unblinking eyes. "I favor my father…Colin Macleod."

The man's face did not change. Only a slight narrowing of his eyes sent a warning chill down Meg's back, but she kept her stare even.

"Colin Macleod," Boswell said through thin lips, "was a rejected suitor. Isabelle came to me a maid." A small drop of spit flew from his mouth when he'd said her mother's name. "I am your legal father and guardian."

"I will not discuss my mother's virginal state with you, sir," Meg said, her anger building. Perhaps her mother had healed her maidenhead when she agreed to return with her father.

She turned back to her aunt and uncle who both stood

wide-eyed, their backs to the flames. "I thank you for bringing my aunt and uncle. If you have no further business, I will take them above to rest. You and your men may take your leave."

"Ah, but I do have further business, daughter," Boswell said.

Ewan took a step closer to Meg, his hand on his hilt. "Your business is with Caden Macbain, husband and legal guardian to milady."

"And we both know that he is away today." Boswell peeled a pair of wet leather gloves from his tapered fingers. The sight of them stretched out with overly long fingernails twisted in Meg's stomach. Her poor mother had to endure those fingers against her skin.

"I speak for Caden when he is away," Ewan said, a dangerous glint in his eyes.

"You are not blood to Meg." Boswell said that as if that made a difference.

"Harold and I are her blood, Rowland," Rachel said. Her sneer was obvious and plainly said that Rowland was *not* linked to Meg by bloodlines.

Boswell's head swiveled toward Rachel. "Hello, Rachel. Amazed to see you still alive up here in this heathen country."

"State yer business and depart," Ewan interrupted.

Boswell turned back to the group before the fire. "Meg, you certainly have a lot of defenders." He glanced around the room. "Where is that beast of yours? I hear you tamed a wolf? Not something a God-fearing young woman would spend her time doing. What other unnatural activities do you perform?"

"You are not here to discuss how I spend my day," Meg said, ignoring his insinuation.

He *tsk*ed. "So hostile. I but wanted to reunite with my daughter."

"I am sorry that you came all this way, and dragged my aunt and uncle with you. We have now met and you can return," Meg said.

"I have something to discuss with you. Alone."

All three elders stepped up behind Boswell with their weapons drawn, and Ewan moved slightly in front of Meg.

"If you wish to discuss something with me, you can discuss it amongst us all," Meg said.

Boswell's stare penetrated her, but she refused to even blink. His lips grew thinner. "Very well." He turned, glaring at the elders until they moved over, and walked to a nearby chair to sit and pulled a folded parchment from his jacket. The Tudor seal sat heavy upon it. "This is a dispatch from King Henry requesting your presence in London."

The hairs on the back of Meg's neck rose. She swallowed against her suddenly dry mouth. *Normal. Sound normal. He doesn't have any power here.* "Why would so great a king request my presence?"

Boswell produced a cold half-smile. "Because he values me and I requested it."

"And why do *you* want me to go to London?"

"I have an Englishman of good standing who will marry you, after I make certain you are not tainted by witchcraft nor heresy."

Meg's stomach squeezed as her pulse raced at his casual reference to torture and forced marriage. She fought to keep a still, relaxed stance. Oh, but she'd been right to run. He truly was a monster.

"I am already married. A priest officiated and blessed the union. The contract has been recorded and sent along proper channels. And it has been consummated."

"I did not agree to this marriage and therefore it is neither legal nor binding."

"The marriage was consummated and sworn to before God," Meg said. "The union is binding before the Lord. And since you are *not* my father, it doesn't matter if you agreed to it or not."

"The wedding was witnessed by over a hundred people," Rachel added. "You cannot undo it."

"The king will grant an annulment," Boswell said, his eyes snapping at Rachel. He turned back to Meg and smiled tightly. "Or not, but you have been commanded to London to stand before your king. To refuse to go is treason."

Meg pulled in a deep breath to chase off the sparkles of light at her periphery. "I would not suffer to offend my good king in any way…but I will not go with you to London. I am not a fool."

Boswell stood to his full height. "You are a fool if you think you can hide from King Henry's wrath up here in the north. He will send English troops to your holding if I ask him. He will strip away your lands, throw you from your homes, hang your treasonous people for harboring a traitor if she refuses to return to England."

Nausea pummeled Meg's middle. Good Lord! Would people die because of her?

"King James will never allow it," Ewan said in defense.

Boswell let loose a staccato laugh. "Your King James is no match to the great King Henry VIII. I also understand that your king is suspicious of the Macbains supporting the Protestant reformation. He will support Henry in an effort to keep relations cordial."

Meg's heart hammered against her ribs. Boswell meant every word he spat. She could see it in his stance, his face. And she had no way of knowing how much influence he had over the English monarch or what lies had been told to the Scottish king.

What if Boswell incited Henry to massacre the Macbains? And the Munros and Macleods? She could be responsible for all their deaths. She also knew in her wildly pumping heart that if she went with Boswell she would meet the same fate as her mother, or possibly worse.

Boswell's gaze fastened onto Meg's. "Do your duty to these people, as your mother was dutiful when her father brought her home. Come back with me to England and ask your King Henry if you may marry here in the north. He is a good and just king."

"Who knows nothing of me but what you've poisoned him with," Meg responded.

Boswell's mouth remained grim but a hint of victory shown in his eyes. "Ah, but he will get to know you. If your words are true, you have nothing to fear."

Meg's mind raced. This was a decision of life and death and not just hers. What would Caden do if he were here? Probably slice Boswell's head off. Of course, killing him outright could cause even more problems. She needed a weapon, one just as lethal as Caden's blade, but without the bloodshed.

Unfortunately, all she had were the bits of information from her mother's desperate note and Colin's memory. However, Boswell didn't know that.

Meg summoned a sweet and thoughtful expression. "If I return with you, King Henry will also get to know *you*."

Boswell's confident expression softened. "He already knows me."

Meg kicked a charred piece of peat into the hearth. "Not the Rowland Boswell you wish him to know." She turned to him. "The Rowland Boswell who conspired to kill him when he was a young and untried king. The Rowland Boswell who even now may still be plotting to assassinate him."

Boswell's frown sharpened into a sneer. She'd just poked a sleepy viper with a stick. The man nearly hissed. "You spew lies like your mother. And she burned for them."

At the open threat, Ewan stepped in front of Meg and slid his sword free. She placed her hand on his arm and stepped to the side, almost as if she were playing a child's game of seek.

"Lies?" she asked. "The ones you wrote in your own hand? I wonder if our good and just king will see it that way."

"Show me these letters written in my own hand."

Meg created an expression of innocent confusion to barely hide the victory surging inside her. "Letters?" She tilted her head. "Did I say letters?"

Boswell pursed his lips tighter.

Meg stepped out from behind Ewan's large body and walked closer to Boswell, showing him that she didn't fear him. "Rowland Boswell, I am Meg Macleod Macbain of Druim

Castle. I am daughter to Colin Macleod, chief of the Macleods. I am niece to Alec Munro, chief of the Munros. And before God and government I am wife to Caden Macbain, chief of the powerful Macbain clan of Druim. I am nothing to you any longer except the person who could bring about your fall and subsequent traitor's death if you threaten any of my people."

Boswell's face burned redder with each word. His lips pulled back to show even, brown teeth, and his hands fisted at his sides.

Meg took another step toward him, leaning slightly forward.

"You are not welcome here." She lowered her voice to a seething whisper. "And your threats against my very extended family have made these rugged, cold climes very dangerous for a delicate man like you. Rowland Boswell, I suggest you return to England immediately."

With that, she turned her back on him and strode to her aunt and uncle, who were still thawing near the hearth. She didn't miss the pride-filled glances of Angus, Kenneth, and Bruce, who all puffed up like roosters. If she weren't so shaken, she'd have laughed.

She took up Mary's cold, cracked hands and rubbed them in her own, though her own were probably just as cold.

Boswell's shrill voice rang throughout the room. "This is not over, Meg. If you don't come with me, Henry will send back troops ordered to destroy everything in their path. They will not read false letters you've concocted."

The words made sense, but the power had ebbed from his voice. Meg willed herself not to respond. She would set it all before Caden and they needed those letters to see what exactly lay in those caves. From Boswell's reaction, it seemed her mother's letter had been true. Her mother had saved King Henry's life.

"Ewan, escort Lord Boswell out," Meg said with the authority of a great lady of the house.

"Harold, Mary, come," Boswell ordered, and Meg's hands clasped around Mary's arm.

Boswell had obviously forced them to come north to use them in some way against her. To persuade her to listen to him? To trade their freedom for her acquiescence? He'd made a mistake by bringing them into Druim. She wouldn't give them up.

"Nay. They stay," Meg said, her eyes locking onto Mary's.

"If they stay, then they are traitors, too," Boswell said.

She turned around. "And if they go, you will freeze them to death on the return to England." She was close to the cracking point, where anger would blend with exhaustion, tipping her into tears. And she couldn't weep, not in front of the devil.

Rachel stepped around them, over to Harold, and clasped his hand. "I am so delighted that you and your wife have come to visit me and Alec. I've been asking all these years, and you finally came. We will throw a banquet in your honor, brother." She turned to Boswell. "I think your good and just king would have no law against a subject visiting his own sister in a peaceful country."

Uncle Harold stood taller next to Rachel. "I do not think to flatter myself to wonder if my good king would even notice that I am gone from his kingdom to visit my kin. I am but a humble farmer and pleased to visit my sister until the roads south are more hospitable. For the safety of my wife."

Meg could feel Mary's muscles relax.

Boswell turned on his heel and grabbed his wrappings. Without a single farewell, he strode out of the hall, Ewan close on his steps.

As the door slammed in the entryway, Meg moved over to a chair and collapsed into it, shaking. Tears threatened, angry tears that she couldn't do more, frustrated tears that she was a woman and couldn't take out her vengeance on Boswell's wickedness.

The three elders stood before her and bowed.

"Definitely the daughter of a Highlander," Angus said with pride thick in his brogue.

Kenneth struck a fist against his heart. "The fire in ye, lass, why, it made me proud."

"If that devil knew ye had a bow, he'd be watching his backside right now as he scurries away," Bruce added, and Angus laughed in agreement.

Meg gave a nervous exhale and pressed the back of her hand against her mouth.

"Isabelle," Rachel said, her eyes tearing up, "is smiling right now from heaven."

With the wet sparkle to Rachel's eyes and the mention of her mother, Meg's own tears wouldn't stay down. They spilled out on her cheek and the four elderly men started poking in their pockets for handkerchiefs.

Uncle Harold found one first. The square was a bit soggy from the snow, but Meg took it and wiped her eyes. Angus handed another to Rachel, who took it gratefully.

Evelyn poked her head back in the room, holding a long knife. "Are the English gone?"

"Aye," Angus called out. "Our Meg here scared that devil Boswell off. Didn't even need us."

"Oh, I definitely needed all of you," Meg said and stood to hug Mary again. "Now let's get you two into some dry clothes."

Mary took Meg's hands. "I am so proud of you, child. Oh my! You've grown so much in the last month. You're even wed!"

"I've so missed you," Meg sniffed.

"No tears," Ewan commanded as he came back into the room. He grabbed her in a fierce bear hug, swinging her around. Meg squeaked.

"Hurrah, Meg!" he cheered and set her down. "Now ye're definitely one of us," he said. "Tough and clever as a Highlander, snubbing yer pretty nose at the English."

Harold cleared his throat.

"Present company excepted," Ewan said without breaking stride. "Wait until Caden hears. Yer words at the end." He shivered dramatically. "I still have chills."

Meg couldn't help but laugh at his enthusiasm. "I don't know, Ewan. I may have just yanked the devil's tail."

"Oh, but he certainly asked for such," Mary said. "The bloody devil."

"Mary," Harold said.

"He treated us terrible," she continued, unhindered by Harold's warning. "Threatened us if we didn't go with him, fed us so little, I swear Harold lost ten pounds. Even when we stayed at that drafty old castle, we couldn't get warm."

Ewan's jubilation faded. "At which castle did ye stay? I

don't know of any abandoned castles near Druim."

"Oh, 'twas fully occupied," Mary said.

Ewan turned to Harold.

Harold answered the unasked question. "Gilbert Davidson."

The name squeezed like dank meat in Meg's stomach.

"No wonder Boswell knows so much," Rachel said. "That Caden and most of the men were away today. That you were here and married. He must have known before, even when he sent the letters to each of us." She turned to Harold. "How long have you been at Davidson's castle?"

"A fortnight," Harold answered.

Meg's breath caught. "You've been here since a week after I arrived. He must have received news immediately that I was in the Highlands." She turned to Ewan. "Could Girshmel have told Gilbert and he have contacted Boswell?"

Angus rubbed his beard. "Gilbert wouldn't have known yer worth or that Boswell was trying to find ye so soon unless he already had dealings with the man."

"What would Boswell want with a contact up in the Highlands?" Meg asked. "I don't know of any business or trading that he'd be involved with."

"He must know the letters are up here somewhere," Kenneth said.

"Perhaps he's been keeping an eye on me," Rachel suggested. "Only the devil knows the mind of one of his demons."

Evelyn made the sign of the cross and the room stood motionless for a long moment while everyone's minds spun.

Mary shivered. "Evelyn, do we have another room to house

my aunt and uncle?"

"They can share my room," Rachel said. "Alec is gone and I will follow him as soon as he returns. I have a banquet to prepare for you two."

Meg laughed. "Beware, she says she will plan a banquet, but let's see if it actually happens."

Rachel turned to Meg. "Ah, but you had a much grander celebration here." She looped her arm in Mary's and gestured to Harold. "Come up to your rooms and I'll tell you what amazing events have been happening since Meg came to Druim."

"She makes it sound like a story," Meg said, and followed her.

"I hear Jonet and Ann have already started another tapestry with ye as the central figure," Ewan called.

Meg glanced at Elspet dying on the great hall tapestry. Would she bring England down on these noble people? "Good Lord," she whispered. "What have I done?"

• • •

"Hail, Druim!" Caden's voice broke through the hushed mist as he halted before the wall.

"Hail, The Macbain," Hugh Loman yelled back. "Open the gate."

"The herds come," Caden called to two other men who ran out of the bailey. "Into the bailey tonight. We'll corral them beyond tomorrow after the sun has worked through this fog." He jogged up to the steps of the castle and swung down.

Ewan stepped out of the great doors, his expression a mix

of relief and concern.

"Meg?" Caden asked, his heart leaping as he waited the scant second it took Ewan to respond.

"Sleeping," Ewan answered.

Caden breathed in fully, the weight of worry dissolving with that one word. He'd thought of her all day—worried, really. Yet she was safe, in bed, warm. He hadn't been able to wake her this morning to say good-bye. Perhaps he'd have an easier time waking her if they were both naked.

The moos and bleats pulled his attention back to the cold night around him as the animals rushed through into the bailey.

"The portcullis was down," Caden said.

"Boswell paid us a visit."

The tightness pressed in on Caden's chest. "With troops?"

"Only ten men and Meg's aunt and uncle from England," Ewan shouted over the din of animal noises.

Caden glanced behind at the sea of cattle and goats. His men moved among them, blanketing the young and throwing out hay. The troughs were filled as the animals crowded around, drinking away their thirst.

He waved to Colin and Alec to follow him. The other men would tend the animals and find their own beds. As he walked inside, Angus and Kenneth pushed out of their chairs by the fire. Bruce's snores vibrated through the great hall until Kenneth thumped his arm.

"What?" Bruce mumbled and then spotted Caden. He unfolded his body and followed the other two.

Only something important would keep these three in the great hall this late. Caden grabbed a mug of ale on the table and guzzled the liquid down his parched throat. He eyed the three elders and Ewan as they waited. Alec and Colin also found ale.

"What has you three up so late?" Alec asked.

"Boswell was here today," Caden said.

Kenneth frowned at Ewan. "Did you already tell him how Meg sent him away speechless? We wanted to tell him what she said."

"Aye, you said we could tell him," Bruce said and belched.

Caden's focus bored into Ewan, his gut tightening. "You let him talk to Meg?"

"She wouldn't go upstairs," Ewan said. "And Rachel wasn't likely to budge, either."

Alec snorted. "If Rachel wants to stay put, she stays."

"You should have heard our Meg," Kenneth said.

"She did us proud," Angus added, puffing up his chest. "Made that devil turn bright red and retreat. She wouldn't even let him take her aunt and uncle back with him."

"Aye, the bastard dragged that old couple up from England in this cold," Bruce added. "Kept them locked away at the Davidsons' for a fortnight."

"Gilbert Davidson," Caden said, his calm voice covering the rush of battle lust through his veins.

"You were right," Ewan said. "Davidson was not the leader. Boswell is and he has a letter from King Henry summoning Meg to London to marry an Englishman."

"Bloody hell she will," Caden swore. Battle energy surged through him, his hand instinctively grabbing the hilt of his sword.

"Meg seemed to have the same opinion." Ewan grinned.

"She threatened to take the letters her mother hid to King Henry if Boswell doesn't leave immediately. She cut all ties to him and England before us all."

"'Twas royal, Caden, you should have seen her," Kenneth said. "Ewan kept standing in front of her to protect her and she kept stepping out and defended us all, Macbains, Munros, and Macleods. Using her cleverness and words as her weapons."

"That woman's a warrior," Bruce said and all three elders agreed loudly.

"She did a mighty fine job with the options she had," Ewan said, but his grin faded.

"He didn't even call farewell when he left, he was so mortified," Angus said. "Red puffed-up face," he added, laughing.

Caden's eyes were still on Ewan. There was more to this story. "I need to wash this animal stink from me."

What he needed to do was run his sword through Davidson and Boswell together.

"Colin and Alec, too. Ewan, follow us to the kitchens where we can wash," Caden said. He nodded to the elders. "And you should find your beds."

He could still hear the three old warriors cackling about Meg's bravery as he walked down the corridor toward the kitchens behind the hall. "And the rest?" he asked Ewan.

Ewan lips pinched into a tight line. "As the bastard was leaving, he stopped me on the steps. He said that if we don't deliver Meg and the letters to the Davidsons' within a fortnight, he would leave for London."

"As the bloody devil should," Alec muttered.

"He said," Ewan continued, "that he would return in the spring with English troops to burn the crops and houses and kill every person standing in his way—man, woman, and child of the clans Macbain, Munro, and Macleod."

"Ha!" Alec said. "Let them try."

"That our lands," Ewan said over Alec's comment, "will be given over to Scots nobles faithful to England and its king."

"Rowland Boswell can't do that," Colin said. "He holds no rank in England."

"Boswell said his king would easily persuade our King James to concur with their actions against us, rather than starting an open war against England. True or not, it's what the man said."

"We will send our petition to Edinburgh first," Alec stammered. "England can't just send troops here as if they ruled this country!"

Ewan kept his gaze on Caden. "He insinuated that King James was not happy with you right now and that he would not defend us."

Anger burned in Caden's chest. "Davidson."

"My thoughts, too," Ewan said and took a deep breath.

"Bloody devil talks too much," Alec grumbled.

"He wanted me to ask you, Caden," Ewan said, "if you placed more value on one little woman than on the men, women, and children of three clans. And if you were willing to wage war with England on Meg's account."

Caden's chest squeezed on an indrawn breath. How many times had he spouted the wisdom of the truce with the Munros? That one woman wasn't worth the lives of hundreds. How many times since he'd decided to steal away an English woman and use her to bring peace had he justified it with those words? He'd married Meg to end a feud, but staying married to her could start a war.

Chapter Thirteen

2 June 1518—Primrose: yellow flower in early spring. Dry the root or use whole plant fresh. Use against body stiffness and gout. A tincture with the green plant will help a person sleep. Use the dry root against headaches and the phrensie.
Primrose will bring peace to the lonely wife as she waits for a time to return to her husband near the western sea. Abundant in woods and pastures along the North Road.

"Why can't we go today?" Meg asked. Caden and Colin sat with her at the long table in the great hall. Unease chewed at her insides, despite Caden's return to her in the dark of night. Apparently she could be woken if he was creative with his well-placed kisses.

"Someone at Druim is trying to scare me or worse, and if that doesn't stop me, then Boswell is going to petition the king for troops to send against us. We must prove he's a traitor to the crown."

Meg's stomach rolled as she replayed the threat that

Boswell had given Ewan upon leaving. Caden had told her just before they'd come down to the hall. She could imagine those black eyes in the red face, his words so firm and sure. They needed those letters.

"Meg," Caden said calmly. "There is a foot of snow out there. We were lucky to get the herds back yesterday."

"And we're not certain that the incidents at Druim are related to Boswell," Colin added. "The pebbles. The mushrooms."

"We aren't even sure that the letters will show Boswell is a traitor," Caden said.

She sat down on the bench beside Caden. "Why else would my mother have Colin hide them, risk her life and mine to steal them in the first place, and then tell me so in a letter urging me to run?" She shook her head, her hands clasping together in the folds of her gown. "What else can we do other than send me to England?" Even the words made her body shudder.

Caden squeezed Meg's hand. "Ye're not going to England."

Colin scratched the short beard that had begun to grow back. "We could send one of our men to represent Meg with the petition."

"And hope he leaves with his life?" Meg asked in frustration. "People lose their lives based on King Henry's whims. And he's none too fond of the Scots."

"Perhaps going through Scottish Parliament would be best. They can deal with Henry," Colin advised. "Father Daughtry may be able to write to King James refuting the allegations of hearsay."

"I'm not sure what Father Daughtry thinks about me," Meg

said. "Ann says he's been asking about my gift." They didn't have time to convince the priest of her goodness, not if one letter from Boswell could convince King Henry that they were a threat. "Maybe I do need to go to London to present my case."

Caden turned his fierce eyes to Meg. "Not without me."

"And not without those letters," Colin said.

"So we are back to needing to retrieve them." She nearly stamped her foot like a child before these big, stoic men.

"Let this snow spell pass, next week," Colin said. "Boswell won't return to England until spring to bring English troops back here, and they will be led by someone other than he."

"We can show the letters to that commander," Caden said. "He will have to take them back to London, which will give us more time to prepare."

"Prepare for what?" Meg asked, her stomach tightening. Apparently, Caden hadn't told her everything Boswell threatened. "For war with England?"

Caden and Colin passed a silent communication between them. Caden was the one who replied. "War with England has always been a possibility, as long as they sit against our borders."

"I won't be the cause of war," she said firmly.

"We could leave," Caden said. "Meg and I, to the colonies or France."

Colin snorted. "Now that I have a daughter, I have a desire to know my grandbairns." He scratched his beard again. "And a desire to teach impudent Englishmen that this is our country, not theirs."

"War. You would really go to war? Against the English? Because I came here?" Meg couldn't sit another moment. She let her legs carry her away while her mind fumbled around the word "war" with a numbness that invaded her whole being.

...

"Meg," Caden called after her. She continued to the entry and threw a cloak around her shoulders to step out into the snowy world. Worry that had nothing to do with the threat of war clenched his chest. The pain in Meg's eyes, it was like...terror.

"Let her calm down a bit," Colin said.

Caden signaled Donald, who'd passed Meg on his way in. Donald walked over to them, broke off a bit of bread, and promptly turned to follow her. The man had been tasked to follow Meg since the moment they found her—or rather, since she'd found them.

Alec and Rachel walked down the steps together, arm in arm.

"Sleeping in, Munro?" Caden indicated the trencher of cold venison and bread.

"Woke at dawn," Alec said, puffing out his chest. "My sweet lass of a bride had other ideas," he waggled his eyebrows.

Rachel slapped Alec's arm and sat down to eat.

"That's what you need to do, lad," Colin said over his ale. "Keep Meg busy, her thoughts off retrieving those letters."

Caden stood. "You just want grandbairns, old man." Though the thought of keeping Meg locked up in their room definitely had its merits. Could he kiss the terror out of her eyes? He'd definitely try.

He pushed out into the chilly autumn morning just as Donald barreled back up the steps.

"She's taken her horse," he said, panting, "and is walking it through the village."

Caden picked up his pace and followed her small footprints through the snow.

"Do you really think she'd try to leave alone?" Donald asked.

She'd done it before with hardly any preparation. And that was just to save herself, not three clans. "She's at least considering it." Caden's heart pounded as he broke into a jog. "I would."

"I'll talk to Hugh about keeping a closer watch. Don't want anything to happen to our lady," Donald called and ran off.

Caden followed discreetly behind Meg. Didn't she know the risk she was putting herself in, just by walking alone through the village? With the foot traffic alone along the village paths, Boswell or Davidson could be waiting to nab her.

Caden scanned the path she followed, watching, waiting, ready to spring into attack. His blood pumped, his palm resting on the familiar hilt of his sword.

People passed and most eyed her horse, yet no one halted her. No one bloody halted her! Would she really leave? Leave him?

Caden watched her straight shoulders as she continued to the edge of the village, where the cattle beyond nosed through the snow in search of covered gorse. He moved with stealth behind cottages until he stood close enough to catch her if she mounted. She put two fingers to her mouth and whistled a high, piercing call. The cows flitted their ears and lowed.

Meg pulled the hood over her head, covering that lustrous

auburn hair. She whistled a second time.

At the edge of the woods a dark-furred animal loped out onto the moor. "Nickum," she said, and gathered her horse's reins in one hand.

As she hiked up her skirt to mount, Caden surged from behind the house. "Enough!"

In three strides he was upon her. He grabbed her arms and spun her to him, his rage barely controlled. He may have felt pride in her thoughts of self-sacrifice, but watching it unfold in reality was entirely different. The wolf paused, as if to watch.

"What are ye doing?" he yelled. He stopped when he saw the tears on the brim of her eyes. He lowered his voice and trailed a thumb across her cheek. "What are ye doing, lass? Ye can't leave me. I...I won't let ye leave me."

"A war, where babies and mothers, husbands and brothers will die," she said. She shook her head. "I won't be the cause of it. I have to do something."

"Don't repeat yer mother's sacrifice, Meg." His words pushed the tears over and they wet a trail down her cheeks. "She should have stayed here. Ye should stay here." He swallowed against the pain in his throat. "Ye *will* stay here."

"Am I a prisoner again, then?"

Caden closed his eyes and let the air move in and out of his lungs. He opened his eyes and stared into her watery ones. What could he say that wasn't a lie? "I won't let ye go. If that makes ye a prisoner, so be it."

"I could stop a war. Just me, one single person, could save many."

Caden bent so his eyes were level with Meg's. "If it comes

to war, ye wouldn't be the cause. Boswell would be the cause."

"Because of me. If I go away—"

"I will slice through every Englishman until I've skewered Boswell's black heart," Caden finished, and pulled her shivering form into his warmth. "If ye go away there will be no one to stop me from taking my revenge on England." He held her close, watching the large wolf slow his gait across the moor. Would it have attacked him for grabbing her? Perhaps his wee wife was safer than he thought.

"Nay, Meg. If ye leave, we leave." He pushed back her hood and ran his palm down the silk of her hair and inhaled the fresh scent. "Together." He paused. "I would have yer word on it."

Meg blinked and looked up into his eyes. The tears remained but something else shone through, strength perhaps, something more. "Together then, if it comes to it, to prevent a war. We go together."

"Ye swear on it."

"I swear." She fell back into his arms. Relief surged through him and he finally drew in a deep breath. He watched Nickum run back to the forest's edge. "Yer pet awaits."

"I haven't seen him since he was healed. Could he think I abandoned him?"

"Time for a visit," Caden said and lifted Meg, sitting her on the saddle. Though she'd sworn, he still held tight to the horse's reins. The unease of almost losing her sat like a fresh wound across his chest. What if he'd listened to Colin and given Meg some time? And she'd ridden out in the cold without direction? "Together," he said, his voice harder than he'd intended.

He mounted behind her and tapped Pippen into a run

across the moor. The wind whipped into their faces, yet Meg didn't shy from it. She laughed for a moment before the wind ripped the melody away. He leaned into her. "I love to hear yer happiness, love."

She turned and her joy melted his anger and fear. The pure happiness lit her face from within, sparkling through her long-lashed eyes, flushing her cheeks. The edge of her tongue touched her lips, wetting them. His blood rushed, filling him with heat.

Before either one of them could respond, Pippen halted to a walk and danced to the left, away from the huge wolf. Even though Caden knew the wolf was tame, its mere size and emotionless eyes awakened a core of caution.

Meg turned and patted Pippen between his twitching ears. "Nickum won't hurt us."

"He's been out in the wild for three weeks. Be careful," Caden warned. The bloody beast stared at him, neither of them moving.

Meg slid down breaking their locked gaze. "I've missed you." She approached the wolf that stood up to her stomach on all fours. One false movement and Caden would yank his short sword from his boot and strike.

She threw her arms around the wolf's neck.

"Meg!" Caden jumped off the horse's back. Luckily, the wolf just stood there while she hugged the beast like a long-lost child.

"You have cuts on your feet." She lifted a paw the size of her hand, turning it over. Caden shook his head, amazed what the animal allowed. Nickum even nuzzled her side. Caden relaxed, moving his hand away from the short sword. The wolf sat when he did so. Had he been aware of the weapon the entire time?

Meg closed her eyes and Caden saw a faint outline of blue light against the wolf's body where she touched him.

"Now I can fix you without that stinging ointment." She stroked his face and scratched behind his ears. "Where have you been?" She paused as if she thought he'd answer.

Could she understand the wolf? Ridiculous, Caden thought, though she was a witch. He hadn't yet fully contemplated what that meant. It didn't matter. Meg was his wife, witch or not.

"Have you been waiting out here for me?" she asked, but then inhaled sharply.

Caden turned to where Meg's eyes fastened in between the trees. Another gray wolf stood still, blending in with the mottled dead leaves of a bush.

"You found a friend?" she whispered, and took a step toward the smaller wolf.

"Meg, that one's wild," Caden warned.

She stopped. The smaller wolf retreated farther into the forest, but stayed close.

"Your friend won't leave you," Meg said to Nickum, and wiped a long stroke down his back. She leaned in and kissed his head. "I won't, either, but I'm living in the castle now and can't get out to visit as much." She hugged him tight. "You don't seem thin and there's plenty of animals for you…and your friend."

"Meg, we need to return," Caden said eyeing the dense, silent woods. Two swords against an army of English? Not good. Although with the wolf on their side, the odds were better.

"Boswell and Davidson could be close and yer pet could get hurt protecting ye again."

That made her move. She hugged the wolf and hurried to Pippen. Caden lifted her up and climbed behind. Nickum jogged back into the woods toward the smaller wolf. Caden glanced back once at them and then the two ran, blending in with the wild winter grays and browns.

He steered Pippen across the frozen heath. Clods of white blew up behind the horse's feet. Caden watched the edge of woods surrounding them on the west to the three mountains behind Druim Castle. His eyes lingered on the third one on the right.

"The letters seem so close," Meg said, her words carrying back to him on the wind.

"They're safe, Meg." Caden tucked her in against his body. "We'll get them. I promise."

• • •

Meg rolled over, her sleep-warmed body shocked into wakefulness by the cold blankets on Caden's side. She tossed back onto her own side and snuggled in deep. Blinking, she noticed the bright sunlight filtering in through the thick glass of the small window. Maybe the frigid temperatures and heavy snow, which had made their trip to the mountain impossible over the last four weeks, had finally abated.

Each day she'd watched to see if the piling snow would melt, but it hadn't. So her days had taken on a pleasant routine of learning the running of a great household. Meanwhile, Caden's scouts had kept tabs on Boswell, and the man seemed holed up at Davidson Castle. Apparently, the devil didn't like the frigid weather, either.

"Just how late is it?" she mumbled. Caden had obviously been up for enough time that all his body heat had evaporated from the layers of blankets and furs. And the man certainly had a lot of body heat. Meg snuggled, naked, down in the bed, remembering just how hot her husband's skin became. Even with the chill that had settled over the Highlands, they'd had to throw the blankets back for fear that they'd singe the linens.

Meg giggled and stretched. The two of them had certainly ignited, but the linens had remained intact, unlike her ripped shift that lay piled on the floor. She should just stop wearing them to bed.

She reached under the blankets, her hand sliding over her abdomen. And stopped.

Something was different. She had always been aware of her body's functions, the changes that happened each month with her cycle. Those changes had stalled, but she thought it was due to the stress of her escape into the Highlands and her new marriage.

Meg called upon her magic to lightly probe her body, her womb. And there it was, small, new, rapidly changing.

Her eyes glazing with joy-filled tears. She was going to have a baby. Caden's baby.

The budding life was still so new that she couldn't tell anything about the growing ball except that it radiated health. She channeled her magic through the rest of her body. Things were already changing as the balance of particles and fluids moved throughout.

She hugged herself tight and listened to her stomach rumble. How soon before she became nauseous? Some mothers began earlier than others and some not at all. Would it be a girl, whom she could teach to appreciate her gift of healing? Or a boy, tall and strong like his father?

A chill ran through her at the thought of a son, sword in hand, standing against an English battalion. She splayed her fingers across her abdomen.

War. They might be on the verge of it. Instead, would they abandon their countries to journey abroad? She couldn't even imagine Caden away from the Highlands, let alone raising his son in another land. Meg closed her eyes.

No. She couldn't think of that now. She tuned into the vibrant health of the burgeoning life within her and coaxed the joy to return. This baby would be a blessing in this terrible time. Colin would be so happy. First a daughter he knew nothing about and now a grandbairn on the way. And Caden…

"Ye are up, milady," Fiona said from the door. "Would ye like some breakfast? A bath?"

"Both would be wonderful." Meg tried not to blush as Fiona scooped up her ripped shift. "How late is it?"

"Halfway to noon." Fiona brought in a tray of bread and cheese. She stuck her head back out the door and yelled, "She wants a bath," then turned back to Meg. "Ye're sleeping late today. Are ye ill?"

Meg thrilled inside over her little secret. "Just tired, I suppose. The day is sunny. Is it warmer at all?"

"Aye," Fiona said as she directed the men, who averted their eyes from Meg.

"*Moran taing*," Meg said, calling her thanks as they hurried out.

Fiona tended the fire while Meg sank into the warm water.

"Is it warm enough to hike to a mountain?" Meg asked as Fiona handed her a small bar of sweet-smelling soap.

"Seems it is," she said.

Meg sat up straight, splashing a small wave of water over the side. "Goodness! They didn't go without me, did they?"

"The men are gathered down below discussing the route."

Meg breathed relief and sank back in the basin. "Then they won't leave today. Tomorrow, perhaps."

"Aye." Fiona helped Meg wash out her long hair. "Caden sent word to Munro Castle for Alec to join him and Colin." Her uncle had been more than anxious to return home so Alec, Rachel, and Searc had departed Druim through the snow a week after the herds had returned.

Tomorrow, then. Meg's stomach churned with excitement. Within a day she could have the evidence to protect the clans and her baby.

For now she'd keep her secret. Maybe she would tell Caden about the baby when they found the spot her mother and Colin had handfasted. He would be so happy. She would find the perfect moment to tell him that he'd soon be a father.

The next morning Meg braced her hand on the stone wall as she hurried cautiously down the steps. No more pebbles had been spread in the dark stairwell, but she wasn't taking any chances with the baby inside.

Meg waved a greeting to Sarah and Aunt Mary as she grabbed a piece of bread from the table and a mug of watered wine. She ran out through the entryway into the bailey and stopped on the steps, breathing hard. Before her, ten men sat atop their horses. Pippen shifted, his saddle vacant.

Murmurs of greeting came haphazardly from the group. Alec, Colin, and Caden were mounted along with Ewan and a few other warriors she knew. Meg took a drink and chewed on the fragrant bread. She'd woken queasy, but the food would help.

Caden grinned. "So ye decided to wake."

She walked to him and returned his smile, even though her stomach still twitched and tossed at her rapid dressing and breakfast. "Did you even try to rouse me?"

He leaned down, close to her. "Ye must be used to me shouting yer name, lass, for ye barely moved."

Meg's breath caught in her throat at the sizzle of passion that sparked through the whisper. She swallowed and focused on the slushy ground to calm her stomach. She took another bite of the bread.

"Ready to go?" Caden asked and she nodded as she sipped from her mug.

"Are there provisions? Bread, cheese, water?" she asked, already thinking that she'd need continual food to keep her stomach strong on the ride.

"Aye, plenty," Caden answered. He frowned. "Ye are a little pale."

"I'm fit as a Highlander," Meg said.

Caden jumped down from his horse and followed her over to Pippen. "Are ye ill this morning?" He touched her forehead.

Meg's eyes rolled upward, as if watching his hand. "See?

No fever. I'm just a little dizzy and hungry." She forced herself to take another bite of the bread that had balled up in her stomach. She didn't want to tell Caden about the baby until they were in the cave and it was too late to leave her at home.

Caden pulled her cloak tighter around her neck. "I have another blanket for ye."

She swallowed another drink when Caden suddenly lifted her up on Pippen's back. At the same time the horse next to Pippen released a pile of horse dung and a stream of urine. The smell hit Meg like hammer in the gut. Only Caden's warrior reflexes saved him as he sidestepped and pointed her face toward the ground while she vomited.

Men shouted. Horses danced. Meg stared at the ground as embarrassment tore through her. Caden moved the horse forward and gently lowered her back to the ground away from her breakfast. "Meg?"

"I think you lifted me too fast." She wiped her lips with the edge of the blanket. In actuality the purging had calmed her stomach, perhaps enough to replace some of that food. "If I could just get another fresh piece of bread, we can be off."

"Meg," Caden said. "Ye vomited. Ye're sick, lass."

"I am not ill," she said, louder than she'd intended. "You just caught me off guard." She waved her hand in front of her face. "And that horse stinks."

"Wait here. We will bring yer mother's letters back." He signaled to one of the stable boys to take Pippen away.

"No!" She grabbed Pippen's reins. "I'm well," she said shaking her head. "Perfectly healthy. I would know if there was something wrong with me, wouldn't I?"

Caden frowned. "Healthy people don't vomit their breakfasts."

The stable boy tugged on the reins that Meg wouldn't drop. Poor Pippen's head yanked from side to side.

"Ye are ill. Alec, I'm sending for Rachel." Alec agreed as Caden barked instructions to Kieven.

"I am perfectly healthy." Frustration picked at Meg's temper. She wanted to go, to see where her mother had been happy. This special place where she had married Colin Macleod and spent time with the man she loved. "Please, Caden. I am full of health."

"Nay."

Ugh! No, no, no! She just had to go! Now that she was truly happy, she wanted to be in the place where her mother had also been so.

"Losing yer stomach is not a sign of health," Caden said low, and worked to unfold her fingers along Pippen's reins.

"It is if a woman is with child," Meg said.

A collective silence descended in the bailey. Even the birds seemed to stop their songs to listen. Holy Mother, had she said that out loud? Hell! That was far from the perfect way she'd imagined telling Caden.

"We've only…been married five weeks," Caden whispered.

"Apparently you are quite potent and I was quite…ripe," she whispered back.

"How would ye know?"

"I sense the physical changes in my body like I can with other people." She placed her hand on her abdomen. "The babe is growing, changing, as it should at this early stage."

Caden's eyes fastened on her belly, a slow grin breaking out along his face, banishing the frown and the furrow. Then his gaze moved to her eyes.

"You see, I'm perfectly—"

He grabbed her up into a fierce hug and twirled her around. "Love," he said and set her down gently. "Thank ye."

"Well, I haven't done much yet," she teased, still tingling at the word "love."

Caden turned to the group. "She's carrying my bairn!"

A resounding "Hoorah" echoed about the bailey and Colin jumped from his horse. He charged toward her but halted a step away and then gingerly pulled her into his arms.

"I will be a grandpapa," he said, and then released her.

Caden scooped her up in his arms. "I will be right back," he said to the men and carried Meg to the steps of the keep.

Alec snorted. "At this rate, we'll never see that cave," he groused, but murmured a blessing to Meg as Caden walked by.

"Caden, I'm perfectly fine. The babe is healthy. I'm healthy. Even the queasiness is better." Her words trailed off as Caden continued to stride toward the keep. She'd just given him an even better reason for leaving her behind. She sighed loudly. "You realize that after this babe is born, you will be taking me up there."

His eyes met hers.

"I wish to be in the one place my mother was truly happy."

"I swear," Caden said.

She laid her head against his heart as he carried her inside and set her on a bench by the long table.

"I'll return by nightfall if all goes well. Don't stay awake waiting." Caden leaned in and kissed Meg on her forehead. "Och, lass, a bairn." He ran his thumb along the contour of her cheek.

Meg sighed and he turned for the door. Evelyn passed him on the way.

"Make sure Meg eats," he said as a parting order.

Evelyn stared back and forth between Meg and Caden. "I know, she needs some more meat on her," she said and walked toward the kitchens.

After a quick breakfast of cooked oats and a slice of cheese, Meg busied herself helping Jonet and Ann with their tapestry, though it made her blush each time she saw the beautiful depiction of herself.

She'd had fun in telling Aunt Mary and Uncle Harold about the babe and Evelyn had to sit down, she was so amazed. Since it was still so early, she asked them not to spread the word, although everyone in the bailey had heard.

Late in the afternoon, Meg couldn't stop yawning. "Evelyn, I think I will rest up in my room. Could you let Donald know that he doesn't have to follow me around for a bit?"

Evelyn left Meg alone in the cozy kitchen. Meg hummed as she leaned over the cook hearth. Caden's babe. She ran her hand over her still-flat stomach. She loved it, just like she loved its father. Yes, she loved Caden Macbain. She loved his honor, his intelligence, his passion…even his Highland stubbornness. This little babe was the product of that love.

"Meow." The faint sound caught at Meg's thoughts. "Meow." A kitten, from the sound of it. She remembered the little ball of orange fluff that Bess had retrieved for her son.

Had it gotten lost in the castle again, or were there other little balls of fluff roaming the corridors?

Meg followed the faint cry to the back of the castle. The cat seemed to be moving farther away. Under a shadowy archway a door stood open. She'd never seen this particular door open before. Could one of the elders have ventured in and left it ajar?

"Kitty, kitty," Meg called. She lit a short candle. Where did the corridor lead?

She crept along the dark path. "Kitty," she called as the kitten mewed pitifully.

Meg trailed her fingers along one rough wall and held the tallow candle higher to guard her steps. The ground sloped downward. She shivered as the chill sunk into her skin.

She'd never gone below ground like this before. Uncle Harold's root cellar had been deep enough for her, and she'd never liked to tarry long there. Perhaps it was good that she wasn't venturing into the caves today with Caden. The dank smell and low, dark ceiling caused her heart to race. She almost turned back, but the sad cry of the kitten kept her feet shuffling forward in the pool of candlelight.

Perhaps the passageway led down to the dungeons. She shivered at the thought that she could have been housed down here rather than in the warm rooms above with floors covered by thick rugs to block the cold seeping up from the stone.

A narrow set of steps led nearly straight down. *I should go back.* The kitten let out a mournful sound. The little beastie was so close.

Meg stepped cautiously into the black hole. When she reached the bottom step, her foot slipped and she leaned into the wall for support. Icy stone, like sharp fingers, sunk a chill through her gown. She jumped away from the wall toward an open cell and tried to ignore the stench of rotting hay and urine. "Where are you?"

Meg held her candle higher and spotted the small ball of fluff toward a corner. "How did you ever find your way down here? Were you chasing a mouse?" she asked. "You are Peter's kitten."

She pulled the kitten into her lap and tried to stand but the cat meowed as a tether pulled at its neck. "What's caught you?"

Meg frowned and the hairs along her nape prickled. A thin twine ran from the cat's neck to a chain loop burrowed into the granite floor. The cat was tied to the loop with a double knot. Meg set it down and turned just in time to see the barred door swing shut with a *clank*. A cloaked figure stood on the opposite side.

Meg's heart rate flared. "Who are you? Why are you doing this?"

The cloaked figure lowered her hood. Bess Tammin stood there, eyes wide. "'Tis for the best. She says that if you go, the English will stay away. I won't lose my boy, too."

"Who says that?" Meg asked on a panicky exhale. So someone did blame her for bringing the English to their doorstep. Someone who was willing to hurt her to get rid of her.

Bess turned and nearly flew up the ladder.

"Bess, please!" Meg yelled. "Don't leave me here. Peter's kitten," she called, trying to give the woman any reason to return. "Don't forget Peter's kitten." The woman continued up, her boots clicking as she ran back through the dark tunnel.

Meg realized that her breathing was shallow when small sparks moved into her periphery. She concentrated on taking full, long inhales and exhales while trying to ignore the pungent decay smell filling her.

Think! She tried the barred door, but it had been set to lock as soon as it clicked shut. She rattled it, tried to squeeze through it, pounded on the bars around the cell.

"Meow!"

Meg turned.

"We're stuck," she said and pulled the kitten into her lap. Her mind whirled around in a panic as she worked at the tie around its neck until the knot released.

Meg smoothed the fluffy orange tuft of fur. How long would it take for them to miss her above? Would Bess come back, or the person who had convinced her to trick Meg down here? What were they going to do with her? Just let her waste away, starve to death?

She glanced around the filthy, smelly cell. Her breathing had picked up again to match her pounding heart. She shut her eyes and imagined the open sky above her when she walked on the top of the keep. Blue, gray sky like Caden's eyes.

Oh, Caden! He would be so angry when he found her gone. Would he think she left without him, broken her oath? No, not with a baby growing in her. He couldn't possibly think her so foolish, so cruel, could he?

Her eyes flew open and she jerked on the iron bars once again. The walls pressed inward, making the room seem tiny.

Meg's breathing became shallow. Could air find her down here below ground? Good lord, what a terrible time to find out she panicked in small, dark places.

She paced, searching for anything to aid her. She kicked at the molding straw, rat excrement, and decayed remains of food. A rusted water bucket stood parched in a corner. She wrinkled her nose as she moved away from the other corner, which must have been used as a place for prisoners to relieve themselves.

"Help!" Meg screamed every few minutes, but only her echo answered. Her candle sputtered and she tipped it so the tallow could drip away from the flame. Ugh! How could she be so foolish as to follow the kitten without alerting anyone? She stood in the center of the cell, taking deep slow breaths through her mouth. The kitten rubbed against her ankle.

Little claws caught in the fabric of her gown underneath as the cat pawed its way out. It stepped through the bars. Meg's breath hitched. "Wait! Here, kitty!"

The kitten padded back through the bars and Meg caught him. She glanced down her dress. Around her sleeve was a thin pearl decorative piping. Meg pulled the pins out that held it around her shoulder and tied the scrap around the kitten's neck. No one would think that Peter kept a ribbon of pearls around his cat.

When she'd made certain the scrap was on tight, Meg set the kitten back through the bars.

"Shoo!" she said and made shooing movements with her fingers. The kitten hesitated. He let out a meow and jumped up the first step and sat.

"That's it, keep going," Meg encouraged. The candle sputtered again. "Go now! Shoo!"

The cat jumped up the next step. Meg leaned into the iron

bars and let out a loud exhale. This would take forever. She wrapped her shawl tighter around her shoulders and sunk down to clasp her knees to her chest to conserve body heat. The remaining tallow fat dripped off the candle wick.

"No," she whispered, the single word swallowed by the dank walls. The flame shrank until it was nothing more than a glowing dot in the smothering darkness of the dungeon. And then it was gone.

Meg closed her eyes for as long as she could. Perhaps she dozed. How long had she been down here? She drew her fingers apart to form the blue orb of light.

"Also quite good at lighting dark dungeons," she said aloud with a sniff as the frigid, wet air racked her body.

In the distance, she heard a faint "meow" and the sound of scratching. The kitten was still trapped on this side of the door. Meg let out a sob and leaned against the rusty iron bars. Of course Bess would have shut the door on her way out. What if the door was locked and no one bothered to come down here?

"Help! Help me!" she screamed at the top of her lungs. She blew her light up until it flooded the cell with luminescence. "Help! I'm down here!"

"Hello?" a paper-thin voice called from above. "Oh, a cat," and then a sneeze. "Be gone."

Someone above had heard the cat and opened the door.

"Help!" Meg screamed at the top of her voice. "Help! I'm locked down in the dungeon!"

"Meg Macbain?" a man's voice called.

"Yes! Help, I'm locked in!"

"Oh my, child," the voice said louder.

"Find Donald," she called but the man continued closer. She could hear his footfalls. He landed on the bottom step with a small huff of exertion.

"Father Daughtry? Father, help me," Meg called and actually reached out with one hand.

The priest stood staring at her other hand, the one she'd forgotten was holding the blue orb. "Good and holy Lord, I will not suffer a witch to live," he murmured and backed up the steps.

"I had no light!" she screamed. "Please don't leave me here! Get Donald! Help me!" Meg continued to scream, hoping someone else would hear her because she wasn't sure if the priest would help her or lock her back in.

Cold and exhaustion weighed heavy on her as she let the blue light dissolve on her fingertips. She blinked against the darkness and squelched the sob that sat in the back of her throat. Wait, was that...? A flicker of firelight crept along the wall of the steep steps.

"She's down here?"

"Aye, she's in the dungeon," the priest replied.

"Help!" Meg called.

"Meg?" Donald! Thank the good Lord Father Daughtry hadn't left her there to rot.

"I'm down here."

"Why are ye in the dungeon?" Donald jumped down the steps into the pit.

"I heard the cat. Donald, Bess Tammin locked me in here."

Donald grabbed the large ring from the shadows where it must have been hanging. Apparently, he was familiar with the dungeon. He turned the key and the door swung open.

"She said that she wouldn't let me start a war and something about not losing Peter, too," Meg said as he threw his own wrap around her shoulders. "I think she is working with someone else."

Donald's face was grim. "Are ye hurt?"

"Just cold. A bit thirsty."

"Let's get ye upstairs," he said and went up the steep steps ahead of her. "Father?"

"Here," Father Daughtry said. "I think someone else is coming down. I heard—"

The priest's words were cut off with a gasp. Meg stepped up quickly out of the dungeon pit. Donald grunted at the same time someone lit an oil lamp. Her heart hammered so hard she couldn't draw breath.

Girshmel pulled his sword from Donald's chest and the warrior slumped to the floor, his own weapon clattering against the stones. "Good to see ye again, milady," he said with a mocking smirk.

Chapter Fourteen

4 July 1518—Comfrey: green, leafy plants, yellow to pink flowers in summer. The best comfrey has a hollow root stalk. Boil root in water or wine to heal inward pains, wounds, and bleeding. Restrains the spitting of blood. Roots applied externally will heal fresh wounds, scrapes, and broken bones. Use against gout and swelling, intestinal maladies, the cough, and boils. Smash the whole plant and use hot mash to apply externally as a poultice. Found along maze-like paths near sources of water, mountain streams. Do not get lost searching, using a map is key.

"Holy God, save us!" Father Daughtry prayed where he slouched against the wall as if he'd been pushed. Another man stood next to him, sword before him.

"Forgive me, Father," Girshmel said, turned, and stabbed his already bloody sword into the priest's stomach. "For I have sinned."

Father Daughtry let out a gasping shrill cry and doubled over, his hands clutching his cross.

A third person stepped into the light of the second man's lantern.

"Gwyneth?" Meg asked weakly, unable to tear her eyes very long from the massacre wetting the floor before her.

The other woman *tsk*ed. "Always in harm's way. Ye found a way out of the other *accidents* I planned, but not this time."

Meg watched the pools of blood growing about the men. They would die in the matter of minutes if she didn't heal them. She took a small step toward Donald and Father Daughtry while the two men watched Gwyneth. Luckily, Donald and Father Daughtry were within reach of one another, but she had never tried to heal two at once. Was that even possible?

"And Simon, let Gilbert know that I've risked much to bring her here. I expect recompense," Gwyneth said. She sneered at Meg. "Don't worry, m'lady. I'll console Caden when ye're gone. He was going to be mine, but then ye and yer bloody sweetness came along."

Simon? That's where she'd seen him before. He'd come with Gilbert to the wedding feast.

Meg refocused on Donald and Father Daughtry. Now or never. She pulled her magic from her core, readying it, imagining what the first thrust may have done to poor Donald's chest muscles and what the second may have done to Father Daughtry's stomach and intestines. Before the brutes could stop her, Meg hurled herself into an act of sobbing. She covered Donald's body and slid her hand under Father Daughtry's chest.

Upon contact her magic was able to find the torn flesh, the ripped muscle, the shattered rib in Donald, and the sliced intestines in the priest. The blade had just missed Donald's beating heart, but the vessels bringing blood to it were damaged. Meg pushed a pulse of magic into Donald, imagining the tissue back together, the vessels mended, the blood replenished. Then she imagined strong, intact intestinal walls and muscle in Father Daughtry. She wailed bitterly as she hid her hands under each victim and cringed at the sticky blood. Had they already lost too much?

Cruel hands yanked her back, breaking the contact. The healing had weakened Meg and she yielded as Simon pulled her.

"None of that, milady," Simon said as he shoved her against the rock wall. "Dear Gwen's told us about yer talented hands and yer witchcraft. I won't have ye fixing Girshmel's handy work."

Meg's eyes stayed on Donald's prone position. She'd been able to fix the worst of the damage, but he'd lost so much blood. The same with Father Daughtry. She needed to touch them again, imagine their veins filled with the life-giving fluid.

"Shhh!" Girshmel held a stumpy finger to his overly wet lips. "Someone's coming down here. Didn't ye shut the door?" he hissed at Simon and moved silently up the dark corridor.

Meg opened her mouth to shout a warning, but Simon crouched in front of her and slapped his palm over it. "Not a word or they die," he seethed. The sting of the slap needled her lips and cheek. She fought to bring in enough air through her nose. The man's filthy hand smelled of horses and dung.

"Meg?" Jonet called over the clicking of her boots. "Meg, is that ye down there?"

Meg willed her to go back but the clicking got louder.

"I found Peter's kitten by the door and I thought I heard ye crying. Meg?"

A gasp, boots flailing against rock. "Not a word, lassie, or ye'll end up dead, too," Girshmel said. He dragged her back down toward Meg.

Jonet's eyes were round above Girshmel's hand. When she saw Simon there was recognition in her eyes and they narrowed. Jonet's foot snapped up and back, kicking Girshmel's knee. He grunted and lost his grip on her mouth as she bit down.

"Bitch!" he yelled and grabbed at Jonet's flailing arms. She hit him in the nose and blood gushed from it.

Meg used her magic to quickly assess Simon's physical flaws. He was all muscle and sinewy strength, but there was bruising all around his ribs on the right side. She jammed her elbow into the sensitive area, and Simon doubled over with a groan. Jonet ran toward the door, but Meg ran for Donald. She reached him just as Girshmel scooped up Jonet. Meg poured her healing thoughts into her fallen friend, fixing the small breaks that remained and replenishing the blood that had drained from his wound. Her hand skimmed Father Daughtry and she sent a blasting pulse of magic with the image of blood-filled veins.

Simon yanked Meg to him roughly. Girshmel laughed and wiped the blood from his nose across his arm. "This one has spirit," he said and grabbed a fistful of Jonet's hair. "Be careful, lassie, or I may take a liking to ye." He bent closer to her and licked from her jaw line to her ear. "And the lasses don't always survive that," he chuckled.

Fear engulfed Jonet's face and she pinched her eyes shut.

"Tie her over here with Meg," Simon instructed. "Until we figure out what to do with her."

Meg knew the two fallen men must be rousing, but if either one moved, they'd be stabbed again. *Stay still!* "Donald and the good Father are dying," she said. "Please let me help them."

"And have the warrior fighting for ye? Or worse, warning the Macbains that ye're missing?" Simon said. "Nay, he can bleed to death and so can the priest. God can take care of him now."

"Where are you taking me?" Meg asked.

"We're taking ye both now," Girshmel added.

"Leave her," Meg said. "I'm the one you're supposed to take, aren't I?"

"Aye, but I like her," Girshmel said.

"*Muc!* Pig!" Jonet spit on the stone floor.

Girshmel laughed softly and sheathed his sword.

"Where are you taking us?" Meg was determined to give as much information to Donald as she could.

"Yer father would like to take a walk with ye, up that mountain," Simon answered.

"Gwyneth told you," Meg said, her eyes flicking to the floor, but both men continued to hold their prone poses.

"Aye, my sweet Gwen hears everything." Simon chuckled.

Could Gwen have heard she was pregnant? Meg prayed the news hadn't spread that fast. "Colin Macleod is my father," she said, using the little strength she had left to sit up defiantly.

Simon laughed. "Ye keep saying that as if that will help ye. I'd start calling Boswell Papa in hopes he doesn't just burn ye for witchcraft himself."

"I think the man would burn his own kin for witchcraft," Girshmel said solemnly and shivered.

What kind of a devil made that giant quake? Meg breathed, trying to slow her rapidly pounding heart. "He did burn his kin," she muttered, and sent a prayer to heaven for help. Not just for herself now, but for her newly forming babe.

Simon looped the rope around Meg's wrists. "Aye, I heard about yer mother being burned." He *tsk*ed. "We'll tie yer hands so ye aren't tempted to use dark magic."

Dark magic? Never had she called upon the devil or demons or anything dark for aid. She was raised as a God-fearing, good Catholic woman. Although, Meg considered, these men didn't know that. She glanced at Father Daughtry but barked out a loud laugh anyway. The noise echoed in the dark hall.

Simon jumped back. "What the hell?"

"I have other dark powers, too," Meg boasted, her lips quirking in a sinister grin. "Ask Girshmel about my beast. Nickum of the Night will stalk you when you take us. He'll follow without a sound. You won't hear him until he leaps upon you, ripping open your throat."

"Shut yer mouth," Girshmel ordered.

"I thought ye shot the wolf at the loch," Simon said.

From Girshmel's face, Meg could tell that Gilbert Davidson had passed along her message, and she laughed. "My wolf healed. He's at full strength and he knows exactly who shot him."

"Stop talking," Girshmel said.

Meg just laughed. Jonet's eyes widened like Meg had grown the devil's own horns. Meg winked at her before turning back to the men.

"I've already placed a spell on all of you," Meg sang.

"A spell?" Simon said and took a step back. "What type of spell?"

"She's lying," Girshmel said and tied Jonet's hands in front.

"A sleeping spell." Meg yawned loudly. "You will soon become very tired. So tired that you will drop right where you are standing."

Just as Meg had hoped, her own yawns had pulled them from all the people in the room. She hoped Donald and the priest could remain still if they were conscious.

"You will all start to yawn and yawn, your jaws opening so wide they will crack and ache. Yawn after yawn after yawn."

Both Simon and Girshmel clenched their jaws.

Meg could barely stop her own. "You will grow so exhausted that you'll barely be able to breathe. Your arms will fall to your sides like you've lugged bricks all day, your legs like they are pulling granite on chains. Even your head is starting to weigh like a boulder upon your neck."

Simon's shoulders slumped a little.

"Yawn after yawn after—"

"Shut yer mouth, witch!" Girshmel hissed in a loud whisper.

"Is Boswell paying you enough to make up for dying under a witch's spell?" Meg pushed.

Girshmel threw a rag at Simon. "Gag the witch."

"That won't stop the spell from working. Leave us here and you will survive."

Simon worked the rag into her mouth, which absorbed all the moisture instantly. She tried to quell her frantic heart. The men wrapped them in large wool blankets, hefted them over their shoulders. An eternity of stopping and running passed before Meg was lowered onto planks, perhaps in the back of a wagon.

"I can't breathe," Jonet called next to Meg. "With that gag, Meg will die and Boswell will slice yer entrails from ye," she said through the wool.

Praise be to Jonet!

"God's teeth." Simon's muffled curse reached Meg as the wagon dipped under his weight. A foul-smelling hand yanked the gag down. She sucked in a gulp of the stagnant air. "If ye make a sound, the gag goes back."

Meg concentrated on the air that she needed until her lightheadedness abated. She rested, letting the stillness replenish her energy. She'd given most of it to Donald and Father Daughtry and nearly the rest to her witch's farce. The act had almost cost her life, but hopefully it was worth the risk. She might be able to save Jonet.

After long minutes, Jonet rolled up against her. "Are ye sound?" she whispered through the folds of fabric.

Meg waited. Should she risk answering? The men continued to talk in the wagon seat. They rumbled slowly along a path, probably out of the surrounding village.

Meg rolled closer to let her know she was awake. "Feign sleep," she whispered and hoped Jonet could hear her. She didn't dare speak louder.

"Sleep?" Jonet asked.

Meg waited, but the men kept talking above them. "When we stop, be asleep. Don't wake."

Simon stopped his banter abruptly and Meg bit into her lip. Had he heard? After a few moments the conversation picked up again.

"Gilbert said that he and Boswell would be at the base of the mountain, after our men take care of Macbain and his troop," Simon said. Meg's ears strained to follow the voices through the muffling layers of wool wrapped so tight.

Girshmel said something and chuckled maliciously.

"Aye, they should be surprised." Simon laughed. "As well as the rest of Druim when our soldiers attack."

Caden and the others were walking into an ambush and the Davidsons planned to storm Druim. Her heart pounded so hard she could barely hear any more words, but then the men fell silent. In the quiet, she prayed.

Dearest Lord, watch Caden's back. Warn him. Her thoughts turned inward to the small ball growing in her womb. *And please take care of me, for our babe.* She sent a quick prayer up that Donald and Father Daughtry were well and that Jonet would make it out of this alive. Then Meg cleared her mind and breathed, resting herself and regaining energy.

The wagon jolted and creaked, dipped and climbed. She'd have bruises from slamming against the wooden side. At last they stopped.

"Sleep," Meg whispered.

Someone lifted her roll out of the wagon and set her on her feet. Her captor grabbed the end and yanked, flipping Meg out onto the ground. She sucked in the freshness like it was life-giving water and blinked in the bright light that filtered through the bare branches of trees overhead.

She pushed up onto her arms. They were in the forest, bare limbs reaching down like gray, gnarled fingers. Snow piled in drifts against trunks, muffling the world. Alone, far from Druim. A chill racked Meg's body.

Two horses stood tethered by one tree. "We go the rest of the way on horse," Simon said.

"Little lass, wake up." Girshmel nudged Jonet with his boot.

Jonet kept her eyes shut and breathed evenly.

"Oh no, the spell has overtaken her," Meg said.

At the mention of the spell, Simon yawned, making Girshmel yawn and curse. The man's hard eyes found Meg. "Wake her."

Meg shook her head, praying that she was doing the right thing denying these men. "I can't. Once she falls asleep only time can wake her. A few days, perhaps."

"*A few days?*" Girshmel picked Jonet up roughly. He shouted in her face. "Wake, woman!"

Jonet continued to breathe evenly. Meg cringed as Girshmel kissed her lips. Amazingly, Jonet remained languid in his arms.

Simon laughed. "What difference if she's awake or not if you are wanting to tup her."

"I prefer some spirit when I pump my way into a lass," Girshmel said with a sneer. He began to carry her to one of the horses.

"We haven't the time to waste on carrying her. Leave her in the wagon. She'll sleep the day away and ye can get her when ye come back down the mountain."

"Nay, I'm taking her," Girshmel said and Meg's stomach twisted. If they would just leave Jonet, she could run back to Druim.

The sound of horses whipped Meg around. Three men she didn't know pulled their mounts to a stop.

"Bring the woman," the man in front said, appraising Meg. "Boswell and Gilbert wait up near the caves." His gaze rested on Jonet across Girshmel's horse. "Who is that?"

"My woman," Girshmel said.

"What's wrong with her?"

"The witch put a sleeping spell on her," Simon said and made the sign of the cross before him.

Meg bared her teeth.

"I'd burn ye myself if my chief didn't want ye first," he murmured.

"Leave the sleeping one," the leader called. "The Englishman grows impatient and she'll slow us down."

Girshmel hesitated and cursed, but pulled Jonet off the horse and toppled her roughly into the back of the wagon. He threw the blanket on top of her. Girshmel climbed on his horse and reached down to grab Meg up in front of him. The smell of sweat and unwashed flesh assailed her, bringing on another bout of queasiness. Her stomach rumbled like far-off thunder.

"What of Macbain and his men?" Simon called as they followed the others up the winding mountain path.

"Dead," the leader called back.

The word hit Meg in the gut. *Dead? Dead! The Macbain was dead!* Her lungs contracted and she couldn't pull in a breath of air. Her hands went to her mouth as unchecked tears pushed out of her eyes. She drew in a gasp and her stomach churned, surging upward.

"Did ye hear that, little lady?" Girshmel said. "Yer big mighty man is dead."

The putrid breath was the last insult to Meg's senses. She turned her head to the side. The vomit that came up flew down along Girshmel's leg.

"Bloody wench!" Girshmel cursed and virtually threw Meg to one of the other men riding beside them. Her sore body banged into the thick trunk of the other warrior. "Take her," he yelled and wiped the frothy waste from his bare leg with the end of his plaid.

"Dead?" Meg whispered.

The man holding her answered. "Shot, he was, by Kendell up there. Must be dead by now."

Meg's hand ran along her abdomen over the small life growing there. To stay alive and to keep their baby alive was her mission. How could a day so full of promise have turned so brutal?

She wiped at her mouth and tears. She had to be strong and clever, for the baby and for Caden, because he just had to survive.

Hope. She must hold onto hope. As the horses climbed along the rock-strewn path amongst the trees and patches of snow, she prayed and pleaded as she concentrated on breathing. *Live, Caden, live! Live, my love, live!*

• • •

"I broke the shaft off," Alec said thickly behind Caden. "Lay back now, lad."

"I will sit," Caden said. The pain in his chest and shoulder shot like fire through his stiff body, causing small bursts of light to pop before his eyes. "Colin, the others?"

Alec squatted down and rubbed his hand over his short beard. "Not good. My man, Seonaidh, is dead."

Caden's mind pushed past the stabbing sharpness of the wound and the difficulty breathing, past his fury for not anticipating the ambush. He forced air down his throat. The breath wheezed on the way back out, and he coughed.

"You're pale. Lay back, Caden." Alec waved another Munro over.

Caden remained sitting against the tree. "My da laid down when he'd been shot and he never rose again. I'll sit."

Alec clasped his shoulder gently. "I've stopped the bleeding with the cloth, but that rasp in your voice says the arrow hit a lung."

"Good thing I have two of them," Caden murmured and tried to keep his eyes in focus.

"Go to Brenon Malley's cottage, the one on the other side of this pass," Alec said to a Munro warrior, one of the men who'd brought up the rear and hadn't been shot in the bombardment of arrows. "Get Rachel—she's there tending a fever—and bring her here." Alec scanned the trees. "Watch for the bastards, but bring her here. Quick as you can."

The warrior ran off, a blur in Caden's peripheral vision that tunneled in and out. He blinked. His eyes opened again on Alec wrapping Colin's plaid around his father-in-law's chest. Colin's eyes were closed, but Caden could see his chest rise and fall on a shallow breath.

Bloody hell, he hadn't even seen Gilbert or Boswell among the attackers, but he knew they were Davidsons, had recognized them. Although he hadn't seen Simon, either. Where were they? Gilbert Davidson may be a bloody traitor and murderer, but he wasn't a coward.

"Alec," Caden said, though his tongue moved thick in his mouth, unwieldy with the taste of his own blood. "Gilbert and Boswell…I didn't see Simon, either. They knew we were gone from Druim…Meg…they…going to get her," he finally spit out with the blood that had collected against the corner of his lip.

Alec frowned. "I've already sent a man back to Druim for help. He will find Meg and make certain she's tucked up tight inside."

Caden nodded—or at least he thought he did—but then Alec's face began to swim farther and farther away down a tunnel surrounded by darkness.

Even though he fought it, the patch of light at the tunnel's end continued to move farther out until it was just a single star in a sea of night. He closed his eyes and spit out the blood in his mouth. *Meg, lass, stay safe, keep our wee bairn safe.* The tree broke his fall as his heavy body fell backward. Just like his da, Caden Macbain laid down on the ground.

...

Meg held tight to the scrap of mane in front of her as she tried not to lean back into the Davidson warrior. The trail threaded up through birch and conifer trees around boulders and along a brisk stream. They stopped once to water the horses.

She sat upon the horse and watched a dry leaf break free of a cluster up stream. The brittle form meandered down over ripples, swirling through eddies to finally stick to a clump of roots. The leaf's wide span clogged the gentle flow, forcing the water to shoot alongside it.

Girshmel stomped through the water, rinsing his leg. "Bloody leg still stinks," he said, glaring in Meg's direction.

Meg moved her eyes back to the leaf and stared, emotionless, aloof. If she allowed her emotions to flow, she'd succumb to weeping. And she couldn't do that, not when her baby's life was still in peril. More leaves followed the strong current, piling up onto the first leaf until a clump dammed the water along the far side.

"Let's go," the man who'd shot Caden called. "Gilbert and the Englishman want her up at the cave now."

Why would they need her at the cave? Meg swallowed hard. They needed a map, but she'd left the key at Druim.

The Davidson warrior named James pulled up behind her again. Had they followed Caden and Colin up there? Would Caden be lying there? Could she reach him in time? Meg's hand tingled with blue heat and she fisted it against her leg. She leaned forward in the saddle.

The horse seemed to sense her impatience and surged forward, making James work hard to keep him under control. "Bloody horse, what's gotten into you?"

Meg's gaze whipped through the trees. Was Nickum near? She moved her fingers up to her lips and stopped. If Nickum attacked she might never find the cave, or at least not quick enough to save Caden. She clenched her fingers and lowered them, still glancing through the layers of frosted forest.

Long minutes later, two riders appeared ahead. The rushing sound of water caught their hail as one raised an arm. Gilbert Davidson. Rowland Boswell sat his horse next to him.

Meg studied the ground they rode over. A blood spot here, scuffed ground there, leaves mixed with reddish slush lay scattered in clumps.

James pulled his horse to a stop with the others near Gilbert and Boswell. Gilbert showed his pristine white teeth at Meg and bowed his head. "Ah, the Lady Meg. Or should I say the Widow Meg?"

Meg sat up as straight as she could. "Show me Caden's body. I see no bodies here."

Gilbert's gaze grew cold. "Caden Macbain is dead. Kendell shot him. See?" He indicated the puddles of blood under the horses' hooves. "Shot through the chest."

She tamped down the panic that pushed bile up her throat. She swallowed, but hid it by narrowing her eyes. "'Tis a trick. I see no body. Did my dead husband walk away, then?"

Kendell shrugged and pointed to the ground. "Dragged."

"You left some of them alive," Boswell said, his hard eyes stared down the man.

Kendell's throat worked up and down. "One or two, perhaps. I had to make contact with Simon to get the girl."

Boswell shifted his black eyes toward Gilbert. "And your other warriors?"

"Ye wanted the Munro Witch taken as well. Half are at Munro Castle and half are at Druim, making sure they are too busy to follow. With The Macbain and The Macleod of Lewis out of the way, we can fetch the letters and be back at my holding by nightfall."

"And after I fetch me woman," Girshmel said. Jonet should be halfway back to Druim by now, if she didn't run into any of the other Davidsons or English.

"Ye'll have yer letters, yer daughter, and the Witch Munro as promised," Gilbert continued.

"In exchange for forty pieces of silver?" Meg asked sarcastically.

Gilbert moved his horse toward her and leaned forward to rub his thumb against her cheek. Meg turned away but found her retreat blocked by James, who pushed forward until Gilbert held her whole face in the palm of his hand. "Gold," he said, his thumb tracing a lazy circle over her cheek. "Weapons, English promises…" His grin hardened into a leer, "…and ye before yer father decides yer fate." The surrounding men chuckled.

Meg's stomach tightened as James ground into her from behind.

"Perhaps ye could be persuaded to share the lass, Gilbert," James said in English. He inhaled dramatically. "She smells delicious."

Gilbert moved his thumb over Meg's mouth, dipping it between her parted lips. "Aye, let's see how many times we can make her beg for release." Gilbert laughed at his own pun and jammed his finger into Meg's mouth like she was a horse being made to accept a bit. Her jaw snapped down over his digit, her teeth cutting flesh.

Gilbert yanked his hand away. "Bloody bitch!"

Whack! His palm slammed into Meg's cheek, sending her reeling backward into James's arms. Gilbert pushed his face into hers. "I can be charming," he snarled, "or I can be cruel. Yer actions, milady, will decide which it will be."

"Enough of this play," Boswell called. "Let us get past this water."

Meg's head throbbed and she had trouble focusing. The trees fuzzed until she couldn't discern their individual shapes. She sucked in the crisp air, trying to rally her magic. The ache alternated with stabs of pain in her cheekbone and head. She sent a small sliver of healing energy into her head, just enough to stabilize the world around her.

James lowered Meg as the others dismounted. Gilbert handed Meg a flask and a linen with cheese. "Provisions for milady," he said, all gallant again.

Meg drank and ate. She had to keep her strength and the nausea became worse with hunger.

The waterfall rushed down into a frothy cistern below. Large rocks jutted upward, breaking the water into huge splashing spray. Meg shivered at the ice edging the top of the rocks.

Girshmel grunted as he lowered a thick log across from the ledge they stood out on. The makeshift bridge fell behind the curtain of water to a barely seen rock ledge, which must have been at the mouth of the cave.

As James pushed her closer and the mist rose up, forming droplets of ice water in her hair. For the barest of seconds, she focused on the jutting rocks below and wondered if her best choice was to jump. Would the simple pain of death be so much less than what these brutes had in mind? If Caden was dead… her hand moved to rest on her stomach. Nay, she couldn't jump, not with so much to live for, so much to protect. She had to stay alive as long as possible. With life there was hope.

"James, go across first," Gilbert said and grabbed Meg's arm. James didn't appear to want to be the first to try the crude bridge, but he didn't argue. With three rapid steps he slipped across the log and behind the waterfall. His head peeked out, a cocky grin on his pockmarked face.

Gilbert glanced at his three men. "Ye stay out here and guard the cave entrance."

Boswell moved across the log with assured grace, though slower than James.

Girshmel glanced around at the woods and frowned. "Best be prepared," he warned.

"For what?" Kendell said. "We slaughtered most of them."

Girshmel lifted his bushy chin toward Meg. "The lass has a beast."

Nickum! Meg stuck two fingers in her lips and blew. A shrill whistle cut through the crash of water, through the trees. She blew again until Gilbert grabbed her wrist, bruising it as he yanked her against him.

"None can hear ye," he said, but his eyes flitted to the bare trees. "Move," he ordered and shoved her toward the log.

Just as her foot stepped onto the slippery wood, she heard the familiar crash through the leaves. A snarl echoed through the trees followed by a scream of pure panic. Nickum's powerful body flew through the air, landing on Simon.

"Move!" Gilbert barked in her ear and pushed her across

the log. Meg's feet slipped and fought for purchase with the big man at her back. "Fast, or ye'll fall!"

Out of the corner of Meg's eye she saw Kendell fall backward over the side. His flailing body thudded against the rocks below. The sound of the crashing water diluted the screams and snarls from behind.

"*Cac!*" Gilbert yelled.

Meg landed on the cold, wet rock floor at the mouth of the cave. A wall of water rushed before her face. She crawled to the edge to see around the flow. The water washed away the melody of death as Nickum and his mate tore into Simon. She winced at the sight and closed her eyes.

"This time you'll stay dead." Meg's eyes snapped back open.

Girshmel held his bow steady and nocked an arrow.

"Nickum!" she warned just as the arrow released. Nickum jumped and the arrow darted through the sheet of water, nearly pinning Gilbert.

Nickum lunged at Girshmel. He darted around the beast and tried to reach the log, but Nickum's teeth tore into his calf, yanking him back. A curse froze on Girshmel's wet lips as Nickum dragged him, the man's nails digging into the frozen earth.

"Pull the log," Boswell yelled at Gilbert. "Or her beast will come across."

Meg stood before the log and whistled.

"Bitch!" Gilbert threw against the outside of the cave with one hand and reached down to yank the log. Nickum turned, his muzzle covered with fresh blood. Too late. Gilbert braced his feet against a boulder and pulled the log off the far edge. "Help me. If I drop this, we'll never get back across!"

James leapt over and grasped the log where thin stumps of branches gave them handholds. The log slid across the chasm, leaving Nickum staring from the edge. His black eyes locked with Meg's. He was a beast, but the expression that passed across his face was human regret, regret for not getting there sooner, not jumping across the log, regret for leaving her with her tormentors.

Meg stood tall along the side of the cave entrance. "You know he won't leave me."

Gilbert spun on his heel and stalked toward her. He grabbed her hair and yanked it back so that he washed her face with his stagnant, fear-drenched breath. "Ye will make him leave, witch."

"Or what?" she asked against the sting on her scalp. "You'll kill my family? You'll kill me? What other threats could you use against me that you haven't already?"

Gilbert's lips crushed down on top of her mouth, bruising, suffocating. He pushed her hard, banging her head, the sharp rocks scoring her back. When he pulled back, the worry was replaced with raw fury. "There are many worse things that can happen to ye before ye die, Meg. Things that can start right here on this rock until ye send yer minion away. Think about it," he said, the spittle from his wet lips speckled her cheeks.

Meg stared at him defiantly but kept her silence.

"Enough, Davidson," Boswell said, stepping out of the cave. "I need her alive to navigate these tunnels."

Gilbert leaned in, his arms braced on either side. "Think about it," he said and pushed backward. He strode toward the cave entrance. Nickum stood there, staring past the edge of the waterfall.

"Find him," Meg called to Nickum and turned before the others could question what she was doing. Whether Nickum understood, she didn't know, but when she glanced back he was gone.

Gilbert lit the dry end of a torch he'd brought out from inside the tunnel. "There are three paths to take," he said and turned to Meg. "The lady will guide us."

"What makes you think that I know which way to go? I've never been here."

Boswell's hands came down heavy on her shoulders. He peered down his hawkish nose. "I've heard of your mother's journal. That there were clues hidden within it." His hand dug into Meg's pocket, down to the very bottom. She stood motionless, though Boswell's fingers sliding against her thigh through the surcoat made her queasy. His hand moved around and his frown deepened.

"I heard there is a key, a map," Boswell said.

"You certainly hear a lot," Meg said, staring into his beady eyes.

"Ah, the lovely Gwyneth." Gilbert said it as if he were sampling a sweet morsel.

"Where's the key?" Boswell asked.

"I gave it to my father," Meg said.

Slap! Boswell's palm burned against her cheek. Her eyes teared with the pain and she swallowed hard.

"Then you will have to remember the way through the tunnels, won't you?" Boswell articulated with cruel precision.

"There are three paths that branch off." He turned to Meg. "Which way?"

She kept her lips shut tight.

"Gwen saw the key," Gilbert said. "She said one line off to the right went the farthest."

The dark victory of Boswell's gaze squelched Meg's breath like fingers pinching a candle flame. "To the right," he ordered.

Gilbert pulled Meg under the heavy lip of wet granite into complete darkness. The contrast between the filtered sunlight under the waterfall and the sharp black of the cave was blinding. Meg blinked several times to help her eyes adjust. Boswell followed them in with the torch, throwing sharp shadows against the moist walls.

"James, walk ahead of her so she can't lose us by running ahead," Gilbert called.

Gilbert gave Meg a small shove. "Ye be thinking of which way we should turn at the first divergence."

Meg followed James but murmured, "I don't know the way."

And it was true. Colin had said the markings were a map, his finger lingering on a spot at the end of the line that extended off to the right, but she hadn't confirmed that it was the hiding place.

Boswell moved the torch closer so that it cast a glow through the circular rock cave. The irregular walls closed in and widened out as they walked. Water trickled along cracks and small mushrooms cropped out at odd intervals. A musty earth smell infused Meg's inhales. The tunnel slanted, curved, and continued like a throat leading into the stomach of the mountain.

Lord, give me strength. She shuddered and tried to keep her breathing regular. The flame flickered as a breeze blew through, followed by a mournful cry. *Mmmaaaayyyyy.*

Meg stopped and rubbed her arms at the chill that had flooded the channel with the wind.

Gilbert turned rapidly, his sword sliding free. "What was that?"

"The wind," Boswell growled and grabbed Meg's arm. "Keep moving."

Rapid heartbeat, sour stomach, veins stretched, unhealed abscess on left foot, poorly healed shin bone on left leg, clot in deep vein of same leg. The infinitesimal details about Rowland Boswell's physical conditions poured into Meg upon contact. She blinked hard as he released her. The clot. Big and dangerous. If it were to break free and travel through his body, much like the clot in Angus or the leaves in the creek…Meg swallowed hard. The clot could kill him. *I could kill him.*

Meg's cheeks filled with heat as she faced the flickering darkness. How could she kill someone? She wasn't a witch who killed with her powers, a witch like the one Boswell had accused her mother of being. She was a healer with a gift from God. Her fears chewed at her heels, fed by years of denial, years of trying to subdue and ignore her powers. What would she become if she gave way and killed a man?

She heard one of them stumble behind her, the torch light shifting sporadically as Boswell cursed. He was winded, probably not used to such a climb. His elevated blood pressure could loosen the clot on its own.

"Perhaps you should rest your left leg. The break in your

shin didn't heal well," Meg said into the darkness, her voice swallowed down the cave's throat.

The torchlight halted, but Meg continued, fading farther into the black, her hand against the wall.

"Hey, where's the light?" James called.

Meg stopped for fear of running into Gilbert's lackey.

"You will burn like your mother, witch," Boswell said.

"Where are ye?" Gilbert called, leaping forward and holding onto Meg's wrist. "Boswell, keep us in sight."

Another breeze moaned through the cave. Meg's curls moved as if an unearthly hand threaded through it. A chill raised gooseflesh on her neck. The same gooseflesh prickled up in Gilbert, along with a leap in his heart rate.

"The cave is inhabited by restless spirits," she said in a soft voice and sensed Gilbert's increasing sweat production and clenched bladder.

James halted at a fork in the tunnel. "Which way?"

"Meg?" Boswell asked.

To the right, Meg thought. Colin's finger had stopped at the end of the farthest right path and all of her mother's clues mentioned staying to the right.

"Left," Meg said and cast her eyes downward as if they'd dragged the answer from her and she harbored guilt over it. "My father said to go left at the fork."

Boswell frowned but flicked his fingers at James. "Continue."

James hurried off into the darkness, the torchlight barely keeping up with him. Meg hung back, not knowing exactly what lay ahead, wondering if she'd been wise or foolish to lead them down a wrong turn.

Pebbles skittered as James shuffled past larger boulders. Meg heard his hand grazing the wall. "Perhaps there is a treasure chest at the end." He laughed over his shoulder. "With the letters. Seems like a perfect place to hide—"

James's words transformed into a gasp and a guttural scream cut through the tunnel. Meg froze. As James's voice grew fainter and fainter, energy to hold herself up drained out of her body. She sagged against the rock wall. Boswell stepped past her, holding the torch high. The light slanted across the sharp angles of stone walls to reveal a sheer drop, so far down into the mountain that the light couldn't reach the bottom.

"*Cac!*" Gilbert cried. "James!" he hollered, as if the man would reply.

The wall supported Meg as she tried to control her breathing, her wildly pounding heart. Gilbert turned on her, fury transforming his face into that of a nightmarish monster. "Ye bitch!" He advanced. Meg had tricked one of them to their death, but would it lead to her own?

"Halt, Davidson," Boswell said, and the angry bull actually stopped. "You can deal with her later. For now, she will lead us through the rest of this maze. I need her alive."

Boswell glanced at Meg. "Thank you for showing me the perfect place to forget a body."

His dark meaning was not lost on Meg. She swallowed hard.

"Now take us the correct way," Boswell finished and shone the light high. "You in front this time."

Meg led them back out to the main tunnel and turned them down the correct path. There were only two more divergences, and she continued to steer them right. She picked up her pace, straight ahead and into the dark. The three of them trod through the tunnel in the small circumference of light. Footfalls and tumbled pebbles echoed with their breaths.

She cringed as Gilbert's huff brushed her hair from behind, but as long as she continued quickly, Gilbert couldn't touch her. A sweat broke out along her spine despite the chill swirling around them. The farther they moved into the heart of the mountain, the milder the air became, as if the summer-warmed cavern still retained its heat.

The belly of the beast. Black nothingness and heavy rock pressed in on her, making her breathing shallow. Meg pushed the panic back into her stomach. The thought that her mother had found happiness here kept her trudging forward at the very fringe of the torchlight circle.

Time passed, the only evidence being the ache in her legs. She spent the time hoping and praying that Caden was alive. Minutes heaped upon minutes.

"Bloody long tunnel," Gilbert swore. "We must have hiked halfway through the mountain by now."

"Halt." Boswell held the torch high. Sweat covered his face. He wiped it with a handkerchief and tucked it back in his vest. He took a drink of water from a bladder he'd brought. "Carry on."

If this rapid hike hadn't dislodged the man's clot, then the hope of it occurring naturally was dim. Meg placed her hand against the slope of her belly. The babe was growing, elongating, protected below the layers of her muscle and skin. Alive, healthy, trusting her to keep it safe.

Her lips tightened into a thin line as she stared ahead. She wasn't an evil witch, plotting to take a man's life at will. Caden had called her a warrior. She was a warrior—a woman warrior with a purpose greater than her own life. And she must use all the weapons available.

Meg rounded the corner. Without the torch glow she could only detect the immense space with an intuition born to her gender. Her arm floundered out to the wall, but only waved in the emptiness.

"Meg!" Gilbert yelled and stepped around the corner with Boswell right behind him. The light flickered around the cavern walls as Boswell held the torch high.

She turned in a circle. Several fist-sized holes of light filtered down near the center where the ancient remains of a fire sat.

"Huh. Could have dug down to it," Gilbert said, staring up at the small holes.

Tears stabbed at her eyes as she surveyed the room. A folded wool plaid sat near the fire. Her mother and Colin had handfasted here in the heart of the mountain. The wind howled along the tunnel, tumbling around the three, chilling the space. Meg crossed her arms and shivered. The wind whipped dried pieces of debris from the fire pit and funneled them upward into mini tornados.

Several large boulders sat around the perimeter of the cavern like ancient monoliths. As Meg stood before the dead fire, directly beneath the holes, she noticed the boulder to the right. Could it be? She squinted in the poor lighting. Yes, a heart. God had molded the large granite stone into the shape of a human heart.

"A cold cave with a warm heart," Meg mumbled, and wiped a stray tear that had escaped her control.

"Where are they?" Boswell tore about the cavern. He flipped open the neatly piled blankets and kicked at the ashes in the fire pit as if attacking the place her mother had at one time been happy. "They've got to be here!"

"Perhaps it was a ruse," Meg said softly. "Perhaps she didn't hide any letters at all."

"No, she took them!" Boswell yelled. "They never arrived or Henry and his little Mary would be dead." His gaze flew about the room. "They must be here."

Gilbert began to kick at the monoliths, scattering stones and sending up dust. Meg spit out the grit in her mouth and shivered as the temperature seemed to drop.

She averted her gaze from the heart stone and prayed Gilbert would stop, but he didn't. With a brutal drive of his heel, Gilbert toppled the heart-shaped boulder. The two halves of the heart slid apart, showing that it had actually been two smaller boulders placed together. A packet of parchment fell out of the rubble.

"There!" Boswell snatched up the dust-covered bundle.

Gilbert picked up a single leaf of parchment, loose from the others. He broke the wax seal and scanned the script.

Boswell plucked it from his fingers and read it himself. "Seems that whore hoped you'd find these," he said and threw the letter at Meg's face.

She grabbed it.

"She always thought of herself as more clever. Her quiet disapproval even when she pretended to be obedient." He laughed with barely concealed insanity. He fingered through the letters. "Thought she'd stop me from proving my greatness."

Meg leaned back against the wall out of Boswell and Gilbert's way. She unfolded the parchment but the torchlight was too far away for her to read what it said. She ran her finger over the brittle paper.

"I love you, Mama," she whispered just above a breath. As she spoke, the tip of her finger began to glow, just enough to light the words. Where was the magic coming from? Not from her.

Meg swallowed hard as the room turned even colder and in contrast the sweet smell of honeysuckle surrounded her. She breathed in the lush scent and read the delicate slanted script.

My Sweet Meg,

May God keep you from harm. I send these letters into hiding with my true husband, your father, Colin Macleod. The letters hold proof of Rowland Boswell's treachery against King Henry and his chosen bride, the Catholic Queen Catherine, in his plans to assassinate his heir, the Princess Mary, and the king himself. Use these letters, your father's support, and any weapons that you have to survive Boswell's wickedness.

Remember that I love you, Meg.

Isabelle Macleod

The pain in Meg's chest forced her to release her breath. Her finger traced her mother's words as the blue light faded away. *Any weapons that you have.* The chilled air blew about the chamber and flickered the torchlight.

Gilbert eyed her from the other side of the cavern. He grinned, his lips shining wet in the fire glow. "Do ye even need Meg now that ye have the letters?"

Boswell glanced at her. "She still must be baptized by fire."

"Och, but not before I have a bit of fun," Gilbert drawled. "Maybe even before we leave this cozy little cave. Ye could even have a go of her, seeing as she isn't yer daughter."

Meg swallowed against the bile in her throat. Blessedly, Boswell didn't seem interested in her as he pored over his old words.

"No wonder the plan didn't work. None of my letters got through," Boswell murmured. He held the parchment toward the flame. "Although King Henry has turned into an easy man to manipulate. Luckily, he will never know." At the first lick of fire against the paper, the honeysuckle wind whipped about the room, bending the flame backward, away from the brittle sheet.

The coldness froze the air around them. Meg wrapped the cloak tightly around herself. "Mama," she whispered into the breeze.

"Damn wind," Boswell said and shoved the parchment onto the end of the torch.

Gilbert strode over to him. "Bloody hell, don't put it out!"

Too late. The flame snuffed out, crashing down the wave of darkness.

Move… Run… The words sang by Meg's ears on the wind. She leapt up, her legs full of energy.

"Get her!" Boswell yelled.

"Where is she?" Gilbert's voice filled the void as Meg skirted to the right around the edge of the cavern. She pulled her gown tight in one hand and with a push off the wall with her foot, she ran toward the spot where the tunnel had been. The wind nudged her from behind, slightly to the left, and she followed, never doubting that it led to freedom.

"Catch her!" Boswell ordered.

Meg ran through the opening into the tunnel. She stumbled into the wall at the first sharp turn, her heart hammering up her throat with each frantic breath. Cursing and stumbling sounds followed. Did she dare? Would they see? Perhaps if she kept the light low and focused toward the ground.

Meg lit a small ball of blue and held it before her stomach in an attempt to hide it. She could see the narrow tunnel and ran forward as the wind surged around her like a wave. She sprinted down the tunnel, afraid to glance behind, afraid to make the light bigger. The curses and shuffling sounds grew fainter. Perhaps she was outrunning them. The thought opened up her chest, allowing for more air.

She wasn't sure how long they had walked in but running out, with death or worse snapping at her heels, made the tunnel seem like an endless path. Her feet pounded against the damp rock and moss until the cramp in her stomach made her stop for breath. She leaned against the rock wall, allowing her little ball of light to go out. Darkness weighed in on her, making her chest tighten with a need for sky and fresh air. She closed her eyes and imagined the open sky above, and slowly, her breathing normalized.

Once the thudding in her head quieted, the thudding on the rock bed behind her grew. Like a monster out of the dark frightening children into staying in their beds at night, the sound solidified into the thunder of footfalls.

Meg shrank back against the wall and crouched. Better than outrunning them, let them pass. Her eyes stared out at the darkness as if she might see the monster coming. Her ears focused on the thuds, just one pair. Gilbert? Boswell probably scurried behind like a rat along the wall.

Along the wall! Which wall would Gilbert follow with his hand so he could maneuver through the dark? Meg stood. Should she move to the center of the tunnel and hope he followed close to the wall? Her ears trained on the sound as it increased. The tunnel wasn't wide enough. If she stood in the middle, he'd hit her. Which wall would he follow?

His dominant hand would make sense. The rapid sound echoed. He was almost upon her. Right side. He'd be following the right side. Her heart leapt at the sound pounding toward her. In a silent leap born on hope, she threw herself through the black width against the left wall, and crouched.

"Damn dark. Bloody damned witch. Used her black magic to blow the light away." Gilbert's curses panted out on each hard exhale as he thudded past. She winced as the edge of his short coat brushed her head, but he didn't stop. She held her breath for long seconds before she dared to exhale. Now what? One had passed and the other crept stealthily behind somewhere. She stilled her breathing and listened to the darkness. No wind, no movement, just her own heartbeat and shallow breaths.

She stood noiselessly and leaned into the jagged wall. She didn't dare illuminate the passage and she didn't dare stumble along making tripping noises. The darkness began to close in on her again and Meg squeezed her eyes shut. Her mind drifted to the blue sky and to Caden.

Please be alive, she pleaded with such intensity that stars sparked behind her eyelids. *Find me!* Meg's hand moved to her belly. *Find us!* She yelled in her head so loudly that she thought she heard a sound.

Her eyes snapped open, the blinding dark mocking her. A voice. She shrank in on herself again, pulling her skirts close, crouching down. Boswell's voice.

"Do you think you can hide from me?" The words came faint from back down the tunnel's throat, like bile rising up from a dank belly. As the voice grew in volume, Meg could distinguish more and more of his calm, precise words, words without exhale. He was walking toward her, slowly searching the corridor. "I will not miss you, Meg." He kicked a loose pebble with his step. She couldn't hear his footfalls, not like Gilbert. His words stopped as if he listened.

"You may not know this but I have an uncanny sense of smell," he continued. "Your mother smelled of flowers. A shame she had to die. She had the loveliest breasts." His laughter crept along Meg's spine, pushing her slowly away from the wall. She grazed the solid rock with her fingertips as she walked, gingerly, picking her feet up high and setting them down without sound. If she continued to walk ahead of him, perhaps he wouldn't find her.

"And I know what you smell like. You smell of that Highlander. However, right now you stink of…fear." He paused to listen.

Meg halted her step until he began to speak again.

"I'm right behind you, Meg," he said, his voice louder.

Her heart raced until she thought she might faint. Would his long cold fingers suddenly touch her hair, wrap around her neck? She held her skirts and walked on, concentrating on even breaths.

"You are making me angry, girl, with this hiding. I know you are out there," he said, his voice quieter now. "If you make me too angry, Meg, I will lose my patience and kill you here, in this black hole where no one will find you. Perhaps I will just throw you down that perilous drop. You can land on that broken Scot at the bottom. Of course, Gilbert will insist on fucking you first." He laughed. "I've thought of you so long as my daughter that the thought of raping you myself turns my stomach."

Although he had the stomach to throw her into a black hole to her death.

Meg listened to his words fade and grow as she walked. She tried to block their meaning. Twice she plugged her ears with her fingers, but pulled them back out. Hearing was the only sense that told her his distance.

"I'm closing in on you now," his words came with a puff of exertion. He inhaled dramatically. "I think I just caught a whiff of your terror."

Her eyes widened. He'd started to walk faster. She kept her feet high as she walked but increased her pace.

"There really is no place for you to go. Gilbert will be waiting for you at the mouth of the cave or I will find you along this tunnel. Either way, I will have you."

Panic skittered between her shoulder blades, down to her wildly beating heart. Run...she had to run! The thought of his hands grabbing her from behind in the dark was overwhelming. Meg couldn't pull in a full breath of air. Her mind tumbled and the corridor seemed to close in. She had to take control, if not of the situation, then at least of herself.

She created a pea-sized ball of light to illuminate the path before her feet and sprinted ahead, no longer concerned what her toes hit as she ran.

Her footfalls resounded in the tunnel.

For several minutes Meg ran, pushing past the stitch in her side, until the sound of Boswell's heavy breathing faded. She forced full breaths through her nose, along with a small channeling of magic and the stitch in her muscles dissolved. She saw the quick turn at the last moment and ran around the corner. Right into a solid wall…of muscle.

Breath slammed out of her. Meg could hardly squeak the scream in her throat as Gilbert's fingers bit into her upper arms.

"Did ye really think ye'd get away?" He laughed and half-dragged her forward, around the sharp bend, until the filtered light through the waterfall filled the cave entrance. "Must have bloody run right past ye."

He released her. Meg blinked long at the pain in her eyes from being so long in total darkness. The rushing sound of water filled her ears. The cold spray whipped inward with the wind, the faint smell of honeysuckle lost in the droplets.

I'm sorry, Mama. Meg fought to hold in tears. She wouldn't let them see her despair. Boswell half jogged and half walked around the corner, holding his side with one hand and the packet of letters with the other.

Meg breathed deeply and tried to focus, but the absolute

impossibility of escaping them beat at her hope. What could she do? What weapons did she still have?

She stood tall. "I command you to release me," she said in her loudest, non-frantic voice. She raised her hands and formed the blue glowing ball. Both men froze for several heartbeats, their eyes round. Gilbert made the sign of the cross. Meg pulled her hands further apart, increasing the size of the ball until it was several feet across. The varying hues of blue swirled within the light.

Power…magic power. This was who she was. There was no denying it. She had a gift, a gift from God. Was it also a weapon?

"Lower the bridge across the gap and release me or I will use my power to kill you," she said succinctly.

Boswell stared at the ball, then at her face. If she wasn't in such dire circumstances, Meg would have laughed at his shock. "You are a witch," he said.

She gave him her best yes-and-I'm-going-to-kill-you expression. "So do what I say or I will use my magic against you."

Boswell's eyes narrowed. "If you were powerful enough to harm us, why wait until now?"

Gilbert seemed to shake off his surprise. "Gwyneth said ye could make some sort of glowing ball, but that it didn't do much except possibly heal people." He walked up to her and grabbed her wrists. Meg's concentration and the ball evaporated. "Unless ye can heal me to death, I'm not worried."

She swallowed the bitterness of fear and fury. If she lost herself to either emotion she'd lose her wits and she desperately needed them. "You'd be surprised what I can do," she replied with icy calm.

Gilbert moved closer until she could smell his dank breath, but she wouldn't back away. "I think it's just about time for me to find out all yer luscious body can do," he said, and grabbed a clump of her hair. He yanked her toward him, his lips bruising hers in a brutal kiss. Meg's hands were free as he forced her head to turn with his. She reached up and impaled the sides of his face with her nails, scraping and tearing the flesh.

Gilbert reared back with a growl. "Ye little hellion!" He touched the side of his cheek that had trails of freshly beaded blood. His eyes narrowed. "So ye like it rough." He spun Meg around to face the granite wall.

"Hurry," Boswell said. "I want to be at your holding before nightfall. If that wolf's still out there, you will want the light to see him."

"There's plenty of time to play, Boswell," Gilbert gritted out. He smashed Meg against the wall. The chill spray of water hit her legs as Gilbert threw up her skirts. She gasped as his knee went between her legs.

Oh God, no! Meg squeezed her legs shut and concentrated on the precious life she protected inside.

Gilbert leaned in to her ear. "Now we'll see just how tough ye—"

His sentence cut off to a yelp and a gurgle. As his hands fell away, Meg twisted and threw herself back against the rock.

...

As soon as Caden loosed the dagger, he bit down on a second one and swung across the chasm. Even though his leg caught the edge of the gushing water, his momentum carried him into the cave entrance. He landed solid and grabbed the dagger from his mouth. "Meg!"

"Caden!" she screamed as Boswell thrust her body before him like a shield. Gilbert Davidson twitched in a pile on the ground, blood gushing around the blade lodged through his neck.

"Let her go," Caden demanded as he held the weapon poised. *Bloody hell!* Her face seemed bruised! Was she hurt? Was the bairn? For a moment he couldn't breathe.

Boswell jammed the razor sharp edge of a knife under Meg's chin, his other arm wrapped around her chest. Caden's control nearly snapped at the thin line of blood on Meg's soft white skin where the blade touched. The only thing that kept him in check was the strength in her eyes as she stared at him. There was no fear, no grimace of pain, only relief and trust. As if she knew he would save her even with a madman's blade scraping her throat.

"You're alive," she breathed.

"Yes," Boswell said, his voice annoyed. "How is that possible? I saw the hit you took."

"Meg's not the only healer in these Highlands," Caden answered as his mind sifted through scenarios.

"Satan's work," Boswell said, his eyes wild.

Colin and Alec swung across behind him, cursing as they slipped on the granite.

"Watch out!" Ewan called as he also landed.

"Enough or she dies now!" Boswell yelled.

"No more men," Caden called above the roar of water, though his eyes remained on the knife. To Boswell he said,

"Release her."

"Why would I do such a thing?"

When Caden had been so close to death, bleeding there cold and blind, he'd made a choice. He'd chosen what he valued most, whom he loved more than life. Meg.

"If ye release her, I will grant ye safe passage off my land, ye and yer letters," he said, indicating the bundle of papers at Meg's feet. "I swear it before these men, on my honor."

"Nay, Caden!" Colin yelled. "He will destroy the letters and bring King Henry's troops down on us."

A wind whipped around them, swirling a chill so powerful it brought bumps up on Caden's arms. Winter's breath, but strangely it smelled of summer flowers.

"I will avenge Isabelle," Colin swore, and pulled back his arm.

Meg shut her eyes as the knife cut against her skin.

Caden held up his hand. "By killing her daughter? Nay! Colin, stand down!"

"That's right," Boswell said, triumph lacing his words, though his eyes remained unnaturally wide. One of them twitched. His hand relaxed against Meg's neck and Caden breathed once more. "Stand down. Let me leave here."

"Release her and ye can leave," Caden said.

Boswell shook his head. "I take her with me."

Steely anger roiled up inside Caden. He swallowed to control his tongue, control his blade.

"You may swear that I have safe passage, but the others do not," Boswell said.

"Do ye really think ye'll live long with Meg with ye?" Ewan

said. "Her beast waits for ye now."

Boswell's eyes flitted to the waterfall where Caden knew Nickum paced.

"Even if Caden let her go with ye, the beast would not," Ewan said.

"And I will not let her go with ye," Caden said slowly. "That is the bargain. Ye let her go and I let ye go."

Boswell narrowed his eyes. "You would really bring war with England down on your clan, on all your clans, because of one woman?"

After years of questioning the logic in a feud that had begun over one woman, Caden's choice was made. Life was not black and white, wrong and right. There were circumstances that colored the world and the wisdom of man. For once, Caden thought of saving one, not of saving the most.

"I said," Caden repeated, "Meg stays."

She carried his unborn child, and she carried his very heart inside her.

Boswell's triumphant face dissolved. *Bloody hell!* The man was realizing that there was very little possibility of his survival.

"I have friends," Boswell said, his arms tightening around Meg. "They know if I do not return that you are to blame. King Henry will send his troops to avenge me."

Sweat dotted his forehead, his hand holding the knife trembled enough to scrape Meg's skin. *Bloody damn hell!* Caden knew that face, the face of a desperate man who would take everyone with him to the grave if he could.

"Boswell, drop the knife," Caden said slowly. Could he reach Meg before the knife sliced her throat open? Could he get her to

Rachel before her life's blood drained out completely?

Meg opened her eyes. She pursed her lips tightly, her forehead furrowed. Her eyes held guilt and resolve as they stared into Caden's.

"God's teeth," Ewan murmured.

Meg's entire body pulsed with a brilliant blue light. Boswell's face pinched in agony, his eyes clenched shut. Caden lunged for the knife, grabbed the handle, and threw it into the rushing waterfall. He yanked Meg into his arms. Boswell crumpled to the ground, grabbing his chest. He convulsed. Colin raised his dagger to throw.

"No!" Meg yelled. "Let nothing mark his body." She watched the writhing man. "Rowland Boswell died of natural causes today, from his exertions climbing this mountain to find his letters, letters my mother intercepted to keep the royal family safe." She focused for a moment on Colin. "Isabelle's name will be cleansed and Boswell's body will be treated like that of a traitor."

Boswell groaned with a shrill cry of pain. He struggled through several stuttered breaths and stopped. The crushing moan of the waterfall filled Caden's ears as the sweet smelling winter air swirled around. Colin picked up the packet of letters.

"Will Henry believe the letters are real?" Alec asked.

"Either way, Boswell is dead," Meg said. "And not by a Scotsman's sword."

Her words were strong, yet Caden could see her shake. He wrapped her in his arms, infusing her with his body heat. "As she says," he commanded.

Ewan knelt beside the prostrate man. "He's dead." His gaze

went to Meg. She nestled her face into Caden's chest.

The ferocious winter air gentled to a breeze, scattering dry leaves and forming a funnel that rose. Colin inhaled and tucked the letters into the leather pouch tied at his waist. The small funnel of debris shot through the waterfall, dispersing. They all stood numb.

"Isabelle can rest," Colin murmured.

. . .

Meg dropped to her knees when she stepped off the log. Nickum pushed his head through the circle of her arms. She hugged him, hiding her tears in his thick coat. He let out a whine and licked the salty tears from her cheek.

"I am sound."

Not far off, away from the Munro and Macbain warriors, was Nickum's friend. Meg's faithful beast turned to sit next to her, his eyes on the female wolf. With timid determination the smaller animal sidled toward Meg, who remained on her knees.

"Have you found a mate, too?" Meg whispered in the hush surrounding them. The female wolf came to Nickum. Meg still held onto his coat, but furtively slid her fingers under to graze the female's foot.

Healthy and pregnant with three cubs. She ran her hand down Nickum's side as she stood. The female wolf trotted off back toward the woods. Nickum's gaze followed her but then turned back to Meg.

"Go," Meg said and smiled. "You have a family starting, too, now." She gave her protector and friend a little push. "I'll always be here if you need me."

New tears wet Meg's eyes as exhaustion and pain from her ordeal weighed heavy on her. She began to crumble back to the slushy mud, but Caden's arms caught her. He swung her up and she rested her head on his chest.

"Time to go home, love," he whispered.

The party rode across the field of broken, churned snow, under sharp moonlight. The horse surged under Meg as she rested her face against Caden's strong heartbeat. Strong, solid, not dead. *Thank you, God.* No matter what came to pass after healing Boswell to death, Meg would never despise her magic. The healing power within her family had kept her love alive.

Meg closed her eyes against the glare of moon on the snow. Caden held her ensconced in his warmth, giving, sharing. He stroked down her hair just before he draped a woolen plaid over her head to block the wind. His blood surged, his muscles strong. His body engulfed her with his own as if he could tuck her inside. He didn't seem afraid of her touch even after he'd witnessed the worst of her magic, the worst of who she was, a witch. Hot tears slipped in silence from her shut eyes. Nay, she would never despise her magic. Not as long as Caden lived.

The warhorse slowed. They must have reached the edge of the village. No sound permeated the wool over her head. The village must be asleep.

Darkness enveloped the landscape, but the village of Druim was alive with torchlight. Her breath caught at the brilliant sight. Along the pebbled, snaking road people lined both sides, Macbains, torches high, a river of fire to mark their way to the open gates.

Shadows and light played across their faces. The edge of

terror bit on the lining of her stomach. Were they waiting to drag her away? The flames danced in the night breeze, and for an instant she thought she saw the woman of her nightmares writhing in one. She gasped.

Caden's arms tightened around her and she forced herself to tamp down the rising dread. They knew. Somehow they all knew that she'd killed a man.

His warm breath touched the ridge of her ear. "They could not be to bed without knowing ye were safe, love."

Meg peered up at him. "Do they know what I've done?"

Caden's brow furrowed.

"Do they know I've…killed?"

"They don't know anything except that we are home."

Meg inhaled and bobbed her head. The fires weren't to burn her, at least not yet. Caden's horse halted in the bailey and she turned to the steps where Father Daughtry and Donald stood. Donald hopped down the steps and ran to hold the horse's bridle.

He beamed up at her. "Ye saved us, Meg, truly."

She sniffed at her tears. Donald helped lower her down. What could she say?

"I laid right there with Father Daughtry until they left. I was able to warn the castle. Everyone was in the walls when the Davidsons attacked." He shook his head in awe. "Ye saved all of us."

"Jonet?" she asked.

"She's well, but resting after her run home."

Meg couldn't help the tears now. Donald frowned slightly and turned to Caden, who had dismounted behind her.

"She's exhausted," Caden said and took Meg's arm. She was barely aware of the warriors and Aunt Rachel dismounting behind her. Aunt Mary and Uncle Harold ran down the steps to hug her. Uncle Harold slapped Caden on the back.

Caden paused when Hugh approached. He grasped the man's one good forearm. "You fought them off, outnumbered. I'm sorry to have missed it."

Hugh grinned. "Aye, you missed the fun," he answered. "I'm pretty good with the stationary crossbow."

Meg heard the conversation but her eyes fastened on the priest who stood at the top of the steps holding his torch. She could imagine him lowering it to a witch's pyre. She released her breath when she saw the approval beaming in his face.

"Let us discuss the details after I get Meg to bed," Caden said and helped her up the steps.

Her eyes remained on Father Daughtry. He waited until she reached the top.

"Meg Macbain," the priest intoned, halting Caden's push. "No heretical witch could have saved a man of God. Ye have a most holy gift from our good Lord. I thank ye for using it today."

She was able to inhale, but her legs wobbled. He didn't know yet. None of them knew.

"Help me, Caden," she whispered and he reached under her legs to lift her up.

Words floated to her on an undercurrent of concern as Caden strode through the hall and up the stairs with her. They didn't know. They thought all she could do was save, but they were wrong.

Meg Macbain was a witch who could kill.

Chapter Fifteen

5 September 1518—Caraway: furrowed branching stem. Feathery leaves with stems that end in clusters of tiny white flowers in summer. The seeds are long, ribbed, and brownish.
Aids digestion. Crush seeds to release the potent flavor in foods.
Mix in wine to dissolve gas in the stomach and intestines.
Caraway will prevent the theft of anything or anyone. Feed it to your animals to keep them from straying. Feed them to your lover to keep them always close to your heart. I was fed caraway once. My heart will never stray. I will find my way home again.

Fire licked up her legs, peeling the flesh from her bone. Meg screamed against the agony and kicked wildly. "No!"

She sat upright, her feet tangled in the linens. Caden grabbed her and pulled her into his naked chest. She blinked, the panic of the nightmare strumming through her.

"'Twas just a dream," he soothed and brushed hair back from her face as she tried to control her trembling. She blinked against the light filtering in from the windowpanes. He rocked her in his lap until her breathing slowed.

Just a dream, a terrible dream.

Concern etched deeply along Caden's face. "Ye're shaking."

Her heartbeat slowed and she wiped her hands down her cheeks. "Just a nightmare," she murmured, and glanced at her arms. There should have been bruises and scratches along her skin. Her fingers touched her face, remembering Gilbert's violence.

"Rachel healed them last night," Caden said, his jaw tense. He gingerly kissed the spot under her eye. "She said the bairn was healthy."

He gaze traveled to the small dark chasm still separating their bodies. Even though his words had been a statement, his eyes held the question.

She assessed the little one's health. Relief melted away the last of her trembling. "And without a care of what's going on out here in the world," she said.

"You're here late," she said and instantly searched for illness in Caden's body. Everything seemed normal, including the healthy erection hidden below the covers. She blushed. "You're still in bed."

He ran his hand along her hair, pushing it back from her cheeks. "Yesterday we nearly lost each other."

She closed her eyes for a moment, the memories of their ordeal washing through her. When Caden's lips brushed her forehead, she opened them again. "I wanted to be here when ye woke."

He kissed her leisurely but pulled back, a hint of merriment in his eyes. "And as much as I'd like to keep us here for another hour or two," his gaze raked down Meg, causing her passion to surge, "we're expected below."

And then to die with his words.

Meg swallowed past the fear that sat in her throat. Had Colin, Alec, or Ewan spread the word of how Boswell died? "I…killed a man yesterday…with my magic. I…I am a w—"

"Warrior," Caden finished her sentence. "Ye defended yerself, our bairn." His hand dipped beneath the covers to stroke her stomach. He halted over the dragonfly birthmark. "Ye used yer weapon to defend our clan, clan Munro, and clan Macleod."

He was being so understanding, but she had to make him recognize what had happened, what could happen again.

"I can't normally do that." She glanced down as the smooth blanket and back up. "Boswell had a blood clot in his leg. I used my healing ability to break it up a little so it would flow through his blood. I knew it would clog his lungs and heart, and go in his brain."

Meg let out a slow breath and spoke in a whisper. "People will think that if I touch them…if I'm angry with them…that I could kill them." She stared into Caden's eyes. "What if I do, by accident? I could have killed Angus when I healed him and…"

"Shhh." He kissed her tenderly. "Rachel will help ye master yer gift." He gave a brief shake of his head. "I am not afraid of yer touch," he said placing her palm on his chest.

"The others."

"Meg," he said. "I have a sword. I carry it everywhere." He indicated the sword in its scabbard on the chest beside the bed. "My weapon is lethal. Are ye afraid to touch me when I wear it?"

"It's not the same."

"Nay? The only difference between yer power and mine is that I'm trained on how to use it and how to not accidentally use it." He ran his fingers through hers and folded them in his fist. "Rachel will work with ye until ye grow accustomed to using yer gift."

He held her against him as he rolled, pinning her into the soft tick. His brow furrowed and he cupped Meg's head in both hands.

"What is it?" she asked.

"Yesterday I almost lost ye without telling ye…" His hand trailed away down the side of the bed. He pulled a thin strip of plaid from the edge and caught her hand in his own.

"The priest may have bound us legally, but the ceremony was really to end the feud."

Meg held her breath, not sure what to say.

"So today," Caden said. "Today I pledge to ye, Meg…my life," he wrapped the cloth around their joined hands, "my love," he wound it a second time, "and my soul." Three loops that held their hands tightly together.

She couldn't stop a little tear from slipping past her lashes.

His breath brushed her lips as he neared. "'Tis true I captured ye, but och lass, ye captured me right back. *Tha gaol agam ort*. I love ye."

Meg melted inside. Currents of joy surrounded her heart and pushed up into her eyes. "And I pledge to you, Caden Macbain, my life, my love, and my soul." She squeezed his hand still intertwined in the cloth. "I love you."

• • •

Meg rested her hand on Caden's arm as they descended the stairs, even though she would have rather clutched it. By now everyone would know what had transpired at the cave. *A warrior, I am a warrior.*

She stalled on the steps. "Where is Gwyneth? Bess?"

Caden glanced down at her. "Locked where they locked ye, in the dungeon."

She shivered, remembering the dank, dark place. They had tried to kill her, but the memory of the place haunted her.

Caden touched her cheek. "They've been given basic needs, warmth, food, water. I'll let them worry for a few days before dealing with them."

"I think it was Gwyneth's plan. Bess seemed…scared, like she'd been convinced to act."

"I believe so, too. Gwyneth will be going to Edinburgh."

"Edinburgh?"

"Aye, the good father has volunteered to journey there to give a true account of the Davidsons' misdeeds in helping the English and their lies about me. Gwyneth will be tried for her part in this misadventure."

"What's happening at the Davidsons?" she asked, even though Caden took another step down, pulling her with him.

"They should be locked in battle over who will lead now that Gilbert is dead. And by the time they have their leadership in place, they'll have to deal with King James and King Henry." Caden brought her knuckles to his lips and kissed them. "Ewan will be transporting Boswell's untouched body to Henry with the letters and a full account of how Gilbert Davidson assisted him in trying to hide his treasonous ways."

A low murmur rumbled from the great hall as if it held a crowd. Without the sounds of minstrels playing, the rumble sounded like a mob. Meg swallowed hard and stopped just before they entered the room. Caden placed his hand on top of hers and squeezed. His love could protect her from their brutality, but it couldn't protect her from their mistrust and hatred.

His warm palm sat on her lower back, gently but firmly pushing her out of the dark corridor and into the mouth of the great hall.

The room hushed.

Jonet stood at the table with Kenneth and Ann. Meg couldn't quite draw in a breath, but then Jonet turned to her and a huge smile broke the worry in her features.

"Meg!" she yelled and flew across the room. She threw her arms around her and squeezed. "Ye saved me," she whispered fervently in Meg's ear. "Ye saved me." She pulled back, tears and joy in her face. "Ye risked everything to save me and the clan."

A nervous laugh escaped Meg. "And you saved me from that gag. I'm so glad you made it home."

Jonet laughed despite her own tears. "I've never run so hard."

She glanced down at Jonet's hand wrapped so tightly with her own. There was not even a hint of concern in the woman's grip, only happiness and relief.

She gazed out at a multitude of Macbain faces, eyes curious,

CAPTURED HEART 387

stances waiting. Donald waved from the back of the room, a large grin across his thin face. They knew she killed a man, didn't they?

Caden propelled her over to the table where they'd sat at their wedding celebration. "Do they…Caden, do they know—?"

"They know, love," he said. "Can't keep something as huge as ye saving us from Boswell a secret."

Father Daughtry talked with some Macbains near the fire. He beamed at her proudly and thumped his chest, making the wooden cross jump on the vestments, as if to confirm that he was fit and hardy again.

Meg and Caden sat and everyone turned toward them. They waited, with only a hum of murmurs.

Donald poked his head out into the entry and then Hugh strode in, carrying a sword held point high. Torchlight flickered along its shiny blade. Hamish, Sean, Eòin, and a line of Macbain warriors followed in two rows. Donald joined at one end, his sword high like the rest. Hugh halted before Caden and Meg.

Caden stood while she just stared. His finger under her chin made her shut her gaping mouth as he helped her stand next to him.

"Hugh Loman, Master Watchman, what are you about today?" Caden asked in Gaelic, but the calm flow of his blood and the relaxed state of his muscles told Meg that Caden wasn't surprised by the show.

"Hail Caden, the Macbain of Druim," Hugh said in Gaelic, his voice booming in the still room. His eyes shifted to Meg. "Hail Meg, Lady of Druim," he said in English.

Meg bowed her head acknowledging the address. Hugh

regarded at her with a serious expression. "We of Druim hail ye and pledge to ye."

At that, all the warriors in the two lines went down on one knee.

Meg's stomach sat in a tight ball as she held her breath.

Hugh lowered his voice. "We were remiss in not swearing our fidelity to the new Lady of Druim, and so we do it now." In unison they lowered their swords and their heads. "We, the warriors of Druim, pledge our lives to the protection of Lady Meg as we protect The Macbain and his people."

A cheer rose up in the room, filling the stone rafters with a glorious echo of acceptance.

Meg's breath shook as she inhaled. "*Mòran taing*. Many thanks," she said as the cheers subsided and the warriors stood.

"Lady Meg." Hugh laid the shined blade of the sword across his stump. "We also gift ye with this fine blade."

Meg's gaze ran across the lovely vines and flowers etched into the steel. The weapon was more slender and shorter than the swords the other warriors held. In the hilt sat a blue sapphire, as blue as the ball of light she could conjure.

"If ye are able to defend us all from the English," Hugh said, "ye deserve yer own sword."

A quick inhale escaped Meg's lips as shock turned to joy. Hugh placed the amazingly light sword in her hands, and Donald raised his high.

"To Warrior Meg, defender of Druim!" Donald yelled.

"To Warrior Meg, defender of Clan Macbain!" Angus yelled.

"To Warrior Meg, defender of Clan Macleod!" her father's

gruff voice boomed from the back of the room.

"To Warrior Meg, defender of Clan Munro!" Aunt Rachel yelled from her place next to Uncle Alec, who raised his own sword in salute.

"To Warrior Meg! Lady of Druim!" Hugh boomed as a cheer rose up like a cresting wave, stealing Meg's breath.

Caden's lips were warm as they moved against the edge of Meg's ear. "See, they love ye, too."

She turned her eyes to him and smiled. Caden took her sword and laid it carefully on the table, turned back to her, and pulled her into his arms. His lips settled over hers in a long leisurely kiss as the cheers swelled around them. Meg was engulfed with elation and acceptance.

The last thought she had before she surrendered to Caden's kiss rushed through her on a wave of joy. She was loved, loved for whom she actually was. She was truly blessed.

Acknowledgments

An immense thank you goes out to the members of Heart of Carolina Romance Writers. Virginia, Katharine, Deb, Claudia, Marcia, Sarra—thank you so much for your advice, support and friendship. You are giants among women (in a legendary way, not a size way)!

Thank you also to Kevan Lyon, Libby Murphy, and Liz Pelletier. Without your amazing talent and expertise, this Highland adventure would still be hiding on my computer.

Thank you, Mom, for drawing the herbs for Isabelle's journal. You are the strongest, most talented woman I know. You will always be my real-life heroine.

Thank you to my Dragonfly-Sisters who remind me constantly that I can write. To my children who put up with my "Not now, I'm writing" and "Hush, I'm trying to finish this scene." To Julie, my beautiful friend and beta-reader, who catches all my eye-color mistakes and gives gentle criticism. To all my chemo-buddies and friends, who tell everyone to read my books. Thank you for being my biggest fans :) To Donna,

Dr. Lee, and Jenny M for saving my life so I could write this wonderful book. And to my own hero, Braden. I loved you before, but after this year, I love you a thousand times more. Thank you too for posing for my cover :)

Since this page is about acknowledgments, I'd also like to call out a sneaky villain that stalks our mothers, daughters, sisters, and friends. Beware, Ovarian Cancer! I will not cower in the corner from you but will stare you down, laugh in your face, and arm women with the weapon of knowledge to use against you.

Symptoms of Ovarian Cancer:
> **B**loating that is persistent
> **E**ating less and feeling fuller
> **A**bdominal pain
> **T**rouble with your bladder

Ovarian Cancer cannot be detected by a PAP Smear. Additional symptoms may include fatigue, indigestion, back pain, pain with intercourse, constipation, menstrual irregularities.

Together, we will "SHOUT against the Whisper" until every woman knows these symptoms.